NO SISTER'S
KEEPER

70125944

Jeanne G'Fellers

Bella
BOOKS
2013

Bella Books, Inc.
P.O. Box 10543
Tallahassee, FL 32302

Printed in the United States of America on acid-free paper.

First Bella Books Edition 2013

Editor: Nene Adams
Cover designer: Linda Callaghan

ISBN: 978-1-59493-307-3

About the Author

Jeanne G'Fellers lives with her partner of ten years. She works to pay the bills, writes to soothe her soul, and gardens because it lets her play in the dirt. *No Sister's Keeper* is her fourth novel.

For Jerod and Bobbi Leigh—survivors just like their mom.

Acknowledgments

Life sometimes gets in the way of the best laid plans and that is exactly what happened between my third and fourth novel in the *Sisters Series*. It would never been completed and found its way to print without the gentle encouragement of my partner, Anna, and my current editor, Nene Adams. I thank you both for the gentle nudges and occasional slaps to the head. They were definitely needed.

Preface

It is difficult for someone who has not lived through long-term abuse to understand why a woman might continue to live in the situation. Why doesn't she just leave? Why, indeed? If only it were that simple. Long-term abuse brings with it two things: a kind of brainwashing and a victim's mentality.

The brainwashing is subtle and begins with a harsh word here and there, indelicate jokes at the other's expense. It is near impossible to detect, especially under the guise of new love. Furthermore, the progression is slow. It's covert, and the victim rarely sees what is going on around her until she has become fully engulfed by her abuser.

What proceeds is a blame game. "I wouldn't do this if you didn't make me so mad. It wouldn't happen if you'd just listen. It's your fault. Why're you so damned stupid?"

To the victim, these are reasonable questions. She has, after all, been trained that the viewpoint of her abuser is the only correct viewpoint. So she tries harder, tries to be what her abuser wants, but it's an impossible task. Then comes a sense of numbness. Nothing matters so she withdraws, going through only the most basic motions of life. She can do nothing but focus on her abuser, be aware of what might happen, be hyper vigilant. Unfortunately, most abused women remain this way, stuck in a vicious cycle of abuse and blame.

Occasionally, a victim finds something to fight for, but that something must be bigger than herself. Something in her must awaken and be angry enough to fight—fight for her very life if necessary. Breaking from her abuser is generally a slow process full of false starts, interrupted efforts and indescribable fear.

However, if the woman succeeds, she will bear the scars and live with the aftereffects, with nightmares, with various ailments derived from the physical and mental stress.

Admire such a woman, because her inner strength is tremendous. Value her perseverance. Honor her courage. Celebrate her survival.

Two such women exist in this novel, the first being Chandrey. Don't judge her until you hear her story, and then place yourself in the same situation, set yourself in the very context.

What would you have done? Would you have been so brave?

The second woman is me, the author. I lived with my abuser for thirteen years and am now just becoming able to really work past the trauma. Conversely, my current relationship, ten years and going strong, is one of utter beauty. My Anna tries to understand why I couldn't leave before I did, why I endured being terrorized. It is difficult for her or anyone else to understand, I know. But I managed to be one of those rare women. *I'm a survivor.*

Here's to all the victims of domestic abuse. Here's to waking up from the nightmare. Here's to survival. So listen closely, my sisters, because this is a survivor's tale.

Chapter One

Rural Farmlands of Myflar

Thrall—under the power of another; a Cleave member raised by Autlachs

Glimma and Tao had just tucked their daughters into bed and settled in for a quiet evening of soothing music and good reading when distant lights appeared through the window of their rural cottage.

"Someone's coming." Glimma placed her recorder and reading spectacles on the chair-side table.

"This late? They should've commed first." Tao glanced out the window. Farm work was difficult and their daughters young, so they very much enjoyed their quiet evenings.

This was more of a nuisance than anything, but Tao was concerned. Her skin began to prickle.

She put her recorder aside and went to the household com, where she tried contacting the approaching launch. "Their com is either off or dead."

"How odd," Glimma said.

Tao looked over her shoulder at her life mate, and then back to the window. "The lights are gone. Maybe they turned off."

"Turned off where?" asked Glimma as she looked through the window. She patted Glimma's hand when it touched her shoulder. "Check the girls, will you?"

Glimma squeezed Tao's hand and went to the children's room where she pushed back the curtain and stood in the doorway, her back to the main room of their small home.

Tao unlocked a worktable drawer and pulled out a plasma bow which she lashed to her forearm. When Glimma glanced at her, she didn't say anything, but quickly phased the children into a deeper sleep and returned to the worktable to strap on her bow as well.

This wasn't first time they'd defended their farm from intruders, but the last time had been before the children and their enemy had been local Auts trying to scare them from their homestead. They'd weathered that problem without scars and now called many of those same Auts friends. This enemy, however, was a new one. There had been a local meeting concerning the two families who had disappeared, but thus far, no Taelachs were missing.

The roar of a launch became audible and the yard's boundary markers sounded an entry, but still, no lights.

"Tao?"

"I'm getting nothing." Tao squinted, trying to phase probe the occupants of the launch.

"Phase blind?"

"Don't know. I'm calling for help." Tao's fingers skimmed across the house com's interface, entering the distress codes for the local authorities, but when the com went blank and the house lights flickered, she cursed under her breath.

"They're jamming us." She squeezed Glimma's hand, which had returned to her shoulder.

"Who is it?" Glimma glanced toward the children's room. "What do they want?"

"I'm going to try the com again." Tao pressed a flashlight into Glimma's hand and pushed her toward the children's room. "They've landed."

Glimma kissed her and hurried to the children's room while Tao tried the com a final time. The distress signal went through, and a face appeared on the screen.

"Your call has been received and acknowledged." A Taelach appeared on the viewer.

While Tao breathed a little easier, she saw the woman wasn't dressed in Kinship military attire, and she wore no life or battle braids. Odd, but not totally unheard of. Like herself and Glimma, some sisters in pursuit of a simple life remained members of the Kinship, but chose to not wear the customary trappings such as braids.

"We're here to help." The woman's odd smile confused her.

She took a second to look at the woman's dress. A heavy hide jacket with back-to-back crescents on one collar, but nothing else to show her affiliation. "Who's speaking?"

"Your judgment." The woman's smile broadened, revealing a chip in a bottom tooth.

"Judgment?"

"You stand accused of living a liar's life, of failing to follow the Mother's Word, and of failing to teach your children the Mother's way."

Tao sucked in her breath. Whoever this woman was, she spoke trouble, but still no matter how she tried, she could not sense the woman's mental presence. Nor could she sense anyone else on the launch, if there was anyone else at all.

"You have a choice," continued the woman. "Let us determine whether your home is satisfactory for raising a Mother's child or die resisting."

"Some choice."

"But it *is* a choice." The woman's smile faded. "I'll give you a moment to decide before we enter." The com clicked off.

Tao turned off the screen and went to the children's room where Glimma waited.

"What do they want?" Glimma sat between the children's bedrolls, a hand on each of their daughters.

"I don't know, but they're Taelach," whispered Tao. She drew Glimma to her feet and pulled her close. "Did you phase them?"

Glimma wrapped her arms around her. "They won't wake no matter the noise."

"Did you kiss them?"

"Of course, but—"

Tao suddenly became aware of other Taelach presences—five proud, indolent presences who exuded greedy anticipation and were closing fast. She reached for her bow.

"I wouldn't do that."

Glimma gasped as Tao pushed her back and turned around.

"What do you want from us?" asked Tao. "Our belongs? Our stores? Take them! Take them all!"

The woman she had seen on the screen only laughed. "If we wanted those, we'd have already taken them." She nodded to her four companions. Before either Tao or Glimma could power their bows, they were separated and disarmed.

"Where're your keepers?" prodded one of the invaders.

"Keepers?" Glimma gritted her teeth as one of the invaders pulled the braid running down her back.

"Answer the fuckin' question," another of the leather-clad women hissed in her ear.

Tao and Glimma looked at each other, seeking a logical answer.

"Why, they're slatterns!" declared the lead woman.

Tao and Glimma were forced to the main room, and thrown prone on the floor as their attackers riffled through their belongings, upending furniture and smashing the recorders holding their readings and music.

"Thralls don't exist without keepers." Someone pulled Glimma by her hair until she perched on her knees. "'The Mother felt pity for her pale-skinned daughters and sent another, stronger daughter to protect the fairer member of her creation.'"

"We know the Word!" cried Tao as she was pulled up by her hair. "Please, let us go!"

"If you know the Word, then you know your crime." The woman holding Glimma pulled out a knife. "You're both slatterns. The Mother damns you for your loose ways and has given keepers the power to punish you."

Glimma's face grayed. Her mouth fell opened in a silent scream.

"No!" Tao threw her captor's foot off her back and reared up, reaching for Glimma.

"We'll be quick with her," promised the lead attacker. "Her mind's not as sharp as yours."

"But you'll witness her Sharing first," laughed another.

Tao was forced prone again. Knees pressed harder into her back, pinning her as the others took turns making Glimma's mind theirs. Tao flailed, trying to throw the woman off her, and almost succeeded before another keeper helped keep her down. This second woman forced her way into Tao's mind, making her "listen" to what went on inside Glimma.

They phased in one after another, shredding Glimma's memories, her hopes, her dreams, tearing her talented mind into nothingness, and then they turned their pain phases into sickening pleasure, taking the last of her for their own satisfaction.

When they had finished, when there was nothing left of Glimma, they withdrew, leaving Tao alone in the shambles of her life mate's mind.

My love. Tao echoed in the void. They hadn't said goodbye, but she chose to remain in the void, holding onto what had been even as she became aware of them taking her as well. They weren't taking her mind, but rather her body, making it theirs. She tuned them out and hid in the quiet until Glimma suddenly shuddered and was gone, launching her back to reality.

When she cried out, someone placed a blade to her throat. "Your children will have a proper upbringing with us." A hand ran down Tao's bare, bruised side. "They'll know the Mother and their proper place. They'll never be slatterns like you."

The woman turned Tao's head so she could watch her sleeping daughters being carried away. "See?" She turned Tao further to look into her eyes.

Tao recognized the lead attacker, the woman from the screen.

The woman still smiled. "Poor little slattern." There was no true sympathy in her eyes. Lust. Greed. Want. But certainly no sympathy. "So lost. No keeper to tell you what to do. I'll end it for you now, little slattern, before the confusion gets worse."

She drew her blade across Tao's throat.

Chapter Two

High Granary Offices of the Sister Farming Coordination Exchange Group, Langus

Keeper—*supervisor, teacher, guard; jailer*

Tyla had been a clerk for over twelve passes, since Creiloff's early days with the Exchange, and despite her annoying habits, had assisted in many ways—some that Creiloff's life mate, Leeshin, would never have approved of.

Tyla might be a skinny, flat-chested example of the Taelach kind and far from Leeshin in looks, but nonetheless, she spent more time with Creiloff than Leeshin, and knew more than Leeshin needed to know about her business dealings.

"I was unable to contact Jandis Gladomain yesterday. Keep trying until you reach her."

"Yes, Creiloff." Tyla didn't look up. "Perhaps after this—"

"My business before your pleasure."

Tyla twitched, but said nothing. Her slim fingers became suddenly mobile on the com. "The storms on Myflar have eased," she said after a long moment.

"Is the connection complete?"

"Still trying." Tyla bit her thin lips as she busied herself at the workroom com. She looked like such a pious woman—tense lips, small eyes, too young for her hair to be dark. But Tyla's phase was good. Creiloff often called on her to record things she could have easily done herself just so they'd be alone.

Tyla was always grateful and discreet, making their arrangement quite suitable and long-lasting. Creiloff had known her long before she'd met Leeshin, but their arrangement had continued even after she and Leeshin oathed. Tyla did her a favor by keeping her more questionable business correspondence quiet and she was rewarded for her silence when need be.

"Looks like one of Jandis Gladomain's life mates is coming on now."

"Interesting. Transfer to the main viewer."

Tyla nodded. The screen behind the worktable burst into life.

"You must be Alexandrous," said Creiloff.

The young woman avoided Creiloff's eyes. "Jand said I not answers com 'cept for Creiloff Commonland, and you Creiloff Commonland." Alexandrous's accent was thick with Aut.

Hearing such a barbaric tongue coming from a pretty woman made Creiloff nauseous. The Cleave, a Taelach fringe generally ignored by the Kinship, found many of its members among lost sisters who, because of their Aut raising, would never have equal status inside the Kinship. These sisters had limited options because of the ineradicable scarring in their minds. They were raised with the Aut mindset of what constituted womanhood ingrained in their heads.

Mental healers had proved with study after study that lost sisters, unless they were rescued before puberty and "reprogrammed," were Taelach in appearance only, incapable of fully understanding and fulfilling a sister's duty to the Kinship.

But the Cleave welcomed them as long as they retained their Aut woman mindset. Aut-like gender roles were part of the Kinship's past, but the Cleave was reviving the trend, calling their settlements clans, and their sisters keepers or thralls depending on their station. Creiloff thought that Alexandrous was obviously thrall to Jand's keeper.

"Where's Jand?" she asked.

Behind Alexandrous, the Myflar winds rocked Jand's private planetary launch, an extravagant but efficient affair. Jand used it for both business and living when she was surveying potential investments on contract for the Exchange. She didn't generally bring any of her life mates with her. Said their place was tending the hearth. But Creiloff had once before seen her bring a new life mate along to "break her in."

Though polygamy wasn't specifically banned by the Kinship, most sisters found it unpalatable. However, the Cleave all but required it, just as some Autlach groups associated with the Raskhallak deity still did. A good Cleave keeper had more than one life mate. A powerful keeper had five or more. Alex made three for Jand.

The Cleave concept was simple, and Jand was a deep believer, Creiloff thought. They based their ideology on the Mother's creation story, specifically the words, "the Mother Maker took pity on her delicate, pale-skinned daughters and saw to their survival, creating a physically stronger daughter, a broadback daughter to assist and love the gentler form of her creation."

What most Taelach saw as the creation of the Oath, the Cleave interpreted as license for one woman to rule over another.

The Cleave generally kept to itself, but as Jand had told her, "business must take place." It frequently did with the Exchange since most other businesses found the Cleave's tenets unacceptable. Creiloff didn't really care about moral idealism as long as the deal was a good one.

"Jand sleeping." Alexandrous looked over her shoulder to where Jand lay sprawled on a folding lounger. "Jand busy last night."

"I'd imagine so," said Creiloff as Tyla stifled a laugh into her hand. "Wake her."

"She not like that, Creiloff Commonland." Alexandrous turned back to the screen, but still kept her eyes averted, as thralls were taught to do when talking to keepers.

This wasn't the first time Creiloff had spoken to one of Jand's women. "What am I, Alexandrous?"

She glanced at Creiloff from the corner of her eye. "Jand not say, Creiloff Commonland, but you looks keeper."

"I *am* keeper," said Creiloff impatiently. "And I told you to wake her up."

Behind her, Tyla cleared her throat. She didn't like the way Creiloff handled Cleave thralls, but they only understood things in familiar terms—keeper terms.

"Wake her, Alexandrous, or I'll tell Jand you got in the way of our business."

Alexandrous gasped and rushed to where Jand lay. She shook her keeper hard, speaking in a low, apologetic tone.

"Get away, Alex." Jand rolled toward the launch's bulkhead.

"So this is how you do business now?" Creiloff shouted through the com.

Jand rolled over to squint at the viewer. "Creiloff?"

"Who else? I've been trying to contact you for two days."

"That's but one day here, my friend." Jand yawned, sat up, and pulled a tunic over her bare chest. She rubbed at her head through her age-darkened, closely shorn hair, and after mumbling something to Alexandrous, crossed the launch in laggard strides to sit in front of her com. "Been storming here."

"My clerk told me." Creiloff could see Alexandrous in the aerolaunch's kitchenette.

She was young to be oathed, no more than eighteen if that. Long, silver hair peeked out of her headscarf—another Cleave throwback. Very young, but pretty despite her simple skirt and blouse. The clothes were ill-made, probably by Alex herself, a sure sign she hadn't been in the Cleave for more than a few moon cycles.

"Damn shame those storms kept you from work," Crieloff went on.

Jand chuckled. "Yeah, something like that." Her image faded and a detailed map took its place. "You can tell my earlier reports are consistent with these findings."

Creiloff peered at the screen. The map contained a multi-dimensional view of Myflar's equator plains, a vast grassland seeded two hundred passes earlier by the Kinship.

Myflar was a cool, rather dry moon of Saria III so grasslands had been a natural choice along the only area potentially suitable for farming. The Exchange's high members would be more than satisfied with the findings, but Creiloff would never be. She'd been Langus raised, and now Langus was being handed over to the Autlach. To give *her* land, the land she and her family had spilled their blood and sweat on to make successful, to give that piece of history and heart to Autlachs to overrun was unconscionable. How dare the Kinship!

"The maps and soil samples were accurate." Creiloff watched as the screen faded back to Jand, who gulped tea while eating bites of bread and dried fruit. "The Cleave still looking to expand nearby?"

"Your leader Benjimena approved our claim to a central homeland. I'm mapping new clan settlements while I'm here," said Jand between bites. "I'm ready to relocate. Damned Kinship is complaining about our ways again."

"More likely about the way you treat your women," mumbled Tyla as Jand continued.

"Takes a strong hand to tame a thrall." Jand snapped her fingers and Alex appeared by her side, kettle in hand to refill her keeper's mug.

After Jand smacked her playfully on the ass, Alex returned to the kitchenette where she retrieved a box of what looked like sewing from beneath a seat.

Tyla grumbled and walked out of the workroom. When Creiloff called her back, she returned only long enough to retrieve her wrap.

Creiloff knew she'd return soon enough. No matter that Tyla was in need of employment, the lure of a good phase always brought her back.

"You letting your thrall walk out?" asked Jand when Creiloff turned back to the screen.

"She's not mine." Creiloff thought briefly of Leeshin, who was away at some volunteer function or another.

When she and Leeshin oathed, they'd decided that Lee should leave her job with the Exchange. Leeshin worked in the procurement department, same as her—in a lower position of course—but they hadn't wanted to be bombarded with nepotism rumors.

Creiloff was rising swiftly in the Exchange, and Leeshin thought she would be in the way. She was right, she would have been in the way. In the way of the long work hours needed to secure Creiloff's future. In the way of her dealings with Jand. In the way of her energetic mind fucks with Tyla. "The one I have is more than enough."

"Discontentment so early?" Jand leaned back in her seat. "How long you been oathed? Two, three passes?"

"Nine."

"No wonder you look frustrated. A keeper shouldn't limit herself to one. It isn't healthy."

More Cleave logic, but some Creiloff might've embraced if she hadn't already oathed. "Who says I limit myself to one?" she asked with wry grin. "What my life mate doesn't know won't hurt her."

"Pfft." Jand threw her hands up in the air. "Keepers don't have to hide their urges in my world, Creiloff Commonland."

"Sisters do in mine." Creiloff was ready to steer the conversation away from private issues. "I'll be to Myflar after the pass-end celebration to finalize the surveys."

"You'd make a strong keeper."

Jand said as much every time they spoke. Creiloff thought she might someday take her up on the offer, but Leeshin would never accept the Cleave lifestyle. Her own raising didn't promote the Renunciation in any form. Life mates should stay together no matter what it took to make things work.

"You attending Saria III's solar eclipse festivities?" she asked.

"Cleave pass-end festivities are much more interesting," Jand said. "I'm leading three devotionals. You should come."

"You recruiting?"

"Always, Creiloff Commonland." Jand popped more fruit into her mouth. "We never seem to have enough keepers to teach the new thralls."

"Not me," said Creiloff. "I have plans."

"In the Exchange, no doubt."

"*For* the Exchange. See you after the pass-end."

"Until then, Creiloff Commonland." Jand was turned, calling Alex for more breakfast before the com clicked off.

Chapter Three

Langus
(ten passes before Chandrey Brava's birth)

Raiser—supporter, parent

"Creiloff?" Leeshin rapped on her life mate's open workroom door. Creiloff didn't look up from the recorders scattered on her desk, but motioned her in with a quick wave.

Leeshin stood in front of the worktable, rocking on her heels. After several minutes of Creiloff's continued inattentiveness, she cleared her throat. Only then did Creiloff look up.

"Yes?"

Leeshin pursed her lips. Creiloff had become disagreeable since they had learned they'd be relocating, paying more attention to the Exchange than anything or anyone else, but she still loved Creiloff in a way she couldn't describe. Creiloff was a good provider, an attractive woman, and fairly well left her to her own devices as long as she didn't spend too many credits.

"We need to talk."

"So talk."

"Well," Leeshin hesitated until Creiloff began drumming her fingers. "The new kimshee for the Aut settlers, Tracemore is her name, just commed. A newborn sister has suddenly become available locally."

Creiloff sat back in her chair and ran her hand through her short locks, twirling her life braid around one finger in what Leeshin had long known as frustration. "How many times have we discussed this? I'm fully against bringing children into our lives. You know that."

"Kimshee Tracemore says this sister was found in a bin of raw hides in the Aut port marketplace."

"Your point?"

"She's had a rough start."

Creiloff ran her hand through her hair again and frowned, an all too common expression on her lean face. "So? Lots of us are found that way or worse."

"It's not that, it's—"

"You and your empathy. What's wrong with her?" There was more curiosity than compassion in Creiloff's voice.

"Kimshee Tracemore said it's minor, probably residue from her abandonment, but nothing that won't wear away with good parenting and time."

"Let me understand this." Creiloff leaned back in her chair. "Despite my insistence otherwise, you've been keeping in touch with the local kimshee?"

"I'd never met Kimshee Tracemore before she commed." Leeshin shuffled her feet and looked away. She knew what Creiloff thought, but she also knew what she felt in her heart. And right then it sang a newborn's lullaby.

"And she commed you just for this?"

"She did."

"I see." Creiloff rose to stand behind her worktable, where she drummed her fingers on the cool hide of her chair's back. "Damn it, why're you putting me in this position?"

"I...I don't mean to put you in any position, Creiloff. It's just that..."

"Just *what*?"

"I'm lonely. When you're home, you're up here in your workroom. And things will be worse when we move. Myflar is remote, and it'll be difficult to receive a child from that distance. The wait will be long, and you'll be busier than ever, and—"

"A profitable business requires constant attention. Besides, I work from home most evenings so you *do* see me."

"Only if I come up here, and then you act like I'm interrupting." Leeshin leaned across the worktable to touch Creiloff's hand. "There's a difference between seeing and interacting, you know."

Creiloff drew back. "What about that group of sisters you volunteer with?"

"Most of them are busy with their own children. Besides, once we move to Myflar I'll never see them. The only other sister I see regularly is Serrina, and she isn't much company."

"Serrina's job is to clean, not entertain."

Creiloff returned to her chair as Leeshin retreated to the room's only other chair, a stiff-backed piece of sister woodworking as uncomfortable as it was interesting, carved from a single trunk with vines and leaves pulled from the wood through fine carving—an overall pretty piece, but too busy for Leeshin's tastes. Creiloff, however, had loved it when she first saw it and had carried on about the low seat which made others sit below her.

"There's more work than Serrina can do since you fired the others," Leeshin said.

"I'll not have Auts supporters in this house for any reason!" Creiloff scowled. "And that has nothing to do with what you've done now."

"I've done nothing but extend my heart to a sister in need." Leeshin crossed her arms and sat up taller in the short seat. "I don't ask for much. I never have. And I insist on even less. But I do insist... no, demand this." She held her gaze steady with Creiloff's, something few dared. "I want this child, and if you won't go to the Association with me to sign for her, I'll sign as a single raiser."

"You know I don't believe in the Renunciation."

"And I believe in this child too much to ignore my feelings."

"You've never seen the kid."

"I feel her in my heart. She needs me."

Resentment flashed across Creiloff's face, but she threw her hands up in the air. "You win. You want the kid. I'll sign. At least then you'll stay out of my way."

Gladly, thought Leeshin as she hurried from Creiloff's workroom. Maternal glee rushed through her, sweeter than any phase. She had a nursery to think of, not that she needed many supplies. She'd been storing items away almost as long as she and Creiloff had been together, knowing her life mate would come around to the idea. Creiloff hadn't always been the way she was now.

When they'd been dating, Creiloff had been eager for children. Leeshin was almost certain the change had come from what had happened three moon cycles after they'd oathed. Creiloff had been on business near Taelach hostile lands on Saria Proper when her aerolaunch was shot down by religious extremists. The pilot and two other passengers were found executed beside the launch, but Creiloff wasn't found until three days later, some twenty kilometers away from the wreckage. She'd been beaten so badly that Leeshin barely recognized her. However, Creiloff had refused to talk about the crash and rejected any counseling.

Things hadn't been the same since. Creiloff had alienated their Aut-understanding friends. The household staff, many of whom Leeshin considered friends, had been dismissed without her knowledge, and Creiloff had hired Serrina, an elder sister and a good housekeeper, whose demeanor left much to be desired—almost as much as Creiloff's did. Their lives had been this way for over nine passes. She was more than ready for a change.

She pulled the boxes from storage, gathered what she would initially need for the baby, and left the items to air. The sitting room beside their bedroom would be the nursery, as intended. She packed a sling of essentials—diapers, covers, blankets and a pacifier—and then made her way to the kitchen, where Serrina was prepping the evening meal.

"I need you to stop by the market and pick up infant formula," Leeshin told her. "And please clean the bottle feeders in the top of the linen closet."

Serrina looked up from the vegetables she was slicing. "What in the Mother's name for?"

"We're bringing our daughter home today!"

"A child?" Serrina slammed her open palm against the cutting board. "I'm no nursery worker!"

"I'm the child's mother, so I'll be caring for her." Leeshin picked up the com and dialed out while Serrina's glare followed her. "Kimshee Tracemore, please. Tell her it's Leeshin Creiloffs."

Third Kimshee Ria Tracemore, a trim woman not far from apprenticeship, appeared on the screen a few seconds later. "Leeshin, nice to hear from you so soon. Good news, I hope?"

"Yes!" Leeshin couldn't contain her excitement. "We should be there within the hour."

"Excellent. I'll ready the forms." Tracemore fiddled with scrolls on her worktable. "If you've picked a name, I'll go ahead and add it."

"A name?" Leeshin's mouth tightened. They'd never discussed such things, but Creiloff's raisers had been named Commonland, Denise and Cancelynn Commonlands. "Cancelynn," she said. "Cancelynn Denise."

"Cancelynn Denise it is." Tracemore jotted down the name and looked up with a grin. "I know you're ready to get here, so I won't keep you."

"Thank you."

"May this be the first of many times we find ourselves meeting. Tracemore out."

Leeshin swept up the sling containing the baby items and climbed the stairs to Creiloff's office. "Kimshee Tracemore is waiting."

"She'll wait some more," said Creiloff around the rolled pilta in her mouth. She lit the end and inhaled, prompting a glower from Leeshin.

"You said you'd quit."

"You have your vices, I have mine." Creiloff exhaled, encasing her head in smoke.

"Must you do this now?" Leeshin placed her hands on her hips.

"I have a deal for you," said Creiloff after another puff. "You don't like my vices. I don't like yours. So I'll keep my vices away from you if you keep yours away from me."

"Vices?"

"The kid." Creiloff ground her pilta into an empty mug. "I'll sign, but that's where my commitment ends."

"Deal." The circumstances surrounding the child's claiming didn't matter, as long as she came home.

Creiloff nodded, rose from her worktable, and smoothed her trousers.

A woman of impeccable neatness, she was never out of full dress—always well groomed, cropped hair cut by Serrina once a seven-day, nary a wrinkle in her clothing despite hours at her worktable. This included evenings, when most would seek the warmth of family and the comfort of casual clothing. The only time she emerged from her office suite during the evening was when she required something, namely Leeshin's body and phase, but even that need seemed to be waning. She often spent the nights on the lounger in her office or on business outside the house, both of which Leeshin took in stride. Sex wasn't everything. But family…

"You call for a launch?" Creiloff asked.

"It's already here," Leeshin stepped aside to let Creiloff pass.

"Let's get this over with." Creiloff pushed past without touching her and led the way to the launch. She stayed silent, her arms stayed crossed over her chest as the pilot glided them down the mountainside to the local Kinship government facilities, the operating base for the local kimshee, a sister trained in the art of obtaining Taelach infants from their Autlach birth parents. No sister waited long for her raisers, especially on Langus.

Kimshee Tracemore met them in the recruiting office's ornate waiting area. "Nice to meet you in person, Leeshin." She clasped her wrist cordially. "And this must be Creiloff." Tracemore extended her hand to Creiloff, who reluctantly returned the courtesy. "Please follow me to my office."

"Can I see the child first?" Leeshin asked with a smile.

"See her?" Tracemore turned them down a side hallway. "Why, you can hold her. She's sleeping in the bassinet in my office."

The child was sleeping peacefully when they entered. Leeshin had to restrain herself from scooping her up. Instead, she reached a finger to her head and stroked her downy white hair.

"My daughter," she whispered, and touched the baby's hand. The baby responded by opening her eyes. "So blue."

"All our eyes are blue." Creiloff peered over Leeshin's shoulder at the baby, and then turned back to Tracemore. "Let's finish this so I can get back to work. I'll need to put in more hours now that we've another mouth to feed."

Leeshin hid her hurt expression and continued to hover over the baby.

"There's not much to do." Tracemore motioned them toward the worktable. "You can pick her up if you want. She's just a few personal marks away from being yours."

Leeshin didn't hesitate to bring the baby to her shoulder, brightening her mood.

"Where do I sign?"

"Here." Tracemore pointed to a multilayered scroll. "And here." She pointed midway down another. "Press hard so the copies take." She passed an inked stylus to Creiloff, who scanned the documents and quickly signed her mark. Creiloff then passed the stylus to Leeshin, who balanced the baby in her right arm as she signed.

Creiloff rose. "I'll be outside." She exited the office, walking slowly but with purpose back toward the launch.

"She has her doubts," said Tracemore before Leeshin managed an explanation. "It's not uncommon, especially when one of the raisers wants a child more than the other."

"I've wanted one for so long."

"There's no shortage. Why didn't you try sooner?"

"I put our names on the list passes ago," Leeshin said. "But I suppose it doesn't matter now."

Tracemore looked to where Creiloff had stood. "To you, maybe, but I wonder about your life mate."

"She's very reserved." Leeshin hoped she sounded convincing. "But she'll warm to Cancelynn after a while."

"I'm sure she will, but take my advice and make a little extra time for Creiloff during the next cycle or two. She's insecure and will need your reassurance." Tracemore opened her office door. "The Mother's blessings on your new family."

"Thank you." Leeshin clutched little Cancelynn to her chest and trotted toward the waiting launch. Creiloff's attitude neared unreasonable when she was impatient, but to her surprise, she wasn't at the launch.

"Sister Creiloff said you should go home without her," said the pilot when she inquired.

"Did she say where she was going?" Leeshin felt almost relieved.

"No, Sister Leeshin, she didn't. Wouldn't let me call her another launch either, just started walking. You want to look for her?"

"That won't be necessary." Leeshin climbed into the back of the launch. "Take us home, please."

"Yes, Sister Leeshin." The pilot slid the door shut and climbed into the front seat, where she looked over her shoulder at Cancelynn.

"Cute, but a bit scarred from the feel of her."

"She had a hard start," said Leeshin. "But it's nothing a little love can't solve."

"Love cures all." The pilot winked, and then turned back around. The land launch began to hum beneath them.

The launch took Cancelynn and Leeshin back to the same hilltop estate she shared with Creiloff, only now it didn't seem as dreary. If anything, the estate had suddenly become something it had never been—a home.

She found comfort in the thought and fell asleep with Cancelynn, her mentally scarred daughter, in her arms.

Chapter Four

Motherslight Community: Saria III
(Chandresslandra "Chandrey" Brava, age six)

Gahrah—first or primary raiser; lesser used Taelach slang for guardian or broadback raiser

Chandrey learned about the Mother from her gahrah, Brava Deb. Chandrey was her gahrah's *only* daughter, and Garah often told her that the Mother wanted it to be just the two of them. Then one day Gahrah sat her down and said something different, that their family was going to be bigger. Life mates, said Gahrah, were put together by the Mother for a reason.

"Two halves make one whole," Gahrah said. "And a whole is unbreakable."

The oath was important, and sisters should think hard about it. Once life mates, always life mates. Gahrah also told her about life mates who broke what the Mother had made. They should be ashamed. They were ugly spots on the Mother Maker's starry skirts. They hadn't kept their promise to the Mother, to each other. Then Gahrah told her stories about sisters who had broken their oaths, how miserable they were, how alone.

Chandrey felt sorry for them, but she also blamed them for their own hurt. When she was grown and the elders asked her to oath, said Gahrah, she should think hard about that promise.

When Kylis came to live with them, her talks with Gahrah didn't happen as much.

Kylis had been a widow for four passes. A dead life mate was the only way a sister could take the oath again, and then the elders in her Mother's Plan group would tell her when she was ready. When the elders said Gahrah should ask Kylis to share the oath, she and Kylis talked the next day.

That night, Chandrey met Kylis, and learned that Kylis's daughter, Seechell, was grown and living in the big city of Polmel on Saria IV.

"A heathen place," said Kylis when they ate dinner that night. "No good can come from her living there."

Gahrah nodded as she did when she had no answer, and sipped her wine. "Chandresslandra is a devoted scholar. Her grades are spectacular, especially in history."

"Every sister needs a solid grounding in the past." Kylis turned her almost clear eyes to Chandrey. "Do you say your prayers every day, child?"

"Yes, ma'am, I do," said Chandrey.

"Wonderfully polite child," Kylis said to Gahrah. "You've done an excellent job on your own."

"I'm always glad to hear such things." Gahrah used her knife to stab small bits of meat from the bottom of her mug. "But 'children do better under the tutelage of two raisers.'"

"Wise Mother's Words." Kylis dropped her head and sat quietly, clearly thinking about what had been said. When Gahrah frowned at Chandrey, she did the same. Knowing all the Mother's Words when she heard them was hard.

Gahrah watched over them for a minute, and then said, "So be," which meant that they could look up again.

"Time for bed, Chandresslandra." Gahrah hugged her when she jumped in her lap. "Kylis will be staying with us from now on. Do you understand?"

Chandrey glanced at the large hide bag Kylis had brought with her. "Are you going to oath?"

"We are. Tomorrow morning, Kylis will be your mama." Gahrah hugged her hard around the neck.

"Okay," Chandrey whispered in her gahrah's ear. "Does that mean you'll hug?"

Kylis cleared her throat.

"Life mates hug, child. You know that," said Gahrah.

"Will you kiss?"

Kylis cleared her throat again.

Gahrah looked red in the face. "She's young and curious, Ky. Please have patience."

"Certainly." Kylis moved her finger around the edge of her mug, making a funny, squeaking sound.

"Are you going to share a bed?" asked Chandrey.

"That is quite enough, young lady!" Kylis put her napkin in her mug and pushed back her chair. "Come see me."

Chandrey did so only after Gahrah said she had to, and then stood in front of Kylis, knowing she was angry.

"Curiosity is only natural," said Kylis after a minute. "It's how we learn." Kylis touched the tip of her tongue to her teeth. "However, you must learn the difference between curiosity and prying. Do you know what prying means?"

"No, ma'am." Chandrey wiggled her hands behind her back.

"Prying means that you are asking things that are best left between others." Kylis looked at Gahrah.

"She's correct, Chandresslandra. You *were* prying." Gahrah shared Kylis's frown.

"I'm sorry." Chandrey shuffled her feet and looked at the floor.

"Give me your hands." Kylis tapped Chandrey on the back of her hands. It didn't hurt, but it made Chandrey mad. Gahrah had never done that.

When she pulled her hands behind her, Kylis told her to look up and say she was sorry again. "With remorse befitting your trespass."

Chandrey looked at Gahrah, who told her to apologize. "I'm very sorry, Kylis. I'm sorry, Gahrah." She looked up, imagining she could see through the ceiling and into the clear night sky where the Mother sat in her watching chair, a look of sadness on her always sunlit face. "I am sorry, Mother. Please forgive me."

"Apology accepted." Gahrah leaned back. "Bedtime, child."

"Yes, Gahrah." Chandrey ran up the stairs to her loft.

Their grotto was built into the cliffs near where Gahrah worked for the Kinship. She was in charge of five sister villages, including Motherslight, the Mother's Plan village where they lived.

Gahrah liked old things and things made by hand, even Chandrey's bedroom furniture, so the house was full of wonderful old stuff. Her loft had a press and a big shelf where she stored her story scrolls, toys and the box where she kept what Gahrah called her little treasures.

"I'm ready," yelled Chandrey when she had put on her sleeping shift.

"We're coming."

Gahrah and Kylis came up the stairs a minute later.

"You've kept this place so nicely." Kylis touched Gahrah on the arm. "And all while parenting alone."

"I've tried." Gahrah sat on the edge of Chandrey's pallet. "Kylis is going to tell you a story tonight."

"Okay." She'd wanted Gahrah to read, not a stranger. "My story scrolls are on the shelf."

"I don't need one." Kylis sat on the pallet too. "I know the Morality Fables by heart."

Chandrey listened quietly to Kylis's words, words she'd heard many times before at children's divinations in the Mother's Temple. Gahrah listened too, her eyes on Kylis's small mouth. Chandrey thought she looked like a fish when she spoke and wanted to giggle, but she didn't dare. No one ever giggled during a Morality Fable.

When Kylis finished, she looked down in Wise Word quiet, so Chandrey did too.

"So be." Gahrah held her arms open for Chandrey to jump into. "Sleep well, Chandrey girl." She hugged her tight. "Mother guide your dreams."

"Yours too, Gahrah." Chandrey looked over Gahrah's shoulder at Kylis. Did she dream? "Yours too, Kylis."

"Thank you, Chandresslandra." Kylis patted Chandrey's head and then went down the stairs.

Gahrah tucked her between the blankets, squeezed her feet, turned down the light, and went down the stairs too.

When Chandrey listened hard, she could hear them talking in the main room below.

"I've missed having a young one around." Chandrey heard Gahrah's big, cushioned chair begin to creak, and then the smaller chair beside it take on a similar rhythm.

"Chandresslandra's been a great comfort." Chandrey heard Gahrah drop her boots on the floor. She hoped Garah's footlings weren't a holey pair.

"You've seen to it that she's an honest Mother's child, a real testament to your faith," said Kylis.

"To *our* faith," said Gahrah. "I've long respected your devotion."

Chandrey heard the little chair rock faster. "I try to be a faithful sister. My only real failing, my great failing, has been Seechell."

"When did you last hear from her?"

"Two moon cycles back. She's living with yet another woman she hasn't oathed with." The little chair moved even faster. "The Mother will see to her misery, mark my words." She stopped. "And this one is a kimshee."

"Some go astray despite our efforts." Chandrey heard Gahrah sharpening her blade like she did every night before bed. "You can't blame yourself."

"Oh, but I do." Chandrey heard the little chair start rocking again, slower than before. "I was young and doubting when I claimed her. If I had been more faithful when she was little, if I had taught her better…"

Gahrah stopped sharpening her blade. "Don't." Chandrey heard her place the knife and stone on the table between their chairs. She never did that. "Doubt taints faith. Remember the Mother's Words."

"Wise Mother Words," Kylis answered, and they were quiet.

"So be," Gahrah said after a few moments. She began sharpening her knife again.

"I see Chandresslandra as my chance at redemption," said Kylis.

"You're far too hard on yourself. I'm certain you've done no wrong in the Mother's eyes."

"I'll do right by Chandresslandra, I promise."

"I wouldn't have accepted the elders' suggestion if I thought otherwise. Hand me your blade."

They didn't say much after that. Chandrey had almost fallen asleep when she heard Gahrah get up from her chair. "Time for bed, Ky."

"I suppose it is at that."

Then Chandrey heard her gahrah do something she'd never heard her do before: she closed and locked her bedroom door.

Chapter Five

Kinship Central Governmental Facilities— Javicks Township: Saria III

Lesson—guided learning; Cleave punishment to teach expected behavior

When Chandrey was twelve, her gahrah, Brava Deb, was promoted to a very important position as second assistant to Grandmaster Benjimena Kim, Taelach of All. With the position came a move to Javicks and an actual freestanding house which Kylis decorated in a combination of Brava's beloved antiques and her own, more simplistic tastes.

Even though they were away from the Mother's Plan group of Motherslight, Chandrey's teachings continued, more so than ever when Kylis found the local schools didn't teach their faith. Kylis taught her at home after that, so she became steeped in the Mother's teachings and Kylis's unique interpretations.

Brava wasn't home much anymore, so Kylis almost became her sole raiser. Her expectations of Chandrey were high and her punishments swift.

More than once, Chandrey hid her bruised hands from Brava. More than once, her backside hurt so badly she wanted to cry when she sat. And Kylis had another form of discipline, one that she found both peculiar and frightening.

Sometimes, when Chandrey disobeyed Kylis's interpretation of the household rules, Kylis phase-forced her to the floor and straddled her with knees pressing into her sides. From this position, she had to lie very still and silent, listening to Kylis repeat Wise Mother Words until she thought Chandrey understood what she had done wrong. If Chandrey were slow in her understanding, Kylis pressed knees into her ribs hard enough to hurt, but never enough to bruise.

She found these punishments humiliating, but as time went on, learned to respond as Kylis wished so the punishment would end.

As odd as things were, as peculiar as they seemed to her, in her isolation she thought them normal enough that she never told Brava. Her gahrah was far too busy with the Taelach of All's requirements to be bothered.

The only time Chandrey got to see Brava for any extended period was during Kylis's twice-a-pass meditation retreats that she spent in solitude, reflecting on the Mother's Word. Brava took leave to stay with her then, and she felt free during these times. They'd play games, read, cook and go on walks together. She valued these times more than any other.

At fourteen passes of age, Chandrey asked if she could take the school exit exams most sisters took right before they turned sixteen and became recognized Kinship members. She knew she wouldn't be considered an adult, but she thought passing the exam would grant her some freedom from Kylis's lessons.

Brava said yes, but Kylis said she doubted Chandrey would pass the exams. Kylis agreed, however, that she should take them if for no other reason than as a "lesson in humility."

To all their surprises, Chandrey not only passed every exam, but passed them with high distinction, receiving a perfect score in history. Brava had fresh flowers delivered to her when she found out. Kylis admonished the gesture as doting and would have thrown them out if her gahrah hadn't come home early that evening to celebrate.

Kylis and Brava's argument that night was the worst Chandrey had ever heard. After it ended, she was granted a bit of freedom as long she studied the Mother's Word for at least two hours a day.

Most days when she finished her studies, she visited Brava's work so she could be close to her and read on the lounger in her workroom. Brava was around, but seldom in her office. Benjimena Kim was elderly, so Brava sometimes acted as much as a caretaker as she did an official assistant.

The scrolls in Brava's workroom were generally Kinship business, but Chandrey devoured them anyway, reading everything from crime reports to grant proposals when Brava wasn't there to censor her choices. The material wasn't the Mother's Word, which was all Kylis allowed at home.

Through the official scrolls, she learned about the Autlach-Taelach Teacher Training and Exchange Program. She was almost sixteen by then and longed for something besides Kylis's oversight, but when she asked Brava about the program, Brava scolded her.

"I'm sorry," Chandrey said, "but it had an Education Workgroup stamp, and you know how much I want to teach."

"When you're old enough for the training, we'll talk."

"But I'll be sixteen right before the next group of sisters is chosen. Can I apply?"

Brava put down the recorder in her hand and came to sit next to her. "You've never dealt with Auts. What makes you think you could teach a room full of them?"

"I don't care if I teach sisters or Auts, I just want to teach. Even Kylis says I have a gift for it."

"'Pride denotes a lack of self-control.'"

"Wise Mother's Words," said Chandrey.

Brava waited a very long moment before she let the silence end. "So be."

"Can I do it?"

"I don't know. Kylis says your faith still lacks."

"I know the Mother's Word in, out, and upside down." Chandrey stopped, knowing the boast would earn her another reprimand.

"I was referring to your spiritual self. Is it strong enough to face the world alone?"

"I believe so."

"That's brave, but is it strong enough to keep the faith in the midst of nonbelievers?"

"I live among them now."

"Yes, but how much time do you really spend talking to them?"

Chandrey bit her lip. Truth was, she spent very little time among the sisters of Javicks because Kylis kept her within arm's reach when they went out. "I had the best of teachers."

Brava smiled. "Well, you certainly know the art of flattery." Her expression grew serious. "Is the teacher exchange program the sole reason you wish to leave home?"

The Mother considered lies a path to misery, so Chandrey had never been able to pull off an effective one, especially with Brava, who seemed to be able to sense her strays from the truth before they came out of her mouth.

"Be honest," Brava prompted.

"It's not you, Gahrah, I promise." Chandrey was being honest, but she knew that wasn't what Brava was asking. Brava's relationship with Kylis had never been overly affectionate, and their regular arguments were often heated, but neither had ever mentioned ending their relationship. It wasn't an option.

"She comparing you to Seechell again?"

"She says I'm on the same path to misery."

"Blast that woman and her—" Brava cleared her throat. "She shouldn't judge."

"That's why I want to go." Chandrey placed an arm around her raiser. "It isn't you. It never has been."

"I understand, child, and I can't say as I blame you, but I worry about placing you among so many older, worldlier sisters. And kimshees too. I worry about their influence."

Again with the kimshees, thought Chandrey. They brought infant sisters to their raisers. It sounded like noble work. "My influences are you and the Mother. That's enough to see me through anything."

"Spoken like a true flatterer." Brava laughed heartily. "Are you certain your calling isn't politics?"

"Does this mean I can apply?"

"Yes, but complete and submit the application from here. Kylis will be livid enough when she finds out. No reason to extend her wrath."

"Oh, thank you, Gahrah!" Chandrey threw her arms around Brava again and squeezed tight. "I'll make you proud, just wait."

"You do every day, child." Brava kissed her face and forehead. "You do every day."

Chapter Six

Kinship Central Governmental Facilities— Javicks Township: Saria III

Training Grounds—Kinship facility for military and public service training

Brava had been right. Kylis was livid about the application, but that paled in comparison to her reaction to Chandrey's acceptance into the program.

"She'll be lost to us, to the Mother's wisdom!" Kylis threw her napkin on the dining table. "How could you even consider allowing her access to such filth! Dear Mother, you know *kimshees* train there."

"The Training Grounds are not without their problems, but they are far from filth. And Chandrey knows about kimshees and to stay away from their loose ways," Brava said.

Chandrey was glad her gahrah had stopped drinking wine. When it became an escape, said the Mother, it was to be refrained from. Besides, water seemed to help Brava keep her wits, which was necessary in a confrontation with Kylis and her knife for a tongue.

Brava went on, "She'll be in a supervised environment with sisters not much older than she is now."

"The Training Grounds are infested with heathens and their lechery," said Kylis in a shrill tone. "Chandresslandra isn't faithful enough to withstand such temptation."

"I *am* faithful enough!" Chandrey jumped up from the table.

"Sit down, Chandrey," said Brava gently. "Kylis and I will discuss this."

"I'm sixteen, Gahrah, or almost, and I won't let Kylis pick me apart any longer. I've a right to defend myself."

"Chandrey," continued Brava, touching her arm, but Kylis held up her hand.

"No, let the girl speak if she wants. I've seen this rebellion coming for a while. Let her get it out of her system while there's still a chance to save her."

"Very well." Brava nodded in her direction. "But remember you allowed it."

"Speak." Kylis placed her mug to the side and leaned forward, her elbows on the table. "Show me you're ready to face the nonbelievers."

"I don't need to prove myself to you or anyone else. The only one I answer to is the Mother, and I know my wanting to teach does nothing to displease Her. 'Share my word as you would share knowledge of all else.'"

"Wise Mother Words," said Kylis, but her eyes narrowed at the use of one of the lesser known of the Mother's passages. The look on her face reminded Chandrey of the the similar expression that landed her on the floor with Kylis's knees in her sides, and she couldn't help the small gasp that escaped her mouth.

But Brava was clearly impressed by her words. "So be, Chandresslandra, and well put."

Kylis glared. "She obviously knows the word, but does she follow it?" She pushed away from the table. "How do you suppose you'll avoid so much temptation when you're in the midst of it?" she asked Chandrey.

"I've spent my entire life learning," Chandrey said. "I'm prepared to be faithful in the midst of temptation, decadence, whatever it takes for me to pursue my gifts."

"Such vanity," said Kylis. "You should be ashamed."

"Are you saying the teaching I received from you and Gahrah wasn't thorough?" She expected an explosion of temper from Kylis, but it never came.

"You twist my words." Kylis turned to Brava. "First you let her wear the robes of an adult, now this. If you let her go, you'll be to blame for her ruin. Just wait. She'll be sick at heart, short of faith, and begging to come home before her training is half over. Kimshees will draw her in with their stories and lies. Her resulting misery will be your doing."

"You talk about everyone else's lack of faith when you clearly haven't got any in yourself or our daughter," Brava said. "We've prepared her as best we can."

"It's not enough!" Kylis burst from her seat and crossed the kitchen to the cloak hooks by the back door. "I'll have no part of her ruin!" She grabbed her wrap.

"She's not Seechell." Brava tried to catch Kylis by the arm when she passed the table. "Where're you going this time of night?"

"Anywhere but this den of stupidity!" Kylis left the house without another word.

Brava placed her head in her hands. "Blasted woman," she said in a low voice. "Blasted, blasted woman."

"Does this mean I can go?" Chandrey asked when things had become quiet.

Brava looked at her from between her fingers. "You're absolutely sure you want this?"

"More than anything."

"Even after Kylis's warning?"

"I'm determined to prove her wrong."

"You're old enough to make your own choices," said Brava. "If you wish to attend the training, then go. You have my blessing."

"Oh, thank you, Gahrah!" She felt giddy as she set about clearing the dining table.

Brava helped her. They sat together most of the evening, going over the items Chandrey would need to pack. Kylis returned in the midst of their discussion. She said nothing, but went straight to the master bedroom and shut the door.

The next morning, Chandrey entered the main room to find Brava asleep in her chair.

Brava opened her eyes when she passed. "Tea, Chandresslandra?"

"I'll make some." She brewed two strong cups, taking them and a plate of breakfast buns to the table. "You slept out here all night?"

"She locked me out," said Brava. "I didn't sleep much. Spent most of the night thinking."

"You look it," Chandrey said between bites. She placed a bun in front of Brava. "Anything I can do?"

"I'll be fine." Brava pushed away the bun. "Kylis and I will simply have to work through our problems. Until then, I'll keep to my study when I'm home. Would you help me move the old lounger from the storage room?"

"Sure, and I'll get you some blankets from my press." The rest of the extra linens sat behind Kylis's barrier.

"Thank you."

She and Brava moved the worn lounger from storage and created a comfy nook where Brava could rest whenever Kylis locked her out. She also brought in a couple of empty baskets for Brava's personal items.

"What about your clothes?" she asked.

"That'll be another battle." Brava turned toward the master bedroom. "Why don't you go on to my work and tell them I'll be late."

"Sure thing."

Kylis was yelling at Brava and throwing clothing at her before Chandrey got out the door.

Chapter Seven

Kinship Training Grounds: Saria IV

Crystal—any storage container for wine or liquor

"There's the launch." Cance took the slice of vine fruit Belsas offered and sucked the juice from the pulp as they watched the aerolaunch float to a stop below their hilltop perch.

Belsas swiped her blade on the grass, sheathed it, and then leaned back against the tree shading them from the sun. One moon, almost white in its reflection, seemed perched above the sun, while another, mainly dark with shadow, was beginning to break above the horizon. She took note of the moons' positions—early afternoon—and turned back to her snack.

"You looking or lusting?" she asked between bites.

Cance's reputation with women was not typical for a kimshee. She held tight to her girlfriends, too tightly according to some of them. Her relationships progressed rapidly and ended abruptly, but no one seemed to emerge unsatisfied, so Belsas never thought too much about it unless Cance was on the hunt, which was often enough.

"Looking, lusting. Same, same." Cance swallowed a mouthful of fruit. "Taylor's too damned independent."

"What'd you expect? She's a weapons officer."

"A little consideration of my needs now and again would've been nice."

"You two fight again?" Belsas was certain the disagreement was the same one Cance always had with her girlfriends—commitment.

"Yeah, we fought."

"About what?"

"Exclusivity." Cance gave the word weight.

"After three dates?"

"I couldn't stand to see her talking to others. She was *my* girlfriend, not everyone else's."

"Was?"

"I broke things off with her when she wouldn't see only me." Cance leaned forward, no doubt to get a better view of the unloading launch where ten women were collecting their bags and smoothing their travel clothes. "But just as well." She smiled over her shoulder. "New skirts for the flirt."

"Can you be any more patronizing?" Belsas popped the last bit of fruit into her mouth. One of the new women caught her eye, but only because of her dress: the simple robes worn by Mother's Plan followers. *Odd*, she thought, but said nothing to Cance. "I read on the boards they're here for teacher training. They're civilian."

"All the better," said Cance wistfully. "They don't know me."

"And you'll be more than happy to introduce yourself, I'm sure."

"Would be my pleasure." Cance sucked juice from her finger, and then waved that finger through the air. "They've got to learn sometime."

"They're civies," reminded Belsas. "We're not supposed to fraternize with them during duty hours."

"We're on break."

"Tell that to the base Protocol Master."

"Since when has she managed to stop me?" Cance turned back to watch the potential objects of her affections. "Besides, all the newbies go to Ballyhoos their first night away from Mama. You coming?"

"Why?"

"I'll need you to take my new girlfriend's friend off my hands. No sister goes there by herself the first time. We didn't."

"I give you that, but how come I always end up going home alone?"

"'Cause you, my friend, have a face that screams academia." Cance chuckled when she turned around to view her. "And you haven't gone out with me in a while. You've had your nose in those musty scrolls."

"It's what I do." Belsas shrugged.

"Yeah, but you're starting to smell like them." Cance squeezed her shoulder when she rose. "Clean up before we go out, okay?"

Belsas looked down at her duty tunic and the dust nestled between its folds. Cance was right. She did wear the odor of old scrolls, but she actually liked the smell. It reminded her of the history she loved to read. Besides, she'd spent three of her five passes as a supply officer trying to convince the Kinship that she would be more beneficial as a historian, and she wasn't about to let Cance's remarks concerning the side-effects bother her now.

"You wearing your dress uniform?" she asked.

"No, then everyone knows what I do." Cance leaned against the tree, waiting for her to stand. "Kimshees are the ones your raisers warn you about, after all."

"Mine certainly did." And that was the truth. Belsas's raisers had objected when she had been billeted to room with Cance, but she had been past the Recognition so their words were fairly well ignored by everyone, especially her. "I really should study."

Cance tapped her fingers against the tree trunk. "You haven't been out in two moon cycles."

"I have an exam in three days."

"Live a little, will you?" Cance didn't try to hide her frustration.

Belsas took in her friend's expression for a moment—the slight raise of Cance's brow, the way she sucked in her bottom lip when she wasn't getting what she wanted. There wasn't any arguing with her, but friendship swayed her much more than Cance's moods or influence.

"You're damned manipulative, you know that?" she asked.

"It's what I do," Cance said with a laugh, helping her to her feet. "I'll buy the first crystal. What more could you ask for?"

"*First* crystal?" Belsas hung back a bit. "Just how much do you plan on us drinking tonight?"

"As much as it takes to get you loosened up." Cance started walking down the hillside to the pad where the empty launch sat. "As much as it takes to get a pretty girl in your arms."

* * *

Ballyhoos was actually a created cavern set into the hills a few hundred meters outside the gates of the Taelach Officer Training Grounds where Cance taught meditation basics to new Kimshee recruits, and Belsas divided her time between her supply officer duties and her studies.

The bar's interior was nothing more than a single room that housed a long counter, stools, and various combinations of tables and chairs scattered around a wooden dance floor set into the stone. Wall-mounted shelves behind the counter held a multitude of wine crystals of different vintages and blends, bottles of harder liquor, a few casks of sweet ale, and the cheap wine popular among the civilian students and low-ranking officers.

In fact, the civilian students had an unofficial ritual of coming to Ballyhoos their first night for a celebratory mug of wine, something that Cance took advantage of whenever she hunted for a new girlfriend.

When Belsas arrived, Cance was seated at one of Ballyhoos' larger tables, already into her second crystal of the fine wine she'd been raised to appreciate, happily sharing it with her favorite preoccupation.

"I thought you'd stayed home to study." Cance poured a brimming mug from her crystal and pushed it toward Belsas as she wedged into the crowded table.

Five of the women they'd seen earlier in the day sat at Cance's table, and every one of them was as pretty as she was young. While this certainly didn't surprise Belsas, it made her uncomfortable, but not enough to more than mention it to Cance through a subtle mind phase.

A bit young, aren't they?

If they're old enough to be here, they're old enough, Cance phased back with a grin and a wink. "Bel, meet Amie, Tamra Jo, Wreed, Allaneara and Chandresslandra, called Chandrey. Girls, meet my best friend, Belsas."

"Charmed." Tamra Jo extended her hand while Amie giggled and Allaneara blushed. Wreed nodded and peered directly at Belsas with a smile, but robe-wearing Chandrey kept her gaze aloof. Typical, she knew, of Mother's Plan members.

These women, save maybe Wreed, were not to Belsas's tastes, but they were appealing, and she felt her doubts fading with her first sip of wine.

"So what you brings you five to the Training Grounds?" Belsas asked politely, her gaze fixed on Chandrey. It wasn't that she found her any more attractive than the others, but the young woman seemed familiar in a way she couldn't place.

"We're here for teacher training," piped Amie, "for the Autlach-Taelach Teacher Outreach Program."

"Interesting," Belsas said, but Cance frowned.

"I thought that program had lost the Aut side of its funding."

"It has." Amie batted her eyelashes at Cance, who was refilling the other girls' mugs. "But several of the Kinship's better-off families have donated enough for the program to be reinstated."

"Do you know much about the program, Cance?" said Wreed.

"Enough to know it's a poor idea." Cance smirked. "Who in her right mind would believe Taelachs and Autlachs should teach each other?"

"How would you know?" Tamra Jo's surprised expression matched her companions'.

Cance had almost inadvertently revealed her kimshee status, but she didn't stumble a bit. "It's obvious the intelligence gap is just too great to bridge," she said. "I mean, really, what's next, Auts teaching sisters?" She motioned for the waitress, a mid-age sister whom Belsas knew was overly familiar with Cance's reputation.

"New crystal already?" the waitress asked.

The civilians whispered among themselves.

"What's on tonight's menu?" Cance asked.

"Hopper ragout. Seven mugs, then?"

"I know Bel and I are hungry for something other than Training Ground food." Cance looked around the table. "But I don't know about our company. Are you hungry, girls? My treat, of course."

"No, thank you." Amie nudged Tamra Jo. "I think we should get back to our dorm."

"So soon?" Belsas rose so the young women could leave the crowded table. "Ballyhoos' food isn't that bad."

"I'm certain it isn't," continued Amie as she and Tamra Jo breezed past. "But we've already eaten, and it's late." She turned to Wreed, Allaneara and Chandrey. "You staying?"

"It *is* late." Allaneara emptied her mug, and then stood. "Thank you for the drinks, Cance." She pulled her wrap over her shoulders. "Nice to meet you, Belsas."

"You as well." She bowed slightly when Allaneara passed, and watched the three women walk away before she turned back to the table.

"Bring us four mugs and some bread," said Cance to the waitress. "And another crystal."

The waitress nodded and walked off.

Now Cance had what she wanted, but Belsas wondered which one she'd end up entertaining the rest of the evening. The answer became apparent as Cance talked softly to Chandrey, who was noticeably uncomfortable with her surroundings.

Belsas downed another swallow of wine and turned to Wreed, who seemed to be taking the bar atmosphere in stride. "Cance is my friend, but I don't share her politics." She topped off Wreed's wine. "There's a definite need for a closing of the gap between the Aut and Taelach education systems."

"I agree," replied Wreed as she sipped.

She was a small woman, curvaceous in the way Belsas liked, but short, something that always made her self-conscious of her own height. She tugged her sleeves down as Wreed talked on about the teaching program and its goals until the waitress plopped four steaming mugs and a heaping basket of hard rolls on the table.

"This is just stew." Wreed poked her blade at the floating chunks of meat and vegetables. "It sounded exotic to hear the waitress describe it."

"She's good at embellishing." Belsas blew across her mug. "And it tastes better than it looks."

"It'd have to." Wreed took a tentative bite from her blade tip. "Not bad."

Across the table, Cance dominated Chandrey's evening, filling her with stories of extensive travels. And Chandrey, with her long, thick mane of hair and heart-shaped face, seemed mesmerized by both the stories and the teller. She sat at arm's length from Cance, but leaned closer whenever the story became interesting, and Cance used these opportunities to touch Chandrey in some small way.

Belsas saw her try to take Chandrey's hand at one point, but Chandrey pulled back. *I'll have to talk to Cance about the Mother's Plan manners*, she thought.

"Fortunately, you don't share your friend's penchant for laying it on thick," said Wreed between bites.

Belsas nearly choked with laughter. "She's not generally so transparent." She liked Wreed, but not in the consuming fashion Cance seemed to like Chandresslandra.

Cance brushed Chandresslandra's hair behind her shoulder and slid a hand down her arm to pat her hand. Chandresslandra pulled back a little this time, but said nothing.

"What does Cance do here at the grounds?" Wreed reached for a second roll.

"She's an instructor."

"Of what?"

It was getting difficult for Belsas to hide Cance's occupation. "A variety of things."

"Like?"

"Weaponry." That wasn't a lie. Cance did teach a weaponry class most terms.

"Oh," said Wreed. "So how'd you become friends? You two seem nothing alike."

"We bunked together during Training Ground basics, and then through school." Belsas broke her roll into pieces so she could clean out her mug. "I guess we've known each other ten passes."

"And you're both *still* at the Grounds?"

"We were reassigned here. Cance teaches, and I'm completing new training."

"What sort?" said Wreed as she watched Cance work her charms on Chandresslandra.

"Historical archivist."

"Chandrey's into history. She wants to teach it." Wreed leaned a bit closer. "Your friend should know Chandrey's younger than the rest of my group."

"Really?" Belsas looked across the table. "By how much?"

"She's just turned sixteen."

"Not good." Belsas shook her head. "I'll let Cance know."

"That's not all. Chandrey's Mother's Plan."

"I recognized the robes."

"And her surname is Brava."

Belsas put down her mug. "As in Brava Deb?"

Wreed nodded. Belsas groaned. Cance was entirely out of her element. Brava Deb was the first assistant to Grandmaster Benjimena Kim, Taelach of All, the official leader of the Silver Kinship and spokeswoman for the entire Taelach population.

Now Belsas knew why Chandrey seemed familiar. Brava Deb was also a lay leader in the Mother's Plan sect, an ultraconservative group which she'd briefly considered joining before she'd fully researched their beliefs.

The Mother's Plan supported Taelach family issues, especially the home as the center of religious teaching. To the Mother's Plan, the oath was for life and could not be undone. While Belsas agreed that the oath was serious, her own raisers had renounced each other when she was young, and neither of them had been miserable after. In fact, they became great friends and better raisers because of the Renunciation.

She wondered how Brava Deb would feel about her daughter sharing a meal with a kimshee. "I've got to tell her."

"If you don't, I will," said Wreed.

Cance poured Chandrey another mug of wine. Poor Chandrey, Belsas thought. She'd obviously been sheltered. Her first venture into adulthood had put her in a kimshee's path.

Belsas wondered what she was doing in a bar in the first place, but when she asked Wreed, she shrugged.

"She needs to get out in the world, so I didn't tell her Ballyhoos was a bar." Wreed smiled weakly. "And now that she's here, she won't walk home without me. We're supposed to stay in at least pairs for the first couple of days. Besides, I'm her roommate."

"Oh." Belsas rose from the table. "Let's get a fresh crystal, Cance."

Cance waved, but didn't look away from Chandrey. "The waitress will be back in a bit."

"I saw her go on break."

"I can wait. There's still some wine in my mug." Cance was clearly reluctant to leave Chandrey's side. "Why don't you get it?"

"I can only afford the cheap stuff."

"No vinegar for this table." Cance patted Chandrey's arm. "Don't go anywhere." She followed Belsas to the bar where she ordered two crystals of Ballyhoos' finest. "What's so important?" she asked.

"How'd you know—?" Belsas began, and then stopped. "Yeah, I know I can use your credit here, but I wanted to talk to you."

"Wreed not to your liking?"

"She's nice enough. But she wanted me to warn you about Chandrey."

"Chandresslandra? What about her?"

"She's only sixteen."

"That's old enough."

"And you're twenty-six, same as me. That's too much difference."

"You're going to have to do better than that. Ten passes is nothing."

"It is at her age. And there's more."

"Yeah?"

"You heard of the Mother's Plan?"

"Yeah, they're some sort of weird religious sect. Chandrey's one of them. Don't you hate those robes? They cover all her good parts."

"Okay, then, how about this: she's Brava Deb's daughter."

Cance popped open one of the crystals to take a swig. "I already know."

"She told you?"

"I picked her thoughts."

"Mother above, Cance. Can you break any more social rules tonight?"

"If I get drunk enough," Cance said with a half grin. "Besides, she never knew I was in her head."

"That's not the point." Belsas popped open the second crystal. "Her upbringing frowns on casual phasing. And do you know what the Mother's Plan group thinks about kimshees?"

"Her mind links everything to her faith."

"So what're you going to do?"

"I'm still working on it."

"The Mother's Word is all she knows." When the wine failed to calm Belsas's nerves, she ordered a shot of bitterwine, which she charged to Cance's account. The drink was sour and thick, but cleared her head fast. "How deep did you go in her head?"

"Not deep. I didn't want to be flooded with her 'Wise Mother Words.'"

"You're tactless when you drink." Belsas tossed back the shot and turned toward the table. "I'm telling Wreed to take Chandrey back to the dorms."

"You wouldn't."

"To keep you out of trouble? Definitely."

"Damn it, Bel." Cance crossed her arms over her chest and spun away from the bar. She spotted Wreed and Chandrey rising. "Fuck! They're leaving."

"Good." Belsas was a step behind Cance all the way to the table.

"Going so soon?" Cance placed a hand on Chandrey's arm, coaxing her to sit back down.

"Wreed reminded me how early we have class tomorrow," said Chandrey, reaching for her cloak. "We must be getting back to the dorm."

"Besides," added Wreed. "Curfew is in less than an hour."

"Curfew?" Cance curled her lip. "You're not cadets."

"Chandrey studies her faith every evening for at least an hour." Wreed's tone did nothing to hide her dislike for Cance. "You know Chandrey's raiser, Brava Deb, don't you?"

"Who doesn't?" Cance scowled at Wreed, and then took Chandrey's hand. "At least let me walk you home."

Chandrey pulled away. "It wouldn't be proper."

"What if Wreed and Belsas walk with us?" prompted Cance. "That'd be proper, wouldn't it?"

"I suppose." Chandrey turned to Wreed. "Will you?"

"Sure." Wreed sounded relieved. "Belsas?"

"Of course." Belsas pushed in the chairs.

Cance collected the two fresh crystals from the bar and passed one to her. "For the walk home."

Belsas took the bottle, more to slow Cance's drinking than to enjoy it herself. "Not on the Training Grounds, Cancelynn. Even for staff."

"Then we've got to the gates to finish them." Cance took a hearty swig. "Let's go."

Belsas watched as Cance took Chandrey by the elbow, leading her toward the door.

"Thank you," said Wreed while they strolled toward the gate. "Chandrey's been so kind that I feel almost obligated to keep an eye on her."

"How did she get into the program at her age?" Belsas watched Chandrey refuse a drink of Cance's wine.

"She's very intelligent." Wreed wrapped her arm around Belsas's. "But her Mother's Plan raising has left her very naïve, something Cance apparently sensed."

"Yeah, she's good at that." Belsas liked Wreed's touch, but it certainly wasn't naïve.

Unlike Chandrey, Wreed wore pants, bucking the current civilian trend toward skirts or jumpers, and she wore her hair in a neat twist high on her head—not a young style, but one that suited her exceptionally well.

"I'm glad she has you to watch out for her," Belsas continued.

"She's a nice girl." Wreed smiled up at her. "You need a Chandrey yourself. Doesn't Cance embarrass you?"

"She's too much into the drink tonight."

"The way she downs it, I thought she always drank heavy."

"Not so." *But then again, I haven't gone out with her in quite a while.*

They were nearing the Training Ground's main gates, Belsas noticed.

Cance downed the last of her crystal and tossed the empty into the bushes clear of the guard's view. Belsas placed her nearly full crystal behind a boulder, trying to make note of its location so she could retrieve it later, but doubted she would need to remember. She had no doubt Cance would come back for it.

After clearing the guard house, the group made its way toward the dormitory that Wreed indicated.

"We'll say goodnight here." Wreed squeezed Belsas's hand and stretched up to kiss her on the cheek. "Thank you for your patience."

She smiled at her embarrassment. "You're almost as shy as Chandrey," she gently teased. "I think it's nice on you." She pulled Belsas's collar until she bent enough to look her in the eyes. "See you again, I hope?"

"Soon," Belsas said when their lips touched. "Soon."

Wreed released her hold and turned her attention to their mutual cause. "Time we got inside, Chandrey."

Cance held fast to Chandrey's arm. "Ballyhoos tomorrow evening?"

"Oh, no, not there." Chandrey touched the hand holding hers. "It wouldn't be proper to be seen there very often."

"Proper." Cance repeated in a monotone. "But of course. I apologize. Where, then, would be proper?"

Wreed sighed. "Chandrey, sweetie, the time…"

"Just a minute." Cance turned so her back was to Wreed and Belsas, blocking Chandrey from view. "The officers' mess tomorrow evening?"

"Officers' mess?" Chandrey tried to peer over Cance's shoulder at Wreed, but Cance was just tall enough in her boots to make eye contact difficult. "Is that similar to Ballyhoos?"

"It's the officers' dining hall." Cance gently but firmly pulled Chandrey toward her. "Come as my guest," she said in a low voice. "I'd be honored."

Chandrey stepped back. "What time will you call?"

"I will be right here at the evening bell."

Wreed looked at Belsas. They exchanged nods.

Belsas had a date the next night, and she felt encouraged for the first time in a very long time. She might not like Cance's behavior, her subtle manipulation of that innocent girl, but supervising the affair might bring Wreed and her together.

Her stomach rumbled from a combination of wine and nerves. Pleasure had been fleeting, true passion for anything but history seldom. She touched Wreed's sleeve as they parted and was rewarded with an unsteady, but far from virginal pleasure phase.

Thank you. Wreed's mental touch seeped deep into her.

Belsas longed to languish in the joy. The history scrolls could wait for once.

Chapter Eight

Kinship Training Grounds: Saria IV

Precious—delicate, helpless; worthless

"Trust me." Cance held out her hand.

Chandrey and Cance stood on the edge of one of the hiking trails just outside the Training Grounds' high stone walls. The steep path was slick with dead grasses and early morning rain, but Cance had begged her to go on a hike—for the exercise, for the time together.

Cance held out her hand a little more insistently. "I won't let you fall."

Chandrey hesitated a second more, and then clasped Cance above the wrist and scrambled up the path, following Cance off the path and behind a boulder.

"Finally." Cance pulled her closer and a bit further from view. "We're alone." She ran a hand down her back.

"Cancelynn, stop." Chandrey took a step away.

"Just a kiss." Cance pulled her close again.

"Another?" Chandrey stepped on her robe hem as she broke away a second time. The hem caught on the heel of her boot and she stumbled backward, sliding a little down the hillside.

Cance grasped her forearm, pulled her back up, and bent to pull her hem loose. "Now that should earn me a kiss," she said as she straightened.

"The Mother says kindness offers its own reward." Chandrey had long since stopped waiting for anyone around her to recognize Wise Mother Words. Cance sometimes noticed them, if she was in the mood, but most of the time they weren't honored. Adult converts to the Mother's Plan were rare, but not unheard of, and she was determined to make Cance her first success. Maybe then, Brava and Kylis would be accepting.

"Your boots are worn out."

"They're functional." Chandrey let their presences mingle as much as she dared, and then stepped back again, much more carefully this time. "My raisers will send my clothing allowance when it's time."

"Brava Deb doesn't know the current state of your wardrobe." Cance seemed upset. "I do, and I say you need some new things. How much does she give you, anyway? Two, three thousand credits a quarter? That's not much."

"That's twice my annual allowance!"

"You can't be serious." Cance pulled a credit chip from her tunic pocket and pressed it into Chandrey's hand. "I have the means. Let me help. Let me purchase you some hiking boots."

"That'd be wasteful." Chandrey placed the chip back into Cance's hand.

"You're going to get hurt."

"The Mother says one should never accept frivolous gifts."

"Wise Words." Cance frowned. "The Mother doesn't forbid basic needs, does she?"

"Of course not, but—"

"When's the last time you saw Brava Deb?"

"At the pass-end break, you know that."

"That was three cycles ago. How could she know what you need?"

"But—"

"I'm taking you shopping, and that's final."

"What's final?" asked Belsas when she and Wreed appeared just below them on the trail.

"Have you seen Chandrey's boots?" Cance pulled up the hem of Chandrey's robes, revealing the chipped, muddy heels.

"She has a point," said Wreed to Chandrey. "Why don't you get some better ones?"

"Because I don't want to ask for the credits, that's why!" Chandrey snatched her robes away from Cance. "Kylis keeps the house accounts, and she makes me account for every bit I use. It gets tedious."

"More reason for me to buy them." Cance looked at Belsas and Wreed for support, but they were engaged in a deep kiss.

Chandrey envied their open affection, but she'd been taught differently. The Mother frowned on such shows.

"Tomorrow's market day. I'll take you by a boot maker's stall," Cance continued.

"Custom boots? I couldn't!"

"Why don't you let her?" Belsas mumbled around Wreed's mouth. "She won't shut up until do."

"Wreed?" Chandrey asked.

"Hmm?" Wreed was too preoccupied to say more.

"Okay. We'll go."

Cance seemed genuinely pleased, if not delighted.

* * *

"Cance has the means." Wreed told Chandrey later that afternoon in their room. "Bel says she has more credits than conscious. Let her spend a little on you. It's better than spending it on wine."

"She's cut back since I asked," said Chandrey. "And I did spend the last of my credits on that wrap she thought I'd look good in." She glanced at the finely woven shawl hanging above her rolled bedding. The shawl had seemed like a good idea at the time, but now she wondered what Kylis and Gahrah would say. "I suppose I bought it more to please her than for myself."

"There you go." Wreed looked up from the scroll she was studying. "She owes you."

"I still feel guilty." However, as Cance had recently pointed out, they *were* her credits to spend. How she spent them should be no one else's business as long as she sent her tithes, Chandrey thought. "I should have donated the money."

"That's your raising talking."

"The Mother doesn't want us wasting money when there are others in need."

"Most any sister will tell you there's a difference between necessities and luxuries."

"I suppose. What're you reading?"

"Something Bel wrote."

"Another poem?"

Wreed smiled. "How'd you guess?"

"Belsas is certainly taken with you."

"And I'm with her." Wreed let the scroll wrap around her finger. "You should read some of her research. It's quite interesting. She's compiling Rankil Danston's life history."

"I hope it's better than her poetry," Chandrey gently teased. "The last one you read me—"

"It wasn't one of her best," said Wreed. "And love poetry doesn't have to be good to, well, to be good. What about the one Cance wrote?"

"It's more of limerick."

"But she wrote it with a good heart."

"I thought you didn't like her?"

"I think she asks too much of someone your age."

"Again with the age?" Chandrey plopped onto her sleeping roll and pulled off her boots. "Will you let it rest? Cance doesn't seem to mind."

"You make her look good." Wreed glanced up from the study scroll she had been reading. "But others don't like the difference."

"Like you and Belsas?"

"No. Kylis."

"I still haven't told my raisers about Cance." Chandrey dropped her boots on her side of the room and began pulling off her stockings, the thick, hand-made kind that Wreed loathed, but Kylis sent them both on a regular basis. Wreed used hers for cleaning. "They wouldn't approve of her faith."

"Cance has a faith?"

"Not exactly, but she lets me share the Mother's Word."

"Really? Look, sweetie, Kylis is digging for something bad on you."

"Why do you say that?"

Wreed dug around her worktable for her personal recorder. "She wrote me."

"Dear Mother, save me from my own family." Chandrey balled up her stockings and squeezed them hard. "What'd you tell her?"

"I just got the message yesterday." Wreed handed her the com printout. "I've been deciding what to say." She hesitated. "And how to tell you."

"Oh, please don't tell her about Cance," Chandrey pleaded as she dropped her stockings. "Please, Wreed."

"I don't have a choice." Wreed pointed at the message. "Read it, and you'll see why."

She did so reluctantly, and then looked at Wreed in sheer despair. "How'd she find out I was seeing someone?"

"Who knows? What do you want me to say?"

"I don't know." Chandrey set the message aside and sagged across her bedroll, landing face first in her pillow. "I just don't know."

"Haven't you talked to Cance about your raisers?"

"We've discussed them once or twice, but she keeps telling me not to worry, that we'll deal with them when the time comes." She picked up her stockings and began to twirl them around her fingers. "I haven't had enough time to teach Cance our ways. Kylis is going to say I've shamed my raising and my faith by dating without their approval." She bit her lip hard enough to sting. "Do they know Cance is a kimshee?"

"Why, does it matter somehow?" said Wreed.

"The Mother's Plan doesn't believe in using kimshees to bring in newborns. We're to seek children on our own and in our own time."

"That's ridiculous." Wreed took the printout from her. "And dangerous."

"It's our way." Chandrey tossed the stockings against the wall, watching as they spread and slinked down to land with a soft thud at her feet. "Poor Gahrah, I'm sure Kylis will throw Cance being kimshee in her face. Gahrah is strong in public, but Kylis reigns at home. She just won't listen to my explanations, not like Gahrah does. All she sees are the Mother's Words which she takes far too literally. Rules for how she lives, how I should live. If it doesn't follow her interpretation of the Words, it's not—"

"Proper?" Wreed sat beside her. "The Mother's Plan has always been strict concerning behavior."

"Kylis is even stricter." Chandrey gathered the stockings and began to neatly fold them, just as she'd been taught. "They're going to be *so* upset when they find out Cance is kimshee." She unfolded and refolded the stockings, and dropped them when the potential extent of Kylis's anger became real. "She called the Training Grounds a den of lechery. What if she convinces Gahrah I should go back home?"

"Your grades are perfect. Surely, they wouldn't." Wreed pulled her personal com from the worktable drawer. "So how should I answer?"

Chandrey thought for a moment, and then stood, kicking her stockings to the side. "Let me talk to Cance first." She walked barefoot to the door. "I'm going to use the hall com."

"Use mine."

She heard Wreed speak as she walked out, but she kept going. She wanted to be alone when she talked to Cance, even if it meant using the old-style com outside their room.

Most sisters had personal coms, but not her, not any sister in her family except her gahrah, who had to have one for work. Personal coms were frivolous—at least that was what she'd always heard. But much of what she had learned now seemed wrong. So much wasn't fair.

Wreed had her own com. Belsas had her own. Cance had two—one for work and one for personal use. Chandrey wanted, no, she needed a com. That way she and Cance could talk at their leisure, even after curfew.

Cance. She gathered her thoughts and reached for the hall com.

* * *

Cance suggested they talk over wine at Ballyhoos, which Chandrey thought wasn't an entirely bad idea. The Mother only permitted wine at the evening meal, and then in moderation, but the Mother didn't have to deal with Kylis or worry about disappointing Gahrah.

Cance met her outside her dorm. They walked arm-in-arm to the bar. Things would be fine, said Cance as she patted Chandrey's hand, just fine. They'd figure something out. In the meantime, she should pray and meditate on the situation. It's what she did best, Cance said.

They drank in silence for almost an hour, Cance seeming to down two mugs to Chandrey's one, but she didn't really keep count. While she brooded about the contrast between her raising and her wants, Cance simply drank, an arm around her shoulder, their feet touching beneath the table. It was more comforting than suggestive. She felt safe.

Cance was older and had more experience with this sort of situation, Chandrey thought. She would be able to solve the problem.

"Well," Cance said after their third crystal. "I have an idea."

Chandrey swallowed hard and lay against Cance's arm, fighting back the swimming feeling between her ears. She wasn't sure she liked the sensation, but she wasn't nearly as stressed either. "I'm afraid to hear."

"Don't be, Precious. I'll take care of you." Cance pulled Chandrey deeper into her arms, and drew her head to her shoulder.

Chandrey had no will to resist, even when thoughts of her raisers' reaction flashed through her mind. But how could holding someone be ugly in the Mother's eyes? Brava had held her often enough as a child. Not like this, but still, she had comforted her and that was exactly what Cance was doing.

"I'll talk to them," Cance went on. "I'll make them see my intentions are good."

"*You* will?" When Chandrey tried to pull back, Cance held her close and kissed her forehead. "That's your idea?"

She could imagine Kylis verbally shredding Cance. Kylis's eyes were sharp, her tongue sharper still. She would pick apart Cance, her raising, and her choice of vocations before Chandrey could get a word in edgewise. She'd seen Kylis do it to so many others—to other Plan members, to Brava, to herself more times than she cared to think about.

Sisters kept away after one of Kylis's inquisitions, and Chandrey couldn't fault them. She'd have fled home earlier had it been possible, but where would she have gone? Brava was prominent. She would have been returned home almost as soon as she left, and Kylis would've locked her door and windows from the outside the first moment Brava wasn't around, "for her own protection."

Cance encouraged her to finish the wine in her mug. "Your raisers already know you're seeing someone, so it's only a matter of time before we're found out." She nuzzled into her hair. "And I'll not hide from them or anyone else."

"But you're not of my faith, reason enough for them to forbid my seeing you." Chandrey found comfort in their closeness and the warmth that traveled from her stomach to her lap whenever they touched. "Plus you're a kimshee."

"I won't be forever."

"You don't understand."

"I'm sure they can find a thousand reasons to keep us apart if they try hard enough," said Cance. "But what I feel for you is so strong that I can't be afraid."

"Well, I am." Chandrey placed her face against Cance's neck. "Kylis'll find some way to get between us. I know she will."

"She can't dissuade me from your side."

A curious sensation swept through Chandrey when Cance spoke. An exhilaration, a joy, a fluttering in her stomach so intense, her breath caught in her throat.

Kylis can't get in the way of our love.

"You're in my head?" Chandrey asked.

Cance brought her mouth up for a kiss unlike any they'd shared. The fluttering and warmth spread through her, so sweet she ached for more.

Yes, Precious, I'm here.

Their kiss deepened until Chandrey tingled and longed. She couldn't break away despite the knowledge of her raisers' disapproval. It was too good, too sweet. She felt accepted, totally free, bare, and unencumbered by rules for the first time. The Mother Maker couldn't disapprove of such joy.

I've fallen desperately in love with you.

I love you too. Chandrey's phase reply came faster than she intended. *I can't help but be in love with you.*

"You've never phased before, have you?"

Chandrey opened her eyes to Cance's knowing smile. "Oh, my." Cance's consuming expression made her ache all the more.

"Don't blush." Cance touched her cheek. "It's okay."

"But what about my raisers?" Chandrey heard herself saying as pleasure seeped into every crevice of her body. She knew what it all meant, what Cance wanted, what *she* wanted, but part of her still said it was wrong. The Mother's Plan forbade phasing before oathing. But those tenets weren't supported here, and she had to adapt to her current environment. Besides, the Mother, the Mother she was learning to embrace, wouldn't fault such a trivial lapse between two sisters she'd so obviously brought together.

"I'll contact Brava Deb tomorrow." Cance emptied her mug, and then took Chandrey by the hand. "Tonight is for us alone."

Chandrey couldn't resist when Cance led her from the bar and off the main path leading to the base, didn't think once to object when Cance eased her to the cool ground behind a rise. Her mind was Cance's and her body would have been too, had she asked.

Cance sat behind Chandrey, pulled her into her lap, back to front, and placed her mind into hers. She'd certainly never experienced the phase they shared, and shuddered and moaned as Cance teased her thoughts, but she sensed Cance was restraining herself, not showing her too much too fast. That restraint bore witness to Cance's true respect for her.

Cance carefully taught Chandrey her role as lover, how the phase worked, how it should be when they phased. Cance was the teacher, she the hungry student. This part of their phase satisfied her more than she could have imagined, but Cance clearly needed more.

I've got to taste you. Cance projected vivid images of them together, Chandrey nude beneath her as Cance greedily sank her mouth into her folds. Cance's tongue flicked against her, sucking her in. When she cried out, Cance pushed her mouth all the harder.

Joy overwhelming coursed through Chandrey. She rocked her hips up to meet Cance. Cance pushed her back down, and then pulled on her again, coaxing her to repeat the movement until it became a rhythm to make her explode. And explode she did, instinctively grinding against Cance's mouth.

You learn fast. Cance wiped Chandrey's juices from her face and kissed her way up her body to her breasts, which she consumed with nearly the same voraciousness.

Cance's tongue circled Chandrey's stiff nipples. She bit down lightly, sending exquisite tingles down her abdomen into her thighs. Cance hummed laughter against her breast when she gasped, and then dropped a hand between her legs without warning.

No. Not that, Chandrey sent. *We're not oathed.*

Shh. Don't worry, Precious. This is all in our minds.

Cance pressed Chandrey's thighs wider apart, and drew a hand up her mound, pausing briefly at her untamed pubic hair before she began stroking. Cance didn't stay there long, either, and pressed downward to the last bit of Chandrey's phase virginity.

Her fingers slipped inside before Chandrey realized. She couldn't do more than try to crawl away even as she tried to keep up with Cance. But Cance held her firm, pinning her as she pressed those long fingers deeper into her.

Once there, Cance persisted in her strokes, riding Chandrey until the pleasure threatened to completely consume her. The Mother's wisest words of all rang through her until she could think of nothing else. *Love with every bit of your being. Honor me with your love.*

Chandrey clenched her thighs around Cance's hand until she slowed and the waves finally ceased. Cance kept her fingers inside her, placing gentle kisses on her abdomen.

"I've wanted you since the night we met," Cance said.

Chandrey opened her eyes to find Cance's hands on her knees. They were both clothed, both panting, sweating, tangled on the ground.

"You're even more beautiful inside than out."

Chandrey sat up on her elbows and looked around. They were still behind the rise.

"No one saw us." Cance reached out her hand, her sticky hand, to touch Chandrey's hair.

"You've got something on your—" Then Chandrey realized what covered Cance's fingers. She grasped Cance's hand and held it to her face. "You said that was all in our minds!"

"It pretty much was." Cance wiped her hand across the grass. "I pleasured myself while I mentally pleasured you. I came with you."

"Came?"

Cance's gaze became rapt. "You don't know?"

Chandrey couldn't help feeling embarrassed. "I felt so much."

"When you couldn't stand any more, but I kept on. What you felt then. You came. That's what I mean."

"The waves?"

"Mmm," Cance said. "Yes, the waves."

"Oh." Chandrey's body ached from the inside out. Her joy felt different now, a tired satisfaction that she knew meant the Mother approved of their expression of love. But as much as she wanted to curl up with Cance and sleep, she couldn't. It was late—how late she wasn't exactly sure—but the dew had settled. "I've got to get back to the dorm."

"I suppose." Cance helped Chandrey to her feet, and then stood and watched with amusement as Chandrey tried to smooth her skirts and hair. "You're beautiful, you know that? You're positively glowing. Mind fucks agree with you."

"Must you use that word?"

"Fuck?" Cance pulled Chandrey to her for another deep kiss.

Chandrey's senses went weak again, and she let Cance have her way.

Cance caressed her breasts and back, but her hands stayed above her clothes until they reached Chandrey's neck, where Cance tilted her head back so she could kiss and nibble everything above the collar. "I like the word fuck," she said into Chandrey's ear. "It's primal. Kind of like my feelings for you."

Chandrey's knees threatened to forsake her, so she leaned harder against Cance.

Cance could have taken her again, phased her again if she had wanted, but after a moment she stood back. "You're dead on your feet, Precious. Let's get you home."

Cance wrapped an arm around Chandrey's waist as they walked in silence back through the gates and toward the dorms.

Chandrey wanted sleep, but she wanted it beside Cance.

I agree. Cance stopped on the walkway outside Chandrey's dormitory, drew her into a last kiss—much softer but no less wanton than the others—and turned her toward the door. "Rest well, Precious. We'll talk tomorrow."

Chandrey watched from the stoop until Cance had turned a corner before reaching for the door. It was locked. She was late for curfew. After a moment of panic, she walked to the rear of the building and rapped on the window of the room she shared with Wreed. The shutters were drawn, but the lights were on.

When she tapped the glass, Wreed parted the shutters and threw them back to open the window.

"You're late!" Wreed said when Chandrey climbed inside and closed the window behind her. "The dorm monitor already made her check."

"Oh, Mother!" Chandrey collapsed into a chair and started removing her boots. "What'd she say?"

"I told her you were in the study lounge."

Chandrey hung her head and slunk past her. Wreed had lied for her.

"You've been drinking."

"Just a couple." Chandrey couldn't look Wreed in the eye, so she concentrated on her shoes, one of three pairs Cance had recently bought her. "Sister Rhal believed I was studying?"

"That's where you usually are." Wreed released her arm and reached up to pick something from Chandrey's hair. "What happened?"

"I was talking with Cance."

Wreed held up a blade of grass. "Some talk." But her amusement faded when Chandrey began to undress. "Damn, Chandrey, what *were* you doing?" Wreed took her under-robe from the chair and held it out, revealing the dirt and the decided white spot on the back. "You didn't."

Chandrey's stockings were even more incriminating. They were ruined—dirty, ripped, and showing more signs of intimacy.

"We phased." Chandrey slipped into her sleeping shift.

"You did a lot more than that." Wreed pointed to her neck. "Look in the reflector."

Chandrey released her hair from its band as she gazed into the board. Cance's long, hard kisses had left marks. "Oh, my." She covered them with her hand and turned to Wreed. "Can I borrow one of your scarves tomorrow?"

"I was going to suggest it."

Chandrey pulled her hair over the marks so she could walk to the facilities down the hall.

The dorm monitor saw her when she walked past, but only nodded. "Good night, Sister Chandrey."

"You too, Sister Rhal."

Chandrey slipped into the facilities, the first bay, and sat there, wringing her hands as she realized she should have brought fresh underwear. Her current pair was wet from more than her joy. The crotch was blood streaked and her groin ached. Now she couldn't be at all sure if they had only phased. Now she couldn't be sure of anything. She tried to remember what had really happened, but all she could think about were the sensations. The pleasure. Cance.

But Cance couldn't have done anything wrong, because the Mother wasn't seeing to her misery. She wasn't miserable at all. She was happy. Confused, but happy.

She slipped the ruined underwear into the waste tube and walked silently back to her room. Wreed was still awake and had unrolled their pallets so they lay side by side.

Wreed patted Chandrey's pillow when she shut the door. "Catch the lights."

Chandrey lowered the overhead beams and crawled into her blankets, which were cold. She was cold. She could only think of Cance, her warmth, her touch, her taste, her feel. "Wreed?"

"Yes?" Wreed rolled toward her.

"Do you love Belsas?"

Wreed propped herself up on an elbow. "Why do you ask?"

"Do you?"

"I don't know," Wreed said. "I like her. We have scads of fun together."

"Have you been with her?"

"As in phased? We've played around a bit, but nothing too serious."

"What do you mean by play around?"

"We've lightly phased a few times." Wreed sat up and wrapped the top blanket over her shoulders. "Why do you ask?"

Chandrey had to share her thoughts. "We did more than play around."

"I figured that out," Wreed said. "Can I ask just how far you went?"

"We pleasure phased, but no more—I think."

"You aren't sure?"

"It happened so fast. One minute we were at Ballyhoos, and the next we were outside. She was in my head before I knew it."

"She didn't force herself into you, did she?" Wreed stared at her.

"No, I wanted it. I'm just not sure how far we went. I thought it was all phase, but now my groin aches and I'm bleeding a little."

"That's not unheard of," Wreed said. "Especially if it's your first time. Think about it. Did you stay dressed?"

"Yes."

"Fully dressed?"

"I think."

"Then you just phased. A good phase can seem real enough that your body reacts like it *was* real, and Cance is kimshee. She's trained to use her phase. You were with a strong mind."

"I suppose you're right." That explained everything. Cance was older, more experienced and trained. Their encounter had been *that* realistic. Chandrey closed her eyes when Wreed lay back down. "Goodnight."

"Goodnight."

But her mind was still processing. "Wreed?" Chandrey asked a moment later.

"Yep?"

"Don't tell anyone, okay?"

"Who'd I tell?"

"Belsas."

"I'm sure Cance already has, but I won't unless she brings it up first. Okay?"

"Okay. Thanks."

"Sure thing. Go to sleep."

"I'll try." Chandrey curled in on herself, imagining Cance wrapped around her, holding her tight through the night.

Chapter Nine

Kinship Training Grounds: Saria IV

Pick—*to tease or make fun of; unwanted mental contact to gain information*

Wreed tried to keep her friend's secret, but as time wore on, Chandrey began coming back late more nights than not. And when she did, she smelled of wine.

When Chandrey finally failed to come in at all one night, Wreed knew she couldn't hide the situation any longer—not from Sister Rahl, not from anyone else—so she commed Belsas the next morning and asked if they could meet.

Belsas said she was working in the Training Ground archives most of the evening, but Wreed could come see her there if she wanted.

After the evening meal, Wreed watched Chandrey walk off with Cance toward Ballyhoos, and then made her way to the archives located in the basement of one of the Training Ground's oldest, mustiest buildings. She knew Belsas was working in one of the deeper vaults in a controlled environment room where delicate, old scrolls were kept.

The watch told her that she was expected and pointed down the left-hand corridor. Belsas waved at her when she tapped the clean room glass, so she waited outside until Belsas shed her smock and gloves and came through the air lock.

"Hello there." Belsas kissed Wreed quickly but firmly on the mouth and took her hand, leading her upstairs to a pair of comfortable reading chairs in the corner of the main archives. "You sounded upset this morning." She continued to hold her hand.

"It's Chandrey. She's in trouble," Wreed said.

"How so?" Belsas leaned back in her chair.

"She's phasing with Cance."

"She's *what?*" Belsas sat up straight and dropped her hand. "What of her raising, her faith, her *age?*"

"I asked her that," said Wreed. "She didn't have a firm answer, just said she was happy."

"Who isn't when she learns to phase? But that doesn't excuse Cance. She should've had more respect for Chandrey and her raising." Belsas gripped her chair arms hard enough for the hide to squeak. "I'm so sorry."

"This wasn't your doing." Wreed placed her hand over Belsas's fist. "Neither of us has been very attentive." She leaned forward to rest her head against Belsas's shoulder.

Belsas responded in her typical manner, barely touching Wreed's hair with her lips and wrapping an arm around her shoulder.

If nothing else, Belsas was one of the gentlest sisters she'd ever met, Wreed thought. "What can we do?"

"Not much since Chandrey's of age," Belsas said. "But we can talk to them."

"Chandrey's going to be pissed. I promised her I wouldn't say anything to you."

"Then what do you suggest?" Belsas crossed her legs at the ankles.

"They were going to Ballyhoos. We could go check on them, feel them out."

"Okay. I'm done here anyway." Belsas stretched, and then reached out to pull Wreed over the chair arm and into her lap. "I don't like to see you worried."

"Won't someone see us?"

"We're the only ones here besides the watch."

Belsas held Wreed against her for a moment, and she couldn't help but calm in her careful touch. Belsas was always respectful, sometimes almost too much for her tastes. A bit of aggression was nice now and then, made her feel wanted. But she did like Belsas. Her phase could be as exciting as it was restful, but she didn't offer it right then, and Wreed didn't ask.

"Shall we?" Belsas helped Wreed to her feet and rose behind her, a hand on her shoulder as they walked through the archives and past the Training Ground gates to Ballyhoos.

* * *

Cance and Chandrey sat together in a far corner.

The waitress, the same sister who often served Belsas and Wreed, approached them as soon as they entered. "Tell your friends to keep it down. They're making the other customers uncomfortable." She nodded over her shoulder to where Chandrey sat in Cance's lap. "And while you're at it, tell them they're been cut off."

"Cut off?" asked Belsas and Wreed together.

"They've downed five crystals in ninety minutes." The waitress swept past them. "I gotta work."

"Thanks," said Belsas, turning with Wreed toward the corner. "What're we going to say?"

"I don't know." Confronting Chandrey and Cance had seemed like a good idea, but now that they were here, Wreed wasn't certain of anything.

Belsas touched her sleeve, steering her toward the bar. "I need something for my nerves." She ordered a single shot of bitterwine, tossed it back, dug a credit chip from her pocket, and tossed it to the barkeep. "Want something?"

Wreed shook her head.

"Then let's do it."

Neither Cance nor Chandrey looked up until Belsas cleared her throat.

"Look who's here!" called Cance when she glanced at them. "What're you two doing here so late on a school night?" She tossed back a mouthful of wine. "Hey, Precious, Bel and Wreed are here." She pulled Chandrey from her shoulder, where she had been nuzzling into her neck. "Wanna help us drink this place dry?"

"Not going to happen." Belsas pulled two chairs to the table. "You've been cut off."

"What's that mean?" Chandrey flashed a drunken grin. Her hair was a mess and her robe open low. Wreed's scarf, the one Chandrey often borrowed, was draped over Cance's shoulder.

"It means the waitress is a bitch." Cance scowled at her nearly empty crystal. "Damn!"

The waitress came to them just then. Wreed ordered four mugs of strong tea and a platter of roast vegetable sandwiches, Ballyhoos' special. Cance cursed the waitress while Wreed ordered, but when Belsas told her she'd better shut up or risk being thrown out of the bar, Cance retreated until the waitress had returned and left again.

"Be a friend, Bel, and order us a couple of crystals." Cance had emptied the last of the wine in her mug and Chandrey's too.

"Not me. I plan on keeping my welcome." Belsas bit into the sandwich Wreed placed in front of her.

"Like I've never helped you out of a difficult situation." Cance pushed away her sandwich.

"Helping me study for an exam is not the same as helping you get smashed," Belsas said.

Wreed watched as Chandrey sat up enough to peek inside her sandwich. She shared Cance's expression and pushed it away, but did sip from her tea.

"We need to talk," Wreed said.

"You're correct there." Cance whispered something into Chandrey's ear which Chandrey agreed to in such an uncontrolled manner that Wreed worried she'd hurt herself. "We've made a decision."

"About what?" Belsas stirred more sweet cane into her tea.

"Two days from now, on the seven-day break, Chandrey and I are making a quick trip to Saria III so I can meet her raisers."

"*You're* going to meet Brava Deb?" said Wreed. She looked at Chandrey for clarification, but her face was buried in Cance's neck.

"Don't sound so surprised." Cance ventured a sip of her tea, but pushed it away as well. "Yuck. It's high time I met her raisers."

Wreed chewed angrily on her sandwich. She knew she was breaking her promise again, but she couldn't help herself. She had been there when Chandrey cried at night. She was the one Chandrey talked to about her raisers' expectations. Chandrey was scared of them, of Kylis's disapproval, but more so of disappointing her gahrah.

"If you knew one thing about the Mother's Plan you'd already be there on your knees, begging her raisers' forgiveness for what you've done," Wreed said.

"What's that mean?" Cance sat up more in her seat.

Chandrey looked up with a silent "no" on her lips directed toward Wreed.

"You know exactly what I mean." Wreed kept her eyes on Cance, even as her glare turned menacing. "Chandrey's my friend. I won't see her hurt."

Cance rolled her eyes and pulled Chandrey's head around until they faced. "Have I ever done anything to hurt you, Chandresslandra?"

"Hurt me?" Chandrey seemed perplexed by the question.

"Yes, Precious. Wreed seems to think I've hurt you in some way. Have I? Be honest."

"Why, no, of course not." Chandrey slurred her words and hiccupped. "Can we get some more wine?"

"And getting her drunk isn't harmful?" asked Belsas. "Phasing with a girl her age isn't harmful?"

Wreed thought Chandrey would slide under the table with embarrassment.

Chandrey turned to her, clearly feeling betrayed. "How could you?"

"I did it for you." Wreed didn't look away. Her raisers, specifically her mama, had taught her never to look away when someone looked her in the eyes. To do so was to back down, admit defeat. "I'm worried."

"You didn't literally hold the glass to her mouth, but you might as well have." Belsas leaned over the table, the index finger of her right hand in Cance's face. "You're sharing your problem."

"I thought you were my friend." Chandrey had moved from Cance's lap to face Wreed directly across the table. "I'd never talk if you'd asked me not to."

"I *am* your friend," Wreed said. "I want what's best for you."

"What problem?" Cance swatted Belsas's finger away.

Belsas waved an empty crystal. "This problem."

"A little wine? You kidding me? You don't know a thing about my relationship with Chandrey. You've no idea how I feel about her."

"How can you possibly know how you feel when you're drunk half the time?" said Belsas. "What do you know about the Mother's Plan?"

"I'm not drunk half the time, and I *know* more than enough." Cance turned up her mug in search of dregs. "If you were any sort of a friend, you'd know I've been studying the Mother's Word."

"Wise Mother Words," slurred Chandrey. She turned back to Wreed. "I asked you not to tell anyone, 'specially Bel."

"We're both worried about you." Part of Wreed wished for wine too.

"You've been studying the Mother's Word?" Belsas stifled a laugh. "A kimshee seriously studying the Mother's Word?"

"I'm considering becoming a member of Her Plan." Cance thumped her empty mug on the tabletop. "I've already made a sizable donation to the elders' council."

"Creiloff's wealth won't get you far with Brava Deb," Belsas said as Chandrey continued to berate Wreed.

"It got me a private meeting." Cance sat back with a smile.

"And you're going to tell her, what?"

"That I want to oath with her daughter."

Chandrey stopped talking to look at Cance with large eyes. "Oath?"

"That's what the Mother's Word says I should do." Cance pulled Chandrey back into her lap. "Will you have me?"

"Are you insane?" Wreed yelled at Chandrey and Cance. "Chandrey, you're only sixteen!"

"I'm old enough," Chandrey said between hiccups.

"Bel?" Wreed cried. "Say something!"

"What can I say? What can either of us say?" Belsas pushed away from the table. "Cance has made up her mind."

"But what about Chandrey?" Wreed wanted to smack the smug expression from Cance's face.

"Arguing isn't going to help," said Belsas as she helped Wreed slide into her cloak. "Let me walk you home." She leaned close to close the clasp at her neck. *I'll explain outside.*

This had better be good. Wreed took her hand and turned to leave.

"We still on for handball tomorrow?" asked Belsas over her shoulder.

"Sure thing." Cance waved at both of them, but Wreed didn't return the wave to her or Chandrey. She was far too angry.

"All right," she said just outside Ballyhoos' door. "Explain."

Belsas kept walking. "Not while Cance is close enough to pick our heads."

"She picks her friends?" Wreed was shocked, but not really surprised.

"She tries to pick everybody's heads, especially her friends."

"You?"

"Right after we first met, but I caught her."

"What happened?"

"I told her I'd kick her ass if she ever did again, and she hasn't tried since."

"That you know of."

She and Belsas walked in silence until they passed through the gates. Belsas led her to a bench near her dorm. They sat for a while, neither speaking as they continued to hold hands.

"I've known her for most of my adult life. Cance wants what Cance wants, and she won't stop until she gets it," Belsas finally said.

"I wish I had something more intelligent to say, some grand solution for the problem, but I do have an idea."

"Mind sharing?" The night was cold so Wreed was grateful when Belsas placed an arm around her. She'd soon have to pull out her heavier cloak.

"I'm considering comming Brava Deb myself."

"Wow!" Wreed exclaimed, at a loss for words. "When are you going to do that?"

"Tomorrow if I can't knock some sense into Cance during our handball match."

"Let me know what happens, okay?"

"I will. But will you work on Chandrey from your end?"

"I plan on it."

Wreed kissed Belsas on the cheek when she surprised her with a small, warming phase. It wasn't suggestive of sex or of real pleasure. Belsas offered comfort, calming her so she might sleep that night. She couldn't help yawning. "It's almost curfew."

Belsas's phase turned more suggestive for a moment, and then she leaned back to view Wreed's face. "Goodnight."

"Goodnight, Bel." She and Belsas shared a kiss on the doorstep before she went inside, fully intent on doing her part to prevent Chandrey from making a serious mistake.

The next morning, Wreed realized she couldn't have kept the promise, no matter her good intentions. Chandrey never returned to the dorm that night.

Chapter Ten

Protocol—the standardized way of doing something; something kimshees regularly ignore

Wreed couldn't hide Chandrey's overnight absence a second time.
Sister Rahl knew Chandrey had failed to return to the dorm and thoroughly questioned Wreed the next morning. What could she say except the truth? She left out the sordid details, but she did say that she had last seen Chandrey at Ballyhoos with Cance.

Wreed commed Belsas after Sister Rahl left.

"The Protocol Master already commed me." Wreed thought Belsas sounded tired. "Cance didn't show for her early meditation class."

"That's serious."

"Dereliction of duty. Could cost her some rank," said Belsas. "Her launch took off late last night. She ignored the call to return. Seems she and Chandrey are on their way to Saria III."

"Mother help poor Chandrey."

"That's not all. Ballyhoos's owner commed right after the Protocol Master released me."

"Why?"

"She's worried about Chandrey."

"Aren't we all?"

"And to tell me Cance has been barred."

"How long and what'd she do?"

"Permanently. Around closing time, she phase-pushed the wait staff around and threatened the barkeep with bodily harm if she didn't give them more to drink."

"Where was Chandrey?"

"Outside, according to the owner—throwing up."

"Damn Cance! Please tell me that's all."

"Cance got on her com after that, and then went outside after Chandrey. That's the last the owner saw of them."

"Have you tried Cance's com?"

"Turned off."

"Figures." Wreed didn't know whether to cry or scream. There was nothing she could do. Chandrey could be throwing away her future, wasting her potential, and for what? A drunkard kimshee? She must have growled into the com, because Belsas's tone turned soothing.

"Calm down, Wreed, dear, please. This is out of our hands."

"There has to be something we can do. Can you contact Brava Deb now?"

"I checked. It's the middle of the night there," said Belsas. "Besides, we both have places to be this morning. What say we meet at Cance's quarters for the midday break? I'm coded in."

"What're we going to do there?"

"Raid her kitchenette. I can com Brava Deb from there too. My visual com doesn't reach long distances."

"Mine neither."

Wreed said goodbye and tried to go about her day, determined not to let Cance's idiocy keep her from her studies. Thoughts of Chandrey, however, plagued her all morning. What was she doing? What was she thinking? What had Cance convinced her of now?

* * *

Cance's quarters were not at all what Wreed expected. They weren't a drunk's filthy hovel, nor were they a low-ranking military officer's spartan corner. On the contrary, Cance's space, the typical studio apartment appointed her rank, was immaculate and well decorated, but all within the Kinship military guidelines.

Belsas assured Wreed that it wasn't because Cance was a good housekeeper. She paid another sister, the life mate of a low-ranking officer, to clean regularly. Still, Wreed was impressed. Cance had apparently done something right.

Belsas found them a decent lunch from the precooked packs in the kitchenette cabinets. Wreed reheated them and made tea while Belsas commed Saria III.

As a Kinship official, Brava Deb was not easy to reach, but Belsas made her way rapidly through the necessary channels when she said it was emergency concerning, "Sister Brava's only daughter, Chandresslandra."

After adding sweet cane to their mugs, Wreed paused mid-stir when Brava Deb came up on the viewer.

"You've news of my daughter?" Brava stood before a window where the grandeur of the Kinship's Saria III governmental facilities spread behind her. She looked older than Wreed had imagined and was harried in her movements.

"My name is Belsas Exzal, Sister Brava, and—"

"I know who you are, Second Officer Belsas. My daughter?"

"She's on her way to see you."

"It's earlier than expected, but it doesn't constitute an emergency." Brava stepped toward the screen. "You clog official channels with notice of a family visit?"

"Certainly n-n-not," stammered Belsas. "I am contacting you regarding the purpose of her visit."

"Couldn't she do so herself when she arrives?"

"That may be too late, Sister Brava."

Now Belsas had Brava's full attention. "Go on."

"She's bringing Second Officer Cancelynn Creiloff with her."

"I know." Brava's expression turned sour. "Second Officer Cancelynn confessed their sins. She has begged our forgiveness, and I am prepared to give it provided she and Chandrey part ways permanently, and Chandrey returns home to relearn her teachings."

"I don't think that will happen, Sister Brava."

"Explain."

"Chandrey and Cance are, well—"

"They're what, Second Officer Belsas?"

"They're seeking your approval to oath," Wreed said when Belsas hesitated.

"My daughter, my Chandrey girl, wants to oath with a kimshee?" Brava paced in tight circles, and then stopped so she could look at Wreed. "You're Wreed Tollamae, aren't you, young woman?"

"Yes, Sister Brava."

"My daughter speaks highly of you. What's your take on the situation?"

"Chandrey doesn't see how manipulative Cance can be, or that Cance is taking advantage of her. The Mother's Plan does little to prepare its members for the real world." Wreed bit her lip before she said more.

"Normally, I would take exception if not insult to your observation, Sister Wreed. But in Chandrey's case, I have to agree. My life mate and I did shelter her more than we should have. She had no real test of her faith before reaching the Training Grounds."

"Chandrey is convinced she can convert Cance."

"There is a difference between evangelizing and converting." Brava moved to her worktable, opening something on her viewer. "Exactly when did they leave?"

"Late last night." Belsas took the mug of tea Wreed offered.

"Then they should be here in a matter of hours." Brava drummed her fingers across the table and stood. "Thank you for your concern, Sister Wreed, Second Officer Belsas. I will alert my life mate."

"You're wel—" Belsas began, but Brava Deb had already closed her end of the transmission.

"Now what?" Wreed took her mug and sat on the oversized lounger in the main room.

"We wait." Belsas came to sit beside her. "How long is your lunch period?"

"My next class is in two hours." The food looked good, but Wreed had nothing in the way of appetite. "You?"

"The same." Belsas sat in silence until they'd finished picking at their food. "I usually study this time of day," she said at last. "But I know I won't be able to concentrate."

"Me neither." Wreed set her mug on a side table and reached for Belsas. "Keep me company?"

"Sure, but not here. Want to go back to my place?"

"Your place?" Belsas had never asked before. "Lead the way."

Belsas nodded, returned their dishes to the kitchenette, and took Wreed by the hand. "It's not nearly as nice as Cance's apartment. Cleaning isn't my forte, but it's decent enough."

Belsas was right. Her quarters weren't as well outfitted as Cance's, but they were comfortable, Wreed thought. The basic layout was the same—a lounger, two chairs pushed up to a small dining table beside the kitchenette, and a bedroll tucked into the corner beside a worktable. Belsas's worktable was a wreck of recorders, notepads and scroll reproductions, just as she had imagined, but the rest of the apartment was relatively clean.

Belsas shut the door behind them. "I'll code you in next time you come over."

"Thanks." Wreed sat on the lounger, hoping Belsas would join her.

She did, and with one knee drawn up, turned to face Wreed. "I've wanted to bring you here for a while." She touched her hair. "I didn't know how you'd take the idea."

Wreed grabbed Belsas's hand and brought it to her mouth. "Don't you know?"

"You suggested it before," Belsas said. "But I wasn't sure if it was time."

"It's long overdue." Wreed lay back.

Belsas lowered her leg and moved forward, to lie on top of her. "I've wanted this too," Belsas whispered in her ear and gently kissed her head.

They lay together in silence for a while, not moving, enjoying each other's comfort until Wreed could stand it no longer.

"You know," she said, looking into Belsas's face, "sometimes I wish you'd get a bit aggressive."

"Aggressive?" Belsas knitted her brows. "You want me to be aggressive?"

Exactly. Wreed opened her mind to Belsas, launching a suggestive phase. *Sometimes I wish you would initiate things. I need you, I need your comfort right now, Bel. I want you.*

Just my phase? Belsas reached out, hesitating at Wreed's waist.

Go on.

Belsas untucked Wreed's shirt and reached beneath to stroke her abdomen.

That's a start. I sometimes wonder if you're secretly bound by some religious dictate I don't know of.

Not me. Belsas's hands slid over Wreed's skin. She lowered her head to kiss her neck. *I just didn't want to take advantage of you. Are you sure?*

We've already done everything but. Wreed unbuckled Belsas's duty belt and tossed it aside.

Belsas responded by pulling off her tunic while Wreed removed her blouse. *This isn't because of Chandrey's situation, is it?* she asked breathlessly.

Don't. Wreed looked toward the rolled bedding. *I don't want to talk about them, think about them. Just us. Take me to bed.*

Belsas needed no further prompting.

Soon, Wreed and Belsas were tangled in a snarl of blankets, and would have remained so if they hadn't moved around the room, discovering multiple ways to experience each other. Their phases were ever-present, but those paled in comparison to the physical sensations they enjoyed.

Belsas's body was firm but soft against Wreed's, her hands attentive and insistent as she came to know every part of her. Wreed returned in kind, using her short stature to her advantage when they moved to the dining table. There she tasted Belsas, savoring what she had only imagined until then. Belsas was her first taste, her first physical lover, and very tender.

"Shower," Belsas whispered when they took a moment to catch their breath.

Wreed followed her, wondering how they would fit into the tight confines of the Training Ground's individual showers.

Belsas seemed to have already considered the problem, however, because she turned on the water, set it to pulse, and told Wreed to step in.

As the warmth covered her, Belsas bent her forward, toward the shower wall. Belsas stood just outside the shower. She eased Wreed's hand between her legs, encouraging her to rub herself as she sank fingers into her from behind.

Wreed arched and moaned. Belsas pulled her closer, partially out of the shower, so that the water streamed over her loosened hair. She felt the water and Belsas's touch pulsing in time in her, on her, until her body quivered.

Belsas let Wreed brace against her knees until she became aware that Belsas had removed her hand and was holding her lower lips open so that she could stroke herself more readily.

"Don't stop," Belsas said. She pulled Wreed out of the shower so she could step inside, and then pulled Wreed back in, knees braced for her as before. She maneuvered Wreed closer and pushed her right leg between Wreed's legs, giving her a place to press against.

Lost in the moment, Wreed clamped her legs round Belsas's thigh and let instinct take over as the water ran across them. Belsas held her tight, helping her move. They shared a phase where Belsas imagined Wreed's fingers inside her, moving in and out of her in time with her own thrusts until Wreed cried out and shook against her.

"Wreed?" Moments later, Belsas roused her.

Wreed became aware they were clasped together in the shower, filling the tiny space with a mixture of steam, flesh and sex.

"We've got twenty minutes." Belsas brushed Wreed's hair back and kissed her firmly. "Step out for a minute so I can rinse off, then you can do the same."

Wreed smiled, stepped from the stall, and wrapped in a towel until Belsas finished. She handed Belsas the towel when they switched places.

Belsas had cooled the water, so she showered quickly, drawing her hand through her hair to find the misplaced pins. When she emerged, Belsas handed her a towel, and they both headed to the main room to find their clothing. They didn't say much as they redressed, but kept their minds open, letting their contented emotions mingle.

"Got a brush?" Wreed asked around the pins in her mouth.

"Check behind the towels."

Wreed found a brush where indicated. It was dusty, but usable. "Whose is this?" She twisted her hair into the knot she generally wore.

"The brush?" Belsas appeared in the bathroom doorway. "It's mine. I wore my hair longer until I got back to the grounds. Cut it off when I didn't have time to mess with it."

"With your schedule, I don't blame you."

"It was almost as long as yours." Belsas gathered Wreed's clothing from the floor and held it out to her. "Here. You see my duty belt?"

"Under the lounger." Wreed grinned at herself in the reflector. She was certain everyone would be able to see her satiated state, but she really didn't care. She needed to get to class, so she grabbed her clothing and began struggling into it as Belsas dived for her duty belt.

"Got it." Belsas paused briefly to exchange kisses, and then checked the reflector to smooth her ruffled locks and make herself more presentable. "This is why I wear my hair short."

"So you can clean up quick after mid day sex?"

"No." Belsas grasped Wreed by the waist as she passed, pulling her hard against her. "So I can spend more time having mid day sex." She winked at Wreed's shocked expression.

They both gasped when the afternoon session bell clanged outside.

"Damn!" Belsas let her go and they scrambled for the door. "This is more the reason," she said, securing the apartment door behind them. "I'm always late!"

"See you this evening?" Wreed called as they parted ways.

"Meet me here." Bel called back. "We can eat, then try contacting Cance and Chandrey again."

"Okay."

Wreed turned toward where her class was held, and stopped. Her notebook and recorder were in the dorm. She was going to be late, but felt too immersed in the afterglow to really care. She had dinner plans which didn't include anything that might be found in Belsas's cabinets.

Chapter Eleven

Javicks Community: Saria III

Cleave—to separate from; to cling to

To Chandrey's dismay, Brava Deb and a full security entourage met them at the launch port. Brava hugged her and kissed her forehead as she always did, and then turned to Cance.

"Second Officer Cancelynn, welcome to Saria III." Brava sounded polite enough, but Chandrey could tell by her stiff movements that she was only going through the motions. She seemed beyond upset. "My life mate is waiting." Brava motioned to her guards. They stepped back from Chandrey, but not from Cance, whom they watched closely.

"Thank you, Sister Brava." Cance extended her hand. "I hope my gift found its way to you."

"Your donation?" Brava gave Cance's gesture the briefest acknowledgment, touching her above the wrist in the most formal and distant manner possible. "I passed it on to the elders." She whisked around. "This way, please."

The guards, the usual Kinship trooper honor guard assigned to high officials, walked in front and behind their group. "It's good to see you, Gahrah." Chandrey struggled to keep up with Brava's harried steps.

"You should have let me know you were coming." Brava didn't slow for Chandrey like she normally did. "There wasn't much time to prepare."

"Don't tell me Kylis cooked something special." Chandrey looked over her shoulder at Cance, who seemed unconcerned.

"I hope your family hasn't made a fuss, Sister Brava." Cance moved to walk directly beside Chandrey, forcing the guards to close the gap.

"That isn't your concern, Second Officer." Brava turned down the ramp leading from the landing pad to where a land launch waited for them.

"We could walk." Chandrey glanced at Brava. "It's a pretty day."

"The launch is faster." Brava sat in the middle of the seat, forcing Chandrey to sit beside Cance. She always sat beside Brava when they rode in a launch, but Brava didn't offer so she said nothing about it.

When the guards closed the launch and the pilot boarded, Brava pulled down the privacy screen. "I want to keep this quiet."

"You want to keep our visit quiet?" Chandrey stared at her, unsure what to say next.

"Gossip runs amok here. You know that." Brava looked away, out the launch window. "The less of a stir your visit makes, the better."

Cance's eyes were closed, but Chandrey could tell she was listening. Kimshees were able to meditate and listen at the same time, a skill she admired and wished she could duplicate, especially when it became apparent that Brava had no wish to talk for the rest of their short ride.

When Chandrey realized the truth, she choked back a tear and gazed out the window. She'd never seen her raiser so upset, had never dreamed her disappointment could feel so complete. But she had no idea how extensive her trespass really was until they reached home, and she saw all the things she hadn't taken to the Training Grounds bundled on the front walk.

"I asked Kylis to keep your things inside." Brava stepped over the items and continued to the front door. "As you know, Second Officer Cancelynn, kimshees are not welcome in Mother's Plan homes. If you'll please go to the side yard and wait, we'll join you shortly."

Cance merely nodded, picked up Chandrey's belongings, and walked toward the side of the house.

"But Gahrah," Chandrey protested. "She's my guest."

"Not in this house," began Brava.

Cance called back to her, "It's all right, Chandrey. I understand Sister Brava's hesitation. I am kimshee, and you have taught me what the Mother's Plan thinks of my vocation. I'll see you in a moment."

"Okay." Chandrey choked back a sob and followed Brava inside.

"Gahrah, please," she begged. "Cance is learning the Mother's way. She's even talking about switching vocations."

"Lies!" Kylis emerged from her bedroom. She looked even sterner than Chandrey remembered. Her hair was short, not uncommon for an aging sister, but her clothing—she still had her robe, but it hung open. Her pants, tall boots and oversized tunic were very unlike her, so much that the strangeness all but overshadowed her words. "You're misery bound, girl. You hear me? I tried to warn Brava that the Training Grounds would ruin you, but she wouldn't listen, and now look at you. Phasing before oathing!"

Chandrey stood before them with her head bowed, not ashamed of phasing with Cance, but that Brava and Kylis had found out before they'd oathed.

The Mother could and did forgive phasing before oathing as long as the guilty pair asked for forgiveness and took the oath to correct their trespass. But physical lovemaking before oathing was unforgivable in the elders' eyes—if they found out. Most families kept such issues private. Here Chandrey took heart. They'd only phased. They'd hadn't done the unforgivable.

"Forgive me, Gahrah. My heart ran away with me. I phased with her. I confess. But I'm prepared to make things right in the Mother's eyes."

Brava sat in her chair, her hands folded in her lap. "It's not that easy."

"But it is, Gahrah. It is." Chandrey stood by her side. "Cance loves me. She wants me for her life mate. We haven't done anything wrong as long as we confess and oath."

"More lies!" Kylis gruffly pulled her away from Brava, and to Chandrey's shock, Brava let her. "Your kimshee lover has been more honest than you, girl. She's confessed to having all you offered, your mind and your body without either of you uttering a word of promise to the Mother. Your lust has damned you both."

"What?" Chandrey wrenched away from Kylis's hands to face her raiser. "Gahrah, I…we never—"

"Your Cancelynn confessed, and the elders have spoken." Brava took a printout from the table beside her chair and held it out.

"The elders?" Chandrey's hands shook.

The worst thing, the very worst thing that could happen to a member of the Mother's Plan was shunning—a literal turning of the Plan's back on the offending member. She'd heard of sisters being shunned in other communities, of them being thrown out of the Plan and forced to find their own way, but she had never considered the punishment extending to her.

She was steeped in the Mother's Word. She knew every phrase by heart. She lived by Her dictates. She lived by Her wishes. The fact she had phased with Cance made little difference. The Mother said they would be forgiven if they asked, but the Plan didn't share the idea.

"No." She wanted nothing more than to crawl into her gahrah's lap like she had as a child. "I'm still your girl, your Chandrey girl. I haven't changed. I love the Mother. I want to share her Word. Just because Cance and I—"

"Shush, Chandresslandra." Brava rose from her chair to stand beside Kylis. "The elders had high hopes for your future, as did we. We'd all hoped you would return to teach in the Motherslight school."

"I can still do that."

"No." Brava walked past her and through the kitchen to the side door, which she opened. "You made your choice when you gave your body to a kimshee."

"But I only shared my mind!"

Kylis pushed past her to stand beside Brava. "Your lover confessed. I did what had to be done."

"Cance told you that we—? *You* told the elders Cance and I—?" Chandrey's hands flew to her mouth. That night near Ballyhoos. The blood. Had they actually...? Cance said they hadn't, but they'd been caught up in the moment.

"Misery bound!" Kylis turned her back on Chandrey, but the shunning didn't disturb her half as much as Brava, who reached forward, touched her on the cheek, and then shook her head sadly and turned around.

"Misery bound," Brava whispered as she turned. "Misery bound."

Chandrey's cries fell on deaf ears, but she continued pleading. She could be everything they wanted if they gave her a chance. She would prove to them how much Cance loved her. She would show them how much of the Mother's Word Cance already knew. She needed them. She loved them. They were her family.

"Chandrey?" Cance stood in the doorway, her arms outstretched. "I'm sorry. I should have told you the truth when I realized what'd actually happened, but I was embarrassed and so guilt-stricken that I had to confess to someone."

"To Kylis?" Chandrey wailed. "I told you how she was!"

Cance glanced at Brava's and Kylis's turned backs. "I had trouble contacting Sister Brava because of her position so I had to talk to Kylis. But she said she would tell Brava, and that we could redeem ourselves in the Mother's eyes and in theirs by oathing. I was trying to spare you." She ventured a small step through the doorway. "Sister Brava, I never intended to hurt Chandrey and certainly never intended for any of this to happen."

Brava said nothing, even as her body quivered with a sigh. Kylis, on the other hand, stood tall, tapping her foot. "Get out of my home, kimshee slattern."

Chandrey had to leave. Brava couldn't forgive her and Kylis wouldn't. Cance had suddenly become her only family, but they weren't family, not yet, so she was really alone. The very idea fell on her. Alone. On her own. Without others. *Miserable.*

"Kylis made certain it happened!" She flung herself into Cance's arms. "If they only knew, if only they could see how things really are."

"Someday they'll realize they were wrong, Precious." Cance hugged her tight, and then stepped back and encouraged her through the door. "But for now, we need to follow their wishes. We can't afford to make things worse."

Chandrey took one more look around her childhood home and gazed at Brava, her gahrah. She stared at the back of her head, at the dark streaks in the hair behind her ears. Her gahrah. Her raiser. Her teacher. Her friend.

"Gahrah, I'm sorry. I'll make things right somehow. I promise." With that, Chandrey took Cance's hand, and they walked back to the launch, Cance carrying the bundle of her belongings under one arm. The guards followed at a distance, but other than that they were alone. No one seemed to notice they were there at all.

Once at the launch, Cance directed her to a rear seat and sat beside her instead of taking the pilot's seat. "I'm sorry." There were tears in her eyes.

"You tried to keep me safe." Chandrey wiped Cance's face with her sleeve. "You meant well. I just wish you'd told me the truth."

"I tried to so many times." Cance cleared Chandrey's face of tears with her uniform cuff. "But I couldn't. I was afraid you'd walk away."

"You should've trusted me."

"I know that now." Cance raised the seat across from them to stow Chandrey's bundle with the travel baggage, and turned back to her. Cance's bottom lip quivered. "Oh, Chandrey. Can you ever forgive me?" She threw herself on Chandrey's mercy, sobbing almost uncontrollably.

"Part of me knew all along, I think, but I didn't know how to bring it up, so I didn't. Then you didn't, so I hoped I was wrong. I don't blame you for this. I don't blame either of us." Chandrey touched the back of Cance's head where it rested in her lap. "I blame Kylis. She betrayed us when she contacted the elders. She wouldn't let us make things right."

Cance sniffled and looked up. "I don't understand why she did what she did. Did she have to? Did I misunderstand the Mother's Word?"

"No, you didn't. The Mother's Word says our trespass should be addressed, but not how. Most Plan families settle these sorts of issues privately."

Cance's expression changed from piteous to hurt. Like Chandrey, she clearly felt betrayed by someone she thought she could trust. "So she didn't have to contact the elders?"

"No."

"Then why did she?"

"To hurt Gahrah." Chandrey glanced over Cance's shoulder to look through the launch's front window toward her raiser's home. "She did it to hurt Gahrah."

"You warned me. I should've listened." Cance turned to look with Chandrey for a moment before she shook her head and rose to take the pilot's seat. "The port is asking about our departure." She sat silent for minute. "There's nothing here for us now. It's time we go."

"Okay," whispered Chandrey. She felt hollow when she moved to the seat beside Cance. How a few minutes had changed everything. She had nowhere to go except where Cance was going, back to Saria IV and the Training Grounds, but she soon learned that Cance had other plans. When it entered Saria IV's atmosphere, the launch turned.

"Is there a problem?" Chandrey glanced at the pilot's monitor. The flight plan troubled her. They were headed toward the Taelach/ Autlach city of Polmel, a trade and cultural center, a location the Mother's Plan considered more lecherous than the Training Grounds. "Polmel?"

"Just a short stop on our way back." Cance patted her leg. "I'm going to do what I should have done earlier. I'm going to make honest women out of us."

"You want to oath in *Polmel?*"

"It hardly seems appropriate that we return to the Training Grounds unoathed." Cance banked the launch right. "So Polmel will have to do."

With or without her raisers' approval, she was going to oath with Cance. How bittersweet. She had lost her family, her traditions, but she had gained a life mate. But what of Cance's family? Cance had said little about Creiloff except that the Exchange had made her exceedingly wealthy before she'd removed her interests.

Chandrey had wondered when they'd meet.

"Oh, and Creiloff is in Polmel on business, so you'll finally get to meet her," Cance said.

Chandrey looked at the simple robes she'd donned for meeting her raisers. While her clothing might be humble and fit for the Mother's Plan, it certainly wasn't appropriate for meeting her future life mate's high business raiser. But Cance, like she so often did, had an answer for that as well.

"I'm going to buy us both new outfits before we see Creiloff. I want to show you off."

Chandrey nodded and turned her head away, watching as Polmel came into view. She no longer cared where she went as long as she had Cance and now Creiloff's approval. They were the only family she had left. She would do what it took to keep in Creiloff's good graces, even if it went against her raising—the raising that had rejected her.

Chapter Twelve

Polmel: Saria IV

Oath—*vow, promise; curse*

Amazing didn't begin to explain what Chandrey saw when she landed in Polmel. The port itself was so large the landing pads were tiered, with larger craft taking the bottom levels, and smaller launches like Cance's taking the upper. But as high as the tiers ranged—some twelve levels Chandrey counted—they were small compared to the surrounding buildings.

Expanses of metal and glass dominated the horizon, their façades skewed by waves of rising heat. Chandrey had heard Polmel was hot, both in temperature and in its night life, but she hadn't dreamed the heat would be so visible or so unbearable.

Cance opened the launch door and the humidity rolled in like fog, choking the air. When Chandrey drew a quick breath, Cance smiled.

"Don't worry, Precious, we won't have to walk far. Here comes our ride now." Cance pointed to the ramp and the small land launch climbing it.

"I thought we were going to get something more appropriate to wear before we met Creiloff."

"She's not meeting us here. The launch is for our use."

"Oh." Chandrey reached for the small bag of essentials she had packed. "What about my things from home?"

"We'll sort through everything when we get back. Leave it all."

"Everything?" Chandrey found the idea wasteful.

"Creiloff said we're not to worry about anything while we're here." Cance led her down the launch steps, through the thick heat, and to the land launch, whose cooled interior made her shiver.

The gaunt, elderly sister pilot closed the door behind them and climbed into the pilot's seat. "Creiloff sends her greetings, Cancelynn." She bowed her head in recognition, and then glanced silently at Chandrey.

"Jeri." Cance nodded in the pilot's direction. "I see you got my message."

"It arrived just before Creiloff landed. She's instructed me to take you wherever you wish," Jeri said. "A room in the penthouse has been aired for you, but Creiloff also had me reserve a private suite elsewhere. She said you might prefer it."

A private suite! How exotic it sounded. "How nice of her," Chandrey said. Their welcome here seemed converse to their earlier arrival at her home. Creiloff might not have met them in person, but she was definitely seeing to their needs. "Cance, there's no need for her to spend on extra accommodations."

Cance admonished her concern with a wave. "The suite would be preferable. But don't take us there yet. Take us to Delmoor Market."

"A particular store?"

"Haddigan's, unless I change my mind. I'll com for package pickup when we're ready to leave."

"Yes, Cancelynn." Jeri bowed her head again. "Creiloff also said you were to meet her at the penthouse for dinner," she added as she turned back around. "She said not to make her wait."

"Never mind the com, then. Pick us up in two hours."

"As you wish."

Jeri said nothing else during the flight, but Cance made a game of pointing out various points of interest to Chandrey. Polmel sprawled in all directions—small parks, huge apartment structures, countless walking trails, towering office structures colored with both Aut and Taelach advertisements. Strange. Polluted. A little frightening. But she was with someone familiar with the territory, so she didn't worry much. Besides, she wasn't there to sightsee.

The launch arrived at Delmoor Market a short time later. While Chandrey marveled over the sea of tents and carts lining the walkways,

Cance seemed more interested in the permanent shops behind them. She had expected Haddigan's to be some vast warehouse of fashion, but when Jeri stopped in front of a small storefront, she became exceedingly intrigued. What could such a small place have that the general market stalls didn't carry?

"Thank you, Jeri," Chandrey said when they exited the launch.

Jeri looked very surprised.

"That's not necessary," Cance said when the launch pulled away. "Jeri is Creiloff's personal driver when she's in Polmel. She's being paid."

"I was only being polite." Chandrey didn't feel like furthering her argument, so she said nothing when Cance frowned at her.

"You needn't be so proper all the time. Especially to the hired help." Cance took her firmly by the arm. "Come along, Precious. Let's get you properly dressed for dinner."

Before Chandrey could object, she and Cance walked through Haddigan's door, where she hung back. The clothing in this shop was unlike anything she'd seen. The Mother's Plan side of her was appalled, but the rest of her was awed.

They were greeted by a brightly dressed, middle-aged sister who smiled at Cance and eyed Chandrey with open disgust. "Cancelynn. It's been a while." She bowed reverently to Cance, and then eyed Chandrey a second time. "Doing some charity work this stay?"

"Watch your mouth, Cathraena." Cance pulled Chandrey forward as if presenting a prize. "This is Chandrey Brava, soon to be Chandrey Cances."

A startled look crossed Cathraena's face. "Oh, oh, how lovely for you both. What a surprise. If I'd known—"

"Then you wouldn't have insulted my intended, correct?" Cance pulled Chandrey's hair from its clasp, spilling it over her shoulders. "We need evening attire."

"The occasion?"

"Dinner with Creiloff."

"Say no more." Cathraena clapped her hands.

Three sisters entered from a side door. They swept Chandrey from Cance's arms and back through the door, where they pampered her in a fashion she was not accustomed to. Her nails were manicured, and she was presented with a seemingly endless array of one- and two-piece outfits deemed suitable for the upcoming evening, each more sophisticated than the next.

She simply wasn't used to this sort of attention, nor the choices offered. Mother's Plan robes were solid colors and limited in style, so having options wasn't easy, but she did notice that there were no pants among the selections. However, pants weren't the current high fashion, so she thought little else about it.

She managed to pick a soft, flowing, subtly detailed gown in a stunning shade of emerald, Cance's favorite color. The garment wasn't revealing, but clung to the curves of her body that Cance frequently complimented.

After picking the gown, Chandrey's mind was tired. She simply let those around her make the choices. The sisters curled and pinned her hair into a style she never would have chosen for herself. They didn't give her shoes. A mistake, she surmised, but she didn't say anything. Polmel was hot enough to warrant bare feet.

Chandrey emerged from the side door close to two hours later, feeling exhausted and unsure of herself. She sat in an oversized chair, drinking wine until Cance whistled, picked up a second mug, and came to her side.

"That was well worth the wait." Cance had redressed as well, Chandrey noticed, in fitted black trousers, a crisp white shirt, a long beast-hide vest and new knee-length, high-heeled boots—all very becoming, but very different than the work uniform she was used to seeing.

And it certainly wasn't the kind of fashion Chandrey had been presented. No, Cance's clothing had a hard edge to it, quite the opposite of what anyone in the Mother's Plan or the Training Grounds generally wore. It was a new side of her intended, and she briefly thought about how much she didn't know about Cance.

Cathraena entered the room to fill Cance's mug and express approval of Chandrey's appearance, but Chandrey couldn't help noting Cathraena's radical change in attitude. Now she was a beauty, a wonderful choice, and Cance should be proud. The praise sounded hollow, but still, she was flattered. The pride turned to dismay, however, when Cathraena's staff came through the door laden with boxes bearing her name—Chandresslandra Cances.

"Those can't be mine." She turned to Cance.

"But they are, Precious." Cance set their mugs aside and swept Chandrey into her arms. "I know your raising resists such extravagance, but I plan on spoiling you." She kissed Chandrey's cheek, and then turned to Cathraena. "Have them sent to our suite."

"As you wish."

Cance nodded and turned Chandrey toward the door. "Jeri just pulled up."

"This is nerve-racking," said Chandrey as the launch pulled away from the market. "The clothes, the hair."

"I want to make a good impression." Cance smoothed her trousers. "Besides, you look beautiful."

Chandrey felt a twinge of revulsion as she looked at her gown. It was too much. This was all too much. She simply wasn't raised to accept this. "I wasn't attractive in my robes?"

Cance looked at her sharply. "Of course! But this is our oath night. Creiloff wanted us to follow her family's tradition of fine dining to celebrate. The attire is part of the event. But if you'd rather not partake, I'll let her know."

"Oh, don't do that!" The gown wasn't really that bad, Chandrey supposed. It had a purpose, but that didn't explain all the other clothes Cance had bought her. The finely woven blouses, the skirts that weren't showy, but certainly not of her raising, the fine lace undergarments. It wasn't—*not again with the raising*. She wasn't a member of the Plan, not anymore. Time she enjoyed what the world had to offer.

"The dress is wonderful, Cance," she went on. "I'm just not used to expensive things."

"You're oathing into wealth. Get used to it," Cance muttered. She abruptly turned the topic back to Polmel's hot spots.

Cance indicated more than Chandrey could possibly remember, if she had been listening in the first place. They were oathing—*oathing!* Making the ultimate lifelong commitment. Chandrey was loved and in love with Cancelynn Creiloff, a Kinship officer, and daughter to one of the wealthiest Taelachs of the time. She felt proud despite her losses.

Beside her, Cance smiled. She seemed a little nervous about presenting Chandrey to Creiloff, but she never mentioned it. She wouldn't.

Chandrey had figured out that much about her. It was part of Cance's training. It was all right that Cance had broken down before her at the shunning, but this situation was different. There was a difference between sorrow and nerves, at least where kimshees were concerned.

A short time later, the launch arrived on the private landing pad at Creiloff's Polmel apartment. Chandrey thought the term apartment did the residence little justice.

The landing pad, while located at the top of one of the taller buildings, was surrounded by small trees and a tiny but well kept green space. Nestled stepping stones led to a patio. Creiloff waited for them there, sitting at the head of an outdoor dining table.

Servants dressed in clothing much drabber than anything the Plan dictated scurried in and out of the apartment, setting the table, and dropping off baskets and bowls of exotic foods which Chandrey had only heard of.

Cance sniffed the air and grinned. "Smells like home."

"Smells like beast steaks if you ask me." Creiloff rose from the table to greet them at the patio's edge. "So this is Chandresslandra Brava."

"It is a pleasure to meet you, Sister Creiloff." Chandrey extended her hand.

"You may call me Creiloff, young woman." Creiloff took Chandrey not by the wrist, as was custom, but by the hand.

Creiloff's hand was clammy, but her eyes were bright and her gaze scrupulous. Her hide leggings were unwrinkled, her jerkin perfect in the way it rested across her torso. And her hair, what little there was of it lengthwise, was as dark as her black hide boots. Her dark blue eyes also looked black in the light, making her appear Autlach save for her skin. Chandrey was taken aback. Cance's eyes were sapphire, and her skin paler than her raiser's, but both were attractive women, though in very different ways.

Creiloff turned Chandrey about like they were dancing, and then released her grip and nodded. "She's just as you described, Cancelynn. I approve."

"I knew you would." Cance passed Chandrey a mug of wine from a tray presented by a servant. "To the future." She held up her mug in toast.

"To the oath." Creiloff tossed back the wine in her mug and took another.

"To the oath night," said Cance with wink in Chandrey's direction.

Chandrey wished she could dissolve into the floor. Thankfully, Creiloff smirked, but said nothing. She wasn't sure what to say, so she leisurely sipped her wine while they waited for the meal preparations to finish.

"Cancelynn tells me you were raised under the Mother's Plan." There was genuine interest in Creiloff's tone.

"I was, but I'm no longer a member." That hurt to say, but it was the truth. "They don't approve of Cance."

"I warned Cancelynn that kimshees were unwelcome in their

midst." Creiloff's stare seemed to pierce Chandrey, taking her apart fiber by fiber, almost like Cance's stare on the night they'd met. "But I also taught her to think for herself, which she obviously did."

"Ah, but if I wasn't kimshee, I wouldn't have been at the Training Grounds to meet Chandrey." Cance wrapped her free hand around Chandrey's waist. "The Mother might well have fated us some other way. I'm certain we would have met. Maybe not as soon, but we would have met, wouldn't we, Precious?" She kissed Chandrey's cheek, which heated with embarrassment.

"I'm certain we would have." Chandrey still struggled with open affection, even from Cance. "The Mother works in mysterious ways."

"Indeed She does," said Creiloff between drinks. "'Ours is not to question, but simply to do.'"

Wise Mother Words from her life mate's raiser! Chandrey had hardly expected to hear them or what came from Cance's mouth next.

"Creiloff has studied religion for many passes, Precious," Cance said. "She's much better versed than I ever hope to be."

"It's more of a hobby." Creiloff gave her mug to a passing servant. "I collect texts to study them. I admit I haven't studied much of the Mother's Plan tenets, but I am beginning to read some reproductions of their early scrolls."

"Not much has changed." Chandrey flattened her toes into the grass, soaking in the building's warmth. The evening was cooling, and they had yet to step beneath the patio lights.

"I'm aware there has been little change in the Mother's Plan since its inception." Creiloff slowly guided them toward the dining area.

Cance wrapped her arm around Chandrey's shoulder. Despite Creiloff's initial brusqueness, she was beginning to feel accepted, but curious as to why Cance hadn't told her about Creiloff's faithfulness sooner.

"Actually, I see the Mother's Plan as being vague in its requirements. Too much is left up to individual interpretation." Creiloff stopped along the patio walkway to gaze over the city.

Below them, Polmel's lights stretched to the horizon in all directions. No street went unlit, no park was unusable due to darkness. It was beautiful, but Chandrey would be glad to get back to the Training Grounds.

"Vague?" she asked. After what had happened earlier in the day, if anything, she felt the Plan was too specific in its interpretations. She may not be a member of the Plan any longer, but she still prickled at Crieloff's criticism.

Creiloff looked at her like someone unused to being questioned and raised a brow. "Yes, Chandresslandra, vague."

They came to the dining table. Servants pulled out their seats and placed napkins in their laps while another poured drinks into their mugs—wine in Chandrey's, strong-smelling liquor in Cance's and Creiloff's.

"I wasn't intending on teaching a lesson this evening." Creiloff raised both her brows at Chandrey's expression. "Don't think for a moment that I am devaluing your background, young woman," she continued as her drink was poured. "The Plan has many good qualities"

"I agree," said Cance, reaching for her mug. "But our situation is a good example of the sort of problem she is talking about."

"Go on, please." Chandrey fiddled with her napkin until it covered more of her gown.

"The Plan claims to strictly follow its tenets, but its members have so seldom actually stuck to anything that the Plan elders never know what is really going on." Cance took a hard roll from a basket and broke it in half.

"Correct," said Creiloff. "And this becomes problematic in a situation such as yours. You expected one thing. You logically expected to receive the same treatment as others in your situation, but something entirely different happened. You were held to the tenets when others were not. How unfair. Cance told me as much from Haddigan's this afternoon."

"I didn't know you knew." Chandrey took half of the roll from Cance and spread it with thick berry jam.

"She was distraught by the entire affair." Creiloff motioned to a servant. Dinner began arriving while she continued speaking. "I actually feel to blame for what happened. I had assured Cancelynn that the situation would be handled as a family matter."

"You know more about the Plan than most outsiders," Chandrey said. A plate of sliced fruit and expensive cheeses was set before her. Her appetite suddenly became overbearing, but she didn't indulge her hunger until Creiloff took her first bite. "Probably more than some of the members. And consequences tend to vary even between Plan communities."

"There lies my point." Creiloff placed a slice of cheese on some fruit and bit into it. "If there hadn't been a discrepancy between the way a situation was normally handled and the way it's officially handled, you could be certain of the outcome." Creiloff stopped to chew, and then drank from her mug. "Cancelynn, if you had been certain that the elders would have shunned Chandresslandra, would you have phased with her?"

"Of course not." Cance assembled her appetizer the same as her raiser.

Chandrey copied Cance, delighted by the combination. The tart fruit matched well with the unexpected richness of the cheese. She assembled a second bite while Cance talked on.

"That's what I've been trying to explain to Chandrey, but all I could seem to get out until now is 'sorry.'" She leaned across the table to touch Chandrey's hand. "And I am truly sorry."

"It wasn't intentional." The second course began arriving. Mugs of soup this time. Not much more than savory broth, but it cleansed the palate after the dense, rich cheeses.

Cance's and Creiloff's liquor was refilled as was Chandrey's wine, and the conversation continued as soon as the servants moved away.

"Life would be much simpler if the tenets weren't up to such wide interpretation." Creiloff pushed her soup aside in favor of her drink. "A sister should know the consequences of her actions or not be held accountable for them."

"But is life ever that simple?" Chandrey enjoyed the conversation, the food, the entire evening.

"Ah, but it can be," said Creiloff.

Cance nodded. "When I spoke to Creiloff the other day, she suggested that you might be interested in hearing something about her faith choice. It's like the Plan in a lot of ways."

"What faith path do you follow?" Hints of the main course drifted across the patio. Chandrey was willing to listen to what Creiloff had to say, but very little could convince her to lean toward another faith path. She knew the Plan too well to veer away from it far, shunned or not.

"I belong to a small group of Taelachs who believe that the Mother's Word is not up to interpretation," said Creiloff. "And our role is to teach others the Word."

"I see." Since arriving at the Training Grounds, Chandrey had learned a little about other small faith groups, but the Plan did not recognize or teach of their existence. "What do you mean by 'not up to interpretation?'"

"The Mother's Word is law," said Creiloff.

She continued explaining the concept while they ate the main course. Cance said little during the discussion, but Chandrey didn't think she was unfamiliar with the information Creiloff presented. In fact, Cance listened with interest to what her raiser said, but knowledge seldom denoted true faith—at least in her experience.

Chandrey listened, but didn't speak much either. Creiloff seemed content to dominate the conversation, even through the last set of drinks—hard liquor for all. She had never tasted liquor and would have choked if she hadn't already drunk four mugs of wine.

After a final toast to the night ahead, the very idea of which prompted a laugh from her, Creiloff walked with them back to the launch, where Jeri waited.

"To the suite, Jeri, and hurry." Cance closed the launch's privacy partition and pulled Chandrey close. "So what did you think of Creiloff?"

"She seems more a woman of strong faith than a business strong-arm." Chandrey slurred her words, but she didn't care. It was her night to celebrate. What did it hurt?

"That's only because she wasn't talking business tonight. Wait until you see her in action." Cance squeezed Chandrey's knee. Her hand crept higher. "We'll be at the suite in a few minutes. You ready for the oath?"

"Definitely." Chandrey pulled Cance to her for a less-than-proper kiss. Their mouths came together in a fierce exchange. Cance's hand slid up Chandrey's thigh impatiently.

When the launch began to descend, Chandrey pulled back.

"Something wrong?" Cance dropped her hand to Chandrey's knee.

"Oh, just curious about something."

"What's that?" Cance smiled at her.

"What's the name of Creiloff's faith group? She never said."

"Didn't she?" Cance paused when the landing locks hissed loudly outside the windows.

"No, I don't think so."

"She's a member of the Cleave."

"I've never heard of them. They must be a really small group."

"They're growing. Creiloff joined them after she pulled her interest from the Exchange. Mama had been dead for three passes and I was past the Recognition, so what I know I only know from my visits, but most of the time I meet her here in Polmel. She showed me a copy of their oath when I first sought her advice about our situation, and I liked what I read. Do you mind if I use that version?"

"The path means the same, no matter the wording," Chandrey said.

All thoughts of faith of any sort faded from her mind. What she wanted this night, she could have, however she wanted it. Her night to promise. Cance's night to vow. Their night to share. The faith the words came from didn't matter. What did matter was their meaning.

If Creiloff said the Mother's Word was law to the Cleave, then Cance's choice of the Oath meant all the more to her.

Chapter Thirteen

Kinship Training Grounds: Saria IV

Reconnaissance—exploration, initial test; kimshee job requirement

Chandrey and Cance's return to the Training Ground was anything but glorious.

Cance was taken to task for her absence and so was Chandrey, each receiving her own distinct punishment. Cance was demoted to Third Kimshee, locked in the Training Ground brig for four days, and placed on extra duty for three moon cycles, while Chandrey was placed on academic probation and made to spend her extra hours assisting with some sort of project, which she would write a lengthy paper about afterward.

None of that seemed to fade their optimism, however, and both set about making things right. Actually, Wreed was amazed by their attitudes, and told them as much when she and Belsas finally got a chance to meet up with them at their apartment a few seven-days later. The apartment was a cramped mix of Chandrey's new clothing and Cance's belongings.

"We have to accept our punishment," said Cance between sips of wine. The very presence of alcohol on the base would have gotten her in more trouble. "We took off without warning or authorization. We got off lucky, considering."

"That's what I think too." Chandrey twisted the bead bracelet on her wrist, a beautiful piece, but very unlike anything Wreed remembered her wearing. In fact, her entire outfit was new, much like her attitude.

Chandrey still drank more than Wreed liked, as did Cance, but Chandrey seemed more mature now. Not everything revolved around her Mother's Plan teaching. She seemed to have realized there was more to life than the Mother's Plan.

"Thanks for letting me work with you on your research project, Belsas," Chandrey went on.

"I'm happy to have help. So how do you like the officer apartments?"

"They're okay," said Chandrey as she looked around. "But they're going to be lonely when Cance goes off."

"Lonely?" Wreed looked at Belsas, who seemed just as surprised.

"Where you going, Cance?" Belsas asked.

"Well, you both know I lost my teaching position." Cance ran her fingers through Chandrey's hair. "Now the higher-ups, particularly the Protocol Master, think I'm a bad influence on the students. I'm being transferred."

Chandrey nodded. "And since I'm oathed to an officer and schooling here, they're letting me keep the apartment." She rose to the back of the lounger and began to rub Cance's neck. "She's headed out on a short assignment."

"They won't tell me exactly what." Cance closed her eyes in response to Chandrey's touch.

"It's not one of those quick, earn-your-rank-back doings, is it?" asked Belsas, and then she breathed in with what Wreed knew as her version of "oops" when Cance tensed.

Chandrey quit rubbing Cance's neck. "What's she mean?"

Cance scowled at Belsas. "I wasn't going to tell her until afterward."

"What does she *mean*?" repeated Chandrey when she returned to the lounger. "Tell me."

"It's not as bad as it seems, Precious." Cance paused long enough to finish the wine in her mug. "I do one reconnaissance mission, and I'm a Second Officer again. Then I come back to you and work here until you finish your schooling. Simple enough."

"Reconnaissance?" Chandrey's hand trembled when she reached for her mug. "We agreed you wouldn't take optional missions. You promised."

"I know."

"But you *promised* me."

"Chandrey." Cance sighed with clear frustration. "I'm trying to help us out. If I don't get my rank back, I'll be assigned to some out-of-the-way place you might not be able to go."

"Did they tell you that?" asked Belsas.

"You know how the Kinship manipulates kimshees when one of us gets in trouble."

"Do they do this often?" For once, Wreed felt sympathetic for Cance. "I mean, is this how kimshees normally earn rank?"

"If they've lost it for some reason, yes." Cance faced Chandrey. "I didn't think about the consequences when we took off. Now my foolishness might keep us apart for a very long time."

"You mean our foolishness." Chandrey caught Cance's arm and hugged it. "Where are they sending you and what'll you be doing?"

"I find out after I launch."

"Will you at least com me and tell me?"

"I can't," said Cance. "It's the norm for this sort of assignment."

"You mean it's the norm for a dangerous assignment." Chandrey swallowed and blinked hard. "This frightens me," she admitted. "What if something happens?"

"I've done over a dozen of these assignments. They're observations. Nothing ever happens. In fact, they're pretty boring."

"Then why do they compensate so well?"

It was an honest question, one that Wreed might have asked if Chandrey hadn't. She was glad Belsas never acted so foolishly.

"Anything that takes a sister into Aut lands is considered dangerous, whether it really is or not," said Cance. "I've gone in Aut lands numerous times and never once stepped into hostile territory. The Kinship has Aut agents for that."

"But we'll be apart." Chandrey's expression remained concerned.

"You already missed four days when Cance was in the brig," Wreed reminded her. "She said she won't be gone long and besides, you'll be busy working with Belsas."

"Not long, Cancey?" Chandrey cocked her head as if in thought. "You sure about that?"

"No more than a couple of seven-days." Cance nodded. "And you'll have Belsas and Wreed to keep you company. It'll seem like no time at all."

"Well, I do have exams coming up."

"And your extra work with me as well," added Belsas.

"And this will be the only time, right?" asked Chandrey.

"Absolutely." Cance held up her hand.

"I don't like it," said Chandrey. "But I guess there's some good in it." She went to the kitchenette to get the open wine crystal and refilled Cance's mug.

Wreed finally relaxed. She knew that Cance's eyes were glazed from the wine, but she and Chandrey were still good company, especially when their conversation turned from Cance's upcoming assignment, and the four of them settled into a card game.

* * *

When Belsas and Wreed left, they walked back to her dorm at a slower-than-usual pace. Belsas seemed to be lagging, not wanting the evening to end.

"They're settling in, don't you think?" Belsas asked.

"I do," Wreed said. "But I still worry."

"Same here." Belsas stopped to look at the clear evening sky, and then down to Wreed, where her gaze lingered on her face. "I was wondering something."

"What's that?"

"Well, Cance and Chandrey seem so happy together."

"I've had my doubts, but now I've got to agree."

"It's got me thinking." Belsas glanced above Wreed again, as if avoiding her eyes. "It's got me to thinking that if…well, if they can be happy together why can't we?"

"Belsas Exzal!" Wreed pulled Belsas's chin down until she looked at her squarely. "Are you asking me to oath with you?" It took all her strength not to laugh out loud. She adored Belsas, she truly did, but she wasn't ready to oath with anyone, even someone so wonderful.

"Um, I suppose I am." Belsas shifted her feet nervously and tried to look away, but Wreed wouldn't let her.

"Bel, darling, you have me in your bed and brain whenever you desire. I'm yours for the taking. What more do you need?" Wreed pulled Belsas into a furious kiss, and didn't let go until she pushed away, gasping. "What more do either of us need?"

"But I miss you at night," Belsas said between breaths. "I miss you beside me."

"Now that *is* a problem." Wreed started walking again, even more slowly than before, until she and Belsas came to a bench where they sat facing one another. "But do we really need the oath to solve it?"

"Don't we?"

"Not as I see it." Wreed held her gaze on Belsas. "Now that Chandrey is out of the dorms, the curfew's been lifted. Most everyone sleeps there spottily."

"You'll spend the night sometimes?" Belsas regarded her with an astonished expression that quickly fell into despair. "But you don't want to oath with me, do you?"

"It's not that I don't want to, sweetie. I'm not ready." Wreed kissed her again, much more tenderly this time. "I hope you can see the difference."

"I guess I can." Belsas was quiet for a moment. She nodded slowly. "I can see the difference."

She looked down and away from Wreed before glancing up with a sort of half-smile on her face. The expression was almost comical, but Wreed dared not laugh. She had just been asked to oath and turned it down.

"I think I kinda got caught up in the romance I see between Cance and Chandrey," Belsas continued. "I think I can live with your alternative, as long as you're still offering."

"Oh, really?" Wreed shared her smile. "I don't know."

"You teasing me?"

"Got room for two in that bedroll?"

Wreed moved too quickly to be grabbed, and darted toward Belsas's apartment with Belsas on her heels, apparently eager for another reason to be out of breath.

Chapter Fourteen

Taelach Training Grounds on Saria IV

Suspicion—doubt, uncertainty; the basis of Taelach/Autlach relations

One evening six days later, Belsas was in the Training Ground's archives showing Chandrey how to properly handle texts. They had finished assembling the research they had already pulled and were looking for new records of Rankil Danston's life when the com on Chandrey's belt buzzed.

"Probably Wreed," said Chandrey as she removed her gloves.

Belsas didn't have a belt com, so Wreed had taken to calling Chandrey when she needed something from either of them during their work sessions.

"She'll be wanting to meet us for dinner about now," Chandrey continued.

"Probably so," Belsas mumbled without looking up from the fragile text unrolled in front of her. "We should be done soon."

"Hiya, Wreed." Chandrey set her gloves on a side table and held the com's small viewer up so she could see the image.

"Sister Chandresslandra Cances?" The voice was not Wreed's.

Belsas looked up, over Chandrey's shoulder, and what she saw could mean nothing good. A uniformed sister was on the other side of the viewer. By her markings, she held Master Kimshee rank, meaning a sister with more than twenty passes experience in the Kinship military and unsurpassed kimshee training. She wouldn't contact Chandrey without very good reason.

"Yes, this is Chandrey Cances." Chandrey must have noticed the rank too, because she reached back to grasp Belsas's hand.

"This is Master Kimshee Tinyal Scree. Are you in a position to speak?"

"Just a moment." Chandrey, still holding Belsas's gloved hand, exited the clean room and sat at a worktable just outside. Neither of them removed their smocks—a clean room error Belsas generally wouldn't have made. "Okay."

"Are you with a friend or family member, Sister Chandresslandra?" Master Scree asked.

"A friend, yes. Why?" Chandrey's voice quavered.

Belsas knew she had to be aware that kimshees didn't contact other kimshees' loved ones except for a very specific purpose: someone had to have been hurt or killed.

"As you can imagine, Sister Chandresslandra, this concerns your life mate, Third Officer Cancelynn Creiloff."

"Is she okay?" Chandrey's grip on Belsas's hand tightened.

"She's been injured."

Belsas removed her hand from Chandrey's grasp, jerked off her gloves, and took the com from Chandrey when she seemed unable to speak. "How badly?"

"She has been seriously injured, second officer." Master Scree had clearly read Belsas's work tunic markings. "She is currently being stabilized at the base hospital on Langus."

"Can her life mate join her there?"

"Negative." Master Scree looked displeased. "There have been numerous small attacks on Langus and Saria Proper during the last seven-day. The airspace around both is considered dangerous. Third Officer Creiloff will be transported back to the Training Grounds medical facilities as soon as she is stable."

"Please tell me what happened!" Chandrey's plea abruptly turned into a wail.

"I'm sorry, Sister Chandresslandra, but I do not have that information. Her medical staff will know more." There was true sympathy in Master Scree's tone. "They will brief you when they arrive with your life mate."

"When might that be?" Belsas asked when Chandrey sobbed and passed the com back to her.

Scree flipped through a small reader on her worktable. "The staff has asked the Training Grounds to have care ready for her within thirty-six hours. They should be there around that time. That's all the information I have."

"Have you contacted Cance's raiser?"

Scree again referred to her reader. "No, Sister Chandresslandra was the only emergency contact listed. Would you be willing to do so, second officer? I still have several families to contact."

"I understand. Please keep us informed."

"Certainly. Scree out."

Belsas closed the com, hooked it to her belt, and guided Chandrey up the stairs to the archive's main entrance, where she sat Chandrey in a chair while she commed Wreed.

"Heya Chandrey," answered Wreed. "I was just about to com you two for—what's wrong, Bel?"

"Cance's been injured."

Wreed's smile faded. "How's Chandrey?"

"Not good. Meet us at her apartment?"

"On my way."

Belsas closed the com and turned her attentions back to Chandrey, who sat staring at her hands.

"She said it was boring duty. She said she would be safe!" Chandrey's voice sounded rough from crying.

"She was doing her job," said Belsas.

"It was optional duty!"

"That doesn't matter now," Belsas said gently. "You have to be strong for her. She needs your strength."

Chandrey blinked away her tears and wiped her face on her sleeve. "But she's used to this sort of thing, isn't she?"

"She's been injured in training, never on a mission. She's going to be as scared as you."

"Oh, poor Cancey." Chandrey closed her eyes for a moment, and then reopened them with a resounding nod. She removed her gloves. "Did you say Wreed was meeting us?"

"Yeah, I bet she's there now."

"Okay." Chandrey started for the archive's double doors, hesitated, and turned back. "Will you com Creiloff for me? I'm not sure I can."

"Sure, as soon as we meet up with Wreed."

They walked in silence, Chandrey worrying her hands until they got to the apartment where Wreed waited.

"Everything will be okay, sweetie." Wreed passed Belsas a food container and drew Chandrey down into a hug.

"I'm trying." Chandrey's voice was muffled in Wreed's shoulder. She pushed back after a moment, cleared her eyes again, and ran her thumb across the ID reader to open the apartment.

Belsas and Wreed made themselves busy setting the table for dinner, but kept a close eye on Chandrey, who sat still on the lounger. This was her first medical crisis with Cance, the potential first of many, and she wasn't taking it very well.

She's young. Wreed reminded Belsas when she expressed her concern through phase. *Plus she's still reeling from losing her family.*

From being forcibly removed from their ranks, you mean. Cance had told Belsas of Chandrey's lingering rejection pain.

Not that anyone could blame her. Belsas had been very close to her raisers, even though they had been past eighty when they claimed her. She was the child of second-time raisers. Each had lost a life mate, but found love again with each other. Even though her raisers had eventually parted ways, Belsas thought of them fondly and often.

Their older children were more like special aunts than siblings to her. In some way, she supposed she was raised more by grandraisers, but despite their eventual break up, their wisdom had shaped her into the person she was. She missed them terribly.

It must feel like all of them died at once.

Worse yet, that they're alive, but she's dead to them. Wreed spooned up the casserole she had heated in Belsas's apartment. *Nothing fancy,* she said, placing slices of jam-slathered dark bread beside the mugs. "Come eat, Chandrey."

"I'm not hungry," Chandrey said softly. "Besides, there's only two chairs."

"I'll pull up a clothing cube. You need to eat something." Belsas moved a stack of clothing and scooted the cube up to the table by pushing it with her knees. "Come on, Chandrey. You need your strength."

Wreed patted the open chair. "Come on, sweetie."

Chandrey grimaced, but came to the table where she ate the bread and only pushed around the food in her mug. "My stomach will be in knots until I see Cance for myself."

"Of course it's in knots." Wreed removed Chandrey's mug and set another piece of jam-covered bread in front of her. "Eat this and Bel will contact Creiloff for you."

Chandrey looked at Belsas. "Do you have the contact info? Cance says Creiloff's not easy to get hold of. The channels are more difficult than the ones to reach Gahrah—" She frowned and coughed like she had swallowed something sour. "They're very complicated."

"I'll manage." Belsas accessed her personal files through the apartment com and pulled up Creiloff's hailing codes, something Cance had given her when they'd schooled together, just in case she got into trouble she couldn't get out of.

Belsas supposed this situation qualified.

Creiloff opened her com within seconds of the first hail.

"I just spoke with you less than a cycle ago, Cancelynn. What have you got yourself into this time, and how much is it going to cost me?" Creiloff's expression turned curious when she saw Belsas. "I was expecting Cancelynn." She leaned back in her office chair and puffed on her pilta. "Where're Cancelynn and her pretty life mate?"

Creiloff's office spread behind her when she switched the view from her personal com to her wall com. There were two other women in the room with her, but they sat on hassocks by a large window—one busy doing some sort of knitting and the other sewing by hand.

Unusual pastimes that Belsas would have inquired about under different circumstances, however, now was not the time. "Chandrey is here."

"Then why're you comming and not her?"

Belsas had answered Cance's com for her numerous times when they'd roomed together, and she was long used to Creiloff's brusque mannerism. "Cance has been injured."

Creiloff ground her pilta into a mug and sat up. "Injured, you say?"

"Yes, ma'am."

The women on the hassocks whispered back and forth, but made no attempt to comfort Creiloff, who demanded, "How did this happen?"

"On a mission."

Creiloff motioned to one of the women, who retrieved a mug from the worktable. "She didn't get tangled in that mess on Saria Proper and Langus, did she?"

Belsas wondered how Creiloff had known news that had yet to be officially released. "I'm afraid that's exactly what happened."

Creiloff pounded a fist on the worktable, strewing a stack of recorders across the top. "I fuckin' warned her about Auts. But she wouldn't listen to a damn thing I said." Her tone turned mocking. "'But Creiloff, I want to be the bridge. But Creiloff, I want to keep sisters from going through what I did when I was born.' And what the fuck did it get her?"

Behind her, the remaining woman scurried from view, if not the room itself. "Elisa, bring me a drink!" Creiloff stood, cursing, her back to the screen for a moment before she turned to Belsas. "Where is she now?"

"Langus, but they're transporting her here as soon as she's stable."

Elisa appeared at Creiloff's side and timidly offered a mug, which she snatched with one hand while she waved both women away with the other. She downed the entire mug in a couple of swallows and wiped her mouth on the back of her hand.

"Didn't you say Chandresslandra was with you?"

"Yes. Do you wish to—"

Creiloff's expression darkened further. "And what would Cancelynn think of your taking advantage of her friendship?"

Belsas drew a breath. "Why, my girlfriend's here as well. She's Chandrey's best friend."

"Let me speak to Chandresslandra."

Belsas called Chandrey to the com and moved to the lounger, where she fumed over Creiloff's not-so-subtle accusation.

She's upset. Wreed tried to calm her from where she stood by the worktable, listening to Creiloff talk to Chandrey.

We all are, but you didn't hear me accusing her of anything, did you? Belsas asked.

I know, but—Wreed broke off to answer a question from Creiloff. "Yes, I'm taking good care of Chandrey."

"Continue to do so until I arrive."

Creiloff must have closed her end of the com, because Wreed closed theirs.

"She's coming here." Wreed joined Belsas on the lounger. "The next seven-day is going to be tough, isn't it?"

"Exceedingly." Belsas looked at Chandrey, who seemed to have wilted across the worktable. "She shouldn't be alone."

"I know." Wreed twisted half around on the lounger so she could see them both. "Chandrey, I'm going to stay with you tonight, okay?"

Chandrey lifted her head enough to nod, and then lowered it again.

"She needs rest. Let's call it a night," Wreed suggested.

"All right." Belsas kissed her cheek and rose from the lounger. "Com me if you hear anything." She touched Chandrey's shoulder. "You'll both be in my prayers."

Chandrey shuddered, but patted Belsas's hand. "Thank you."

Belsas opened the door and turned back, watching as Wreed

tried to coax Chandrey into drinking some tea. When neither acknowledged her, she stepped into the corridor, pulled the door shut, and stood there, wishing there was something more she could do to ease Chandrey's hurt, and puzzling over the sensation that had swept through her when they'd touched.

It had been a tingling, an exchange of pain and passion mere friends seldom shared, but Belsas wasn't at all certain if the passion she'd felt from Chandrey had been solely for Cance.

However, Belsas decided that Chandrey was young at sharing her emotions through phase and had probably mixed her signals. Besides, she told herself, she was also being selfish about sharing Wreed for the night. With this in mind, she walked back to her apartment alone, hoping to manage at least at bit of sleep before morning.

Chapter Fifteen

Taelach Training Grounds: Saria IV

Tentacle—extension, something that grasps and squeezes

When Chandrey was finally allowed to see her life mate, she had to be convinced Cance was actually in the bed. Her life mate looked foreign, a tentacled creature fused to a sister in some awful experiment.

A breathing tube ran from her throat, and drains ran from several places in her abdomen. What wasn't bandaged was bruised purple to black or scratched, like she'd been dragged behind a moving object. Only Cance's face remained clearly visible, and it was swollen, specifically her eyes. She'd suffered severe corneal abrasions. There had been dozens of metal slivers in each eye, and she might have suffered permanent damage.

Hardest of all were the two special healers at Cance's side, providing something Chandrey couldn't—constant pain relief.

They were an interesting duo, a raiser and her daughter. One or the other remained with Cance at all times, linked to her mind so that she stayed sedated, but neither left the immediate area. They ate, slept and showered in Cance's medical suite.

"The pain to your life mate would be too great if one or both of us left yet," said Sheelian, the daughter, when Chandrey watched her change one of the drains. "She needs constant phasing to keep her reasonably comfortable."

"On top of pain meds?" Chandrey asked Esther, the other healer, as she injected a syringe into a tube.

"Yes," Sheelian and Esther replied in unison. "Sister Cancelynn has more than twenty broken bones."

Chandrey quietly watched them work. They answered all her questions and let her assist when she asked, but offered little more in the way of conversation.

She was allowed to stay in Cance's room, but occasionally left for her own sanity. Wreed and sometimes Belsas would walk with her in the medical facility's garden. Her friends weren't allowed in the room until Cance regained full consciousness, so she tried to keep them informed—difficult to do without shedding a few tears.

Wreed and Belsas remained supportive, and frequently brought items she needed so she didn't have to stray far from Cance's side.

It took Chandrey almost a full moon cycle to even remotely understand what had happened to her life mate. Esther said Cance had been captured by Aut radicals, but the rest she learned along the way.

Most of Cance's injuries were caused by torture. She had been beaten and burned, among other things, but Chandrey was left to figure out the worst when some of the bandages were being changed and she saw bite marks on Cance's breasts and stomach. No one need tell her what they meant. Even the Mother's Word mentioned their significance. Bite marks were an Aut man's way of making a sister a living, breathing warning to others. The physical scars could and would be removed when they'd fully healed, but she worried more about the mental ones.

Sheelian tried to comfort her. "The mental healers will remove all they can."

Chandrey said nothing, just watched when Cance's bandages were changed. The elder healer, Esther, rested on a lounger beside her bed, deep in meditation. Neither of the healers moved much when they were linked to Cance, so when Esther began to stir, she noticed. The healer moved her head back and forth, mumbling and swatting at something invisible.

"Go away," Esther repeated in a whisper that grew louder. "You've no business here."

"She's sharing Cance's nightmare," explained Sheelian, but Chandrey saw her dismay. "It's near time for us to switch places. My raiser is probably getting tired."

Before Sheelian could cross the room, Esther opened her eyes and screamed, "Get away! No!"

"Mama!" Sheelian rushed to her raiser's side, catching her before she slid off the lounger. "Mama, you okay?"

"I was pushed out." Esther held her daughter's tunic tightly. "There was a second presence."

"A duplicity?"

Esther shook her head. "No, she wasn't trying to compartmentalize to cope. There was someone else there!" Her breathing began to slow, and she accepted the mug of water Chandrey offered. "A distinct second presence exists in this sister's mind."

"There's nothing like that in her military evals," said Sheelian. "She'd never have been able to become kimshee if there were." She looked at Chandrey. "Do you know anything that might explain this?"

"No." Chandrey looked at Cance, who was beginning to stir. What she felt coming from her life mate was complicated, dark and very painful. "She's waking."

"Too soon," said the older healer. "But I can't go back in. Dose her."

"She's on a high dose already," objected Sheelian. "I'll go."

"You'll not." Esther grasped her hand. "It's dangerous."

"Dangerous?" Chandrey asked. When Cance began moaning, she added, "Please, do something to help her."

"I'm going in, Mama." Sheelian moved onto the lounger.

"No!" Esther reached for a vial and syringe. "She can take more of a dose."

"It's not like you to deny standard treatment," said Sheelian. "What're you not saying?"

"Please do something!" Chandrey watched helplessly as pain showed clearly on Cance's swollen face.

"We're going to up her dosage." Esther emptied the syringe into one of Cance's tentacle lines, and turned back to Sheelian, taking her aside to speak to her softly.

The medicine did seem to calm Cance, but didn't ease her back to sleep. She was still waking far too early in her recovery. She needed phased sleep, Chandrey thought—a comatose state in order to heal quickly.

"Not enough." Chandrey smoothed the hair from Cance's face. "If you won't ease her pain, then I will." She closed her eyes.

"Sister Chandresslandra, you can't." Esther touched her sleeve. "We can't let you."

Chandrey opened her eyes. "You won't let me phase with my own life mate?"

"It's not safe."

"We'll phase you unconscious before we let you," said Sheelian.

"How dare you—" Chandrey began, but Esther pulled back her tunic collar.

"Look before you decide." A fresh bite mark glistened on her shoulder.

Chandrey looked from the wound to Cance. "How?"

"We don't know," said Esther as her daughter disinfected the wound. "But the other presence attacked me just before I dropped my phase."

"That's impossible."

"We've heard of it happening, but never experienced it." Sheelian placed adhering gauze on her raiser's shoulder, and then returned to the bed, where she began strapping down Cance's uninjured arm.

"Is that necessary?" Chandrey asked.

Water soaked the bottom of the bandages over Cance's eyes, and a trail of tears ran down the side of her nose.

"It's protocol," assured Esther. She secured a secondary strap to Cance's left ankle and another loosely to her waist. "We've ordered a binder for her too."

"A binder!" Chandrey had never seen a binder, but she had heard of them. They were worn by criminals and the insane, any sister whose phase couldn't be trusted. "But then I won't be able to—"

"You can still speak to and touch her, which is enough until we can explain all this."

"Your life mate is awake, Sister Chandrey," said Sheelian. "We'll step out for a moment."

The healers left the room.

"Cancey?" Chandrey ventured. Cance looked like such a prisoner—bound, bruised and soon to be bindered. She wanted to hold her tight, but she knew she couldn't without causing more pain. "Cancey?"

Cance wiggled the fingers of her uninjured arm.

"I know you hurt," said Chandrey. "The healers are doing all they can." She watched as Cance folded the same fingers, one by one, into a fist. "You're safe, love. And I'm right here, okay?"

But this seemed to do little to soothe Cance. She squeezed and released her fist repeatedly, tighter each time until Chandrey placed her hand in Cance's. "Shhh."

Rage shot through Chandrey the moment they touched. She tried to pull away, but Cance held on, gripping her hand hard enough to hurt. "Let go!" Fear and hatred. Confusion. Agony and vengeance.

Her life mate's mind randomly swung between emotional extremes. "Help!"

Sheelian and Esther burst into the room.

"I was afraid this would happen," said Esther. She filled another syringe as her daughter tried to loosen Cance's hold.

Chandrey gritted her teeth against the pain and rage Cance forced on her. Cance had no clear thoughts, no real idea where she was so she was striking out at everything. Panic. Terror. It was as if two hands were crushing Chandrey's one. She couldn't help crying out.

Esther emptied the syringe into Cance's largest tentacle line. "Give it a moment," she said.

"Great Mother!" said Sheelian as she finally managed to open Cance's hand. "I've never seen the like." She pulled Chandrey's hand free and held it in her own, examining it. "Nothing broken, but let me ice it."

"No, thank you." Chandrey snatched her hand away. It was sore and certainly bruised, but she didn't want anyone touching her. "What happened?"

"Muscle spasms," said Esther, but Chandrey doubted the explanation. That hadn't been a spasm. It was too intentional. A sharing. Cance had wanted her to feel what she did—what they had done to her.

"I've paralyzed her until they bring the binder," continued Esther, but she looked very concerned. "Sister Chandrey, who's Brandoff?"

"You heard that too?" asked Sheelian.

"I don't know," said Chandrey. "I'll ask her raiser when she arrives." She didn't understand why Creiloff was being detained outside the Training Grounds gates, left sitting there for two days under guard while the Kinship determined whether she should be allowed in. Belsas said she would let her know if things changed.

"Please do." Esther checked Cance's straps and began setting up a new tentacle line connected to what Chandrey believed to be an Aut sleep smoker. She slid the tentacle under Cance's nose and set the smoker to a quick bubble, sending air through a thin chemical gel which charged the air with sedating, colored smoke. "By itself, it wouldn't be enough, but combined with the meds, she'll be reasonably comfortable."

Chandrey didn't completely understand what was going on, but felt too tired to object, even when Esther helped Sheelian secure an amber binder around Cance's head and set the alarm codes, Sheelian lowered the lights and produced a pillow and blanket from a cabinet.

"You need sleep too, Sister Chandrey," said Esther.

"Thank you." She curled on the lounger and tried to relax, but couldn't when she became aware of two sister sentries, elite troopers by their uniforms, standing outside the door.

Ignore them. Esther slipped into her mind. *Rest so you might be able to help your mate.*

Before Chandrey could say more, Esther placed her into a dreamless, senseless sleep.

Chapter Sixteen

Training Ground Medical Facilities

Binder—something used to bind, fasten, wrap or limit; contract

Creiloff finally saw her daughter while under military escort. She also wore a binder, which astonished Chandrey until she was informed by the trooper in charge that as a member of the Cleave, Creiloff was not a Kinship sister, so her very presence on a Kinship military base was unheard of. The trooper began to say something else concerning the Cleave, but stopped short when Creiloff turned to glower, her eyes positively crimson beneath the amber binder.

"Her stay here will be short, trust me." The trooper nodded at her subordinates, who guided their charge through the door to Cance's room.

Creiloff was obviously incensed by the treatment, but tolerated it better than Chandrey thought she might. At least Creiloff wasn't fettered, she told herself, following the entourage.

"Wake up, Cancelynn." Creiloff rattled the bed. "Come on, girl. I haven't all day."

"Creiloff?" Cance's facial swelling had eased enough for her to open her eyes more than a slit. Still, her eyes were very red and watered almost constantly when open. "How'd you manage to get on the Training Grounds?"

"It's all in who you know." Creiloff moved to the bedside, where she stood over her daughter. "Auts. Fucking Auts." She spoke slowly, as if carefully choosing every word. "Are they killing your pain?"

"Pretty much." Cance looked at her water mug. Chandrey quickly held it to her mouth.

"You're too weak to lie." Creiloff's joints cracked when she flexed her hands. "Why're you being restrained?"

"Protocol until the mental healers clear me."

"You all but lose your life for them, and they treat you like a criminal." Creiloff bent close to the bed. "The Kinship doesn't understand your needs," she said in a low voice. "Come to my home to heal. You'll be infinitely better cared for there than here." She looked at Chandrey. "Your life mate should be seeing to your care, not strangers."

"Those strangers saved her life," Chandrey began.

Creiloff admonished her with a wave. "Those strangers would have sent her to her death." Her gaze returned to Cance. "Come recuperate at my home. I insist."

"Your home?" Cance's face clouded. "The Cleave?"

"Where else would you go?" Creiloff touched Cance's shoulder, an affectionate gesture that seemed to surprise Cance as much as it did Chandrey. "How did all this happen?"

"Working." Cance winced when Chandrey dabbed water from her eyes. "Can't tell more."

"They've already taken it from you, haven't they?"

"No." Cance let Chandrey straighten her pillow, which frequently caught on her binder. "I remember." She touched the tentacle lines running from her abdomen. "My contact double-crossed me." She looked at her mug again, and Chandrey held it to her mouth a second time. "Can't tell more."

Creiloff motioned to Chandrey. "Wait outside."

Ready for a break, Chandrey walked down the hall to a small waiting area where Belsas and Wreed sat. Belsas offered her chair, but she refused, instead taking a seat on the floor in front of them.

"So that's Creiloff," said Wreed, just above a whisper.

"In the flesh." Belsas looked down the hall to Cance's open door. "I told you."

"What a bitch." Wreed looked surprised when Chandrey chided her. "Well, she is."

"She's upset about Cancey," Chandrey said.

"Don't make excuses for her." Belsas moved closer to Chandrey. "She thinks her power gets her whatever she wants."

"Doesn't it?" said Wreed. "She's on a Kinship military base, and she isn't even *in* the Kinship."

"Why isn't she in the Kinship?" asked Chandrey. "Why isn't the Cleave part of the Kinship?"

"The Cleave and Kinship have very different views," began Belsas, but Wreed interrupted.

"You're sugarcoating."

Belsas shook her head. "You're still mad about Creiloff's reaction when I contacted her about Cance."

"Aren't you?"

"What happened?" Chandrey asked.

"Oh, nothing," began Belsas, but Wreed wagged a finger at her.

"Tell her. She has the right to know."

"It'll upset her."

"It should." Wreed frowned at Belsas. "Tell her."

"Tell me what?" Chandrey tried to keep her voice down, but didn't succeed. "Damn it, someone tell me!"

Wreed and Belsas looked at her with the same awe.

"She actually cursed." Wreed held out her hand. "I win."

"Later." Belsas flashed a grin, and then turned back to Chandrey. "When I contacted Creiloff about Cance, she accused me of being alone with you inappropriately."

"What?" Chandrey drew up to her knees. "We're friends, and I'm working with you on your project. We're alone quite often. There's nothing going on between us."

"We know that," said Wreed. "But Creiloff was quick to accuse Bel."

"She was upset," said Chandrey. "I wouldn't put much into it."

"Again with the excuses." Wreed sighed. "You're good at making excuses for others' bad behavior."

"Now, Wreed." Belsas placed her hand on Wreed's shoulder as Creiloff emerged from Cance's room. The three of them stood when Creiloff approached and bowed a greeting, but Creiloff ignored them.

"Walk me out." She took Chandrey's arm and walked with her down the corridor, the trooper escort a few steps behind, but never interrupting. "Your life mate cannot get out of bed because of her injuries, yet you went to socialize and did not wait outside the door like I instructed?"

"They've been a comfort."

"You should be providing your life mate comfort, not seeking it." Creiloff glared at her. "Especially from Belsas."

"She and Wreed are friends."

"It is overtly clear Belsas wishes more from you."

Chandrey stopped in her tracks. "They're Cance's friends as well. Belsas has been here almost as much as I have."

"Because you're here." Creiloff stopped with her in front of a large window, but didn't let go of her arm. "I know the Plan teaches proper associations, so your behavior's simply inexcusable."

"Belsas and Wreed have been a comfort, nothing more."

"Your comfort is of no concern."

"I know Cance has been through a lot, but—"

"You cannot possibly fathom what Cance has been through, so stop trying."

Was Creiloff chastising her? Chandrey wondered. "I'm doing my best."

"Caring is not understanding." Creiloff relaxed her grip on Chandrey's arm, but didn't let go as she looked past her to the window, which overlooked the Training Grounds. "And comforting her will not change reality."

"I know that." Chandrey tensed her arm, encouraging Creiloff to release her, but her grip suddenly became tighter than ever.

"You know nothing." Creiloff whirled Chandrey around. She struggled, but Creiloff held her fast. "You're nothing but a girl, a child, an ignorant thrall. You've a duty to care for her every need."

"I've spent most every moment with her since she's been back. Please let go."

The trooper in charge interceded. "None of your Cleave crap here. You heard the sister. Let her loose."

Creiloff slowly loosened her grip, but not before growling in disgust. "'Independent thought clouds the greater need.'"

Chandrey recognized the words, Wise Mother's Words, but she had never heard them used in that context. In the Plan, the words were interpreted as meaning that one should not alienate herself from family, not as referring to constant care of one for another. The interpretation confused her. She stared out the window, thinking about what Creiloff had said while she spoke more on what she expected of her as Cance's life mate. They resumed their walk as Creiloff continued.

"Can I ask you something?" Chandrey broke in after a few moments.

Creiloff's mouth tightened. "We do not interrupt where I come from. Furthermore, you are obviously ignoring my directions, so this had better concern Cancelynn."

"It does."

"Proceed."

They neared the medical facility's entrance. Chandrey paused. "Who's Brandoff?"

"When Cancelynn was very young, she had an imaginary playmate by the name." Creiloff reached into her tunic, retrieving a fat pilta. She bit the end off and spat it on the ground immediately outside the door. "Probably called it up in her unconsciousness."

"The healers picked up on it."

"Hmph. Cancelynn used to blame 'Brannie' for a lot of things."

"Thank you, that helps."

Creiloff peered at Chandrey through the binder. "I want her well cared for."

"She will be."

"By *you*. It's your duty. I cannot stress that enough with this chunk of amber on my face."

"I understand." Chandrey rubbed her arm, wondering what the binder had to do with emphasis.

"I'll know if you do less."

A warning? A promise? Chandrey wasn't sure how to take her words.

"I'll see you both when you reach my home." Creiloff turned and exited the building, her escorts in tow.

"You okay?" asked Wreed when Chandrey returned to the waiting area. "You look frazzled."

"I'm fine." Chandrey headed straight to Cance's room.

"There you are." Cance was sitting up more. "Did you see Creiloff out?"

"I did." Chandrey rubbed her arm again. It hurt, probably more because she kept focusing on what had been said during their walk. She was Cance's caretaker right now. Her life mate depended on her. She reached behind Cance to adjust the pillows, and then took her water mug to refill it. "Do you need anything else?"

"Lower the light, then come sit beside me." Cance leaned back against the pillows and closed her eyes. "I'll be damned glad when I get this binder off."

"The mental healer will be here in the morning," said Chandrey, returning the mug to the bedside table.

"Good." Cance watched in silence as Chandrey sat down on the edge of the lounger. "Where'd you go while Creiloff and I talked?"

"Just outside."

"Good." Cance shifted beneath her blanket. "What're you doing when I sleep?"

"Mostly, I'm here with you."

"What about when you're not?"

"I have to shower and change clothes sometime."

"And other than that?"

"I have to eat."

"Is that all?"

"I go for walks."

"With whom?"

"I walk with Wreed and Bel. Why the sudden concern?" But Chandrey knew why.

"Curiosity." Cance yawned and closed her eyes. "You walk with both of them?"

"If they're both here."

"You don't walk alone with Belsas, do you?"

They'd reached the true reason for her questions, courtesy of Creiloff, Chandrey thought. "Sometimes. Why?"

"Don't anymore. It's not right."

"But—"

"Do as I say."

Chandrey didn't want to stress Cance, so she didn't argue. Cance was in pain, and Creiloff had inserted her views into that pain. The scrutiny would pass as Cance healed and things would return to normal. Until then, she would let things stay as they were.

Creiloff wouldn't ruin her friendships, but still, she wondered what Creiloff had meant by saying she would know if Chandrey did less. Less what? Pay less attention to Cance than she already did? She would have asked Wreed or Belsas, but she was too tired.

When Cance fell asleep, she lay back on the lounger and quickly joined her, dreams flitting back and forth between her wants and the expectations of others.

Chapter Seventeen

Kinship Training Grounds: Saria IV

Rot—to degenerate; decline

When Cance was finally released from the medical facilities, she was placed on a strict regime of bed rest and daily physical therapy. She'd been awarded second officer rank again and wore the insignia proudly when she limped to and from therapy.

Chandrey was with her every time Wreed saw them, carrying Cance's therapy clothing, helping her up and down steps along the way. Chandrey had asked and been permitted to fall back another class in her training, but this time she'd been told she wouldn't be allowed to drop back again. Wreed worried for her, as did Belsas, but neither of them knew what to do. She was isolated from everyone but Cance, and Cance seemed thrilled by the attention.

Wreed and Belsas stopped by their apartment on occasion, if for no other reason than for Belsas to drop off work for Chandrey, who still had to complete the reprimand she'd earned when she and Cance had taken off to oath.

Chandrey opened the door when they rang in. "Cance is sleeping," she said in a whisper. "Thanks for dropping off my stuff."

"Do you have the last batch done?" Belsas looked over her head and could see Cance on the lounger, clearly awake.

"Almost." Chandrey looked away.

"I really need them."

"I know. I'm sorry." Chandrey glanced over her shoulder.

"Who's here?" Cance sat up and looked at the door, cursing under her breath.

"Wreed and Bel," Chandrey answered.

"Good, you're awake." Belsas pushed past Chandrey, and Wreed followed, eager to check on her friend.

The inside of the apartment was dark, cave-like, the curtains drawn, the lights off. While Wreed knew the Taelach had spent much of their earlier days in caves, she pulled back the curtain, flooding the room with natural light.

"Fuck!" Cance covered her eyes with a hand while Chandrey rushed to close the curtains.

"Wreed!" Chandrey cried.

"It's depressing in here, sweetie. Not very conducive to healing, if you ask me."

"Cance's eyes are still sensitive. She's supposed to stay in low light."

"There's a difference between low light and no light." Wreed parted the curtain just a little, letting in a stream of light far from Cance's face. Not that the light had even the faintest chance of hurting Cance with Chandrey hovering, she thought.

Belsas pulled a stack of scroll replicas from her carry bag. "I'll place the work on the table." She touched Wreed's arm, encouraging her to enter the main living area. Wreed did so grudgingly and sat in the empty chair. Both Cance and Chandrey glowered at her, but she ignored them, sitting straight and looking at them directly.

"You're looking better, Cance," Wreed said. "Walking better too. I saw you on your way to therapy the other day."

"I'm improving," said Cance after a moment. "Chandrey, a drink for our guests."

"Oh, yes." Chandrey spoke softly, her mouth downturned as if she were being forced into service. "Would you like something?"

"No thanks," said Belsas as Wreed shook her head. "We really just stopped by on our way to eat."

"Oh, well, in that case, thanks," Cance told them.

"Would you like to go with us?" Belsas asked.

Wreed was upset by Belsas's suggestion, but didn't let it show. Not that she didn't want Chandrey with them, but she had trouble finding much sympathy for Cance. True, Cance been injured, but that had been in the line of duty. She'd been doing her job, and now she treated

Chandrey more like a servant than a life mate. And Chandrey took the treatment in stride, like she deserved it. But it was hard to really tell, because an odor so dominated the room that she practically gagged. It smelled like overripe fruit—sweet, yet flawed.

"Aside from therapy, she's still on mandatory bed rest," said Chandrey.

Cance nodded. "I have another half-cycle before my next medical eval. Hopefully, I'll be upgraded then."

"How about you, Chandrey?" Belsas asked. She must have smelled something as well, Wreed noticed, because she rubbed the bridge of her nose.

Chandrey looked at Cance, who waggled a finger. "Thank you, but no. I'm needed here."

"You won't be gone long," Belsas said.

"Cance needs her dinner."

"You can bring her something back." Belsas looked at Wreed. "We won't be gone more than an hour, right?"

"At the most," Wreed said. "We're just going to the officers' mess." But she didn't know if she felt like eating anymore. Actually, she was feeling a bit nauseous from the sweet odor of rot. "Chandrey can order you a mug and roll."

"I don't know." Again, Chandrey looked at Cance, whose expression darkened. "She needs freshly made food, not the half-warm, premade slop they serve in the mess."

"Then bring her back a salad," Wreed replied hastily, more than ready to leave. "You need time out with friends."

"She's with her best friend." Cance took Chandrey's hand.

"I have salad makings in the cooler," said Chandrey. "Besides, it's almost time for Cance's evening exercises."

Belsas sighed. Wreed shrugged, ready to move on, but when she stood, Belsas lingered.

"How goes the therapy?"

"Slow," said Cance brusquely. "They won't tell me when I can go back on duty."

"Don't rush things." Belsas looked generally uncomfortable. She shifted in her seat and rubbed her temple a bit harder. "Why don't we get together to play a game or two on our next off day? It must get boring sitting in this little apartment day after day."

"We get out for my therapy." Cance crossed her arms and looked at the door, making it abundantly clear they were to leave. Still, Belsas sat, even as Wreed drifted toward the exit.

"Suit yourself. The offer stands if you change your mind," Belsas said. "But really, Cancelynn, laying about in the dark isn't good for either of you."

"Are you my healer?" Cance balled her fists in her lap blanket. "You don't know a damn thing about what I need."

"I know you shouldn't stay in the dark." Belsas frowned. "I know Chandrey needs air."

"I'm fine," said Chandrey in the background.

"Air?" Cance looked positively incensed. "She gets out plenty when I go to therapy."

"It's more than that." Belsas pointed to the stack of materials she'd placed on the table. "Chandrey has an obligation to fulfill. I'm going to need her help in the archives soon. The final research deadline is coming up and—"

Cance's eyes narrowed. "I see how it is."

"How what is?" Belsas demanded, her voice low but insistent.

"We should go." Wreed moved closer to the door. Chandrey was no help whatsoever, remaining still and emotionless at Cance's side.

"How what is?" repeated Belsas. "Out with it."

"Out with you!" Cance clenched her fists tighter around her blankets. "I trusted you with my life mate, and this is how you repay me?"

"Wait a moment." Belsas's concern seemed to fade, and she laughed bitterly. "You don't actually believe what Creiloff said, do you?"

"Her observations are never wrong."

"Chandrey and I are friends. We met through you. You encouraged her to work with me on the Rankil Danston project."

"Which you took advantage of!"

"I did no such thing." Belsas turned to Chandrey. "Tell her!"

"I have," said Chandrey in a quiet, glum voice.

"Then tell her again!"

Chandrey's expression became crestfallen. "Please, Bel, just leave."

"This is ridiculous!" Belsas stood, but didn't move toward the door. "I've been your friend for over ten passes, Cancelynn. You know me better than anyone."

"Obviously not," Cance fairly growled. She pointed at the door. "Get out. And take her with you." She waggled her finger at Wreed. "Take the one who helped you make your rendezvous. Take your whore with you."

"Hey!" Wreed would have hit Cance, hurt or not, if Belsas hadn't caught her by the arm.

"She's positively out of her mind from the meds," whispered Belsas. "Let's go."

"She's going to need more when I'm through with her!" Wreed pulled against Belsas's grip. "Let me at her!"

"No." Belsas passed her off to Chandrey, who urged her toward the door. Belsas watched them for a second, and then swung back to Cance. "Medicated or not, that was over the top. You'll apologize when you've sobered."

"Mother be damned if I will!"

"She doesn't mean it," said Chandrey from the doorway.

"Shut up, Chandrey." Cance's tone turned positively venomous. She raised her voice. "I meant every fucking word. Belsas wants you. Wreed is seeing that it happens. Stars! She probably wants some of you too."

"That's it!" Wreed ripped free of Chandrey and jumped over the side of the lounger to take a swing at Cance. Her punch would have landed if Cance hadn't deflected it with her good arm and tossed her to the floor. The effort sent Cance into a coughing fit which brought Chandrey running to her side.

"Please leave." Chandrey sobbed, pushing Wreed away. "Just leave." She quickly mixed a packet of white powders into Cance's water mug and held it to her mouth. "Please."

Belsas helped Wreed from the floor, turned her toward the door, and spun around to stand over Cance.

"We didn't come here for this." Anger tensed Belsas's expression. She shook as she spoke. "You insult me, my girlfriend, and your own life mate. You'll apologize to all of us, but particularly Chandrey when you're able. She's done nothing to deserve your abuse. None of us have."

Cance said nothing, but Belsas stood over her a minute longer and continued speaking.

"And if you think I haven't felt you in my head, you're wrong. You're trying to manipulate the situation." She blinked hard and touched her temple. "You're getting what you want. We're leaving, so stop."

Cance lifted her mouth from her mug long enough to mouth a silent "Fuck you," and returned to her medicine as Belsas rubbed her head.

"I warned you about trying this ever again. Stop it!" Belsas must have launched a phase back at Cance, because Cance gasped and began to cough again. "Chandrey, you staying?"

Chandrey lifted her head enough to whisper a soft, "I'm sorry," and smoothed the blanket over Cance. "You'd best go."

"This apartment needs airing," Wreed said. She went toward the door.

"When Cance is off the meds, have her com me, and we'll talk," said Belsas to Chandrey.

Wreed and Belsas retreated from the apartment without further comment.

"Something stunk in there." Wreed clasped her arm around Belsas's. "Did you smell it?"

"I'm not hungry anymore." Belsas turned, not in the direction of the officers' mess, but back toward her apartment. "And it wasn't the air that stank. It was Cance."

"Huh?"

"You weren't really smelling anything. She was in your head."

"In *my* head?" Now Wreed was beyond angry and wanted nothing more than to return to the apartment, but what would she do when she got there? Try to punch Cance again? What good would that do? She might feel better but poor Chandrey…

"She was in both our heads," said Bel. "And Chandrey's."

"Chandrey's?" Wreed stopped walking. "Why?"

"Don't know, but she's still listening."

Wreed could still smell the sweet stench, just not as strongly. "Damn her," she called into the evening air. "Hear that, Cance? Damn you!" She felt a pinch on the back of her head and the smell disappeared. "Is she gone?"

Belsas swatted at the back of her neck. "Yes."

"It's more than the medicines, isn't it?" Wreed asked when they'd gone a few steps further down the corridor.

"I think so." Belsas frowned in thought. "She's changed."

"What she went through would change you too."

"I know," Belsas said. "But I think it's much more than that. Tell me what you felt."

"I'm not really sure," Wreed said. She continued her slow walk with Belsas, taking the stairs and rounding a corner to the level holding Belsas's apartment. "It was like Cance was all over. Like…well, I don't know how to explain it."

"Like there was more than one of her?" Belsas scanned her index finger over her apartment's lock and the door hissed open.

"Yes." Wreed followed Belsas inside. "She's seriously sick, isn't she?"

"And making Chandrey sick as well."

"Should we have tried to stay?"

"I think we would've made things worse." Belsas dropped her bag by the door and walked into the kitchenette. She stood, staring at the pantry shelf. "There's nothing here I want."

"Me neither." Wreed had followed Belsas to the kitchenette, but now retreated to the lounger and sat down, devoid of thought.

"I'm out of ideas," Belsas said quietly. She drew Wreed to her. "Sometimes there aren't answers," she told her simply, and she was absolutely right.

There were no answers to Cance, only questions Wreed didn't want to talk about. She tried not to think about the situation at all, and lay still in Belsas's arms, watching the evening sun lengthen the shadows near the window. After a while, Belsas kissed her gently on the head and opened her mind.

I'm frightened for Chandrey. Her phase was more polished than Wreed's, but Belsas had assured her it was simply their age difference. Practice made perfect.

So am I. She and Belsas exchanged no more thoughts, but rested in the other's comforting mental presence. She thought they needed the calm after such chaos, but part of her later wondered if she should have tried harder to convince Chandrey to leave with them.

Her instincts proved right, because Cance didn't com—not even after they saw her and Chandrey walking two seven-days later. Soon after, Wreed learned from a mutual acquaintance at the medical facilities that Cance hadn't been allowed to return to duty. She'd failed her final vision and mental evaluations. She was declared unfit for service and would eventually be discharged from the Kinship military. Until then, she was on inactive status.

Cance was still paid, but she and Chandrey were forced to move to an apartment just outside the base, and Cance wasn't allowed on base except for medical purposes.

Wreed ran into Chandrey about a moon cycle later. She was on her way to a nearby marketplace Chandrey said, but she didn't share much else, and even avoided Wreed's eyes as well as her other questions. Chandrey seemed to be in a hurry and practically ran away before she could ask her about the Rankil Danston research for Belsas.

A few days later, Belsas and Wreed went to Cance and Chandrey's new apartment to collect the research materials Belsas desperately needed to finish her project.

Cance and Chandrey had moved into a recent construction known for its amenities, complete with a door attendant who forbade them access.

"Sister Cancelynn just left," the attendant said. "But I'll inquire with her life mate." After a quick com conversation, she waved them through.

They took the level lift to the penthouse. Wreed could already smell the sweet stench of Cance's mind—weak but present—before Chandrey opened the lift door.

"What're you doing here?" Chandrey asked.

"I need my research materials," said Belsas. "Can we come in?"

"Just for a moment." Chandrey opened the door fully, and the grandeur of the penthouse spread before them.

All the furnishings were brand new and very high end, crafted by the finest Taelach craftswomen. An enormous bouquet of exotic flowers sat on the dining table, another bouquet on the console behind the lounger, and yet another on the worktable in the bay window. Chandrey was dressed in a much simpler style than her surroundings. Actually, Wreed thought, the clothing was not much different than her Plan days, richer in texture, but just as concealing.

"Wow!" exclaimed Wreed when they stepped in, but Chandrey didn't offer a tour.

She went to the worktable and pulled Belsas's research materials from a drawer. A scroll replica slipped from her hands and fell on the floor. When she reached for it, her cuff slid back, revealing a dark ring of bruises around her wrist.

"What happened to your arm?" Wreed asked as Belsas took the stack from Chandrey.

"I bumped it during the move," said Chandrey, pulling down her sleeve.

Belsas furrowed her brow. "You moved a moon cycle ago."

Chandrey steered them back toward the door. "I think that's all the materials. Sorry I wasn't more help." She avoided Belsas's gaze.

"You were a bigger help than you think," said Belsas.

"I heard you dropped out of teacher training," Wreed said to Chandrey while taking some of the scrolls from Belsas and placing them in her bag.

"Cance needs too much care." Chandrey was about to open the lift when the entrance com buzzed, startling her. "Yes?"

"Delivery for you, Sister Chandrey," said the door attendant. "Should I send her up?"

"Please."

A moment later, a sister dressed in a local delivery service uniform arrived via the lift, a large bouquet in her arms.

"For you, Sister Chandresslandra." The uniformed woman smiled widely. "Second one in five days. I should be so lucky."

"Thank you," said Chandrey. She placed her index finger on the confirmation pad and took the bouquet. The delivery woman rode the lift back down. Most sisters would have been thrilled by such rare blossoms, Wreed thought, but Chandrey merely set them aside.

"It was nice seeing you again," she said politely, and recalled the lift to the penthouse.

"Take care, sweetie." Wreed kissed Chandrey on the cheek and stepped into the lift when the door opened.

"Com if you need us," added Belsas.

The lift door slid shut in their faces.

"That was odd," Wreed remarked.

"Wasn't it though?" Bel leaned against the bulkhead. "Did you see that bruise?"

"Too black to be old. Why'd she lie?"

"I don't know." Belsas bent to pick up a small card from the door track. It was the type attached to floral gifts. She began to wad it up for the nearest disposal unit, but stopped and unfolded the card to look at it. "Dear Mother, Wreed. What're we going to do?" she asked, stopping the lift between floors.

"What?"

"'Dearest Chandrey,'" Belsas read aloud. "'My passion for you never seems to wane. You are my precious, my beauty, mine forevermore. I know this morning proved difficult for us both, but you can learn from it just as I can. Lessons are never easy for anyone involved. Your lover and life mate, Cancelynn.'"

"Lessons?" Wreed repeated. She took the card from Belsas to read it for herself.

"Lessons," said Belsas.

Wreed felt a white-hot anger rising from her, stronger than when Cance had invaded their minds, stronger than when she had been accused of improper behavior with Chandrey. Belsas reversed the lift's direction, but when they reached the penthouse, the door wouldn't open.

"Chandresslandra! Open this door!" Belsas pounded on the door with both fists.

"Bel? What lessons?" Wreed implored as Belsas pounded harder. "What does Cance mean by lessons?"

"It's Cleave talk," Belsas replied when she stopped for breath.

"The Cleave?" Wreed repeated. "Creiloff's group?"

"Yes."

"The Cleave?" Wreed's heart pounded.

She had recently done some reading on the Cleave. There wasn't much available, and most of that had been speculation, but she didn't remember anything about lessons. Still, what she had read on the Cleave highlighted the group's highly structured makeup. While Creiloff's affiliation had been bad enough, Cance was now apparently associated as well. She was frightened for Chandrey.

"You know for sure this is Cleave talk?" she asked.

"I'm certain." Belsas let out a small cry of desperation and turned back to the door. "It's their word for discipline. Open the door, Chandresslandra! Please!"

"Dear Mother!" Wreed joined her in pounding on the door. "Chandrey!" she cried. "Please. We want to help."

But Chandrey didn't open the door no matter how hard they pounded, and eventually the lift began descending despite their efforts.

Wreed and Belsas exited the lift only to find the door attendant waiting for them. She escorted them to the building entrance and gently pushed them out, telling them not to return again that day. There was nothing to do except return to the base, exhausted, exasperated, and more frightened for Chandrey than ever.

Wreed cried in Belsas's arms that night. They made frantic love to still the anger and fear. It helped, but nothing kept the knowledge away. Creiloff had convinced Cance to forsake the Kinship and join her in the Cleave, and now Cance was grooming Chandrey for membership.

Belsas told Wreed that while some outside the Cleave called those who assumed Cance's Aut-like role by the old term "broadback," inside the Cleave, members were either keepers or women. Often, women were even referred to as thralls, another word for someone enslaved or under the control of another.

Wreed cried harder when Belsas told her this tidbit. She and Belsas returned to the penthouse the next day and the next, but were turned away at the entrance both times. Sister Cancelynn had barred their entrance for the next few days, said the attendant. After that, they would be welcome. But when they returned those few days later, they were told that neither Sister Cancelynn nor her life mate were available. Two days later, they found out why.

As they left Belsas's apartment one morning for class and work, Belsas found a replica scroll with a small note attached to it outside the door.

"I'm sorry for everything," read the note. "Hope you and Wreed are well. Cance has decided we're moving in with Creiloff. Take care." It was signed, "Chandrey."

That was the last either Wreed or Belsas heard from Chandrey or Cance for many passes.

Chapter Eighteen

Kinship Central Governmental Facilities— Javicks Township: Saria III

Shun—avoid; expel

Second Officer Belsas Exzal: Official Recorder, Kinship Vital Statistics.

Belsas loved the way the nameplate looked on her workroom door. She touched it every day when she walked into her office. Wreed had laughed when she'd told her about the habit, but the laughter had been good-natured.

Belsas liked the nameplate and what it symbolized. She'd moved up a level in rank and several levels in importance. Her extra training was paying off. The best part was that, initially, she had occasionally worked with the highest Kinship officials, recording dictates whenever the chief clerk was away. But when the clerk transferred out, she was promoted to chief clerk, making her job more interesting than ever.

Chandrey's raiser, Brava Deb, worked as the personal assistant to Benjimena Kim, the Taelach of All, so they often crossed paths, but never exchanged anything beyond pleasantries.

On the other hand, Belsas didn't get to see Wreed enough. She taught in a rural Aut settlement located some three hours away by aerolaunch, so they only got to be together for a rare bit of carefully coordinated off time.

They commed two or three times a moon cycle, but Belsas missed Wreed dreadfully. She was lonely, but told herself that she could use the new free time to practice her meditation and catch up on reading.

Things would have been so much easier if Wreed had agreed to oath, but she'd refused more times than Belsas could count. Wreed kept saying she wasn't ready. She accepted the answer, trying to be patient, but her patience was beginning to wear thin. Would Wreed ever be ready? Did she even want to oath?

And Belsas wondered about Chandrey as well. Was she happy? Was she at least safe? Knowing what she did about the Cleave, she knew both answers, but hoped, so hoped that Chandrey was okay and thinking about her too, when her mind had a free moment from Cance.

As Belsas's time away from Wreed increased, she found herself thinking about Chandrey more each day. It became her general evening preoccupation. Not the healthiest of pastimes, but there it was, meeting her at her apartment door every night, ready to help her keep awake.

"There is nothing you can do, that either of us can do," Wreed told her one day. They were in her apartment, sharing a rainy and windy day in the best way possible—in bed.

"I just worry for her. That's all."

Wreed had come for a three-day visit, which had thrilled Belsas, but a day into their time together, she was actually ready for her lover to leave. Wreed was pressing her, not for the Oath, not for sex, but to move past Chandrey. Wreed had, so why couldn't she?

"She dominates our conversations." Wreed sat up, taking the blankets with her so that they covered her chest. "And your thoughts."

"That was an accident." Belsas sat up and began to rub Wreed's shoulders. "I'm sorry."

"You could have controlled it if you'd really wanted." Wreed shrugged off her touch. "But it wouldn't have bothered me much if it'd been just once. But this makes three times, including my last visit."

"I said I'm sorry." Belsas frowned when Wreed batted her away a second time. "We all have our fantasies."

"That was one vivid fantasy." Wreed reached for her tunic.

"I've come across a few in your head." Belsas touched Wreed's arm, encouraging her to come back under the blankets. "It's natural."

"Natural?" Wreed pulled her tunic over her head and reached for her leggings. "Do my fantasies involve Cance?"

"I certainly hope not." Belsas's smile disappeared when Wreed scowled at her.

"Do they concern anyone you know?"

"Now, Wreed—"

"Do they?"

"No, they don't." Belsas knew she had betrayed Wreed in their phase, but she didn't know how to fix the problem, or even if she could. "Can you forgive me?"

"If it had been anyone else. But Chandrey?" Wreed tied her waist lacings and turned back to confront her. "You used my body to fantasize about Chandrey," she said flatly. "You were with her, not me."

"Please don't go. Not now. Not like this." Belsas wrapped a blanket around her shoulders and moved to the hide-covered chair at her worktable. "Please, Wreed. We need to talk."

Wreed closed her bag and turned back in search of her boots. "We've nothing to discuss," she said with such calm, Belsas couldn't help cringing. "You made your choice."

"But I choose you, Wreed, you," said Belsas. "How many times have I asked you to oath?"

"Twenty-three." Wreed stopped in front of her. "And I wanted to say yes every time."

"Then why didn't you?" Belsas couldn't understand why neither of them were crying.

"I was waiting for us to be alone." Wreed dropped her boots and sat in Belsas's lap, placing her arms around her neck. "But we never were. Chandrey was there the night we met. She was there the first time we made love, the first time you asked me to oath, and every time since. She's here now." Wreed placed a hand on her forehead. "She's right here, sweetie, right here. All day, all night. You love Chandrey—deep, complete, and in a way you never can me."

"But..." Belsas knew Wreed was right and that nothing she could say would keep her there, but loving Chandrey wasn't logical. Chandrey was oathed to Cance. She belonged to Cance. In Cleave terms, Cance owned Chandrey, but she still loved her.

"I'll miss you," she said softly.

"I'll miss you too." Wreed continued sitting in Belsas's lap while she pulled on a pair of boots, and then touched her face again before she rose. "Good times, huh?"

"Yeah." Belsas puzzled over her own sense of calm.

"Com me every now and then so I know you're alive?"

"Yeah." Belsas watched as Wreed pulled on her cloak and picked up her bag. "Be careful."

"You too, sweetie, you too." Wreed disappeared into the rain that had darkened the afternoon, leaving Belsas alone with her perpetual preoccupation.

After Wreed left that day, Belsas threw herself into work, spending extra hours at her terminal, sometimes sleeping on her office's small lounger rather than face an empty apartment. The work wasn't hard, but it did occupy her. She often entered statistics into the Kinship mainframe and compared them to past records, looking for trends. It wasn't exactly what she'd been trained to do, but it was close enough that she couldn't complain.

During the early fall of her second pass working at the Central Governmental Facilities—or a half-pass "post-Wreed" as she often thought—she began to notice an increase in the number of sisters leaving the Kinship and a rise in the crime rate along Kinship, Autlach and Cleave borders. The incidents appeared to be border disputes, but people were getting hurt, and occasionally a whole family, sister and Aut alike, lost its life or simply disappeared.

Generally, Belsas noticed, any daughters in the Taelach families disappeared while their raisers were murdered—a dangerous trend. When she alerted Benjimena Kim to the trend, Benjimena didn't agree with her only explanation.

"This isn't the Cleave's nature," she told Belsas in her quiet, tired voice.

Brava Deb, now Benjimena's almost constant companion, nodded. "They've yet to actually cause a problem inside Kinship lands, so Benjimena feels they aren't likely involved."

"But girls are missing, and by these numbers we are losing sisters to the Cleave in record numbers," Belsas explained. "The Cleave is—"

"Growing," finished Brava Deb. "We're aware. But they serve a purpose, and as long as they stay within their borders, the Taelach of All believes them of little consequence. Families living near the borders have long been aware of the risks."

Belsas knew how the Cleave served the Kinship. They took Aut-raised sisters, long considered unable to assimilate into the Kinship, off their hands, but at what cost? And Brava Deb's own child was among them. She bit her tongue.

"You are very concerned about something, Belsas." Benjimena extended her hand. "Share with me." She didn't speak often, and her health wouldn't allow for her to move without assistance, but she did phase extensively with those around her.

Belsas had to obey. She sat by Benjimena's lounger and opened her thoughts, explaining her concern over the statistics while trying to hide her personal worries. Benjimena, however, easily saw through Belsas's block and opened their conversation to Brava Deb.

She worries about your daughter.

I have no daughter.

Come now. Benjimena opened her eyes to gaze at her assistant. *Shunned or not, she's still your child. Your thoughts turn to her often enough.* Her eyes turned to Belsas. *And our clerk knows more about young Chandresslandra than she's willing to say. Tell her, Belsas. Brava wants to know, whether she'll admit it or not.*

Sister Benjimena, please. Brava rose to stand in front of the workroom window. *She's lost to me.*

She may be lost to the Plan, but not to you. Tell her, Belsas.

No. Brava turned toward the door. *I cannot.*

That is the Plan speaking, not you. Benjimena cleared her throat. "Come back and sit down," she said in a voice stronger than Belsas had ever heard.

When the Taelach of All spoke, others listened. Brava shuddered, but turned back to sit on the end of the lounger when Benjimena motioned her to do so.

Belsas has information concerning your daughter. Benjimena expanded her mind to fully include both her companions. *Listen to what she says.*

Then tell me, Belsas, so we might continue the day. Brava Deb rolled her shoulders forward so her elbows rested on her knees. *Tell me so this is over.*

Brava, reprimanded Benjimena in a loving tone. *Listen.*

I'm trying. Brava squared her shoulders. *Belsas?*

Belsas shifted to the edge of her seat. *Chandrey did oath to Cance.*

She did the honorable thing. I expected nothing less. Brava's mental tone softened. *Is that all?*

Shortly after they oathed, Cance was severely injured in the line of duty.

Chandresslandra knew the risks of their relationship. Despite her bluntness, Brava looked concerned. *Did Cance survive her injuries?*

Technically, yes. Belsas wasn't certain how to explain the changes in Cance. *She's always been rather temperamental and a bit—*

Manipulative? supplied Benjimena when she hesitated. *Your memories will explain more than your words.*

Benjimena, in a hard, practiced push that only came to sisters through advanced age, dug into Belsas's mind, pulling out the memories of her last few meetings with Cance and Chandrey: the argument, the bruise, the note, all of it spilled out for Brava to see.

Dearest Mother. Brava drew a protection symbol across her chest. *My Chandrey girl's there, with them? With the Cleave?*

The last I knew, confirmed Belsas.

Why there? Brava absently tucked Benjimena's foot back under her lap blanket. *What possible reason would they have to go there?*

Cance's surviving raiser is a member.

Brava gasped, but Benjimena seemed unaffected by the information. *The Cleave is a fundamentalist group, same as the Plan, so Chandresslandra can follow the Word just as she was raised. She's safe.*

Safe? Brava paused. *They're not part of the Kinship! How did this happen? How did I not know? Did Chandrey go willingly?* She stopped and leaned back against the lounger's pillows. *She couldn't have known much about them. The Plan doesn't recognize the Cleave, so Kylis and I saw no need to educate her. How did Cance get involved with the Cleave? She's Kinship military—a kimshee.*

Cance's raiser joined the Cleave after Cance left home, phased Belsas when Brava's confusion threatened to thicken again. *But Cance left military service.*

She left the kimshee ranks? Brava's hands tightened around nothing in particular. *Chandresslandra mentioned something along those lines the last time we spoke.*

She didn't do so voluntarily. She was found too unstable for duty. Belsas glanced at Benjimena, who appeared to be sleeping.

I'm here. The Taelach of All didn't physically move, but her mind shifted, creating a slight wave confirming her presence. *Belsas, go to my worktable terminal.*

I'll do it. Brava began to rise.

Let Belsas, said Benjimena. *Help me sit up.*

Brava looked confused, but helped her superior into a sitting position as Belsas moved to the terminal. *What am I doing?* She glanced at Benjimena, who was now upright and apparently having a private mental conversation with Brava.

What list? Asked Brava when the conversation came to include Belsas.

The tracking list of sisters who have chosen to leave the Kinship.

We track them? Belsas stared at the terminal screen, unsure how to access such information.

Use my secondary interface board, said Benjimena.

Brava came to the worktable to reach under it, producing a much smaller, almost com-sized board that she placed on the table. *I only know of its whereabouts, not its contents.* She looked at Benjimena. *I knew there was a list of former members, but I didn't know they were tracked afterward.* Brava's internal voice had become agitated.

Need to know. Benjimena's eyes opened to view Belsas. *Now Brava, I am going to exclude you while I give Belsas the proper codes.*

Brava sighed and ran her hand over her face. *I don't understand.*

Benjimena removed her from the link and fed Belsas the information, which she quickly entered, revealing a long list of files organized by date and location. She hesitated.

Last pass, fourth cycle, Motherslight, said Benjimena.

Yes, ma'am.

Read the list aloud.

Belsas read out the names one by one. She thought she recognized a couple of them, but Brava apparently recognized several.

"I knew her from the Motherslight community," Brava said of one name, and, "I schooled with her," of another. "Some of these were prominent community members. They were faithful sisters. Has the Cleave infiltrated the Plan?"

They learned another way, said Benjimena when she expanded her thoughts to Brava again. *The Plan and the Cleave share many of the same principles.*

Not that many, said Brava.

You are too close to your faith to see, but the Plan and the Cleave are very much alike. And the Cleave is just as harmless to the Kinship. Benjimena didn't share her assistant's pained expression.

So you believe the Cleave harmless? Brava asked.

Any group that embraces the Mother's Word is peaceful in principle.

So what is Belsas going to show me?

Patience, my friend.

I'm trying.

Stop there, said Benjimena in a voice only for Belsas.

Belsas had found what Benjimena wanted her to see, and it pained her to no end. Brava drew a double protection symbol across her chest. Benjimena leaned forward enough to place her hand on Brava's back, absorbing her pain as if it were her own.

"Don't get so upset," she said softly. "Belsas, open file last pass, second cycle, Myflar."

Belsas fought back a surge of white-hot anger that she hadn't felt in some time. She had expected what she had read, but to actually see it…"Cance's name is here."

"I thought as much." Brava didn't look up. "Chandresslandra?"

"Yes," said Belsas.

"Read it as written." Benjimena's gnarled hand gripped Brava's shoulder.

"Cancelynn Denise Creiloff." Belsas slowed, hoping the symbols changed before she reached them. "Life mate of Chandresslandra Cances and two unknowns."

"Two *others*?" Brava gasped and jumped up to pace the room.

"Aut-raised. We've no names for them," explained Benjimena. "See, she isn't alone."

"But is this correct?" Belsas looked up from the viewer. "Are we certain?"

"Yes. I thought knowing she isn't alone would bring you comfort." Benjimena's breathing had become shallow, but she refused to lie back, even when Brava moved to help her. "Sit, Brava. You'll wear holes in my new rug."

"And you're far too calm concerning my daughter's plight." Brava sat in the chair by Benjimena's head. "You know the Plan doesn't accept polygamy."

But she's still there. Benjimena smiled as she tried to smooth the blankets tangled between her fingers. *So she must be content.*

"This goes against everything she was taught," said Brava. "How can I be certain she's content if I haven't heard from her?"

You shunned her. Benjimena leaned her head to glance at Belsas. *She probably thinks you don't care.*

"Nothing could be further from the truth." Brava turned to Belsas as well. "Second Officer Belsas, you have been privy to some very delicate information. It goes no further. Understood?"

"Yes, Sister Brava."

Very good. Benjimena closed her eyes. *As long as the Kinship serves the Cleave as it has for the last century, things will remain as they are.* Exhaustion leeched through the link. *This meeting has thoroughly drained my energies. I can sleep even without your encouragement, Brava.*

"You'll outlast us all, Sister Benjimena." Brava eased the blanket from the Taelach of All's hands and smoothed it over her before motioning to Belsas. "She's asleep." She closed the curtain between Benjimena's workroom and her own. "One hundred and thirty-three passes of age and she still needs an occasional phase nudge."

"Did she say the Kinship served the Cleave?" Belsas turned toward the workroom.

"Another logic mishap. Stay." Brava cleared the scrolls and recorders from her lounger and encouraged Belsas to sit. "Benjimena is obviously unconcerned about the Cleave, but I don't share her ease."

"Neither do I."

"I'm afraid her mind lingers in the past, when the Cleave was nothing more than a few repressive separatists with an affinity for Aut-raised Taelachs." Brava sat back in her chair. "But they're much more, and my daughter is among them." She twisted her life braid around her finger. "Chandresslandra needs me."

"Forgive my candor, Sister Brava, but she needed you long before now."

"I deserve that," said Brava. "I should have listened to my heart instead of the elders and Kylis. I felt something wasn't right with Cance, but I ignored it."

"I suppose we're all guilty of that at some time or another." Belsas became aware of Brava's scrutiny, as if they were first meeting.

"Benjimena wouldn't have called you into her office today unless she knew she could trust you." Brava leaned over her worktable to look Belsas in the eyes. "You seem an honest sister and an intelligent one, but you're young and low-ranking. She thought you personally vested in the conversation and that puzzles me."

"I know Chandrey from the Training Grounds," Belsas said.

"Yes, I remember our com chat about her visit. You worried for her even then."

"I won't speak of her whereabouts, if that's your concern."

Brava brushed the idea aside and joined Belsas on the lounger, scattering her work materials across the floor. "It's anything but. You've proved yourself trustworthy again and again. It's what's lurking in the back of your mind that concerns me."

"You picked me?" Belsas felt her eyes narrow.

"Absolutely not." Brava moved a little closer, closing the formal gap between them. "At one time, Benjimena would have called such things to my attention, but these days, she seems incapable of sensing what I now can."

"I don't understand." Belsas wished to regain the formal distance, but was afraid she'd insult her superior.

"I wouldn't have, either, at your age," said Brava. "So I'll be blunt. You're hiding something."

"Hiding?" Now Belsas was extremely uncomfortable. Besides

work habits, she knew little about Brava, but Brava seemed to know everything about her.

"You've suppressed something for so long, it's become habitual."

"I'm angry and worried. That should be apparent." She frowned at Brava, who had come to sit directly beside her. "The Cleave is far too powerful to be dismissed."

"I'm not talking about the Cleave."

"What then?" Her voice cracked, revealing her unease.

"I'm sorry if I've upset you, but I need to know for my own sake." Brava's expression softened and her tone became gentle. "You had a problem with your last girlfriend, didn't you?"

Her heart skipped a beat. "You spoke to Wreed?"

"Certainly not. But I did notice when she stopped visiting."

Belsas's private life was being called into question in a way she had never expected. "We broke up nearly three cycles ago."

"Over seven by my estimate, but that's not the point."

"Then what is?"

"My daughter." Brava took Belsas's hands. Brava had gentle, strong hands, and she could see where Chandrey got her empathetic nature. "You're in love with my Chandrey girl. I saw it when you read from the list."

"I—"

"There's no need to explain." Brava turned to look directly at Belsas, to touch her face—to sympathize. "You don't need to hide it anymore."

Belsas broke into tears, letting her heart boil over. Wreed had seen the connection build, and it had driven her away, and now she hated herself for denying the truth.

"We both failed her." Brava touched her forehead to Belsas's in a sign of approval and affection. "But now you have an ally in me, and I have one in you." She wiped tears from her eyes and sat up. "We'll get her back."

"Yes." The word came out as a mumble, the best Belsas could do without losing control again. Beautiful, bright, her heart's only wish—Chandrey reduced to servitude. Subservient. Subjugated. Suffering. All because of them. "We'll get her back."

"One way or another," said Brava. "But we have to do this carefully."

Her legs shook when she rose. If she could move, maybe she could think straight. "I—I don't know where to begin. Where do we start?"

Brava thought for a moment before answering. "Did Benjimena remove that password she phased you?"

"She forgot," said Belsas. Her mind moved the digit string to long-term storage, keeping it safe from casual picks.

"For once, her diminished capacity works in our favor." Brava cast her a tired, determined smile. "She's given us an inroad, so that's where we'll begin."

Chapter Nineteen

Cleave Lands—Myflar

Voiceless—*unable to speak; without right to speak*

"Silence her."

Those were the last words Chandrey heard before Cance left her in the hands of a Cleave surgeon. Moments later, she was phased unconscious.

She awoke late afternoon the next day in a small room in the Central Medical complex. Her throat hurt badly, but she knew she'd find little sympathy from the healers or anyone else. Her voice was gone, like so much of her before it. She sipped from the mug of cold water beside her bed, surprised to find it contained a numbing agent which eased the burn.

When she sat up, she could see out the window to the elegant garden, more than likely kept tidy by studs, the Autlach men the Cleave "acquired" for their breeding program. Studs were carriers of one-half of the genetic combination which differentiated an Autlach from a Taelach. They were often used for field and gardening work too delicate for machinery. Cance had said the exercise kept them in shape. She had often seen the studs working, but had never seen what she saw now—breeders.

Three Aut women, each in a different stage of pregnancy, walked about the garden. They carried the other half of the genetics needed to produce Taelachs, and now they all carried Taelach babies. Chandrey knew that, but the specifics of the breeding program were strictly keeper knowledge.

Two elder Cleave thralls—widows, or so Chandrey surmised, since they didn't look old enough to be hags—watched the pregnant Auts from beneath the shade of a tree. Neither the Auts nor the thralls seemed thrilled by their situation, but they were tolerant of each other, and after a while, the breeders were called back inside.

"Were you told to sit up?" Creiloff seemed to materialize by her bedside.

Chandrey had been expecting the clan leader's appearance, but she was still startled. Creiloff seemed to have a penchant for surprising her, considering Chandrey her "special" project. Creiloff believed that, like all thralls, she required constant supervision and discipline, but since she hadn't been Aut-raised, she also required a "tutor," a senior clan member who helped Cance teach her the proper path. And Creiloff, as clan leader, was expected to do the job.

"Get back in bed." Creiloff pushed Chandrey onto her back and jerked up her chin, showing her neck. "You'll go home tomorrow."

Creiloff dropped Chandrey's chin, causing her to flinch, but didn't stop there. She climbed onto the bed, on top of Chandrey and pressed her knees into her sides, pulling her shift across her front.

"Not running off at the mouth now, are you?" Creiloff pressed her knees inward so the fabric stretched tighter. "'Silence keeps false words away.'" She recited the Mother's Word as she briefly ground against Chandrey's hip in a show of dominance.

As leader of the Cleave's Granary clan and Chandrey's tutor, Creiloff was justified in this means of discipline, so no matter how disgusted Chandrey might be, she had to comply. Resistance could have her disciplined at a Sharing, at the hands and minds of every Granary keeper who chose to take part.

Thankfully, Creiloff pulled back after a few seconds. "Remember your place," she said simply. "I'll be watching." She climbed from the bed to exit the room.

Chandrey had no doubt Creiloff would make good on her word, and lay very still for a long while after she was gone, afraid Creiloff was indeed watching or secretly in her mind.

While Creiloff didn't return, one of the healers, a kind-hearted local keeper named Zhastra, slid into her mind at some point, insistent that she sleep.

Chandrey woke the next afternoon, fully dressed and back at home, but not in the master bedroom. Rather, she was in the second's room. It was small, mainly a nest of blankets and pillows piled on the floor, but it was comfortable, though not as much as the master bedroom's luxurious bedding. Cance liked to be surrounded by nice things, especially in bed.

Chandrey stirred and looked around the room. Her throat was still on fire. Cance wasn't there; but she wouldn't have been. It wasn't her role. It wasn't her place as a keeper. *Damn Cance.* For once, she could think that, because Cance wasn't in her head. Cance would be back soon, though, and life would continue as it had, with Cance dominating her mind and will. Keeper and thrall. Master and servant.

Chandrey clutched her neck when she sat up. The window was open and a breeze blew across the grain field nearest the house, creating a little rippling sound. The grain was half-grown now, but at harvest, the heavy machinery would arrive. With the machinery came more keepers.

She sighed. She would be expected to feed the guests and keep them in drink. As Cance's favorite, she ran the household, but how would she do so now? They'd taken her voice too. She'd have to phase Cance's other thralls until they learned to read her lips. She hated phasing them. Their phases were rough at best, painful at worst, and always uneven.

Chandrey touched her neck again, feeling the small metal plate surrounding her larynx. It was a temporary method of silencing an unruly thrall, a punishment that could and would be reversed if she learned how to behave before the scar tissue became too thick.

The old surgeon who had placed it had been kind by keeper standards, almost sympathetic, but she'd been keeper nonetheless, and had slapped Chandrey for resisting her phase.

Movement just outside the doorway caught Chandrey's eye. It was Atchia, Cance's youngest life mate. Atchia had only been in the house a couple of moon cycles, and she already hated her. Not for being another life mate to Cance, but for spying. Atchia told Cance everything that happened in the house, most of the time before Cance had a chance to probe her and Mitsu, the third life mate, for information.

Chandrey liked Mitsu, even if she was sometimes naïve to the point of irritation.

Atchia appeared in the doorway a second time. "You wakes?"

Chandrey could only nod.

"Cance saids you cares for Mitsu." Atchia pointed to the corner, and then disappeared into the main house.

Mitsu was there, but Chandrey didn't see her until she moved closer to the corner. What she saw distressed her. Mitsu's eyes were swollen and her arms, what she could see above the blankets, were black and blue with bruises. Cance had beaten Mitsu after she and Chandrey had been caught reading.

Chandrey had been secretly teaching her for some time, and Mitsu, a quick student, had absorbed the knowledge. Now when she smoothed the hair from Mitsu's face, the woman stirred, but didn't wake. Her tunic and skirt lay wadded by her head.

I'm sorry, Chandrey mouthed. She picked up the clothing for the laundry, but tensed, dropping the clothing as a familiar shadow filled the doorway.

"See the trouble you caused?" Cance, in her grain-dust-coated work leathers and boots, stepped on the bedding to pull Chandrey to her. "Show me your neck."

Chandrey stood still as Cance pushed down her collar to inspect the incision site.

"Better not scar." Cance jerked Chandrey into a brusque kiss. "See that it doesn't." She lowered herself to the pillows, taking Chandrey with her. "What were you thinking? Huh?" Her voice was almost gentle. Almost.

Chandrey hung her head. What could she say that would possibly satisfy Cance?

Mitsu had been eager to learn. She had asked…no, begged Chandrey to teach her, and she had been starving to do something worthwhile.

Only keepers teach. Cance entered her head with such ease these days, Chandrey seldom noticed her presence until she spoke. *You knew what'd happen if you were caught. Didn't you?* Cance squeezed her arm hard when she didn't answer. *Didn't you?*

Yes, Cancelynn. I knew.

Worse yet, you made me look bad in front of Creiloff. Cance shook Chandrey by the shoulder, causing an explosion of pain in her neck. *She thinks I can't control you.*

I'm sorry, Cancelynn.

Sorry doesn't fucking cut it, Chandresslandra. Cance shook her harder. *Creiloff wanted you Shared, you know that?*

Yes, Cance. I know.

But I loved you enough to save you. I convinced her to silence you instead.

Cance used her free hand to push the hair away from Chandrey's face. *You should appreciate that.*

I do. Thank you.

Thank you for what?

Thank you for saving me from being Shared.

I'm the only one who can do that, Chandresslandra. I'm the only one who can save you from your foolish self. In one swift movement, Cance moved her hand from Chandrey's hair to encircle her neck, which she began to squeeze. *Not a new lesson, Precious, but a reteaching.*

Chandrey had expected this, and had learned long ago not to fight a lesson, no matter the pain.

What should you have done when Mitsu asked you? Cance asked.

Said no. She couldn't swallow.

Wrong. Cance squeezed harder, until Chandrey's eyes rolled back and she sank into the bedding. *What should you have done?*

Told you.

Say it like you know it without a doubt. Cance jerked her upright by the throat.

I should have told you!

Cance released her hold and Chandrey fell back onto the pillows. *That's my Precious.* She kissed her lightly on the forehead. *You'll remember this time, won't you?*

Yes, Cancelynn. Chandrey gasped.

Good girl.

Cance moved on top of Chandrey, straddling her so that her knees pressed into her sides. From there, she offered a dual phase, one that soothed some of the pain in her neck, another which pushed deep into her mind, shutting down her will to resist.

Cance drew her hand up Chandrey's side, following the curve of her breast until her hand reached her shoulder, where it lingered on the simple collar of her tunic.

You're my first and favorite, my love, and that grants you a position of honor and trust. Don't violate that trust again, Precious, or next time, I'll offer you at a Sharing myself. Understand?

Yes. Chandrey lay numb beneath her.

I knew you would. Cance kissed her forehead again and rolled off her. *Move Mitsu to the sunporch, then bring Atchia to me.* She sat up enough to pull off her boots. *The girl needs practice.*

Should I come back too? Chandrey perched on her knees, waiting further instruction. The room reeked of sweet stench.

Very considerate, but you need to tend the evening schedule. What's for dinner?

Whatever you want, Cance.

Cance smiled and reached forward to pat Chandrey's cheek. *That was a good lesson. You choose the menu, Precious, but make it a good choice.*

Yes, Cance. Chandrey looped her arm under Mitsu's shoulders and pulled her upright, which caused the woman to cry out when she woke.

She shook her head at Mitsu and eased her to a standing position. Mitsu stood by herself after a moment, gaining her bearings while Chandrey pulled fresh clothing from the press.

Cance glared as Chandrey helped Mitsu dress. "You're too stupid to get yourself dressed, so what the fuck made you think you could read?"

"I—I don't knows. I'm sorry, Cance." Mitsu hung her head and began to back out of the room, leaning on Chandrey as she went.

"You got what you earned." Cance kicked out as Mitsu passed, narrowly missing her leg. "Get her out of here before I send *her* to a Sharing," she said to Chandrey.

Chandrey led Mitsu to the sunporch, placed her on the lounger, and spread a light blanket across her lap. The day was beginning to wane and the porch was shady. It wouldn't be long until dinner. She had to get busy, so she ignored Mitsu's questions about her throat and turned back to the house. *Rest. You'll be needed to serve soon.*

Atchia met her in the back hallway. "Cance says you watches Mitsu. Why you not?"

Chandrey made a hissing sound when she grabbed Atchia by the arm.

"Ouch! Lets go!" Atchia dug in her heels as Chandrey pulled her to the room where Cance waited.

Tattletale, Chandrey mouthed. She shoved Atchia through the door and pulled the curtain closed. The house's kitchen hag, a thrall too old to be someone's life mate, should have finished the daily cleaning and would be waiting on dinner instructions. She swept into the kitchen and stood before the woman, ready to recite the menu before she remembered her new handicap.

"Just think it to me and get outs," said the old woman with a sigh. "I don't wants you in my head any longer than needs be." She grimaced when Chandrey relayed the message, and then backed from her mind. "Your head is sick sweets," she said. "Rotted justs like everyone else around here."

Chandrey watched the old thrall begin assembling the meal just as instructed. Satisfied for the moment, she turned to the dining room where she spread a purple cloth across the table and began to set for the evening meal. Everything from the linens to the mugs had to be immaculate, including herself, so she finished her prep work and turned to the main bedroom.

Cance's voice and Atchia's squeals echoed down the back hall and into the room, but Chandrey tuned them out. She had to shower and dress for dinner, which she did without further thought, drying and curling her hair in a way that Cance particularly liked, and choosing a dinner gown she knew Cance would approve. It paid to make Cance happy. It paid to follow the laws, no matter how—she stopped. The law was the law. She was wrong to disobey and deserved what she received. Cance had every right to punish her. Cance, she knew, was listening.

She returned to the kitchen just as the main course, beast tenderloin in a savory broth, emerged from the oven. Chandrey tasted the broth, nodded her approval, and went once again to the sunporch, carrying two mugs of tea.

"Thank you." Mitsu sat up to give Chandrey a place to sit.

Neither she nor Mitsu attempted conversation as they sipped their tea, choosing instead to watch the shadows lengthen on the porch.

"I'm sorry," Mitsu finally whispered.

So am I. Your eyes hurt?

"Some. Your throat?" Mitsu asked aloud. She couldn't yet phase speak in Taelach, and Chandrey's Autlach was spotty at best.

Some. Chandrey looked at Mitsu, unsure what to say next. Mitsu couldn't be caught reading again and she couldn't be caught teaching her. The risks were too high.

The sweet stench of Cance's mental presence was almost continuous. It only faded when she took one of her other thralls to bed, when she was…Chandrey's mind cleared as Atchia's cries spread to the porch.

Chandrey raised the hem of her skirt so Mitsu could see her bare foot—shoes were not worn by Cance's thralls, not even her favorite—scratching across the fine sand on the floor. Mitsu nodded, raised the edge of her skirt, and made the same markings.

"Floor?"

Chandrey shook her head. *Foot.*

Mitsu traced the marking and repeated it to herself.

That was all they managed before Chandrey felt the first tinglings of Cance rousing from Atchia's head. It would take passes to teach

Mitsu this way, but time, it seemed, was all they had. She smoothed the floor, motioned Mitsu to follow her, and returned to the kitchen, where Mitsu assisted the kitchen hag.

Cance would be back in the master bedroom soon, wanting Chandrey to help her dress for dinner. Creiloff and her favorite of some time, Lauriel, would be there very shortly.

As a clan leader, Creiloff had earned six life mates. She was allowed children as well, but had chosen not to have them "under foot." Chandrey wondered how long it would take for Cance to decide they needed a daughter. She'd also wanted children at one point, but now she wanted nothing of the sort. Cleave-born children, those born to the Aut "breeders" housed in the medical facilities, were raised to be keepers. They were horribly behaved, disrespectful, aggressive toward their thrall raisers, and treated harshly by other keepers so they would "toughen up."

Chandrey was glad she had been spared the trouble of children thus far.

"I'm waiting." Cance's impatient call brought Chandrey to their bedroom.

She helped Cance remove her work leathers and tunic—Cance seldom indulged in physical sex with the lesser thralls—and washed the grain dust from her neck before helping her into trousers and a close-fitting shirt.

I hope you kept Creiloff in mind when you chose the menu. Cance looked at her from where she stood at the room's full-length reflecting board, smoothing the stray hairs on her head.

Yes, Cance, I did. Chandrey stood nearby, holding footlings and a pair of freshly polished, high-heeled dress boots.

Very good. Cance took the items and sat in the room's only chair. *Is Mitsu still up?*

She's in the kitchen.

Good. See that Atchia cleans up and helps serve.

Yes, Cance. Chandrey shuddered when Cance pushed enough phase into her for her thighs to tingle.

Your mind is decidedly more delicious, Precious. And your body—Cance patted her backside when she passed. *I'll take care of you later.*

Yes, Cance.

Chandrey picked up her pace, moving into the hall before Cance decided to indulge then and there. Cance always wanted her mind and body after phasing with Atchia. The girl's phase was still rough and inexperienced. She turned the corner into the second's bedroom just as Atchia began to sob.

"She saids my head's too stupid to makes her feels good." Atchia brought her knees to her chest to hug them. "But I tried, I really dids."

Chandrey wanted to defuse the situation quickly, so she ventured a phase. *The more you do, the more you'll learn.* When she tried to back out of Atchia's mind, Atchia held on.

You her favorite. Teach me whats she likes. Atchia opened her mind wide to Chandrey, spilling the memories of her unsuccessful pleasure phase.

She'd kill us both. Fix your hair. Chandrey pushed Atchia from her mind. She went to the bedroom's sink and wet a cloth, which she brought to the girl, who said nothing else, but sobbed once more while she cleaned her face.

"I wants to make her happy."

Chandrey pulled Atchia up, took the cloth from her, and guided her to the kitchen, into the smells of well-made food.

Tell her dutiful service is her only concern, she phased to Mitsu before she went to the dining room where she stood behind her seat, waiting quietly as was expected, for obedience was the only thing that kept one in a keeper's good graces.

Good service, and now silent service, was the only thing keeping everyone, including Chandrey, safe.

Chapter Twenty

Kinship Governmental Facilities: Saria III

Senility—confusion in advanced age; weakness

"New reports, Sister Brava," said Belsas when she rapped on Brava's open workroom door. She knew she could be honest with Brava about her feelings for Chandrey, and Brava was determined to find a way to free her daughter from Cance and the Cleave even if it went against the Plan's dictates concerning the oath.

"The oath was meant to be a commitment of lifelong loyalty and devotion, not a contract for bondage," Brava had told her in a quiet moment. "And nothing we have learned about the Cleave suggests anything but slavery for thralls."

Brava was frequently in her workroom, handling the official business that Benjimena could no longer manage. Since her latest stroke, the elderly Taelach of All slept most hours and her healers gave little hope of her condition improving. Her body had been slowly failing for several passes, and until recently, her mind had been sharp, but after the stroke, Brava started attending official functions and maintaining correspondence in her stead.

What Belsas and Brava found in the private files preplexed them both. Benjimena had been ignoring the Cleave for over six decades, recording again and again that they were, at most, a minor nuisance, even granting them a homeland on Myflar so they were conveniently off Kinship soil and out of public view.

"Come in, Bel. I'll be finished in a moment." Brava continued typing into her board, and then pushed back from the table and looked up. "Okay."

"Another sister couple has been murdered near the Cleave border." Belsas placed a recorder on Brava's table. "Their daughter, age two, is missing."

"Just the right age to be easily assimilated." Brava pushed back in her chair and motioned Belsas to sit. "I've pored over this newest list of active Plan members for days, and I still can't find any possible link to the Cleave." She twisted her life braid thoughtfully around her finger. "Aut families disappearing, Kinship members murdered for their children. This has got to stop. I need to talk to Benjimena, but I need a witness to what she says. Come with me."

Brava pushed back the curtain between her workroom and what had become the Taelach of All's hospice. "Wake her," she demanded the healer on duty.

"She needs sleep."

"This can't wait." Brava held Belsas's recorder in her hand. "Do it."

"She's very weak."

"Do it!" Brava insisted. "Do it, then leave."

"Very well," said the healer, moving closer to Benjimena. "But I doubt she'll be coherent."

"That's for me to decide." Brava watched as the healer reached into Benjimena's head to rouse her. "Go now!" she repeated.

The healer swept past her and out of the room, closing the door with a bang which startled Benjimena into opening her eyes.

"What? Ah, Brava. Did I fall asleep again?" Her voice was barely audible.

"Just for a while." Brava drew a chair next to the bed that had replaced Benjimena's worktable. "Second Officer Belsas is here too."

"Belsas?" Benjimena squinted at Belsas. "Do I know her?"

"She's our records clerk." Brava cast a worried glance over her shoulder. "You're too weak to talk more. Let's phase. Belsas will be joining us, if you don't mind."

"Yes, yes. Nice young woman," mumbled Benjimena.

Belsas opened her mind to both the Taelach of All and Brava.

Did I fall asleep again, Brava? Benjimena's mind was a mass of jumbled memories that Belsas found difficult to hear until Brava expanded her phase deeper into the ailing woman.

No, said Brava patiently when she touched Benjimena's hand. *We need to discuss the Cleave.*

Oh, yes, the Cleave, chuckled Benjimena. *How I miss my home. Those faithful, beautiful women need a permanent home, so I've been thinking of giving them one of the Myflar tracts.*

Benjimena's phase caused Belsas considerable discomfort. It took both her energies and Brava's to steady Benjimena, but even then things wavered between mild pleasure and pain.

Her mind's stuck, said Brava around their steadying efforts. *She said the exact same thing yesterday.*

Benjimena rambled in the background, speaking of old events as if they had only just happened. The Cleave did good work and helped the Kinship, so simply giving them what they needed would be best, and then they'd be content. Hadn't the first three crop turns on Langus been successful? Who was this Belsas again? And, oh, she needed to repair Ryan's com, and when was dinner, and...

Misses her home? asked Belsas above the rambling.

Babble, nothing more. Brava sighed and nudged the old woman back to sleep. *And Ryan was her life mate. She died nearly forty passes ago.* She looked at Belsas. *The healer was right. This goes no further.*

I understand.

After they left the Taelach of All to her thoughts, Brava remained in Belsas's head, prodding her for ideas. The Taelach of All was a lifelong office. As long as Benjimena breathed, the problems with the Cleave would go unchallenged. Sisters would continue to die and disappear. Auts would be executed for simply being Auts, and Chandrey would remain a thrall.

My daughter is no one's slave, seethed Brava through their link. She stood beside Belsas. *And if Benjimena can't help, then we must take the situation into our own hands.*

But how? asked Belsas. *We'll have to convince her during a lucid moment.*

Then we'll be waiting forever. Didn't you feel how the time barriers have broken down inside her? She's unable to tell past from present.

I felt it, said Belsas. *But the laws—*

Those laws were written in a time when the Taelach of All nearly always died in battle, not from long wasting. Brava looked at Benjimena, then at Belsas, nodding and shaking her head as if their three-way conversation was still taking place. *There are cameras in here. Both the healers and security use them. They can't record our thoughts, but we need to make it look like we're having a heated discussion.*

Belsas glanced at one of the cameras. *Okay, but mind telling me why?* She gestured with an arm as if emphasizing a point.

Brava took a deep breath before she continued. *Taelach of All Benjimena Kim is most distressed by the current border disputes, and is sending a diplomatic team to negotiate and end the unrest.* She shrugged. *That's how she'd put it if she were able.*

And where are these diplomatic discussions taking place? Belsas returned her shrug.

Myflar, on the Cleave/Kinship/Autlach borders.

I see. Belsas motioned to Benjimena, further highlighting their imaginary conversation for the cameras.

Very good. Brava patted Belsas's shoulder. *You're going to the talks.*

Pardon? Belsas definitely didn't remember Benjimena saying anything about her joining a diplomatic team. Only senior officers were permitted on diplomatic details. She simply didn't have the experience to support the rank. Early promotions were only allowed during war time, and the Kinship was not at war.

That all depends on your interpretation, Brava continued inside Belsas's mind. *During her prime, Benjimena would have considered the kidnapping of sisters along any border an act of war. The Kinship's continual inaction makes us look weak. The Cleave is using it to their advantage.*

I can see Benjimena sending a diplomatic team, but I don't see how I can be allowed to take part or why I would be allowed.

There needs to be an official recorder to draw up any documents, said Brava. *And as for rank…* She stood and extended her hand officiously, just touching Belsas above the wrist in the most formal manner. *Congratulations, First Officer Belsas. I'll finalize the paperwork after our meeting and have new uniforms expedited to you. You'll have them when the team leaves, day after tomorrow.*

I'm honored. Belsas touched Brava's wrist with the same formality. *I don't care much for even simple symbols of office, so this phony display is simply awkward. Can we finish this in your workroom?*

I was about say the same thing. Brava nodded acknowledgment to Belsas's salute to Benjimena, and they both quickly exited to her workroom.

Chapter Twenty-One

Myflar—Kinship/Autlach/Cleave Border

Memory—a collection of past events; recalled experience

Brava introduced Belsas to the rest of the Kinship diplomatic team at the preflight meeting in one of the smaller conference rooms. Master Protocol Officer Cyan Lupinski, an impossibly lean woman with close-set eyes, a loud voice, and a reputation for strong negotiation skills, and her assistant, First Officer Quall Dawn, whom Belsas had met once or twice at the training grounds, would be among her traveling companions.

One of the Autlach negotiation team was already present too. He worked regularly at the Kinship governmental facilities, so he would make the trip with them. His name was Adallum, he spoke fluent Taelach, and he was unlike any Autlach that Belsas had ever met.

"He's worked among the Kinship for many passes and is partnered with a sister," said Brava with an accepting shrug. "She's a pediatric healer specializing in Aut disease morphology. No accounting for tastes, but I've heard they're a very good pair."

"Interesting." Belsas watched Brava move off to speak to Master Lupinski.

"Nice to see you again," said a voice behind her.

Belsas spun about to see Quall Dawn holding out her hand. Quall was large, both in height and girth, and she knew that was one reason why Lupinski had chosen her as an assistant. Quall's sheer size served as an intimidating reminder of Kinship might when firearms weren't allowed around the negotiation table.

Quall grasped her wrist cordially. "How's Wreed?" she asked.

Belsas remembered that they'd met at a junior officer's social. "We're no longer together." She grasped Quall's wrist in the same greeting gesture.

"I'm sorry to hear that."

Their conversation ended when Brava called everyone to the table.

"Let's get the preflight briefing over with so you can be on your way." Brava indicated the coms in front of them. "Sister Benjimena could not be with us today, so she has asked me to express her wish for a quick resolution to this problem."

"Excuse me, Sister Brava," interrupted Adallum. "But Benjimena Kim hasn't been seen in public for a while. Rumor has it—"

"Rumors?" Master Lupinski guffawed. "If we lived by rumors—"

"If we lived by rumor we wouldn't be here," said Adallum. "But the fact remains that the Taelach of All hasn't made a recent appearance. Some say she's either dead or on her death bed."

"She's neither." Brava seemed unfazed, and Belsas assumed the response was a practiced one. "But she cannot attend this briefing." She moved to the wall viewer, activating the room's large screen. "The Cleave is headed by three pedagogues: the Missionary in charge of educating others to the Cleave way, the Practitioner in charge of the health and proliferation of the population, and the Harbinger, deliverer of the Mother's direct word."

"Do we now who fills the roles?" said Lupinski.

"The Practitioner is Tavince Bonwell. There's no Kinship record of her, so she's likely Cleave born." Brava pointed to the central viewer where Tavince's image appeared—a grainy, covert picture, but she was clearly small-boned, thin, dark-headed, and wore a domineering expression.

"Could she have changed her name?" asked Quall.

"Few keepers change their name when they join. It's their way of thumbing their noses at the Kinship."

"Do we know the other pedagogues?" asked Adallum.

"Cleave-born Jandis Gladomain is the Harbinger," continued Brava as an aging, heavyset woman in ceremonial robes appeared on the viewer. "She's the longest serving and therefore chief pedagogue, but we've no indicator of the Missionary's identity or origins."

"Since that position's maxim is 'education through infiltration,' it wouldn't do to be upfront with her identity," said Lupinski. "Okay, now that we have the current Cleave leaders, what do they want from us?"

"Peace talks," said Brava, "but on their terms."

"Of course." Lupinski chuckled. "And what are those terms?"

"They'll only talk to those who fit their definition of keeper," continued Brava. "I'm sorry, First Officer Quall, but your ponytail goes. Under any other condition I wouldn't indulge such ridiculous demands, but—"

"Master Lupinski said that might be a problem, so I'm prepared." Quall nodded to her supervisor and walked from the room.

"Where's she going?" asked Adallum as she squeezed past.

"To cut her hair," said Lupinski. "Unless you'd rather we do it in free fall."

"So we can all wear it? No thanks." Adallum turned back to Brava. "What else do they expect?"

"We're to come unarmed and bindered."

"Are we requiring the same?" Lupinski asked.

"We are," said Brava.

Adallum stifled a laugh.

"Something funny?" Lupinski furrowed her thin, arched brows at the Autlach.

"Actually, my people are thrilled by the binder clause. It keeps you out of our heads and from phase speaking behind anyone's back."

Lupinski smiled. "Oh, but we, like your people, sir, have many ways of communicating that aren't readily apparent."

"Share some?"

Belsas soon discovered that their quick rhetoric was the result of over a decade of working together.

Lupinski stifled a laugh and turned back to Brava. "Is that all they require?"

"Pretty much. They've given us touchdown coordinates for a site exactly on the borders of all three peoples." Brava made a small chopping motion with her hands, dividing the air before her into thirds. "We'll all be on our own land."

"Isn't that kind of them?" said Adallum. "But a few meters either way isn't the problem."

"For any of us." Lupinski looked to Belsas, who had thus far remained out of the conversation. "First Officer Belsas, why do you believe they'd wish to meet at such a balanced location?"

"To create the illusion of equality." Belsas wondered why she had been asked about the obvious diversionary tactic.

"Most observant," said Brava with an approving nod. "And illusion is very apropos."

Lupinski pocketed her com in her flight jumper. "Are we ready then?"

Brava touched Belsas's shoulder when they exited the conference room. "Bring her home to me," she whispered, pressing a small recorder into her hand.

After she'd settled into her compartment aboard the Battleship Tempest, Belsas plugged the recorder into her com and sat for hours, replaying the images until they were ingrained in her mind: Chandrey as a small girl, as a happy child, as an adolescent. Chandrey playing, reading, studying, singing. Chandrey celebrating her twelfth claiming anniversary. Chandrey, a sleeping infant rocked in a younger Brava's arms.

Chapter Twenty-Two

Myflar—Cleave/Kinship Autlach Border

Farce—fake; to mock

A negotiations tent had been erected in the shallow dale where the borders came together. The tent was nothing impressive, an old Kinship military setup probably stolen from a hiding cave, but the Kinship symbol had been carefully marked out and replaced with a large version of the Cleave's crest of two back-to-back crescents.

Guards stood on the hills above: elite troopers on the Kinship side, specially trained sentries on the Autlach, and a line of leather-wearing keepers on the third. Everyone involved wore binders, but only the negotiation teams went unarmed. While this surprised Belsas, she knew the weapons would not be allowed in the tent.

The Kinship aerolaunch landed precisely where instructed, and the team disembarked to stretch and get their bearings in the morning haze before proceedings began.

Back in the launch, Belsas, Lupinski and Quall dressed in their ceremonial uniforms and reviewed the facts: twenty missing children, thirty-five sisters killed, all in the last pass—a total of one hundred seventy-two within the last five moon cycles.

The Autlach team, whom Adallum joined upon landing, had similar numbers, though only eight, six women and two men, were considered missing.

"How I hate all this pomp." Lupinski struggled to fasten her high collar.

"You always say that, Master Lupe." Quall ran her hand over her shorn head. "My ears are cold."

"You get used to it," said Belsas, running a hand over her own short cut.

During the last two days, she had grown to like and respect her fellow team members. They were very knowledgeable concerning diplomacy and readily shared their experience with her, even talking at length about what her specific role would be during the negotiations.

Belsas's job seemed simple enough, but there was much more to it than she'd suspected. She was not only to scribe for the Kinship, she was to watch the body language of the other teams. Hand gestures and the smallest of motions could be forms of silent communication. Those forms, Lupinski had told her, were just as important as verbal and, while she might not recognize their meanings, she should detail them so they could be reviewed between sessions.

And then there was Belsas's mission of the heart. A Kinship spy was supposedly among the keepers in attendance, but she wasn't sure what her contact, Quincy Moralez's, position would be or when they would meet. Brava has shown her a com image of Moralez, but with all the keepers sporting similar hairstyles, identification would be difficult. Moralez would have to make first contact.

When the time arrived, two troopers, their holsters and sheaths conspicuously empty, arrived at the launch. One trooper nodded and motioned for them to follow her while the other took step behind them, steering them toward the tent.

The haze was beginning to lift and the day looked hot and dry. Belsas was glad to see their Kinship aide placing sealed water bottles at their places. She licked her lips and took her place at a small table just behind Quall and Lupinski. While her view was mainly of their backs, if she shifted slightly she could see the Autlach team already in place and, if she leaned just a bit the other way, she had a clear view of the Cleave's arm of the triangular table arrangement. Their seats were empty. They'd probably be late and make a dramatic entrance, she thought as she assembled her equipment on her tiny worktable.

She was right. The Kinship and Autlach teams stared at each other impatiently until a string of no less than eight unarmed, black-clad keepers led in the Cleave team. They met all of Belsas's expectations—heavy leathers, very little hair on their heads, growling expressions.

Belsas drew from her water bottle while she watched the

keepers finish setting up. They'd actually brought what looked to be, of all things, educational materials. Were they recruiting? Well, they certainly wouldn't find a receptive audience among the other negotiators, so why had they brought the items in the first place?

When the proceedings began a few minutes later, it became readily apparent that the Cleave team was indeed actively recruiting the Kinship members present. No one took their prodding seriously, but the Autlach contingent became very incensed, as they should. The Cleave believed the Autlachs nothing more than vessels for increasing Cleave numbers.

"Are you finished insulting us?" Adallum asked. The rest of the Autlach team had already removed their translation earpieces and stormed from the tent. "This was to be a negotiation, not a propaganda spewing."

"Keepers are teachers," said a Cleave member. "And from our teaching you will come to understand the Mother's requirements of your people."

"We were obviously brought here under false pretenses." He gathered his robes and stood. "The Autlach contingent protests this blatant political stunt and will have no part in its continuance." He too stormed from the tent, prompting a volley of cheers from the Cleave team and their security.

"We require a recess." Lupinski motioned to Quall and Belsas. They followed her out of the tent with much of the same flourish as the Autlach team.

"Tighten the security around our launch," Lupinski told the lead trooper outside the tent. She led the way inside, the only space they had to speak in confidence.

"What was that?" Quall loosened her uniform collar as she collapsed into one of the seats.

"That, First Officer Quall, was a fantastic power play on the Cleave's part." Lupinski brought her hands together, miming silent applause. "They wanted to dominate these proceedings and got their wish."

"Yes, but Adallum and the other Autlachs are leaving," said Belsas as the roar of a launch became audible. "This ends the negotiations."

Both Quall and Lupinski shook their heads.

"No, Belsas, this is just the beginning," said Lupinski. She slid into the seat beside her. "The Cleave didn't want the Autlach team here to begin with, but the Kinship insisted. The Auts could have stayed if they had so chosen. I'm certain Adallum recognized the subterfuge, but the rest of his team took such quick offense, they left him little choice but to leave as well."

The ground shook a little as the Autlach launch took flight.

"There they go," said Quall, glancing out one of their launch's tinted windows. "So how long do you think we'll have to wait, Master Lupe?"

"Ask the Cleave team." Lupinski shifted her binder lens and pushed her seat to a reclined position. "They're in charge." She closed her eyes. "Until then, my able staff, I suggest you rest."

* * *

Two hours later, the Cleave asked for an informal meeting, just Master Lupinski and the lead Cleave diplomat outside the tent, with only one guard each. Lupinski sleepily agreed to the request and left with a trooper on her heels. Quall and Belsas barely had time to discuss the possibilities before Lupinski returned to the launch.

"Very interesting," she said after she closed the doors. "Seems we've been invited to supper."

"Supper?" repeated Belsas and Quall simultaneously.

"Yes." Lupinski turned the seat in front of her, placed her feet on it, and lounged back, clearly amused. "Yes, the Cleave has asked that we spend a relaxing evening at their expense before talks resume tomorrow."

"And we're actually going?" Quall stiffened. "We're eating food *they* prepare?"

"Seems so." Lupinski placed her hands behind her head. "Good thing I made certain one of our trooper escorts was trained in culinary supervision." She closed her eyes. "Every dish must meet her scrutiny before it is set in front of us."

* * *

The meal was indeed superb. Spit-roasted herd beast from Cleave pastures, breads soft and hard from Cleave grains, cheeses from the Cleave's best dairy, and fine wines from Cleave orchards—a healthy bit of advertising, but Belsas longed for a good green salad. The food was heavy and weighed her down as the evening progressed.

She and Quall kept together while they mingled among the Cleave in attendance. Lupinski circulated with one of the higher-ranking Kinship sentries.

Fortunately, Belsas recognized Moralez among those present, though only as a guard, which might prove problematic.

Moralez, however, had things planned. She nodded politely when Belsas passed, and then motioned with her head, indicating the two simple latrines the Cleave had dug into the side of a nearby hill—a Kinship owned hill, Belsas noted.

Saved the Cleave a mess to clean up, she quietly mused as she walked toward the rough wood shanty. She would rather have used the cramped facility in the launch since, with its self-cleaning capabilities, it was at least hygienic, but it would be out of the way to return to the launch and she would be forced to ask for an escort.

"You Belsas?" Moralez whispered between the slats once she was inside.

"Moralez?" Belsas could just see her through the gaps in the boards.

"Yep." A rustle came from Moralez's location. "I saw Chandrey two days back. It was only from a distance, but she looked okay."

"You're getting her out?"

"I said I'd try," Moralez said. "But things have changed."

Belsas made rustling sounds of her own, lest someone come to investigate her continued absence. "How so?"

"If I take her out, they'll kill my family."

"Then take me to her."

"You crazy? They'd kill us both, and they'd take their time doing it." Moralez pressed her hand against the slats. "Best you forget about Chandrey." Belsas saw her rise. "And accept what will be."

Before Belsas could respond, Moralez was gone. She waited a few moments, and then returned to the tent, seemingly relaxed and mingling as she searched for her team members. She saw Quall first, sitting at the Kinship table, and moved to join her.

Quall looked at her and said nothing.

Keepers stood near them, but none close enough to hear her whisper, "Where's Lupinski?"

Quall drew her gaze slowly to the middle of the tent. Lupinski was at the end of that gaze, standing beside the lead Cleave table and leaning against the main tent pole. Keepers surrounded her. Belsas didn't see their trooper protectors anywhere around.

"Let's go."

"Can't." Quall never took her eyes from Lupinski. "Not until they're through."

"Through with what?" When Belsas leaned forward, Quall shook her head, eyes wide.

"They said we can leave when they're done." Quall cringed as a metallic grind rose from Lupinski's general location.

Belsas turned at the sound and shared Quall's reaction. The keepers had parted so they could see. Lupinski had been forced to the ground, her arms extended across a plank like those used for the latrines. A keeper was drilling a screw through Lupinski's right wrist. Lupinski made no sound as she was fastened down, but tears streamed from her eyes.

"Stop!" cried Belsas.

Quall grabbed her wrist. "That'll make it worse." Quall pulled her hard, forcing her to sit as another keeper descended onto Lupinski, climbing on top of her to press her knees into the Protocol Master's sides as she punched her face twice.

"Dear Mother," whispered Belsas to both Quall and herself. "Why?"

"It is a Cleave lesson." Moralez sat beside them, a confident expression on her face. "When her lesson's complete, First Officer Quall can take her master back to the Kinship so she can report on what she learned about us." She ignored Belsas's betrayed stare. "Your Master Lupinski has yet to beg. She's a good student."

"You?" Belsas heard a second screw being turned, she assumed, into Lupinski's other wrist.

"I'm doing the Mother's work." Moralez's smile tensed. "And securing my family."

"Where's the rest of the Kinship team?" Belsas asked.

A final crack signaled the end of Lupinski's lesson. The other keepers began clearing the tables and collapsing the empty chairs.

"Digging." Moralez began to clear dishes from the Kinship table. "Remain silent and sitting until you're instructed otherwise." She pulled Quall, chair and all, from the table and motioned Belsas back.

Left without options save death, Belsas did as she was instructed, trying to find a silent means of communicating with Quall. Outside the tent, blaster shots echoed through the dale. The troopers, she mourned, had dug their own grave.

"First Officer Quall will follow me." A keeper grabbed Quall by the collar and pushed her hard, sending her sprawling on the ground in front of Lupinski.

"Master?" said Quall in a low voice.

"Do exactly as they say." Lupinski's voice shook.

"An excellent student." Moralez sat once more beside Belsas.

Belsas dared not look at her nor express her horror at the "compliment." She watched in silence as Quall was instructed to help Lupinski stand. She wasn't allowed to remove the screws from Lupinski's wrists, nor was she to break away the wood, but she managed to get her master standing. Lupinski looked only briefly at Belsas when she stumbled past and out of the tent, and Quall was ordered to follow her. Belsas thought of the troopers' fates, but the blaster fire she expected was actually the sound of a launch—the Kinship launch leaving without her!

"They were instructed to leave you behind," said Moralez. "Master Lupinski was too old, her assistant too fat, but you're ideal."

"I have no p-p-political value," stammered Belsas when she rose. "I'm nothing but a recorder, a record's clerk—" She looked out the open tent flap to see the Kinship launch fade from sight. "What do you want with me?"

"Only to deliver you," said Moralez. She motioned Belsas to sit. "Don't be difficult."

Belsas backed toward the open flap. She didn't know where she'd go or how she'd get back to Saria III, but she had to get away. A keeper stood just outside the tent flap, but she seemed unaware of what was going inside.

"She's smart," said one of the other keepers as she watched Belsas back away.

"And well built." Belsas heard another say. "She'd be keeper if she hadn't been chosen for the project."

"That strong body will be an asset," said a third.

Belsas reached for her absent blade, cursed under her breath, and glanced around for a weapon. The tables had been cleared. The chairs, save for the occupied ones, were folded away. She only had her hands and her bindered mind, which scrambled to remember the battle moves she had reviewed. The binder, she thought. They'd kill her if she tried to remove it.

She backed away a few more paces, and then turned to grab the keeper standing just outside by the neck, spinning her around so they both faced the interior of the tent. "I get a launch out of here or she dies."

"What energy!" said one of the keepers in an admiring tone. "You certain she can't be Shared?"

"Practitioner Tavince insists she be fresh," said Moralez. "Come now, First Officer Belsas. Don't make this needlessly difficult."

"A launch, now!" The keeper in Belsas's grasp didn't fight, but rather went along with her rough handling, moving only when she moved.

"Your records indicate you've never killed." Moralez stepped toward her. "Not going to make this girl your first, are you?"

They'd seen her service record? How? Belsas tightened her hold on the keeper's neck. "I'll do it."

"I expect you would," said Moralez. "But you see, if you kill her, there will be consequences, and you won't like those consequences." It sounded like she was reasoning with a child, which frightened Belsas even more. She was certain this was some weird sort of lesson.

"If you kill a keeper," Moralez continued, "even a young one, you will be Shared, and while you might survive the Sharing, you won't be in any shape to participate in the project, and I will be forced to take your place, which means giving up my thralls and daughters." Her smile waned a bit. "Since I enjoy my life, you've put me in a bit of quandary."

She nodded ever so slightly. Several hands grabbed Belsas from behind, wrenching her arm from the young keeper's neck.

"Fuckin' bitch!" swore the young keeper, but Moralez blocked her punch and twisted her arm until she cried out.

"She's to stay fresh!" Moralez kept twisting until the keeper sank to her knees. "You were warned." She jerked the binder from the keeper's face, pushed back her own, and the keeper screamed again, falling at Moralez's feet. "Lesson learned, young one." She kicked the keeper in the ribs and turned back to Belsas.

"See what I do to protect you?" Moralez pulled Belsas's binder from her face and sank in a sedating phase she could not fight fast enough. The phase consumed her, lifted her from the ground, and dropped her into Moralez's waiting arms.

* * *

They were on a launch, maybe just the two of them and a pilot, but Belsas couldn't be certain. The lights were low. Was it night? She couldn't tell, but Moralez had taken off her binder and was holding her, looking down at her and stroking her head where it rested in her lap.

Quite attractive. Moralez paused her stroking at the tips of Belsas's hair to look thoughtfully down. *The Kinship and its slattern ways are behind you now. The Mother has called you into service.* Moralez shook her head slightly when she pulled away from her touch. *Accept what is.* She looked hungrily over her lean, uniformed body. *If you'll come back to me when your service ends, I'll teach you to be keeper. Or an atypical, but enjoyable and obedient thrall, your choice.*

Moralez pushed a phase that sent a faint wave of pleasure down Belsas's spine, and then pushed a second which forced her back toward unconsciousness.

You'll do both the project and the Cleave proud. I know you will.

Chapter Twenty-Three

Granary Clan Lands

Compassion—sympathy, desire to assist or make change; an undesirable keeper trait

Chandrey and Cance were awakened before dawn by Mitsu's screams. They rushed, Chandrey wrapped in a blanket, Cance nude, to the second's room to find Atchia, clad only in a short, white shift, hanging from one of the room's higher clothing hooks with one of Cance's hide belts wrapped around her neck.

"Damn it." Cance moved to the side, just enough for Chandrey to slide through. "Check her," she said to Chandrey. She looked down at Mitsu. "You do this?"

Mitsu could only sob and pull the blankets higher.

"Never mind." Cance kicked the overturned dressing stool aside and turned back toward the master bedroom. "Take care of this after daylight, Chandrey."

We can't leave her here. Chandrey comforted Mitsu, who collapsed against her in a heap of soggy grief. *It's okay.* She looked up at Cance. *Please help me take Atchia down.*

"She'll keep." Cance stood in the doorway, looking from her dead life mate to her breathing ones. At most, Chandrey thought, their keeper seemed inconvenienced by young Atchia's suicide. "Quit your blubbering, Mit, or you'll hang beside her."

Mitsu gasped and buried her face in Chandrey's shoulder.

Please, Cance. At least let me take Mitsu to the front room and stay with her until daylight. She shouldn't stay in here.

"Mitsu can sleep with the kitchen hag if she wants. I said we're going back to bed." Cance grasped Chandrey by her shoulder and pulled her toward the door.

Sweet rot filled Chandrey's mind, but she managed to push it aside, a task she was becoming proficient at. Cance tightened her phase hold, but she still resisted, physically pulling away. When she moved toward Mitsu, Cance grabbed her, jerking her arm and wrist back and then up. The resulting pop and snap brought her to her knees.

Cance sighed, motioned Mitsu to leave the room, and left the room herself, returning a few moments later in her dressing robe.

"Get up." Cance stood over her.

Chandrey, bare of her blanket, struggled to rise. The pain in her shoulder throbbed down her side and into her back, but she said nothing, and no tears fell.

"Tell me why you pushed away." Cance grasped Chandrey's shoulder between her hands, maneuvering it until it reduced back into place with a second pop.

Chandrey said nothing.

"Why did you push me away?" Cance persisted.

Chandrey sniffed away the tears that had formed during the reduction. *I did it without thinking. Atchia was just hanging there. Mitsu was hysterical...*

"Fuck the both of them." Cance pulled up Chandrey gruffly, twisting her wrist until another crack sounded. *What am I going to do with you, Chandresslandra?*

Her phase was consuming, but Chandrey resisted, shaking her head until Cance tightened her hold. *Stop fighting me!*

Chandrey fell toward her, but Cance stepped back so that she slipped to the floor, and phase-squeezed her harder. The phase nauseated her, burned her, disgusted her, but these sensations paled in comparison to the pain in her wrist, couldn't compare to Cance's next tactic.

Cance placed Chandrey on her back, and then disrobed and straddled her head. She smelled of excitement, of sweat, of lust, of the granary—of deep, sweet rot.

Apologize, Cance's pain-and-pleasure mixed phase demanded.

Chandrey performed as ordered until her jaw ached, until Cance shuddered over her a second time and rolled off. *All right, now you'll finish your lesson on Mitsu.*

Please, Cance, no! But the phase hold was so deep, there was little she or Mitsu could do but comply.

Cance took time undressing and caressing Mitsu, and ordered Chandrey to perform a second time on a reluctant recipient until she lay silent, sticky, exhausted and in multiple layers of agony which deepened when Cance fucked her long and hard with a balled up fist while Mitsu lay phase-stunned beside them.

Afterward, Cance lay between her and Mitsu, pulling their heads to her shoulders. *Look up*, she told them in a lazy, contented, but still powerful phase.

Chandrey glanced up in direct obedience to view Atchia hovering over them.

"See what you missed?" Cance smacked Atchia's foot, knocking her body into a gentle swing. "See what a treat you missed, Atchia girl?"

She kissed Mitsu and Chandrey on their foreheads before sitting up to examine her handiwork. "And what did we learn tonight?" Her tone was proud.

Chandrey felt her keeper's eyes on her, so she phased her answer, the only answer that would suffice. She listened as Mitsu repeated the words in a flat tone.

"'The Mother Maker took pity on her delicate, pale-skinned daughters and saw to their survival, creating a physically stronger daughter, a keeper to guide and teach the gentler form of her creation.' I am lost to the universe without my keeper. I need her loving lessons to understand my role."

"That's right," whispered Cance. She phased Mitsu to sleep when she left the room.

Chandrey was ordered not to move and left awake—and in pain—nauseous and shamed at the feet of Atchia's silent, swinging form.

Her wrist was broken again, she knew that much by looking at it, but Cance made her wait until mid morning, until Atchia's body had been taken away to the pyres, before allowing her to go for medical treatment. Mitsu helped her dress after Cance left for the granary, but they weren't able to look at each other.

On her way to the infirmary, Chandrey passed Creiloff's residence. The exterior was simple, as were all Cleave homes, but since she was clan leader, it was bigger than most. A large picture window dominated the wall of Creiloff's favorite room, her spacious office.

Chandrey hurried by the window, but Creiloff must have either spied her or felt her presence, because a moment later, Lauriel appeared on the front porch.

"Creiloff says you come in."

Chandrey slowly turned, feeling every movement in her thighs and belly. The burning ache paired well with the throb in her hand, she thought scornfully when she moved. She was limping when she got to the door, more so when she stopped outside Creiloff's office. She wondered how she would make it to the infirmary.

"Enter." The room smelled of pilta and wine, much like Creiloff's mind. "Does Cancelynn know you're out unaccompanied?"

Yes, Creiloff, she does. Chandrey pressed her thighs together to still the hurt.

And where are you going?

The infirmary. She clutched her arm tighter to her side.

Why now? Cancelynn send you? When Creiloff sampled Chandrey's mind for the truth, her expression turned odd. She cleared her throat and shifted uncomfortably in her chair.

Yes, Cancelynn sent me. Chandrey chewed a bit on her bottom lip before she found control enough to answer the other question. *I fell and broke my wrist again.*

Creiloff looked doubtful. *Twice in three cycles? No one's that clumsy.* She waved Chandrey closer, grasping her arm just above the wrist when she extended it as ordered.

Chandrey couldn't help sucking in her breath, though Creiloff didn't grab hard. She examined the injury, turning her arm very carefully while mumbling.

You fell? Creiloff looked critically at her.

Tripped, please, phased Chandrey.

Creiloff prodded her mind, but she'd responded like Cance had told her. *Over what?* Creiloff released her hold so Chandrey could cradle her arm again.

My own stupid feet.

Just like last time? Interesting. Creiloff reached out with her mind a second time to pull the entire truth from Chandrey.

Now Creiloff knew everything about the morning. Chandrey braced for her punishment for the lie, for her disobedience to Cance, but the punishment never came. Rather, Creiloff leaned back in her chair and sat silently for several moments.

"You'll take a launch to the infirmary," she said, and called for one over her com. Then she commed Cance, but received no answer. "Is Cancelynn tending Atchia's pyre?"

She didn't go with the body. She just called for pick up.

Creiloff pulled a fresh pilta from her desk and began to chew the end. "Where'd she go?"

Work.

"When is the pyre-side scheduled?"

I don't know.

"Wait in the front room." Creiloff pointed to her office door.

Chandrey gratefully shuffled off, but Creiloff entered her mind again before she could exit, sliding in and out with a quick blast of rough, but well-placed pain relief aimed not to her wrist, but her thighs and shoulder.

"What?" Creiloff taunted when Chandrey glanced at her.

Chandrey removed herself from Creiloff's presence, moving easier to the formal parlor which graced the front of the home, and sitting gingerly on the padded bench nearest the door. Lauriel crossed the parlor into Creiloff's office, passed through again to the deeper part of the house, and returned with a small tray.

"You eat." Lauriel held out a tray of simple toast and tea. She was a beautiful woman in her late twenties, and wore her silver hair very long, loose, and curve hugging down her back—impractical for work, but with five other thralls and three hags in the house, Chandrey doubted she did much besides serving as Creiloff's household manager and hostess.

Chandrey shook her head. *No, thank you.*

"Creiloff says you're to eat." Lauriel placed the tray on the bench beside her and marched off, no doubt to some other task she'd been assigned.

Chandrey stared blankly at the tray, at the jam-slathered toast and steaming mug of herbal tea—a small kindness from someone she'd least expected to be kind. It confused her, blending with the dull ache of her body to put her in a funk which lasted until the launch arrived. The tea and toast were mostly gone by then, and so was Creiloff's thoughtfulness.

Chandrey shuffled painfully to the launch and rode in silence, a captive audience as the chatty young keeper pilot bragged about her new infant daughter, her little tyrant in the making.

* * *

"Granary Manager Cancelynn's Chandresslandra," called the healer in the examining room. Chandrey jumped to her feet and moved to her proper place just inside the doorway. "You again?" The healer frowned.

Chandrey was glad to be in Healer Zhastra's care.

Zhastra was a lifelong member of the Granary Clan, but she wasn't without compassion. In fact, Chandrey felt safe and wanted in her presence. But Zhastra, with her azure eyes and age-darkened, home-cut hair which seemed to go every direction at once, also intrigued her. She'd heard rumors about the healer's odd family. Zhastra had so many thralls, her general healer's allotment could barely clothe and feed them all.

Zhastra wore simple, handmade tunics and leggings, and walked around in worn boots that were big if the curled toes were any indicator. Neither did she go heavily armed, preferring her personal blade and one more dagger to the small arsenal other keepers carried.

"Let me see." Zhastra pointed at Chandrey's arm and took her wrist into her hands, holding it gingerly as she looked at the swelling.

When Chandrey winced and pulled away, Zhastra cocked an eyebrow, but waited until she held out the hand again.

"It's likely broken," Zhastra said flatly, but her mind opened to Chandrey's, delivering a dose of relief while she gleaned some needed information. *I'm sorry if I hurt you.*

"Show me your shoulder." The healer rose from her worktable to check the injury, her gentle, long fingers feeling along the joint. "It'll be fine, but it needs rest." She pointed at the metal examining lounger in the center of the room. "Remove everything from the waist down."

When Chandrey hesitated, Zhastra cocked her brow a second time, a common keeper warning to a thrall, but her phase spoke differently. *You're in obvious pain. I should to check the damage.*

Damage. Chandrey hung her head as she removed her skirts and climbed onto the table.

"Knees apart, feet together."

Though the healer never touched her, Chandrey began to shake. *You're safe.* Zhastra pushed a calming phase into Chandrey that loosened her grip on the lounger's edge. *Damn it!* Fury permeated Zhastra's mental tone. *I've reported Cance more times than I can count, but they do nothing.*

"No bite marks this time, but a fair number of shallow lacerations and contusions." Zhastra patted Chandrey's arm and motioned for her to dress.

Those born into the Cleave know their role is to teach, not torture, Zhastra phased. *I don't agree with what's happening to you and many of the others these days. These new keepers, the ones who've bought their way into the Cleave, use their power to abuse their life mates. They're changing things, leading us down the wrong path.*

I don't understand. Chandrey struggled to pull her skirt up.

They're power hungry. Zhastra rolled her eyes toward the visual recorder snuggled into the corner of the room. *Cleave tenets say we teach, not torment.* She cleared her throat.

"I'm no emotional healer," Zhastra said when she returned to her worktable. "But you've got to be more careful around your keeper." She produced a small imager from the cabinet beneath her worktable.

After Chandrey redressed, Zhastra pointed to the empty chair. When she sat, the healer ran the imager over her wrist and said, "It needs more than a splint this time."

Zhastra entered her findings into her worktable com, and then called to her apprentice, a younger keeper whose rough touch Chandrey loathed. "Bring me a sling and call an escort to Central Medical."

"Done." The apprentice healer appeared in the examining room a moment later with the sling. "Receiving just commed. The newlings are on their way."

"Before they're decontaminated?" Zhastra deftly slid Chandrey's wrist into the sling. "Send her keeper a voice com saying Chandresslandra will be housed at Central Medical overnight. Afterward, no lifting, lightest of household duties only, and for the Mother's sake, let her heal before bedding her again." With that final humiliating bit of instruction, Zhastra breezed from the room and into her office.

The apprentice healer recorded exactly what her mentor had said and took Chandrey by the elbow of her well arm to lead her back to the waiting area. "Sit," she mumbled and disappeared into the examining room.

Chandrey had just found a comfortable position in the straight-backed chair when seven thralls, herded by heavily armed keepers, burst into the waiting room. She averted her eyes—no thrall dared make eye contact with that many keepers at once—but she had long perfected the skill of surveying a situation from the knee down.

The thralls were in various states of dress—ragged hems, bare legs, and dirty, bare feet—and they stank of foreign air. Their minds were blank. Chandrey couldn't gain the slightest mental impression of them. *Binders.*

One of the keepers ordered them in the Autlach tongue to sit on the floor. All but one obeyed. This woman had filthy feet, untrimmed, talon-like nails and thin legs without a bit of meat on them.

Starved, Chandrey thought.

When the keeper ordered her again, the woman screamed something back.

Chandrey watched in silence as an amber binder fell to the floor. In the chaos that followed, someone pushed her to the floor beside the other thralls and ordered her to stay. She knew better than to move.

The combative woman's mind poured the sour, sweet stench of instability into the room, which followed her as she evaded the closest keepers in her effort to escape. When the mental stench faded, the room quieted. Chandrey ventured a glance. Only two keepers were left to watch the remaining women who huddled together, whispering and anxious in their stares.

"You, the one in the sling," said one of the armed keepers in Taelach. "Get off the floor." She gave Chandrey brusque assistance to a chair. "Don't know why they shoved you down there, but I'd get deloused if I were you."

"Maybe her keeper likes it dirty," laughed the other armed keeper. "She already likes it rough."

"Watch your moronic mouth." Zhastra appeared in her office doorway. "She's Granary Manager Cancelynn's favorite." The armed keepers quieted as Zhastra sat beside Chandrey to check her wrist. "But she's right about lice."

Zhastra led Chandrey back to her office, where she adjusted her sling before sliding into her mind, dulling her pain again. *Chandrey?* She pulled Chandrey's chin up until their eyes met. *You deserve better. If you weren't Cancelynn's favorite—*

She left the rest unsaid. Her mental touch was the only tenderness Chandrey had received since coming to the Cleave, and she clung to it until the healer softly pulled away.

A fine woman. Cancelynn isn't likely to let go of you, but I'll see what I can offer to persuade her. Zhastra let go of Chandrey's chin as a warm sensation crossed her mouth.

Only a fleeting thought, a tiny phase, but Chandrey longed to bury herself in it.

You deserve to experience how a beautiful, intelligent Cleave woman should be treated. If you were just mine... With a touch to Chandrey's shoulder, Zhastra escorted her back to the waiting area and pointed to the nearest newling.

"You first," Zhastra said—Chandrey understood that much Autlach—and returned to her office with the woman and one of the armed keepers.

Hers? Chandrey pondered as she continued to wait. *Not Cance's? We're oathed.* But that didn't seem to mean much in the Cleave. Thralls changed hands all the time. To think, no more sweet-rot mind smell taking over, no more—

The newling, the one who'd shed her binder and run off, had felt like Cance. Uncontrolled. Just as volatile. Chandrey shivered.

She worried the point until her escort arrived and she was delivered to Central Medical and the surgical ward, where the surgeon on duty pushed the idea and the rest of the day from her mind with a phase.

The next afternoon, Chandrey returned home to an entirely new level of chaos. Not only did Cance pick her head for the details of the infirmary, but she did so with mind-raking, pain-riddled thoroughness.

In her post-surgical haze, Chandrey was unable to defend herself, to shield anything including the newlings and Zhastra's comforting. After quizzing her for every detail of the talon-toed escapee, Cance turned rageful, took a belt, and whipped her across the back of her legs until they bled. Afterward, she lay atop the bedding, parched for something, anything that would take away the terror Cance inflicted.

"Fuckin' Zhastra. I knew she'd set herself on you the first time she reported me. And you! You like her! You actually like that raggedy old bitch. You wish yourself hers!"

Cance tightened her phase grip until Chandrey felt squeezed nearly in half. Breath escaped but didn't come back. Just as well. It lessened Cance's pummeling. It lessened everything until Cance allowed air, leaving her gasping for a moment before Cance launched into her again.

Sweet rot filled the air and Chandrey's mind as Cance punched her abdomen. The kitchen thrall's singing filled the background, a poor attempt at drowning out the sounds.

Mitsu stood in the bedroom doorway, sobbing and bartering. "Please, Cance. Please. Come see me. I'll makes you feel better." She stepped forward to touch Cance's shoulder.

Cance kicked back, knocking Mitsu off her feet, "Shut up, or I'll give you to Brannie." She pounded her fist into Chandrey's face.

All breath escaped her again, but this time Chandrey swung her arm wildly, turning up the hard side of her splint.

Cance fell back, touched her chin, and examined the blood on her hand. "I see." A new expression formed on her, one Chandrey had never seen. Absent. Void. Lecherous. A smile that meant something Chandrey couldn't define as anything but terrifying. "Be wary, Precious."

Cance wiped her hand on her trousers and rose to all fours. She leaned...no, she loomed over Chandrey. "For every action, there is an opposite and equal reaction." She hovered over her a second more, and then punched the pillow beside Chandrey's head and jumped to her feet, extending her sweet rot mind to Mitsu, paralyzing her.

"Hitting a keeper is a Sharing offense." Cance ran her hands down Mitsu's trembling curves and undid the fabric belt at her waist. "You forgot, I know. But that's no excuse. You sorely need the lesson, but since you just had surgery, I can't send you." She bound Mitsu's hands behind her. "Mitsu'll go in your place."

A whimper escaped Mitsu's mouth as a gut-twisted scream escaped Chandrey's mind.

Dear Mother, Cancelynn! No! Please! I beg you! Healer Zhastra was just trying to comfort me, and I took her compassion too much to heart.

"Comfort you? Why? And don't beg *my* forgiveness, Precious." Cance tightened Mitsu's binds. "You've merely bruised my image a bit. I've tried to be there, to give you what you need, to be your guide, but I guess it wasn't enough. I can live with that. I can overcome the hurt, bear the shame."

She sank a final time into Chandrey's mind, sweet-rot glazing her thoughts. *But from now on, you'll know your disgrace every time you see Mitsu. That's your lesson, Precious. Sometimes what we do has painful repercussions.*

Cance smiled in a manner to melt glass, kicked Chandrey in the ribs, and pulled Mitsu from the room. Chandrey heard thuds down the front steps, moving away from the house. A few minutes later, the horns sounded five blasts—the signal for a Sharing. Keepers would leave their homes, their jobs, their families, to help Cance with her lessoning. Creiloff would be there—it was her job as clan leader—and then she'd come to Cance's home to continue the lesson.

Mother, Mother, Mother. Chandrey prayed between hard breaths. She tried to follow them, to beg Cance to take her instead, but got no further than the bedroom doorway before collapsing. *Mother? Have you forsaken me? I atone for my sins. I try to live by your Wise Words, but I'm in pain, Mother, and my pain has spread to others. Please help Mitsu. Put me in her place. The sin of a wandering will is mine, not hers.*

Chandrey lay against the doorjamb, feeling the brunt of her beating, aware that these injuries were just the first wave. *Have you forsaken me, Mother? Have you left me to misery? Were Gahrah and Kylis right?* She ceased thinking and crawled toward the front door, begging for escape before Creiloff found her.

Chapter Twenty-Four

Kinship Governmental Facilities: Saria III

Warfare—strife; to destroy another

She still breathed—ragged, halting, but Benjimena Kim still breathed.

And as long as she breathes, Brava Deb thought day after dragging day, *the Kinship suffers*. She spent long hours in Benjimena's workroom turned hospice, and had taken to sleeping in the room most nights, not that Kylis noticed or even cared.

Kylis was on another spiritual retreat and had been gone for almost two moon cycles this time. While Brava always enjoyed these reprieves from her less-than-palatable life mate, she found the lingering absence puzzling. But then again, Kylis's retreats had been longer since Chandrey had left, and now she was gone more often than she was home.

Brava tucked her robes tighter around her legs. The night was chilly. A healer on duty sat outside the room, watching Benjimena's vital signs, but other than that, she was alone with the Taelach of All.

What an empty title, she thought. *Benjimena is the leader of nothing, ruler of less*. The Kinship was at a standstill until Benjimena either regained her senses or died. Every sister knew that: it had been the law since the formation of the Kinship. However, very few seemed to fathom the dark state this archaic law had created.

Brava emerged from her thoughts long enough to watch the healer clean Benjimena's tracheal tube. *Her breathing isn't easing when her tube is cleaned.* She closed her eyes again, quite used to the wheezing, gurgling sounds of lurking death.

Death. I sent poor, loving Belsas to her death. The negotiation team had returned with Lupinski in bandages, Quall Dawn barely able to speak about what had happened, and thirty elite troopers shot and buried in graves like common Auts. No last rites, not proper pyres. No way to the Mother's side, and it was too dangerous to retrieve the remains. The Cleave was building a new community near their graves—on Kinship land. No rest would come for those souls. The Cleave had seen to that. The Cleave was seeing to a lot of things.

Three Kinship communities, two with less than five hundred sisters and the third with nearly five thousand, had been infested by the Cleave. Cleave members had been hiding among the residents, living dual lives until they had been called into action. And act they had.

The leaders of one of the smaller communities, very near Brava's own beloved Motherslight, had successfully overtaken their neighbors without anyone knowing the truth until the community borders had been closed and communication cut. Even though she had known some of these women for most of her adult life, there was no negotiating. She was not Cleave, not keeper, so with her robes and shoulder-length hair, she must be thrall, and they didn't negotiate with thralls.

Send a keeper, they had said in their only communication. *Send us Benjimena Kim.*

Brava would have cut her hair or shaved her head if it would have helped, but she wouldn't remove the robes of her faith. She pulled those robes tight again, and looked at Benjimena. It was sinful to wish someone dead, sinful to think of how it could be done, but she could imagine so many ways, so many easy ways, all for the greater good.

So went the night for Brava as did most nights, dozing to Benjimena's death wheeze while healers came in and out.

The days were different. The days proved difficult on a grandiose scale. Council meetings. Updates on new Cleave "holdings." Inquiry after inquiry as to when Benjimena was going to do something. Everyone knew the Taelach of All was seriously ill, but very, very few knew she lay comatose. Other sisters suspected, but they didn't *know*, so Brava could still effectively serve as Benjimena's mouthpiece in every regard except one—warfare.

Only The Taelach of All had the power to stop the Cleave, to call out anything larger than a local militia to quell their advances. No assistant could say the words. Benjimena had to speak in front of her highest council, the very council Brava had to meet with that morning.

The council members wasted no time barraging Brava with questions concerning the Taelach of All's status. Where was Benjimena? How was she? Rumor had it—

"Rumor?" Brava guffawed at the young councilwoman who had spoken. "Rumors bring nothing."

"But they're often based on truth," countered another council member. "We need evidence."

"Evidence of what?" Brava pointed at the empty chair at the end of the table. "If Benjimena were dead, we'd be tending her pyre. But we're not. What more do you need?"

"We need our leader," said a council member from across the room. "We need her or knowledge of her whereabouts. Nothing more. Nothing less."

"You know where she is." Brava turned toward the councilwoman.

"You twist my words. We need her presence."

"We need her war declaration," said a third council member. "My district has lost nearly a hundred to Cleave influx."

"Nearly as many here." A councilwoman waved at Benjimena's empty seat. "They're crawling out of every corner, but our leader does nothing to help."

The council needed more than assurance, Brava knew. They needed troopers, seasoned fighters, officers trained in Cleave tactics. "Patience," she said. "I'm doing all I can."

"Patience?" said another. "Will patience save my peoples' lives? Save them from the Cleave's warped version of justice?"

"I agree. We all agree," said the council member across the room from Brava. "You expect us to tell our people to be patient?"

"What're the odds?" came another voice, thin with stress, from the other side of the room. "What're the odds Benjimena will say the words?"

Brava looked away from the voice, away from the council members, and at the ceiling, her prayer silent and solemn, her thoughts grim. What could she say? The truth? That certainly wouldn't help. Benjimena had thought, when she had possessed thoughts, that the Cleave was nothing but a minor nuisance.

There was the crux of the matter—thoughts. Benjimena had no real ones. She hadn't in over a moon cycle. Memories, but not thoughts, not cognitive, no recognition of her surroundings. Was one alive without thought? No matter. Brava was bound by law and the law stated that she, as Benjimena's assistant, was to protect her life and power. It was her sworn duty, second only to her duty to the Mother.

"Brava," insisted the thin voice a second time. "My daughter died with the label slattern." The pain in the council member's voice was unbearable. "They sent me images of her as a lesson. She was only seventeen."

A parent's grief—the one thing Brava could not refuse. She could no longer protect Benjimena. "The Taelach of All is alive." The words weighed heavy in her tongue. "But alive is a relative term."

"Your meaning?" asked someone.

"She breathes."

"Of her own accord?"

"With assistance."

"Show us." The thin voice, though still trembling, had become stronger. "Show us."

Brava finally did as asked without further explanation, dismissing the healers in an official flourish so the higher council members could crowd the room. The rest stood just outside the doorway, waiting until the others filed past Benjimena and through Brava's office access to stand outside Benjimena's doorway again.

For all its somberness, it might as well have been a funeral procession, and in a manner it was—an end of an era, the end of the longest lived leader in Kinship history.

After a quick, unanimous vote, the healers were dismissed. Only council members and Brava were allowed near Benjimena, and then only as observers. The Taelach of All would be allowed to pass in her own time. They must wait for that, but certainly it wouldn't be long. Until then, the council would remain officially assembled, camped in chambers and in Benjimena's office, waiting for the change.

There would be no time for elections, no time for the mourning the law called for. The Kinship needed an immediate leader. But the law also dictated that in times of crisis, a temporary Taelach of All could be named by the council until elections could be safely held.

The council voted again—not to declare war, they had no power to do so—but to address the current situation. Kinship citizens would be evacuated from the proximity of any Cleave activity and the border protection would be doubled. It was a stopgap measure, just until Benjimena passed.

But Benjimena did not die easily, Brava noted as days passed. She wheezed, gurgled and choked, drowning and resurfacing. A death without dignity.

When she seemed to have left, Benjimina emerged again, gasping and throwing up fluid. She was kept clean and outwardly comfortable, but no one cleaned her tracheal tubing or gave lung clearing medications. She was no longer fed or given water.

No one could stay in her room for long without wearing a binder to shield her mind. Going unbindered caused one to sense Benjimena's drowning. It drew you in, Brava thought, pulled you under, and more than one council member emerged from the room coughing up fluid herself. Even then, no one bindered the Taelach of All. No one dared.

Benjimena eventually passed, not in sleep as everyone prayed, but beneath a sudden fluid wave so large it streamed from her eyes and ears. She pulled a final breath and seized against the wave, and then succumbed to it, gushing out a line of bubbles which ran down her chin.

Brava was sitting with her when it happened. She quietly cleaned the worst of the mess from Benjimena's face before removing her binder and bending her head in prayer, as relieved as she was uncertain.

When the council voted a few hours later, the result was unanimous. A temporary leader was put in place, a leader who knew what was at stake, who would declare war against the Cleave.

Brava Deb, the new Taelach of All, wasted no time doing so, but she included stipulations. Keepers were the only enemy. Thralls and daughters were innocents. No thrall or daughter was to be killed except in self-defense. Every keeper was to be disarmed and bindered, and any keeper caught teaching a lesson would be killed on sight.

Chapter Twenty-Five

Granary Clan Lands

Change—*difference; newness*

"Stays still." Mitsu laid a cool cloth on Chandrey's forehead. "You hurts? Zhastra says to lets her know if you do."

How? Chandrey managed.

"Creiloff saved us," said Mitsu. She stepped out of the room, returning a moment later on healer Zhastra's arm.

"You look good, considering." Zhastra slid into Chandrey's mind long enough to deliver a needed phase. "I suppose Mitsu has updated you."

Creiloff?

"She helped carry you here." Zhastra sat at the foot of the bed where she played idly with the blanket. "You won't be returning to Cance."

Mitsu?

"Do you always think about everyone but yourself? Yes, her as well."

How?

"A clipped phase means a hurting head. I'll mix you some powders." Zhastra began to rise.

Please. Chandrey phased after her. *Where'll we go?*

"I took care of that," Zhastra said. "Mitsu can share the particulars." She disappeared from the room in a flourish of worn fabric, but didn't go far. "Mistu best hurry too," she called. "I intend for you to sleep."

When Chandrey looked at Mitsu, she began rattling off information as quickly as she could in her faltering Taelach. As soon as Creiloff had gotten to the Sharing, she'd been mad at Cance, something about her overstepping her role. So mad, in fact, that she hadn't allowed Mitsu to be Shared. She'd smacked Cance hard in front of everyone, told her she was out of control, and would be out of the Granary Clan if she didn't stop. She had ordered her daughter locked in the Granary office until she sobered and told everyone who'd come to the Sharing to go home.

Wow!

"Then we wents to get you. You were on the front porch, looking something awful."

I feel awful.

"Five broken ribs, a fractured eye socket, and forty-seven stitches," called Zhastra from another room. "Awful is an understatement."

"But when we gots here," continued Mitsu, "Zhastra told Creiloff she would take respon—responsibil—ity for us. That you needs to heal a long time, and I was needed to helps." At this point, Mitsu became excited.

Creiloff okayed that?

"She kinda shrugged and walked off."

How odd.

"Creiloff has much more to deal with." Zhastra returned with a small mug. "That newling is still loose."

The one from the—

"Yes, the wild woman is still at large." Zhastra held out the mug. "You'll drink, and then you'll sleep a long, healing sleep."

Cance? Chandrey choked down the bittersweet orange liquid.

"She has no claim on you anymore."

She'll come for me anyway.

Zhastra shook her head. "I signed my mark on the papers."

For some reason, that didn't ease Chandrey's mind. *Oh. The wild woman?*

"Why do you ask?" Zhastra came to sit beside her.

*I...*Chandrey hesitated. *I thought I might know her.*

"You couldn't possibly." Zhastra took her uninjured hand. "She was raised on Saria Proper."

She's old for a newling.

"That she is." Zhastra, despite her brusqueness, had an underlying gentleness that she demonstrated by rubbing the back of Chandrey's hand. "Time was she wouldn't have been brought here at all."

Age? Chandrey's eyes began to close.

"That, and she's too unstable." Zhastra laid Chandrey's hand by her side. "But such things are not your concern," she said softly. "Sleep."

Mitsu? Chandrey managed to phase.

"I've already coaxed her to rest." Zhastra let Chandrey open her eyes long enough to see her companion curled on the room's half-lounger. "Should I coax you as well?" Her hand drifted to Chandrey's face. "Rest. Repair. Rejuvenate. My home is active, so you must be on the mend before I move you there."

Chandrey didn't want to reply to or ponder over Zhastra's last comment. Sleep was enough. Sleep was welcome. Sleep, for once, was safe.

* * *

Chandrey didn't emerge from her infirmary room for three days, and then it was only for short jaunts down the hall. Not until her second day of walking, made agonizing by her stitches, did she notice someone in the room across from hers. It took another two days to find out who the bindered woman was—Belsas.

She only caught a glimpse between the guards posted outside the door, but that glance was enough. Belsas's hair was longer, she'd put on weight, but it was Belsas, awake and lying on her side on a bare bed. Her feet were chained to the frame.

"So you know her." Zhastra said later that day when she came to redo a few deeper sutures that Chandrey had pulled loose.

Know who?

Zhastra raised her brow. Chandrey looked away. The healer, although kind, was as thorough at mind picking as Cance, though much more subtle and warming in her mental touch.

Yes, I know her, Chandrey admitted.

"But not her reason for being here, I'm certain." Zhastra reached for her scissors. "This will scar badly if you don't quit popping the stitches." She trimmed off a bit of loose suture. "Forget what you saw."

She's my friend.

"Forget for your own good." Zhastra pulled the sheet back over Chandrey's legs. "Turn over."

Chandrey, still on her stomach, looked over her shoulder at her new keeper, full of questions she was afraid to ask.

Zhastra sighed, placed her instruments aside, and came to sit on the bed after Chandrey turned. "No, she hasn't been injured. No, she hasn't been Shared. No, you cannot speak to her."

I wasn't going to ask.

"But it was in the back of your mind." Zhastra helped Chandrey sit up, all the while mindful of her broken ribs. "No, I don't know how she came to be among the Cleave."

Why's she here?

"You ask too many questions," said Zhastra. "We'll work on that."

I've missed my friend. Chandrey didn't dislike Zhastra, but found her touch a confusing mixture of curiosity, sensuality, experience and self-control. Maybe it was Zhastra's age—an easy two generations older than herself. Maybe it was fear of being touched at all.

"Once you're in my home, you'll have more companionship than you can bear." Zhastra touched Chandrey's hair. "Mitsu's readying the room you'll share."

Thank you.

Zhastra didn't move her hand, not even when Chandrey tried to pull away. *I know you've been badly hurt.* Her phase soothed. *But you must learn, and learn quickly, that I won't harm you. It is against my very nature.*

Yes, Zhastra.

"I admire that you strive to understand. Your intelligence is most alluring, if not exotic." Zhastra eased Chandrey back on the bed and pulled the blankets higher. "None of my other mates were Kinship born." She glanced over her shoulder toward the guards in the hallway. "Your curiosity, however, could get you into trouble. Remember, a good life mate doesn't meddle in keeper affairs."

Keeper. That was all Zhastra really was, all Zhastra ever would be. Chandrey bowed her head in compliance, but the healer saw through the façade to her thoughts once again.

You go through the motions, but think otherwise. Interesting. You are going to take some time to teach.

Chandrey couldn't help wincing.

Teach, not beat, reminded Zhastra. *You were raised in the Mother's Word, but the Plan's interpretations of Her Words stray from their true meaning. With my help, you will learn what's right. It will take time, but you will come to accept and eventually believe.*

How Chandrey wished her mind were her own again, if only for a moment. She smoothed the blankets over her lap. Her wrist still hurt, but everything hurt in some way. *If I do this, may I have my voice back?*

Certainly. Zhastra touched Chandrey's throat just enough to feel the plate. *You'll need your voice to teach.*

Teach? Chandrey looked up. What could she possibly teach that the Cleave would allow?

Zhastra was quick to answer that question as well. *My mates should be able to read, and write, and do mathematics. They should also know Cleave history. Regretfully, I am often too busy to tend to the task very well.*

Creiloff silenced me for teaching.

Education is up to the keeper to give or deny. Most deny, but I see it as counterproductive to an efficient, happy home. Zhastra smiled in an offhanded manner that Chandrey could interpret several ways. "I'll have the throat plate removed before you come home, but it will take some time and effort for your voice to return to normal." With those words and a wave, she left Chandrey to her thoughts.

Those thoughts quickly returned to Belsas.

Late in the evening two days later, during one of her jaunts down the hallway, Chandrey briefly crossed paths with Belsas as she slowly paced the hall. The guards were chatting, arguing some point so intently that she and Belsas dared share recognizing glances. Chandrey knew her face was still dark with bruises, and Belsas's face was masked by a binder. Dressed in a robe, Belsas shuffled along on swollen, bare feet. In fact, she looked swollen all over.

Chandrey tried to keep her eyes averted, but she wanted to look, to question, to grab Belsas and never let go. But she passed Belsas and walked to the end of the hall so she could turn around and possibly pass Belsas again. Belsas's shuffle picked up pace behind her, and they faced each other again.

Why? Chandrey mouthed when Belsas looked toward her.

Belsas looked down at herself and back to Chandrey. "You," she whispered as they passed each other.

Chandrey returned to the opposite end of the hall and turned to cross paths with Belsas a third time. You okay? she mouthed this time.

Belsas shrugged. "You?"

Will be.

"Cance?"

They walked apart again.

Chandrey touched her bruised face when they neared each other the fourth time. Cance did this, she mouthed.

"Damn her." Belsas opened her mouth, no doubt to whisper more, but a low groan came out instead. She clutched her side.

Chandrey stopped in front of her, unsure what to do, but Belsas placed a hand on her shoulder as she doubled over. "Another one," she whispered. "They're killing me."

Belsas's second groan, louder than the last, drew the guards' attention. They hurried her back to her bed and ordered Chandrey to hers. She obeyed, but not without slipping on a puddle where they'd stood. A trail of blood led back to Belsas's room.

Zhastra arrived a moment later and someone shut the door to Chandrey's room, but if she listened closely, she could still hear the confusion. Someone called for assistance. Zhastra called for calm. Belsas's angry cries rose and faded moment to moment until Zhastra finally called for orange powder to be mixed.

After that, things quieted for a while, and then a sharp cry rose from Belsas again, but this time, expressed far more than physical pain. Sorrow washed from her faster than the tears which flowed from Chandrey's eyes. Binder or not, Bel's emotions were clear.

"I won't go back!" she insisted. "You'll have to kill me before I go back!" Chandrey heard terror in her words. "Four times! Four! I can't do it. None of us can. You want the impossible!"

But even Chandrey knew Belsas would be sent back to wherever it was she didn't want go. The Cleave didn't negotiate. Keepers kept repeating their attempts until the desired lesson was learned, or until…she sucked in her breath. They were slowly killing Belsas in some torturous way, but how?

You hear too much. Zhastra appeared in her mind, troubled and disappointed. *Your meeting was most unfortunate and ill-timed, but she will be leaving here tomorrow, and you are to spend the day having your throat plate removed.*

The door slid open and Zhastra stepped into the room.

Where will she go? Chandrey dared to look the healer in the eye. *Is she okay? What happened?*

Zhastra raised her brows and looked hard at Chandrey. *Exotic, but terribly aggravating. I will indulge you on this, but only because you were a partial witness. Something unfortunate happened, but it has happened before and to others.*

Four times.

To her, yes. But this was the first time I was in attendance.

What happened?

The subject—

Her name is Belsas.

Absolutely infuriating! Zhastra glowered at her, but continued speaking after dropping her phase. "She was brought here in the hope that the quiet would make a difference. Obviously, it did not. She'll heal." She moved to stand over Chandrey. "That is far more information than you warrant."

Whose is she?

Zhastra looked shocked. "Didn't Cancelynn teach you *anything*? Slatterns don't belong to anyone."

Chandrey could think no more so she simply closed her eyes and rolled onto her side away from Zhastra, ignoring the pain of the stitches.

However, after a moment, Zhastra entered her mind again, gentle but direct. *I'll cut your pain so you can rest. The surgery to remove that plate can be complicated.*

Chandrey phase-pushed her away, though more warily than she had Cance. *Please leave me alone.*

You want to hurt like your friend? Zhastra pushed harder against Chandrey's weakened defenses. *I should leave you in pain?* She pushed again.

Chandrey had to concede. She hadn't the strength to do otherwise.

Take the comfort. Zhastra came to lie against her and caress her hair. *You've a lot to learn, more than most keepers would have the patience to teach. But I'll succeed where they've failed.*

Chandrey numbed in Zhastra's arms, thinking nothing, feeling nothing, being nothing except what her new keeper wanted. Beneath it all, however, deeper than Zhastra could easily sense, her soul cried for Belsas, for the pain she was in, for the things they hadn't been able to say. Above all, she tried to comprehend the tiny, mourning blue-wrapped bundle she'd seen carried from Belsas's room.

Chapter Twenty-Six

Cull—reject, remove; destroy

Zhastra's home was actually a wing of the infirmary—a bit medical in its odors, but a hotbed of activity. Besides Chandrey and Mitsu, a dozen thralls lived in the house, all equally receiving Zhastra's attention. She was insistent that her home, filled with an eclectic collection of repaired and castoff furniture, stay organized, and that the daily routine flowed in a consistent manner, but she was reasonable and surprisingly patient with everyone.

All the thralls were Zhastra's life mates, but more than once, Chandrey heard a visitor call them Zhastra's "oddities" instead. She supposed they were all different in their own ways.

No one in the house bore the title of hag, no one was less valued than any other, and they all readily shared their clothing so Chandrey and Mistu each had a few outfits since Cance had made a spectacle of burning everything they'd possessed.

There were children in Zhastra's home as well, four daughters between the ages of two and fifteen whom Zhastra doted on. They were being raised keeper, but Zhastra's version of keeper was very different from the rude Cleave daughters Chandrey had been exposed to.

Zhastra's sleeping habits were unusual as well. No main or second's bedroom, but like the other wing of the infirmary, the long hall had rooms on each side, twelve in all: ten used for sleeping, two for storage. The older women had their own rooms, but the younger, including Chandrey, Mitsu, and the children shared.

With one exception, Zhastra slept beside one or the other of her life mates every night, but at least once every three nights she spent with Chandrey and Mitsu in their tight little room. She seemed to care little for the mental or physical couplings which were her right, at least where they were concerned.

Chandrey welcomed the fact and worked through her grief together with Mitsu, finding peace and a sibling-like affinity for each other. On their nights with Zhastra, she explored their minds with gentleness and respect, handling their memories like museum pieces, but doing nothing to remove or revise a single thought.

"It would change you," Zhastra told Chandrey one night after Mitsu had fallen asleep. "And that is not my intention."

Despite Zhastra's thoughtfulness, Chandrey couldn't help thinking of Belsas.

Every evening after dinner, Zhastra assembled her family in the gathering room, the only sizable room in the home aside from the large eat-in kitchen, and led a Cleave version of a Mother's devotional. These tedious lessons would sometimes last the entire evening, and Zhastra quizzed her family afterward, particularly Chandrey, whom she was intent on converting.

Chandrey appreciated being back in the Mother's Word and hearing verses she had grown up with, but seldom agreed with Cleave interpretations. The Cleave ignored the context of the Word in favor of a line-by-line meaning which frequently angered her, but she knew better than to speak up.

Besides, Zhastra allowed her to express her thoughts when they were alone. While Chandrey reveled in these free moments, Zhastra would never answer her inquiries about Belsas. In fact, this was the only time she ever saw Zhastra grow angry. Eventually, Belsas's name was banned from the home, but that didn't stop Chandrey from thinking about her.

It wasn't a bad existence, fathoms better than Cance's home. Chandrey was grateful, but this wasn't the life she wanted. She wanted her freedom, her thoughts valued instead of usurped by obscure interpretations, to laugh spontaneously without someone wanting a reason.

She was physically healed by this point, the scars on her legs and a stiff wrist the only physical evidence of her time with Cance. Zhastra allowed her to participate fully in the household, including making some of the more domestic decisions, and with the oldest keeper daughter as an escort, going to the community stores for supplies and pantry staples.

At the stores, she heard rumors about Cance's activities, of her two new life mates, and how Creiloff had leashed her daughter's bad behavior with nothing more than a few knocks on the head. The general consensus was that Creiloff was a good leader. And Cance, since she had been relieved of her disobedient thralls, had those same makings. Her thralls had driven her to near insanity. She was well rid of them.

Such comments naturally came with scowls aimed in Chandrey's direction, but no keeper approached her when she had the proper keeper escort, child or not.

No keeper except Cance.

The first couple of times they met on the pathways, she ignored Chandrey, but the next, Cance slid her shoulder pack low to brush hard against her as they passed, even though Chandrey had moved well to the side as was expected.

"You'll pay," mumbled Cance. She spun on her heel to face Zhastra's eldest, Emre. "You need help controlling your thrall?"

"Sorry, Granary Manager Cancelynn," said Emre, drawing up to her full height. "I thought she'd moved."

"What's she doing out anyway?" Cance balled her hands into fists, but Chandrey kept her outer expression in check. Emre stood her ground. Zhastra would be proud.

"She's been retrained. Zhastra wouldn't allow her out if she couldn't behave." Emre deferred to Cance, moving aside as well. "You have my apologies. I'll report the incident to Zhastra. May we pass?"

"Not yet." Cance reached over young Emre's head to grab Chandrey by her cloak hood. "This thrall needs an immediate lesson."

"Zhastra doesn't allow others to discipline what's hers." Emre stepped back onto the path and broke Cance's grip on Chandrey's hood, but Cance swung with her right arm to plant her fist in the middle of Emre's face.

"A lesson for two then." Cance reached again for Chandrey.

"Is there a problem?" A roaming guard approached at a trot. Guards had been on constant patrol since the wild woman had escaped. "Hey, Cance. How ya doing?"

"Fine, thanks, Raja. No problem here." Cance flexed her hand as her mouth slid into a lecherous grin aimed at Chandrey. "Got a problem, Zhastra's child?"

"No." Emre covered her nose with one hand. "We were just on our way."

"Me as well," said Cance as she sauntered down the pathway toward the silos which designated her work. "Have a good day."

The guard shrugged and followed Cance down the pathway.

"I'm sorry," said Chandrey when she and Emre resumed their walk home.

"For what?" Emre sniffed, and then returned her hand to her nose to stem the slow bleeding. "Zhastra warned me it might happen."

Still, Zhastra wasn't happy about the episode when she learned about it.

"I'll send someone else with Emre until things calm with Keeper Cancelynn," she said over dinner, glancing at Emre's black eyes. "The medicinal herb beds need cleaning. Chandrey and Mitsu can work on them for now."

The lesson that evening was brief, but had everything to do with what had happened. It was a lesson on wielding power, who wielded it, and when she should. Chandrey thought of it as a lesson on giving lessons, Zhastra's way of denouncing Cance's behavior without openly blasting another keeper in front of thralls.

Afterward, Zhastra took Emre aside for a short talk, and afterward called an early night, telling Mitsu to sleep beside Giana as she took Chandrey by the arm.

"I'll share your space." Zhastra escorted her to the bedroom and turned away. "Be back shortly."

Chandrey obeyed, used to Zhastra's sense of humility.

Zhastra dressed in her private study located at the end of the hall. Chandrey had been permitted in the space for some of their discussions, and had emerged to the amazed and confused faces of the others. Few of the other thralls had ever been in the room except Zhastra's first life mate, Giana, and even she claimed in her halting speech, the result of a recent stroke, not to have been in the room in several passes.

Chandrey slid into her shift, unrolled the bedding, and sat on some stacked pillows, ready for one of Zhastra's thorough mind-pickings.

But the evening was focused on conversation—voice, not phases—and was accompanied by wine, a rarity in Zhastra's house.

"Something different." Zhastra settled back with her mug. "I know you're aware of the rumors and have chosen to ignore them. Cance has painted a rather ugly image of you and Mitsu."

Chandrey sipped her wine. "I know." Her voice still didn't sound right. Zhastra had said her vocal cords would return to something near normal, but at present, she sounded very raspy.

"She's popular among the younger keepers." Zhastra looked concerned, if not haggard, by the day's events. "I need to understand why."

"She's kimshee trained. They're taught to be manipulative."

"Disturbingly so." Zhastra regarded Chandrey for a moment. "This is difficult for you."

Chandrey looked into her half-filled mug. "I'm simply tired this evening."

"You don't sleep well."

"Mitsu moves around so."

"And your nightmares—"

"Are horrendous," blurted Chandrey. "So are Mitsu's." She curled a bit smaller on her pillow. "Does it matter?"

"Yes, they're horrendous, but unlike Mitsu, you've yet to accept my assistance in stopping them." Zhastra moved into a cross-legged position. "Why do you keep rejecting me?"

Chandrey set aside her empty mug and looked balefully at the wall. "How can you ask that knowing what I've been through at the hands of a keeper like you?"

"I'm nothing like Cancelynn." Zhastra made no attempt to comfort her apart from topping her mug again. "But I know you see her in the other young keepers. They think she can do no wrong. Even Emre found her actions today justified. She believes you were unfairly singled out, but she also thinks Cance's punch justified. Emre said she was disrespectful of an elder."

"By keeper teaching, she was, wasn't she?"

"Not by *my* teaching," said Zhastra. "No Cleave teaching I know justifies unwarranted aggression."

"If they can justify beating and sharing thralls," Chandrey said indignantly, "then what's punching a kid?"

"The Cleave I know doesn't discipline without very good reason," countered Zhastra in a rising voice. "The Cleave I know—"

"The Cleave you know is dead!" Chandrey shouted before she could stop herself. "This New Cleave is the only one I knew until I met you." She and Zhastra were arguing on equal terms. She wondered how long it would last. "This Cleave—"

"Don't push my generosity," warned Zhastra, but her tone softened. "So what draws them to her? What drew you to her?"

Chandrey considered the question as she drank the wine, glad she'd eaten beforehand. "Cance knew what I wanted to hear," she said hesitantly. "She made me feel valued, like there was nothing she and I couldn't conquer together."

"Intriguing." Zhastra shifted so her tunic slid lower on her patched leggings. "I know enough of you to know how you felt later, but I never considered she could be so initially charming."

"I was mesmerized." The conversation proved exhausting. Chandrey yawned despite her efforts, earning a smile from Zhastra.

"Perhaps you'll sleep better tonight." Zhastra divided the rest of the bottle between them. "You're relaxed enough for some honest discussion."

"You could have picked it from my mind if you'd wanted."

"I could have." Zhastra slid down to rest her head on her pillows. "But I wanted your direct observations, not your emotion-tainted memories."

"Tainted?" said Chandrey.

"I'm not used to being questioned." Zhastra rose quickly to draw in very close, eye-to-eye, both brows raised. A challenge, not a warning. "Yes, tainted. Even though it was a façade, part of you misses that early Cance."

"That's the Cance I oathed with." She was torn between anger and agony, but she could not draw her gaze away from Zhastra, from her kind eyes, her keen interest and understanding.

"I know." Zhastra's sharp tone eased as she took Chandrey's face in her hands. "I know." She pressed her lips to her forehead, and for once, Chandrey didn't try to pull away. "Come lay beside me. I promise to stay free of your thoughts unless I'm invited in."

"I don't—I can't—"

"You can't what?" Zhastra seemed insulted. "You can't understand why I would desire you when your heart so clearly rests elsewhere?"

"I hate Cance."

"Yes, but you love her in some small way as well," said Zhastra. "What a terrible conflict." She wrapped her arms around Chandrey, encouraging her to lay back. "And then there's your love for Belsas."

Chandrey couldn't deny it so she tensed, ready for some sort of punishment. "I'm sorry."

"Don't lie." Zhastra pulled her closer and moved to kiss her cheeks: left, and then right. "She came here for you, you know, to take you back to the Kinship, but look what it got her. Lost to this New Cleave. I banned her name in the hope you'd eventually forget her." Zhastra looked deep into her eyes. "But that won't happen, will it?"

Chandrey didn't look away, but neither could she answer.

"Then I must admit defeat." Zhastra looked away. "Others told me you weren't tamable, but I didn't believe them. I knew I could make you into a good life mate with enough patience. I even tried to appeal to you with logic."

"Nothing about the Cleave is logical to me."

"The harder I pushed, the more you questioned. How did Cance manage you so long?"

Should she tell? Would Zhastra do the same? No, Chandrey decided. She was simply curious. "She never left my head."

"How maddening for you both." Zhastra examined her for a moment more, following the line of her face, her lips, and her neck with a finger.

Chandrey didn't want to stop her. "I thought all keepers handled thralls that way."

"I loathe the term thrall," Zhastra said after a moment more of tracing. "And one's life mates shouldn't need controlling."

"And the ones that do?" Chandrey dared to capture Zhastra's hand.

Zhastra laced their fingers together. "Some call me a salvager, even a collector. I see true value in those who might otherwise be culled."

Chandrey gripped Zhastra's hand. "We were to be culled?"

"Cance dubbed you both unmanageable." Zhastra wiggled her fingers in Chandrey's grasp. "But I knew from the beginning the accusations were untrue."

"So you took us in." Chandrey released her hold, but Zhastra now took her hand, which she brought up to kiss.

"Yes." Zhastra's voice was tender. "I've saved every one of my life mates, and I never expected any of them to love me for it, but they all do, each in her own wounded way. But not you. I know you'll never feel that way. Appreciation, yes. I sense that, now that you know the truth, but no love. You're far too intelligent to confuse the two. You'll never be truly mine, no matter my kindness or cruelty."

"I—"

"Shh." Zhastra touched her fingers to Chandrey's mouth where they stayed in a nervous hover. "You're more of an equal than I've known, and I find that very exciting. I could easily fall in love, lose myself to you, but I know it'd be futile. You don't belong here, in this house, among the Cleave—you don't belong with me."

"I never wanted this."

"The Cleave I know wouldn't have brought you in. You're an outsider, unable to understand our ways. But this New Cleave is unpredictable." Zhastra shook her head. "It'll destroy what it can't control. I can't let it continue consuming such vibrant women."

"Then help me." Chandrey was aghast at her own brashness.

"These walls are thin." Zhastra pushed back Chandrey's headscarf to expose her ear. "I can give you time to finish healing," she whispered. "Time to plan. Your friend needs you. You'll need to rescue her—Belsas—before her spirit is completely broken."

"But I don't know where she is." Chandrey's heart pattered rapidly, feeling ready to fly to freedom without her.

"You know where she'll be sooner or later." Zhastra glanced back toward the infirmary wing. "I can teach you what you need to know for when the time comes."

"You'd set me free?" Chandrey was close enough to smell the wine on Zhastra's breath. It wasn't a bad smell, and she wondered about her own.

"I'd see you happy." Zhastra lingered close, obviously breathing her in.

We're both feeling the wine, thought Chandrey, her breaths quickening the same way.

"But I ask for something in return," Zhastra continued.

"What?" Chandrey's voice caught in her throat. She had nothing worth giving. Not anymore.

"Oh, but you do." Zhastra's fingers quivered atop Chandrey's lips. "Teach me, and I'll teach you. Let's trade lessons. Let me experience you as an equal, as a woman can experience a woman, not as the keeper I am. In return, I'll teach you skills you'll need: how to fight, where to hit, where to strike with your blade to do the most damage, give you tools that will undo some of her damage, give you back some of the confidence she took."

Chandrey placed her cheek in Zhastra's palm. "I lost myself to her."

"Then let me restore you," said Zhastra, "before she tries to make you forget again."

It wasn't a question, but an observation of something they both knew and needed to forget, if only for one night. Chandrey kissed Zhastra's trembling palm, a hand that had healed her and wished to do so again. "She's not finished with me."

"Not with any of us, I'm afraid." Zhastra replaced her palm with her mouth, drawing Chandrey in with such passion, there could be no doubt. This wasn't love, but a partnership, one she could accept in all its forms. "May I?" Zhastra asked when they parted.

"What about Mitsu?" Chandrey removed her headscarf.

"Still thinking of everyone but yourself?" Chandrey felt Zhastra's smile against her. "She's a bright woman, but doesn't understand the world like you do. She'll be safe with me."

Her hand now rested on the top edge of Chandrey's shift. "May I?" Zhastra's expression implored as much as her words.

Chandrey toyed with Zhastra's unhooked collar. If this was going to be an equal partnership, she would give as much as she received, something totally different from her previous experience and a delicious prospect. "Gently?"

"As gentle as the breeze, as long and hot as a Sarian summer," whispered Zhastra. She cocooned Chandrey, ever so true to her word.

Chapter Twenty-Seven

Addict—*dependent; obsessing over*

Chandrey felt eyes on her every time she and Mitsu worked in the medicinal garden.

The garden at the back of the infirmary was surrounded by a high wall, but Chandrey still sensed someone watching her, noting her movements, lying in wait. Her skin crawled at the height of these sensations, but she never saw physical evidence of an intruder.

Mitsu, content with their current task, often sang Aut ditties under her breath.

Shadowed by a wide-brimmed hat, Chandrey labored until the Sarian sun reached its apex, and then retreated to the herb shed to process the harvest per Zhastra's written instructions. Some plants were hung to dry while others were stripped of their leaves and placed in the large dehydrator. And some, always the worst smelling it seemed, were set to a low boil in a sealed cooker. It wasn't that Zhastra didn't use modern medicine. Rather, she knew the old ways as well and used the best method available. Early on, she'd taken Chandrey for a walk through the garden, giving the names and preservation methods for each plant.

On a rainy day, Mitsu had been detailed to household duties, but Chandrey had been instructed to work in the herb shed, changing out the dehydrator, and peeling slip root, a particularly volatile natural compound. Zhastra had warned her to wear gloves.

While the foul-smelling root simmered under a ventilated hood, Chandrey cleaned the dehydrator and found she had extra time before Zhastra returned to check her progress, so she explored the shed, finding machinery, storage bins and vessels, small pouches for single dosages, and yellowed hide scrolls giving detailed mixtures and exact dosages for various herbal combinations.

She wanted to know more about the individual herbs and found the plants she was familiar with amid the scrolls. Slip root bark, she learned, was not to be handled by Autlach women of childbearing age. Reason: spontaneous abortion.

"Ground slip root bark, mother's hat leaves and silver rod thorns in equal portions create that orange powder I gave you for pain." Zhastra stood in the shed doorway. "Mix them light in water and the patient won't feel any side effect. Mix them too heavy…" Zhastra paused before continuing, "The normal dose is one fingernail depth per two fingernails of water with a hefty bit of sweet cane to mask the taste."

Chandrey repeated the healer's instructions verbatim. "Can it be mixed in other liquids?"

"Wine works well."

"Covers the taste?"

"Yes." Zhastra looked down at the scroll in Chandrey's hand. "I forgot you read at such a high level." She didn't try to take the scroll, instead turning to the simmering slip root. "Such a horrid smell for something so effective." She donned gloves and moved the steaming mixture from beneath the hood. "Bring me an empty dehydrator tray and I'll show you the next step." She spread the mixture on the tray and loaded it into the dryer. "Only process one tray at a time."

"Should I prep another pot?"

"No, I've a good supply after this batch." Zhastra removed her gloves and rinsed her hands. "I've a patient waiting, but I'll be back in a while. Practice your lunges while I'm gone." She squeezed Chandrey's shoulder as she passed, one of the few times they'd touched since that night. "After that, there's a recorder on one of the shelves containing a medicinal plant database. Thought it might interest you."

"Thanks," Chandrey said, but Zhastra was gone in another of her harried walks.

She watched Zhastra until she'd cleared the infirmary doors, and then reached for a couple of small pouches. Zhastra hadn't picked her mind since their night together. She didn't worry about being caught because the healer stayed true to her word and didn't get in the way of her preparations.

At this point, Chandrey had no idea what those preparations might be. She had ideas: wait until Belsas returned to the infirmary and get past the guards long enough to set things in motion, but then what? She had a kitchen knife hidden in her blankets and would bag some of the orange powder mix just in case.

Her skin began to crawl. Someone was watching. Not Mitsu. Her mental presence was easy. No, this presence was there but not. Phase blind? Bindered? She wasn't sure.

"I know you're there, Zhastra," she said. "You can't sneak up on me like you used to."

When Chandrey turned toward the door, a silhouette flew at her, knocking her backward. Her head cracked against the stone floor. She lay there, recovering her senses as the shadow figure tore around the shed, sniffing and tasting one herb after another, discarding them all except the orange powder mix. The entire bin of mix, in fact.

"Hey!" Chandrey stood up as the shadow figure, wearing a dark cloak, inhaled some of the powder.

The figure spoke something in Autlach and kicked out, sending Chandrey staggering across the room and into the far shelves, showering her with empty containers and scrolls. Before she could escape from beneath the pile, the shadow sprung on top of her, grabbing her by the collar and shoving a handful of orange mix in her face.

Within seconds, Chandrey's world began to recede. The shadow figure said something to her, maybe Autlach again, but she couldn't tell. The door between her and the conscious world suddenly slammed shut.

Chapter Twenty-Eight

Sacrificial—giving of self; a good keeper's trait

Chandrey woke in the infirmary to find Zhastra sitting on one side of her bed, and to her dismay, Creiloff standing, arms folded across her chest, by the other.

"Who attacked you?" Creiloff drummed her fingers against her arm. "Quick, girl. Time is wasting."

"I—I don't know." Chandrey's swallowed to discover a soreness she hadn't felt since the throat plate's removal.

"I induced vomiting as soon as I found you." Zhastra held a mug of water to her mouth. "Small sips." She looked to Creiloff. "I picked her for details as soon as she stabilized. She doesn't know who attacked her. It happened too fast. By the time she sensed the presence, it was too late. The attacker was after the medicines, and she got in the way."

"Start locking that shed," Creiloff said simply and walked from the room.

Chandrey stared after her. "Something else happened. I feel it." She peered up at Zhastra. "What didn't she say?"

"You're too observant." Zhastra seemed to try, but failed to summon the smile she usually had for Chandrey. "Creiloff's Lauriel was found dead late this morning. She's on her way to the pyre."

"What happened?"

"Someone or something broke her neck." Zhastra's gaze shifted to the open doorway. "Yes, Chloe?"

"Giana saids I should bring these." Chloe nodded at the basket propped against her hip. She had lost her right arm to an infection after a beating by her former keeper, but the lack didn't seem to get in her way. "And she saids that since Chandrey knew Lauriel, she should go too, if she's able."

"She has a point," said Zhastra as she relieved Chloe of her load and kissed her cheek. "Good work, Chloe. You may go."

"Yes, Zhastra." Chloe nodded pleasantly and turned back toward the household wing.

Zhastra pulled out the basket's contents—neatly pressed clothing—and placed the garments on the foot of the bed. "I know you're wobbly, but—"

Chandrey pushed aside the blankets and sat up, swinging her feet over the edge of the bed. She was indeed wobbly, she found when she tried to stand, more than she anticipated, so she sat for a moment. "I'll need some help."

"Someone will be close to steady you," assured Zhastra. She separated their outfits. "I understand the Kinship wears mourning blue sashes to their pyres, correct?"

"Yes." Chandrey saw nothing blue in the basket. "What does the Cleave wear?"

Zhastra held up an unadorned sheath dress obviously meant for Chandrey. "The living wear pure, uninterrupted white." She added a pair of slippers and a headscarf in the same shade. "The dead wear mourning blue."

Chandrey thought about the significance of the switch as Zhastra helped her dress. In the Kinship, the dead wore a white shroud as a sign of the fire's purifying process. They were ready to move on, free of life's complications, ready for a new start at the Mother's side. How could they do so trapped in the color of grief? she wondered.

* * *

With one critical exception, the Cleave pyre service was even simpler than the Kinship version. Since Lauriel had been a clan leader's life mate, all of the clan attended. The more important the community member to the deceased, the closer to the pyre she stood. Of course, Creiloff was closest, and her other life mates stood in single file behind her, ranked by Creiloff according to their status. The space directly behind her, usually reserved for Lauriel, was empty.

Zhastra found her life mates all equally important, so she arranged them by age. Giana naturally directly behind her, and then the rest, with young Tamberly last. Tamberly was perhaps fifteen, but no one, not even Tamberly, knew her real age. She was short as an Aut child, deaf as a stone, and much more a thrall daughter than a life mate to Zhastra.

Chandrey stood in front of Tamberly, unsteady on her feet, but able to place her hand on Chloe's shoulder whenever she needed balance. Mitsu stood beside her, holding her erect when her knees went weak, which was often enough. Their line was by far the deepest.

Creiloff must have cared for Lauriel in her own manner, in a keeper's way, thought Chandrey as she turned her gaze toward the ground. It was a deeply internal thought, kept close and safely tucked away, but someone in the crowd still heard her and replied—with laughter.

Chandrey looked up to find only one other person looking up and looking at her.

Someone had to die, Precious. It was supposed to be you, but when that didn't work the way I planned, Lauriel went in your place. Funny how others keep taking your punishment. Wonder who'll be next?

Chandrey glanced around when Cance dropped her phase, but no one else had heard. Cance knew her mind enough to focus solely on it if she was close enough. But her former life mate soon wouldn't be, she reminded herself, grateful when the service ended moments later.

Zhastra and the others helped her back to the infirmary.

"One more night, just until you regain your bearings," Zhastra said. "And your vital signs are high again. Interesting how a distant someone's pyre can stress us so."

"We need to talk." Chandrey pushed her exchange with Cance deep within her. Proof, if Zhastra needed it.

"Okay, but the bed won't record your vitals if you aren't in it." Zhastra's hand lingered on Chandrey's hair. "I think I'll stay with you so we can discuss whatever's bothering you."

"All I want is talk."

"Not if I do things correctly," said Zhastra. "I'll be back."

"But—"

"It will wait." Zhastra left Chandrey alone for much of the evening, returning wearing her faded, patched evening tunic and leggings when the house side of the building had grown quiet.

"I thought you'd never get back," said Chandrey. "Chloe said you were with a patient. Is everyone okay?"

"Yes, minor injury. I see someone brought you dinner," Zhastra said, moving the tray from the bedside table. She read the viewer above the bed. "You've recovered nicely." While she skimmed the input board, an odd chirp sounded from somewhere in the bed, and all the sensors turned off. "I don't want to confuse the infernal thing," Zhastra added.

"Something happened during the pyre today." Chandrey slid over and flipped back the blanket. "I need to tell you."

"Why so rushed?" Zhastra slipped in beside her.

"Cance." Chandrey rolled to one side and propped on an elbow. "She phased me during the pyre."

"Very rude of her, but you seem unharmed." Zhastra tugged on her arm, pulling her back on the bed. "I've news."

Chandrey pushed up again. "Let me talk first."

"If you were anyone else," Zhastra warned. "What?"

"Cance said she killed Lauriel."

Zhastra shook her head. "I thought about the possibility, but she couldn't have killed Lauriel."

"But she told me," said Chandrey.

Zhastra shook her head again. "She's playing mind games with you," she said crossly. "And you're letting her."

"But—"

"She was at the Granary when Lauriel died. Other keepers saw her there. She's guilty of a lot of crimes, but not this." Zhastra's expression dulled. "Now I've got news for you. It isn't good, but you should know nonetheless."

Chandrey couldn't dismiss Cance's phase, but she put it aside for the moment. "Does it have anything to do with the keeper gathering?"

"How would you know about that?" Zhastra lay beside her.

"Keepers forget someone can be on the other side of the garden wall." Chandrey smiled a little. "I simply overheard."

"And didn't forget like most in your position would," said Zhastra. "Glad you aren't staying with me. I'd forever be cleaning up after you."

"Just as well then, huh?" Chandrey patted Zhastra's face. "What was the gathering about?"

"Betrayal." Zhastra's smile faded.

"What?" Chandrey sat up again. "Who?"

"Keeper Jana."

"Cance had Jana and her favorite to dinner once."

"They caught her at the border with her life mates." Zhastra shook her head. "Joining the Cleave as a keeper requires something near the oath. It's a lifelong pledge."

Chandrey caught her breath. "What happened to Jana? To her family?"

Zhastra looked away. "I had to be there, but I didn't take part."

"She's dead? They're dead?" Zhastra didn't have to answer. Chandrey knew, but had the worst happened? "Were they—?"

"Not her life mates."

A small relief at best. "Keeper Jana?"

"She was a Kinship spy," said Zhastra. "No one knew until then, until they'd dug deep enough."

"You stayed for *that*?"

"Stars, no! I haven't the stomach for such things. I heard word of mouth." Zhastra cast her a wounded look. "How could you even think I'd take part in a Sharing?"

"I hoped you wouldn't."

"I've never appreciated that little custom, and it seems to be used far too much these days." Zhastra brooded for a moment before she spoke again. "And there's other news as well."

"Is it Bel?" Chandrey asked eagerly. "Is she coming back?"

"Listen closely."

"It's Bel, isn't it?" asked Chandrey.

"Shh. Calm down," said Zhastra as she pulled her down. "Patience." She captured one of Chandrey's legs beneath her own, preventing her from rising again. "She'll be here tomorrow, but bide your time where she's concerned."

"Absolutely not." Chandrey pushed her leg aside.

"I can speed things, but she'll need to heal before you make your move." Zhastra moved more forcefully, pulling Chandrey to the middle of the bed to move on top of her. "Be patient."

"What're you doing?"

"Making you listen." Zhastra pushed Chandrey's arms over her head and held them tight. "You can't go until I say."

"You said you wouldn't stand in my way." Chandrey struggled against her. "You gave your word!"

"Damn it, Chandresslandra, listen to me." Zhastra pressed hard against her. "She can't leave here until I undo what they did to her in the lab. She could bleed to death away from care."

Chandrey tried, but couldn't relax. "What'd they do?"

"Nothing I can't fix, but it will temporarily weaken her further." Zhastra wouldn't move from on top of her. "Slip root," she whispered. "Its side effects can be useful."

Chandrey stopped when she remembered the blue bundle she'd seen carried from the infirmary. "No!" She withdrew against the bed, away from Zhastra. "You knew?"

"Not until she was brought to the infirmary." Zhastra's expression implored her to understand, but Chandrey wasn't interested. "I don't like it any more than you, but I'm only a local healer, not a researcher. Those sorts of experiments are carried out by specialists at Central Medical."

"Oh, really?" Chandrey sneered. "So you've nothing to do with the Aut breeding program either?"

"My daughters came from that program," said Zhastra without shame. "But no. The studs come here to work on occasion, but that's the only contact I have."

Chandrey stared intently at Zhastra, demanding the truth. "If you've nothing to do with any of this, why is Bel being brought here?"

"Because it's a calmer environment. She progressed better here— to a point." Zhastra grunted and pushed down harder when Chandrey tried to slide out from under her. "Damn it! I'll take your suspicions, but not your judgment. You'll stay with me until I tell you it's safe. You'll listen!"

"Keeper talk." Chandrey didn't hide her disgust. "You sound like the rest of them."

"I sound like them, because I *am* one of them." Zhastra sighed and lowered her voice. "For Belsas's sake, listen, Chandrey, please." She began to rise, hesitated, and returned to her position though her body lay lighter across Chandrey's. "I'm not stopping you. I'm helping you."

"I've been patient for over four passes." Chandrey twisted beneath Zhastra.

"Then what's a bit longer?" Zhastra let go with one hand to smooth her palm across Chandrey's forehead.

"Longer?" Chandrey couldn't feel a phase coming from the healer, but she felt her outrage fading, and after a moment, her breathing settled.

"I knew you wouldn't take that very well." Zhastra moved to her side. "But I never imagined—" She propped up on an elbow as Chandrey had before. "You're quite powerful when motivated. It's positively erotic." She cast one of her multi meaning smiles. "But you're also horribly impulsive. Patience is a crucial skill, a tactic. I can help you master it, if you'll let me."

"You've done quite enough today, thank you." Chandrey lay still beside Zhastra, thinking of all the things she still had to gather. She and Belsas could escape the clan, but how far overland would they have to go to escape Cleave lands? And she needed binders. If the Cleave could sense them, they could track them.

Slow down. Zhastra gazed sidelong at her. *The storerooms probably hold most everything you need, aside from a map.* She pressed tightly against Chandrey. *You have time enough.*

Zhastra studied her for a moment, and then eased her leg over, pulling Chandrey's legs slightly apart as she raised her shift. *Patience.* Her phase deepened as well.

I thought—

Patience. Zhastra slid her hand down Chandrey's side, to her hip and inward.

I—Chandrey sucked in air as Zhastra's phase hold crept out further than her fingers to press into her.

Shh. Patience. Zhastra's fingers were persistent, peeling her from the blankets. *One more lesson. A grand one.*

Zhastra smiled thoughtfully as she pressed, raising Chandrey close to pleasure, and then slowing so the sensation waned just enough. *Patience. It will happen in time.*

Chandrey writhed beneath Zhastra's fingers.

Zhastra, clearly enjoying her agony, was perfect in her timing. Another near explosion and Chandrey sank again, begging for release. *Quit rushing.* Zhastra removed her hand for a second, but only a second. *Not until I say.* She moved in again, just as insistent as before.

Chandrey muffled a moan in her shoulder.

Wait. Zhastra's phase voice steamed.

I can't. Please. Chandrey pounded her hand against the bed.

Quiet. Zhastra pulled Chandrey's leg tighter to her, separating her thighs more. *You'll do this because you must.* She dove in again, one hand on Chandrey's shoulder, the other held flat, palm down. She rubbed hard, but Chandrey managed silence under her, as intent on the sensations as she was on keeping control.

Excellent. Zhastra kicked Chandrey's legs wider apart to replace her hand with her body, smacking down in short bursts. *Embrace what comes, but don't let it win until I say.* She rose long enough to slip off her leggings, slide a pillow under Chandrey's hips, and ease Chandrey's hands above her head where she held them. *'And you'll learn from the suffering.'*

Wise Mother Words. Chandrey could only mouth her recognition.

Zhastra felt harsh against her, pushing, gritting her teeth with the effort. *Hold it.* Her phase commanded above everything else.

Chandrey complied, biting her tongue to keep her cries at bay.

You'll wait! Zhastra didn't slow this time, didn't stop, gave no sign of ending her joyous torture until Chandrey began to beg again. *Silence.* Zhastra tensed against her, shifting her push to a steady grind as her breath quickened. *Soon.* She reared back to grind harder, and then dropped and slid her mouth over Chandrey's, tangling them even closer together.

Sweet Mother, finish me, Zhastra, I beg you.

When I say. Zhastra pulled back to look at her. *Only when I say.* She combined Chandrey's hands under her right hand, and reached down with her left, running a finger down Chandrey's side.

The slightest touch caused Chandrey to arch her back, all but losing control. *Yes.* When Zhastra repeated the sensation, Chandrey's concentration shattered and everything shook, something Zhastra mirrored.

Now!

The explosion which followed consumed them both.

Times like these, I realize how old I really am. Zhastra's entire body quaked as she fell to one side and released her phase. "Now, if you can contain yourself through that," she said, mopping the sweat from her face, "you can certainly wait a bit longer."

"I think you're right." Chandrey curled into Zhastra's side, too drained to move or say more.

"Patience, beautiful woman," mumbled Zhastra against Chandrey's head. "Your freedom will come soon enough."

* * *

Chandrey woke alone.

"Place her on the table," someone said.

Chandrey heard a thump in the next room.

"Keep pressure!" cried someone else.

Panic clearly filled the area. Chandrey wanted to know, but was still a bit woozy, and a thrall who stuck her head in the middle of a keeper crisis might just lose that head, so she stayed put and listened. Patience. She'd find out soon enough.

"Step back!" Chandrey heard Zhastra pushing other women aside. "Dear Mother! What happened to—don't stop the pressure!"

"Keep her leg still." That came from Zhastra's apprentice.

"Where's her daughter?" asked someone. "Anybody commed her yet?"

"Blood's everywhere."

"Anyone see it happen?" Zhastra again.

"I just heard the yell."

"Me too." Zhastra's apprentice again. "I grabbed my kit and came running, but it took a few minutes to find her."

"How long from then until you got here?" The bed in the other room pulsed through its scan, setting off a series of alarms. "How long?"

"Ten minutes?"

"Thereabouts."

"Too long," said Zhastra. Someone turned off the alarms. "How much synth-blood has she had?"

"Everything in my kit," said her apprentice. "Five more since she got here."

Chandrey felt the anxiety which permeated the now silent room as a new alarm began to sound, long, low, and steady until someone turned it off.

"It wasn't for lack of trying." Zhastra sounded winded. "The synth-blood wouldn't have mattered anyway. She bled out as quick as we put it in." Chandrey heard her open, and then close the tall cabinet against the wall. "All of you, go home and change. No reason for the family to know how it really was. I'll move her to another room and clean her up."

The others mumbled, but they did leave, and the room fell silent again. "Chandrey?" Zhastra tapped on the wall. "Come see."

Chandrey slid back into her shift, pulled a blanket over her shoulders, and padded to where Zhastra stood in the doorway.

"Look past the blood. Past the mess," said Zhastra. "Look at the face."

Blood didn't bother Chandrey, it never had, but the face...the pale-on-pale face of a dead Taelach moved her deeply. This face, however, brought a mix of emotions. "She bled to death?"

"Both femoral arteries were cut." Zhastra pushed a gurney against the cleaner side of the table, and with some effort pulled the body onto it. "You know what this means?"

"Aside from another pyre, not really." Chandrey moved to assist, but Zhastra waved her away.

"Provisional power is familial. Her daughter has control until the pedagogues choose a replacement."

"Uh-uh." Chandrey stumbled back. "She can't be put in control—no, Zhastra. No!"

"Go to your room in the house wing and remain there until I come for you."

"She'll send for me as soon as she finds out." Chandrey looked around the room for a weapon. Any weapon.

"She can't make any claims until after the pyre." Zhastra pushed the gurney into the room across the hall. "A pyre you won't be attending." She turned back to grasp Chandrey, shoving her toward the family wing. "Go."

"She'll be here tonight."

"Yes, but she doesn't have power."

"But she'll feel me. She'll know I know."

"She expects you to be frightened," said Zhastra. "Give her what she wants so she won't suspect." With that, she shoved Chandrey through the door.

I wasn't wrong about patience. Zhastra's phase followed her to her room. *Now you'll need it more than ever.*

Chandrey buried her face in Mitsu's back and tried to stay calm by repeating prayers.

* * *

Ten of them came—the future clan leader and nine of her followers against one aging healer in her nightclothes.

"Bring her!" Cance's voice rose from just outside the locked door. "Or so help me, Zhastra, you'll be treating yourself for serious injuries."

"I know the laws, Cancelynn. She's mine until morning."

"Don't spew archaic decrees to me, you old bitch. I'll work my way through every one of your pitiful thralls to get her if that's what it takes." Supportive jeers leached through walls that were every bit as thin as Zhastra had warned.

"They've done nothing to deserve your rage."

Chandrey imagined Zhastra, wizened by time and strong in fortitude, facing the challenge.

"Which one should I start with? Stroked out Giana? She'd break easy enough. Oh, no, I'd pick little Tamberly. I bet she's a delight to fuck."

"Don't."

Chandrey could all but see Cance beaming at the implied admission. "Oh, so you haven't? Unfortunate. Well, I'll be certain to share the details."

Chandrey couldn't understand their next exchange of words, but a moment later, Cance's tone hardened. "Come tomorrow, I can take any or all of them, Chandrey included. Should I wait and expand my thralls by fourteen, or will you give me what I came for?"

Mitsu stirred against Chandrey and turned onto her back. "Whats you doing?" she mumbled.

"Shh." Chandrey looked down at Mitsu as she phase nudged her back asleep. Cance would be taking her as well. It was Mitsu's greatest fear, which she had tearfully admitted during one of their healing talks.

Chandrey watched her sleep for a moment: content, wanted, valued and oblivious to what was happening nearby. She'd learned to read quickly once she'd been allowed to do so. Cance would fault her for it, beat her so she'd forget, always be watching to ensure she didn't pass on the skill. All of Zhastra's life mates would endure the same treatment. All those unique, talented minds that Zhastra had saved.

Chandrey burst through the door between the infirmary wings. "Leave them alone!"

"Well, well, well." Cance clasped her hands. "I knew if I pressed hard enough someone would crack, but I hadn't suspected it'd be you."

"You'll not!" Zhastra pulled Chandrey to her. "The laws clearly state—"

"Will you shut up?" Cance motioned to Chandrey. "Come on. I haven't got all night."

"It's okay." Chandrey kissed Zhastra on the cheek. "I have to go."

Patience. Zhastra grew calm against her, understanding, accepting. "We must obey." She stepped back. "The clan leader has claimed you."

Cance held out her hand. "Chandresslandra."

Chandrey lowered her head and stepped forward. "Clan Leader Cancelynn." Her hand slid into Cance's.

"Such obedience." Cance twisted Chandrey's arm behind her back. "Let's see how long it lasts."

She spirited them away from the infirmary in such haste that Chandrey could barely keep up. Cance's cronies followed behind. They spoke little, but oh, their leers when she looked back! Chandrey refocused on the path in front of her. One step at a time. One breath at a time. Patience.

Moments later, she and Cance stood on the doorstep of Creiloff—no, Cance's home. Cance told her cronies when they should return and opened the door. Creiloff's five remaining life mates, in various states of dress, obediently lined the front foyer alongside Cance's two thralls. They didn't look up, but Chandrey saw them observing just like she did, by watching feet. She was barefoot. They were barefoot. Another for the slaughter.

"Welcome home, Precious." Cance dragged her past the others and up the stairs leading to the second-floor master suite. Inside the door, she tore Chandrey's shift from her, pushed her prone on the bedding, and stood over her. "Scars?" She slapped the backs of Chandrey's legs. "Where'd those come from?"

"You." Chandrey made certain her voice rose above the pillows.

"Oh, yeah. I forgot." Cance crawled on top of her, pressing her knees into the small of Chandrey's back as she pulled her head back by the hair. "Thought you were safe, didn't you? Thought that bitch Zhastra had saved you? Ha!"

She slipped her legs down and ground her crotch into Chandrey's back so hard, her hide pants rubbed away the skin. "So where should we begin? A lesson to help you remember what I like?" Cance hummed as she continued to gyrate and push, and with every move, her hands tightened in Chandrey's hair. "No, that's not enough of a welcome home gift."

"How kind." Chandrey clenched her teeth against the burn as Cance dropped her head in favor of her shoulders.

"You have no fucking idea how kind I'm being." Cance lay fully on top of her, shoving Chandrey's face into the bedding as she picked up speed. "You'll be showered with gifts tonight and every night from here on out, Precious." Cance tensed and grunted, and then stopped her grinding. "Our oath night was better, but who am I to criticize?"

She rose and flipped Chandrey onto her back, smiling when she winced. "Oh, did that hurt you, lover? Did it burn? Are you raw?" Cance looked down at her leathers. "Oh, you bled. So sorry." She cleaned the hide with Chandrey's shift. "Certainly better than what Zhastra gave you tonight."

"Jealous?" Chandrey bore the punch to the stomach she received as answer.

"And she said she'd retrained you." Cance balled her fist for another blow.

"Oh, she trained me." Chandrey blocked the next punch and landed a return blow on Cance's jaw.

Momentary bedlam ensued. Chandrey fought Cance in every way Zhastra had taught her. Cance returned as much as she received, and soon both of them stood gasping in the middle of the room.

Chandrey's leg was scraped badly from a fall against a clothing press. Cance's tunic was torn and her face marked by a trio of deep scratches down one cheek.

Only then, in the heat of their physical battle, did Cance push her mind into Chandrey's. But she even met resistance there. Zhastra had taught her how to shield herself from phase attacks. The defense wasn't perfect, but Cance had to spend a significant amount of energy tearing the shield down, leaving considerably less power at her disposal.

"The old bitch really did teach you a thing or two," gasped Cance after her third unsuccessful attempt at control. "You're a little bit of a challenge now."

She suddenly kicked out, sweeping Chandrey's legs out from under her so she fell back onto the bedding. *Emphasis on little.* Cance was on Chandrey then, her mind as quick as her kick in its assault.

Chandrey cried out and grabbed her head. "Stop. Stop. Stop!" Cance's phase-burn consumed her. She swallowed hard and tried to focus on the energy, wanting to turn it, but nothing happened.

"Nice try." Cance pulled a strip of hide from her pocket and secured Chandrey's hands. She sank her face into Chandrey's hair and nosed her ear, sending a disgusted chill down her spine. "What? You don't like our playtime? I'm wounded, Precious. I really am." She sat back to pull Chandrey upright on the bedding. "You changed our game without telling me. Imagine my surprise. If I had known…"

Chandrey wouldn't answer the taunt.

"Oh, wait, I know what I can do to bring things up to your new standards." Cance smiled broadly. "You'll like this one, Precious." She tied Chandrey's feet with a second piece of hide, paralyzing her with a phase when she resisted. "I can hardly wait to see your expression."

She left Chandrey alone in the dark, locking the door from the outside. No one would help her. No one could. She had no outlet, no recourse at that point—only time.

It was early morning. Chandrey was cold so she began to work at opening some bedding. It took effort, but she managed to unfold a comforter and wiggle beneath. The comforter was soft and she was exhausted enough to sleep.

"Precious." Not Cance's voice.

Chandrey started. The heavy drapes blocked all but the smallest streaks of light. She sensed no mental presence. There was no noise at all. A dream. She began to settle again.

Something moved beneath the comforter.

She cringed as something warm and tendril-like touched her leg.

"Who's there?" Chandrey kicked her bound feet and the tendril disappeared.

Someone chuckled and the comforter slid away. The tendrils returned. Hands this time, scratching across her belly. The nails were long, digging in to knead her flesh.

Chandrey scooted back. "Get away."

"Why shoulds I?" The accent was undeniable—Aut-laced Taelach.

"Who are you?" Chandrey furthered the distance, pushing back with her legs.

"Not gonna tells." A hand grabbed her ankle, dragging her back for more aggressive pinching and scratching.

"Stop it!" Chandrey squirmed away again, flailing with her elbows until she hit something solid—the wall.

"Gotcha now." A body slipped beside her, pulling her down. Sharp hip bones poked her side. Thin legs ran along her own. Hands jerked her arms above her head and held hard to her wrists. The someone smelled of herbs, of pungent slip root and sweet Mother's hat, and of filth, of dirt, spoiled food, sweat and—

"Let's plays." The someone descended fully upon her, crueler than Cance had ever been.

Chapter Twenty-Nine

Abend—inevitable end, crash, sudden halt

Zhastra paced the hallway outside Belsas's room. She'd fed her the slip root, mixed in jam, but Belsas hadn't eaten much of it on her bread and now the tray lay outside her room.

Zhastra stopped at the tray each time she passed, glaring as if it were somehow guilty. If the root was going to take effect, it would be soon. That's the only way things would begin to happen, the only way she could—

"Someone, please." Belsas's call sounded weak. She'd fought two post surgical infections this time and now verged on a third.

Zhastra slipped between the guards, entered the room, and closed the door. Belsas had the right to this much privacy, at least in her infirmary.

Belsas had been borne to the infirmary in formal fashion by armored land launch and carried in on a float. The Practitioner's orders were direct. Belsas's cervix had been sealed, sewn this time, and she was bedbound until the process completed. Tavince expected daily reports.

Zhastra saw that Belsas had rolled on her side, clutching her stomach as her feet strained against the bonds.

"Don't fight it." Zhastra moved to the side of the bed. "Let it happen naturally."

"Let it happen?" Belsas ventured a look at Zhastra. "They sealed me like a tomb."

"They can't stop the inevitable," soothed Zhastra. "They can't force what the Mother never intended."

"Please. If one lives, they say they'll let me go."

"We both know better." Zhastra gazed at the monitors above the bed. Belsas's blood pressure and respiration were high. The woman was necessarily stressed, but she couldn't let the stress be known, so she hooked a recorder into the monitors, replacing Belsas's true vitals with an earlier recording. "You give them one, and they'll insist on twenty more. This New Cleave doesn't keep to its promises or laws." She touched Belsas's forehead. "You're fevered."

"I've stayed sick this time."

"Our bodies are designed to reject invaders." Zhastra wet a cloth and returned to the bedside, where she cleaned Belsas's face. "This one will kill you if I don't intercede."

Belsas couldn't answer right away. She bore through a wave of pain, and then dared another look at Zhastra. "Why me?"

"Chance. Circumstance. I don't really know." Zhastra stepped from the room, returning a moment later with a glass of orange powders mixed to the consistency of syrup. She slid the door shut again. "This will give you what you want." She kept her voice hushed.

Belsas took the glass with trembling hands. "Why help me this time and not before?"

"Everything has changed." Zhastra motioned her to drink, which Belsas did without further comment. She gave the glass back to Zhastra and lay down to wait, bearing another wave before the strong mix began to take effect.

Zhastra removed Belsas's binder to make her more comfortable. "It'll be over soon."

Belsas slipped away for a moment, but awakened when Zhastra began gathering surgical instruments. She pushed in a phase. Belsas slipped away again, deeper than before, unconscious so long she feared that in the woman's weakened state, she'd become comatose.

When Belsas woke, Zhastra stood at the barred window, gazing at the medicinal garden.

"You lied." Belsas reached up to touch the binder.

"How do you feel?" Zhastra didn't look at her.

"Like a fool." Belsas didn't seem as fatigued or uncomfortable.

"Then we feel the same." Zhastra finally turned to look squarely at Belsas. "You thought I was going to end your life."

Belsas said nothing.

"But you're still here so now you think me as cruel as the rest."

Belsas nodded ever so slightly.

"So did Chandrey when she first came to me."

"Liar." Belsas crossed her arms over her chest. "Cance would never let her go."

"But she had to for a while. And when she did, Chandrey came to me."

"Then where is she?" asked Belsas.

"Cance." Zhastra said the name with such abhorrence, she knew Belsas would understand she had an ally. "She took Chandrey four days ago."

"And you let her?"

"She went of her own accord." Zhastra held up her hand. "When Cancelynn threatened my household, she rushed out. She sacrificed herself to protect them." She stood at the end of the bed, where she cast Belsas an appraising look. "She was planning to rescue you this time."

"And you'd have let her?"

"More like help her. Neither of you belong here." Zhastra looked to the closed door. "Time was when guards weren't needed. Time was when you could trust your clan." She returned her gaze to her patient. "Time was when you could rely on your clan leader."

"Creiloff?"

"Cance, now."

"How?"

"She has someone doing her dirty work."

"Someone always does her dirty work. I did without thinking until she got out of hand."

Zhastra raised her brows at the confession. "You know her?"

"Very well." Belsas explained her history with both Chandrey and Cance, how they had all met, how Cance had destabilized after her injuries. She seemed tired by the end of the conversation, but eager to make her own plans—plans to save Chandrey.

"Impatience must be a Kinship trait," said Zhastra. She had left Belsas's room once that evening to retrieve dinner from the household side of the infirmary. Their mugs sat untouched on the bedside table. "Though you are more organized in your planning than Chandrey."

Belsas glowered. "You picked me?"

"While you were unconscious. I had to see what Chandrey found so compelling about you." Zhastra was a bit saddened by the admission. "What made her choose you over me."

"Choose me?"

"You seem surprised."

"I never knew until now."

"Did I miss something in my examination?" Zhastra squinted at Belsas. "You don't look blind."

"No, I was just in denial."

"The curse of the young." Zhastra rocked on her heels, and went to the head of the bed to tinker with the monitor settings. "I took a long scan when you first came in and began looping it before your procedure. They won't look close enough to notice the difference."

"Procedure," repeated Belsas dryly. "How clinical that sounds."

"Nothing that happened to you is natural." She passed Belsas a blunt eating blade and one of the dinner mugs. "It's Sabra's turn to cook." She sniffed her own mug, feeling none too pleased. "You're warned."

Belsas took a few bites and set her mug aside. "I'm not much hungry." She lay back and pulled her blanket higher, mumbling when she found her ankles still bound to the bed.

"You'll eat." Zhastra thrust the mug at her. "Sabra's stew isn't burned beyond recognition this time, and you need the strength."

Belsas sat back up to eat. "When will you release me?"

"When it's time." Zhastra frowned when something crunched in her otherwise overcooked dinner. "When it's safe to proceed."

"And when will that be?"

"When you're stronger, but before Cance finds out you're here."

"My shackles?"

"Guards outside, remember?" Zhastra nodded toward the door.

"Apparently not." Belsas managed to finish dinner and lay back a second time.

She appeared exceptionally tired now. Zhastra thought this was probably the most conversation she'd had since her abduction, and the interaction itself was healing.

"Rest." Zhastra pulled a second blanket from a cabinet and covered her patient. "I owe you an apology." She touched Belsas's forehead. No fever.

"For?" Belsas yawned.

"For judging you. For judging everyone outside the Cleave."

Zhastra touched Belsas's hairline, and then reached behind to loosen her binder. The electronics beeped. Belsas sighed as fresh air slid across the bridge of her nose.

"You're strong of faith. Strong of heart. A true Mother's child, just like Chandrey," Zhastra went on. She stood over Belsas a moment more, observing and coming to some sort of peace within herself. "'When ten thousand split a million ways and the world hangs over the rift, one shall shed her disguise—strong of heart, strong of faith, a child of the Mother shall rise to unite them.' Do you recognize the verse?"

"Yes," said Belsas. "Wise Mother Words."

"They're about change, about the need to change." Zhastra turned to the door. "They're about what's happening now." She paused and glanced over her shoulder. "You're no prophet, Belsas, but the Mother has put you here for a reason." She opened the door. "Don't let Her down."

Chapter Thirty

Kinship Governmental Facilities: Saria III

Vessel—*container; carrier; agent*

Fifteen passes together and Brava knew almost nothing about her life mate.

For the first time ever, Kylis returned early from a retreat, but certainly not of her own accord. Brava had called her back when Benjimena passed, when her appointment had been finalized, but Kylis failed to answer her com messages, even the emergency flagged ones. In fact, Kylis had to be physically tracked down, and had been positively irate when she'd been forced back to Saria III "by order of the Taelach of All."

Brava was briefed before Kylis's arrival on where she'd been found, relative to a recent Kinship-Cleave skirmish site. Furthermore, reported the trooper in charge of the detail entrusted with Kylis's protection, a small disposable com had been found in the lining of her baggage.

"Cryptology has it now," said the trooper with a bow as another trooper led Kylis into Brava's workroom.

"I'm being treated like a common criminal!" The amber phase binder on Kylis's face couldn't hide her displeasure. "Remove this binder."

The trooper shook her head when Brava looked inquiringly at her. "I'm sorry, Sister Kylis, but I can't remove the binder until you've been completely cleared by security." She deferred to Brava. "I'll be just out the door, Grandmaster Brava."

Brava, not used to hearing the Taelach of All's military title applied to her own name, took a second to acknowledge, and then she looked at Kylis. She searched her life mate's expression, trying to see some external change, some clue that she had missed anything, but she saw nothing, sensed nothing. Kylis simply looked like Kylis, as pious as ever.

"Sit down, please," she said.

"You're Taelach of All?" Kylis asked when they were alone. "When did this happen?"

"It's temporary until elections," said Brava. "I thought you were on Saria IV. Why'd they find you on Myflar?"

"The Saria IV meditation facilities were unusually crowded, so I moved to a more rural location." Kylis half smiled at Brava. "What do the Plan elders say about your new position?"

"I didn't expect their support, but the Kinship needed me."

"All the way down to the uniform." Kylis's smile faded. "Why am I bindered?"

"Security protocol." Brava rested her hands on the arms of her chair. Her robes had been put away and she was in military dress, but her position and the war dictated what she wore at the moment. "Why were you so difficult to find?"

"I always turn off my com during my retreats. You know that." Kylis looked around the room. "Benjimena's things are still sitting here. You'd work better if you'd make it yours."

"In time." Even through Kylis's binder, Brava felt her life mate's presence. "The emergency features of your personal com were deactivated. You know that's illegal."

"I wasn't aware they were off line." Kylis laced and unlaced her fingers together in her lap. "If you're busy, I could help you redecorate."

"Later." Brava wrapped her hands tighter around the arms of her chair, Benjimena's former seat. "Your launch's flight recorder was deactivated as well."

"Was it?" Kylis smoothed her robes. "Maybe someone should check the leasing service."

"It's being done."

"You're so formal," said Kylis. "This new position must be stressful."

"Stressful?" Brava pondered the dichotomy between her life mate's concerned tone and the anger she sensed. "We're at war. Sisters are dying. Our daughter—"

"Is dead to us." Kylis looked at Brava with sad, amber-tinted eyes whose expression finally matched her voice. "Why do you torture me by mentioning her?"

"She's among the enemy," said Brava in a near rage. How could she know the truth? Why was she so certain Kylis lied? "Did you know about the com in your bag?"

"Of course not." Kylis touched her binder. "I barely use the one you make me carry. Why would I possibly need another? A new rug would brighten this place up."

"The rug is new. Quit changing the topic."

"Then explain your sudden suspicion," said Kylis. "Those troopers descended on me in the middle of silent meditation. They wouldn't even let me finish my prayer! Really, Brava, you simply must do something about—"

"They were acting on my orders."

Kylis stopped to stare. "But why?"

"We're at war, Kylis. At war!"

"You're at war. The Kinship is at war. You know my views, the Plan's view on violence." Kylis clasped her hands. "They used to be your views too."

"Not when sisters are dying because of their judged lack of faith." Brava drummed her fingers on the worktable. Kylis was bindered, so what did she sense? "There isn't a Wise Mother's Word to explain or justify what's happening along the Kinship borders."

"You exaggerate." Kylis dismissed everything with a wave. "Auts and sisters will always be fighting. They're but tiny skirmishes. You're really making too much of all this."

Brava's mood darkened. She sat forward in her seat, leaning across the table to face her life mate. "This is Taelach on Taelach fighting."

"Bah," spat Kylis. "Sisters of faith don't kill each other."

"The Cleave kills everyone they deem slattern—including daughters above toddler age."

"The Cleave doesn't kill little girls."

"How would you know?"

"I know what I overheard during my forced return." Kylis leaned forward as well. "I know what I know from fifteen passes with you. You've gotten what you've always wanted—power within the Kinship. You're its voice. Its political mouthpiece. Now you're making up lies about a minority group to further your power." Kylis scowled. But her mental presence, Brava noted, was almost amused. Again, Kylis was bindered, so how could she be sensing her at all? "'Power is a consuming distraction. It draws the wielder from the path, blinds her to the way.'"

"Wise Mother's Words," said Brava, but she didn't back down. "That verse concerns trust, not murder."

"So you interpret the Word as well?" Kylis scoffed. "How power hungry you've become. What's next, openly attacking the Cleave for their beliefs?"

"What do *you* know about the Cleave? What do you know about *any* of this? You've been gone for three cycles, Kylis. Three!"

"First the Cleave, then what? The Plan? When will our beliefs get in your way?" Kylis became calm and deliberate in her choice of words. "Should I give myself over to you now, Brava? Because nothing you say or do will make me forsake my beliefs." She held out her hands, wrists up in submission.

"Drama." Brava slid back in her seat. "How do you think it looks when the Taelach of All's life mate is found near a skirmish line and in possession of an encrypted com?"

"Looks bad, doesn't it?" Kylis reached across the worktable to stroke the back of Brava's hand. "Sorry about what I said. These are troubling times, and I'm worried. I'd hoped to spend a little time with you when I got back, but things have suddenly become so complicated."

"They are complicated." Despite herself, Brava enjoyed the touch. It had been a very, very long time.

"I know." Kylis continued to hold Brava's hand as she rounded the table to slip into her lap. She laid her head on Brava's shoulder and kissed her tenderly on the neck.

Brava felt her tensions release, so she turned her head to kiss her life mate back, first on the face, and then the mouth.

Kylis responded in kind. They pressed together in brief passion. "Let me out of this binder and take me home, my beautiful, brave Brava."

Brava opened her mouth to call in the trooper, and then paused and pulled back. Kylis never called her pet names, never exhibited the sort of affection she was now. They hadn't kissed in passes or made love since their second anniversary.

When Kylis moved in for another kiss, Brava wrapped a hand around her head to pull her closer. Midway, she stopped, and leaned back and away, avoiding Kylis's mouth.

"I knew I could feel you a bit too much." Brava pushed Kylis from her lap, forcing her to stand as her binder sagged on her face. "Get away."

"Why?" Kylis spun around as Brava spoke into her desk com.

"She's ready for escort."

Kylis shook her head at the three troopers who entered. To Brava's mortification, the troopers backed off. "And to think, it only took fifteen passes to begin figuring things out." Kylis pulled the binder from her face in one hard pull and motioned to the troopers.

Brava was bound with the same binder before she could fully comprehend what was happening. She felt far more than betrayed by Kylis. She felt forsaken—used. Seduced and abandoned. No wonder she had been miserable with Kylis. The Mother had absolutely nothing to do with their being brought together.

The lead trooper who had been in charge of the investigation cleared her throat.

"Where do things currently stand?" Kylis turned back to the trooper as Brava was spun around to watch.

"The council has been gathered per your order." The trooper frowned. "Will your life mate be joining them?"

"Call her that again and you're dead." Kylis returned to the worktable where she lounged in the Taelach of All's seat. "Perfect fit." She and the trooper exchanged smiles. "She witnesses the council's lessoning. Proceed as planned, Keeper Lionel."

"As you wish, Missionary." Lionel motioned to the other troopers.

Brava was dragged away. She was powerless, removed from the room, from power, from hope. Worst of all, she'd never seen any of it coming.

Chapter Thirty-One

Feral—*wild, to be wild after domesticity or capture*

Close to the ground. Head down. Binder tight.

Belsas didn't need need the reminders, but she practiced them just the same as she lowered her body over the grass. It felt good to have control over herself, felt good for her body to be her own. She still had twinges, but Zhastra had said she would for a while. It was part of the healing process, her body returning to its normal shape. And she was stronger now, both mentally and physically. Zhastra had helped there as well.

Belsas found her an odd woman, a dichotomy of keeper and healer. Hard but empathetic. Demanding but educating. Zhastra was a Cleave keeper in the classic sense, she'd surmised during her time in the infirmary, and one determined the Cleave should return to its original principles—caring for the Kinship's rejects, even if it meant defying the current powers.

She glanced back at the infirmary. She'd spent too much time there, but it had been necessary. It had taken almost thirty days for Belsas to regain her strength. Zhastra had made the most of those days, filling her with strengthening herbs and teaching her muscle toning-exercises she could do without drawing her guards' attention.

Two seven-days before her planned escape, Zhastra had started taking her outside her barred window in the predawn hours to work on her endurance. At that time of the morning, the guards didn't notice, but a small dose of powder in their morning tea, brought to them by Zhastra, didn't hurt, either.

Now Belsas checked her binder again and tightened her backpack. She'd scaled the infirmary garden wall without much trouble, followed Zhastra's directions to the Granary Leader's residence, and now hugged the ground outside.

Chandrey was inside, in the second-floor suite. Zhastra had found that out from her apprentice, the only healer allowed to treat Cance's household. Chandrey had been treated twice, once for a deep laceration to her shoulder, again for dehydration. She'd become animalistic, said Zhastra, functioning on only the most primal level.

From the brush near the house, Belsas took time to watch the comings and goings at the house. Guards walked lazily across the grounds, messengers and deliverers came and went, thralls came out to hang laundry, but no Chandrey. The upstairs curtains were drawn and the windows bore what Zhastra had said were recently installed exterior bars. Chandrey was up there, she was certain, but where was Cance? Her plan depended on Cance being away.

Four hours passed. At midafternoon, Cance emerged with two guards on her heels as she walked toward the main granary buildings. She passed near Belsas, but she was rushed and the binder hid any mental signs.

Belsas waited until Cance faded. When the remaining guard pair retreated to the shady porch, she moved carefully within the landscaping to the edge of the yard where she crouched behind a damp blanket that dragged the ground under the clothesline.

When the household quieted, Belsas removed her binder and went into action, walking boldly to the back door and knocking, just like a keeper would. One of Cance's thralls, Elisa by Zhastra's description, parted the door.

She looked briefly at Belsas, and then looked down. "Cancelynn says business comes through the front."

Elisa obviously thought Belsas keeper, and she did look the part. Zhastra had supplied her with leathers, a closely fitting jerkin, tall boots and the all-important close haircut. The clothing and boots were worn but serviceable, and the haircut was bad, but in a general keeper style that matched the back story Zhastra had given her.

Belsas was supposed to be from the Shepard clan, a community of a half-dozen families who came into contact with the rest of the Cleave only once or twice a pass for trade purposes. They were a very self-sufficient group and believed in using everything until it couldn't be patched anymore—hence Belsas's worn clothing.

Zhastra had said it would get her into the house, and she was right. After a few simple questions, which Belsas replied to in an irritated, keeperesque tone, Elisa let her in and led her to Cance's workroom, where she asked her to wait in one of the low chairs. Cance would be back in a while, she said and left.

Another thrall appeared a moment later with a mug of wine which Belsas took, but set aside as soon as she was alone.

Neither thrall had looked her in the eye, only Elisa has spoken to her, and that had been in the briefest and politest fashion. The thralls weren't stupid, but they were certainly naïve and very afraid of crossing a keeper. She hated to exploit them, but it would get her to Chandrey.

While she waited for the right moment, she crept into Elisa's mind, learning the home's general layout, the location and activities of everyone inside the home, and the thrall's absolute fear of her keeper and those who followed her.

When everyone seemed occupied with their given duties, Belsas slipped from the workroom and up the stairs to the suite. The door was locked from the outside.

"Damn." Belsas dropped her pack and examined the lock. Simple mechanism, four number code, but what numbers? She only had five tries before the system triggered an alarm.

What numbers might Cance have used? Most used something familiar, so Belsas thought hard about which numbers which might be important enough to Cance. Her claiming date? The lock clicked, but didn't open. The date she joined the military? Two clicks, but nothing more. Date of her Langus injuries? Three clicks, a hiss, but that was all.

Belsas stopped, considering whether she should keep going. She had one more try without consequences, so she moved quickly, clicking out a simple code—the entrance code to their first dorm room together. The numbers took and the bolt slid back with a faint clunk.

The room was silent, save for a faint rustle of blankets. She felt one presence—Chandrey's, she thought. Somewhat different, darker, more complex than she remembered, but people changed, and Chandrey had had plenty of reasons.

Belsas slid on her pack, stepped inside, and pushed the door to, but not quite shut. "Chandrey?"

Across the room, a curtain moved, allowing in a narrow ray of morning sunlight. Belsas saw a trembling hand, the nails bitten to the quick. "Shh."

"It's Bel." Belsas felt along the wall in search of a light. "Can you get up?"

"Shh." Chandrey moved so she showed in the light. She was gaunt, her hair matted and mussed, and naked from what Belsas could see.

"Where's the light?" Belsas moved the other direction, feeling blindly along the wall, but never taking her eyes from Chandrey.

"Shh." The sound was hard, desperate.

"Okay," whispered Belsas. "But Cance isn't here. I saw her leave." She gave up on the light and began to move slowly across the room, trying not to catch her feet on the miscellaneous shadows on the floor. *Bedding*, she thought as something gave against the toe of her boot.

She'd gone halfway across when Chandrey hissed at her, a low warning.

Belsas stopped. "What?"

"Shh."

Belsas took another step and Chandrey hissed again, deeper, longer, lower.

"I don't understand," whispered Belsas. Chandrey didn't move. "Can you come to me?"

Chandrey shook her head.

"Are you hurt?"

Chandrey shook her head again.

Can you phase speak? Belsas tried.

Chandrey let out something of a mental growl, and then pushed Belsas from her mind.

"Then help me," said Belsas. "What do I do next?"

Chandrey looked down and shook her head, but she crept forward, her back against the wall. "Shh," she repeated and moved a bit more, edging along very slowly.

At this rate, we'll be here all evening, Belsas phased at her. *Cance will be back sooner or later.*

Chandrey hissed and closed off her mind, but she continued moving, stopping just on the other side of the window. She pressed against the wall, her breathing rapid. She looked at the floor. Belsas followed her line of sight, but couldn't see what she focused on.

"Chandrey?"

"Shh!"

Belsas froze. Something moved in the bedding in front of

Chandrey, who breathed raggedly, her mind slipping open to fill the air with panic.

"Whats you doing up?" An Aut accent? Belsas held her breath. "Comes here."

Chandrey disappeared from view as a shadowed arm reached out to pull the curtain closed.

In a sudden burst of pure adrenaline, Belsas bounded over the form and jerked the curtain back, flooding the room with afternoon sunlight.

Chandrey shrieked and cowered in the corner as the silhouette covered its face.

When Belsas's eyes adjusted, she became aware of her adversary—Taelach, bindered, naked, cadaverously thin, but quick, alive and furious as she grabbed for the blade strapped to her bare ankle.

"Who's you?" demanded the woman in a sleep-gruff voice. She looked somewhat like Cance.

Belsas squinted at her, trying to make sense of what she saw. "Who're you?" She pulled her blade—a worn, but well-edged knife given to her by Zhastra—from her belt sheath.

The woman smirked and twirled her blade as she rose to her full height. "Cancey said kills anyone who comes in besides her."

"You do everything Cance tells you?" Belsas motioned for Chandrey to stay still.

"Whatcha doings here? Huh?" The woman stepped forward. "Whatcha wants?"

"To leave." Belsas took a single step back. "With Chandrey."

"Not happenin'." The woman made a lean, toothy grin and licked her cracked lips. "Cancey gaves her to me." Behind her, Chandrey began to edge around again, "Don't you fuckin' moves," she snapped over her shoulder. Chandrey shrank against the wall.

"Oh, no, Chandrey, come right on." Belsas pushed her way into Chandrey's mind as much as she dared while watching Cance's long-haired, sickly looking double. *No one owns you.*

Chandrey broadcast one word before pushing Belsas out. *Brandoff.*

"Brandoff?" repeated Belsas, and the woman started.

"Hows you know my name?" The woman glared at Chandrey. "I'm gonna cuts your tongue loose for that one." Her gaze returned to Belsas. "But you firsts."

Brandoff dropped to the floor and swung out with one leg to knock Belsas off balance, but she leaped over the kick and came down on either side of Brandoff's leg, catching her thigh to pull and twist.

Brandoff growled and struck with her knife, grazing the side of Belsas's calf until she let loose and stumbled backward beside Chandrey.

"Gots you both now." Brandoff leered. When she rose, her twisted leg refused to cooperate. She dropped back to the floor in obvious pain.

"Cance fell for that once too." Belsas kicked the knife from Brandoff's hand and lunged out to grab the woman by the binder, but the amber barrier refused to move, so she used it like a handle and drove her head into the floor.

"Gonna kills you!" Brandoff grabbed Belsas's wrist and dug in with her claw-like nails.

Belsas held on, repeating her blows until Brandoff grew still and went limp. She bound her at the wrists and feet, and shoved a wad of pillowcase into her mouth, covering her head with the rest.

After taking care of Brandoff, Belsas tended her own injuries, wrapping her wrist and leg with more pillowcases. Chandrey never offered assistance, never moved from her corner. She watched at a physical and mental distance, hissing under her breath until Belsas pulled two binders from her pack and held one out to her.

"They can't track us if they can't feel us."

Chandrey began to pull the curtain closed.

"Keep it open," said Belsas as she slid on her own binder and held out Chandrey's a second time. "You have any clothing?"

Chandrey released the curtain and crouched before the window, looking from Belsas to Brandoff again and again.

Belsas saw the bruises mottling her body. "Let's get you out of here."

"Brandoff," Chandrey whispered. "Cance."

"Yes, I know." Belsas found a cloak among the bedding and placed it beside Chandrey. "Come on."

"Shh."

"We have to get out of here."

When Chandrey tried to pull the curtain again, Belsas began to understand. Since Chandrey operated on the most basic of levels, she had to respond in kind. "Chandresslandra," she said, her tone demanding, "put the binder and cloak on and be quick about it."

Chandrey responded obediently, slipping into the gear without further hesitation.

"Don't make me wait again." Belsas took Chandrey by the arm, slung her pack onto her back, and with Chandrey in tow, moved from the room.

The door closed with a locking chirp as Belsas pushed up her binder long enough to feel where everyone was. All the thralls were occupied downstairs, but there was no clear path to the back door. "We need a diversion," she said.

Chandrey stood stiffly beside her.

Belsas glanced at her, but continued to think. Five thralls were currently in the house, two guards on the front porch, no one in the yard or on any near paths. Only two thralls were in their way, so she'd handle them directly. She hated using her phase in such a way, but there wouldn't be any real harm, at least not by her hand.

"Keep hold of me and stay quiet." She placed Chandrey's hand on her shoulder and descended the stairs, looking in every direction as they descended the stairs.

Elisa encountered them first, just outside Creiloff's office. "You wents upstairs?" She gasped when she saw Chandrey. "She can't be down here. Cance will lessons us all if she gets out." Elisa glanced toward where the guards lounged out front, but when she opened her mouth, nothing came out. She clutched her throat and fell forward into Belsas's waiting arms.

"I'm so sorry." Belsas lowered her binder and laid Elisa on her side, the safe way for someone who'd been phased unconscious. Outside, the guards stirred, but neither of them bothered to investigate.

Chandrey returned her hand to Belsas's shoulder when she straightened.

Belsas was thankful for the reminder. She patted Chandrey's hand and moved through the elegant dining room toward the kitchen. One more thrall stood in their way. She couldn't be certain which one or of her abilities, but she was thrall, so her mind couldn't be well developed.

Unfortunately, the thrall's mouth worked too well. She screamed when she saw them and threw a full mixing bowl, drenching their faces with batter.

Belsas wiped the worst of the mess from her binder, knocked the thrall aside, and burst through the back door, dragging Chandrey behind her. She grabbed an armful of clothes as they passed the clothesline, and bounded through the neatly trimmed hedges and into the fields as the guards erupted from the back door.

"Down!" Belsas pulled Chandrey beside her as blaster fire flew over their heads.

The black grain field they hid in wasn't tall, but tall enough if they crawled on their bellies. Belsas whispered sharp orders whenever Chandrey faltered. Their pace was slower than she wanted, but after a few minutes, the blaster fire stopped. The last she saw of the guards, they were still on the house grounds, yelling into their coms.

Belsas and Chandrey slipped through the field and into a creek bed at the end, shimmying through ankle deep water until she felt they could stop.

She cleaned their binders with a damp towel she'd harvested from the line and placed Chandrey into a pair of leggings and undershirt which she'd gleaned from the same source. Chandrey was still barefoot and her feet had bled, but...

At least she has some dignity, thought Belsas, though she also wondered if Chandrey felt much of anything anymore. She stowed the remaining items, mainly hand towels, until they could stop longer. For now, they had to keep moving.

"Keep up," Belsas told her.

They crawled on their hands and knees along the creek bank until the sides ran deep enough for them to crouch and eventually stand.

She stopped for a moment more so she and Chandrey could drink from a clear spot in the water. It wasn't always safe to drink from wild sources, but she wanted to save the water in her pack. She encouraged Chandrey to drink deep, did the same, and they were off into nearby woods, headed in the general direction of the border with cover dictating their exact path.

At dusk, Belsas stopped in a low spot partially covered by a fallen tree. She gave Chandrey some of the fortified bread Zhastra had packed and a bottle of water, both of which Chandrey took when she was told, but didn't move to consume.

Belsas ate her own share, drank less than she wanted, and then went to work on Chandrey's feet, cleaning and wrapping them in a few rags and hide strips from her pack.

"Eat." Belsas patted her ankle. "You need the energy." Chandrey looked from her to the food and water, which she slowly opened and drank in rhythmic swallows.

"Well, at least you made some sort of choice for yourself." Belsas put away the remaining bread and settled back against the log.

The woods were quiet, but not the kind of quiet indicating trouble. The little sounds had returned, the scurry of small animals, the buzz of insects—a safety sign. Belsas relaxed. They could stay here until morning, nine hours away in Myflar's lunar orbit. After dark, Cance would likely send search launches equipped with heat sensing technology. The trees would provide some cover against the sensors, and the log would give more, provided they hid fully under it.

She cleared the worst of the rot from inside the log and lined it with fallen leaves. "It'll do," she said, turning back to Chandrey, who had stopped watching to scratch her head furiously.

"How long's it been since you bathed?" Belsas asked, cutting a triangular wedge from the better part of the log and carving a few shallow teeth into the thinner end. "Here." She tossed the crude comb to Chandrey.

After staring at the comb until Belsas instructed her, Chandrey attacked her matted head with a vengeance, pulling out the worst of the knots between digs at her scalp. Her hair was greasy, but what she did was an improvement, to a point. She still dug at her head until hairs came out between her fingers.

"Stop it." Belsas took the comb and used it to carefully lift Chandrey's hair in layers. Knots weren't the problem. She saw nits and lice. Brandoff had shared a horrid infestation. "That's got to be uncomfortable." She looked up at the waning light. They hadn't much time, so she dug in her backpack and tossed Chandrey a hide strip. "Tie it up."

Chandrey obeyed, flipping her head over to gather her infested tresses in a high ponytail.

"Stand up." When Chandrey stood, so did Belsas. "Bend over."

Chandrey gave her a frightened glance, but didn't hesitate, flipping her ponytail forward. Belsas grasped the hair at its base, drew her knife, and sawed it off. She buried the hair in the leaves a dozen meters away.

"Don't stand up yet." Chandrey made little gasping sounds, but she didn't fight when Belsas poured half a water bottle over her head. "Cold, I know," she said, aggressively combing Chandrey's hair forward. "This won't get them all," she went on, standing Chandrey up again. "But if we do this whenever we can, maybe we'll keep it under control."

Chandrey ran her fingers through the chin-length cut, drawing out the last of the water.

"Sorry for the hack job." Belsas shook the hide strip free of potential passengers, and stowed it and the comb in her pack. "Ready to bed down?"

Chandrey looked through her and continued fingering her hair.

"Chandrey." Belsas tried to keep her voice calm, but Chandrey started anyway, cringing and looking down. "I made a bed." She pointed to the nest-like space under the log. "Climb in."

Chandrey craned her neck to look.

"Go on."

Chandrey looked up at Belsas with large, panicky eyes.

"They won't find us under all that wood," assured Belsas as she sat beside the opening. "I cleaned it best I could. The leaves are fresh. We'll be warm if we lie close."

Chandrey hissed and drew her cloak across her body.

"Keep your cloak. I'll use the emergency blanket." She pulled the gauze-like sheet from the pack and shook it out. "See?"

Chandrey simply stared.

"I know it feels like everyone's betrayed you," began Belsas, but she stopped. She was cold and too damned tired. "Tie your cloak up and get in the log." Her tone became keeper hard. "Scoot back and make room for me."

Chandrey moved slowly into a fetal curl until Belsas made her straighten her legs.

"You sleep," Belsas said simply. She pulled the gauze sheet to her chin. "I'll keep watch."

But Chandrey didn't sleep. She lay wide-eyed beside Belsas, although her breathing slowed after a bit.

*If I could get into her head…*Belsas gazed at the log above her, concentrating on its lines. *If I could get into her head, I could help her fight what's consuming her, but not here.* She scratched her head. *I'll just have to stay her keeper until we're safe.*

* * *

"Shh."

Belsas woke to Chandrey's warning hiss. Lights showed above and to their right, but none were close to their location. "Stay still." She rolled back to nudge Chandrey deeper into their hiding spot.

Chandrey's heart pounded against her, and she clutched her back. She might not be verbal, but she had come to accept her as her protector. It was a step, Belsas supposed, but she wanted the Chandrey she knew, not the instinct-driven creature cowering against her. When the ground lights grew brighter, she rolled to face Chandrey.

Chandrey drew away from her, tighter against the log until voices became audible, and then she hid her face in Belsas's shoulder.

"Keep still," Belsas whispered.

Chandrey whimpered, but remained otherwise motionless, even when Belsas slipped an arm underneath and around her. They lay silent, holding their breaths when the voices became clear.

"You track down that blip?"

"Hopper." One of their pursuers stood in front of the log. She wore thick-heeled keeper boots with sheathed blades sticking out the tops.

"This wood's thick with them. Gonna have to remember this place." Ground cover crunched to their left. A boot landed on their log, showering them with tiny bits of wood.

"Good eating, hopper."

"Yeah, hoppers spread faster here than on Saria Proper. Okay, they're not here. Probably kept to the water. I would've. Let's head back."

The footfalls faded and the lights receded, finally disappearing altogether.

Belsas breathed deeply and rolled out of the log, giving Chandrey more room, but to her surprise, Chandrey rolled with her, laying her head on Belsas's shoulder.

Belsas gazed down at her, afraid to move. She'd dreamed of this, though it wasn't the way she'd envisioned, but she'd take any small comfort, so she let Chandrey rest and eventually sleep against her. She didn't sleep, but she did worry.

Cance had managed to insert Chandrey so completely into a thrall's role, she believed she needed a keeper to secure her safety, to make her decisions.

For the first time, Belsas missed Wreed's fierce sense of independence.

Chapter Thirty-Two

Flight—to move using air currents; to flee

While there were ten launches docked at the Granary's landing pad, only one was big enough for Zhastra's brood.

Before Belsas's escape, Zhastra walked by the pad almost daily, noting the schedules, pilots and normal cargoes. Two supply flights a day, in by dusk. Two pilots, both keepers older than herself. She knew them, but she couldn't trust them, either. She couldn't trust anyone, not with the ones she loved.

Stores were the normal cargo, generally fresh foods from the Cleave central stores so the launches were empty overnight, every night. While this was good, she still had to determine how many guards walked the paths after dark and their exact schedules, if they had them.

Zhastra hoped Chandrey and Belsas were managing, but she had to concentrate on her family. She'd packed a bag of medical supplies and her life mates' various medications, but she waited until the evening of their flight to share her plan.

Emre, in particular, was aghast. She argued with her vehemently that the New Cleave was just, that times were simply difficult, and that difficult times called for—

"Murder?" Zhastra cut her off. "You'll come with us, daughter. If you don't, you'll be Shared for my choice."

"Then don't go," said Emre. "You're putting us in danger."

"We're all in grave danger come tomorrow."

"You keep saying that, but you won't say why."

Zhastra looked to where her life mates had assembled, each with a change of clothing and one or two sentimental items tucked into pillowcases. Her three younger daughters were there too, the youngest resting her sleepy head on Tamberly's shoulder. The little girl adored Tamberly like she was an older sibling. She even used some of the same hand signals, indicating their bond.

"If I were sixteen—"

"You aren't, so hush." Zhastra hated her short answers.

Emre said nothing more, but her eyes projected everything she didn't vocalize. She'd been engulfed by the New Cleave, by their promises, their grandiose ideas.

Zhastra knew then that Emre wouldn't go willingly, that she might even sound the alarm. But Emre was also her eldest. Her progeny. Her daughter. "Finish packing."

"No."

Behind them, the others gasped.

"We're leaving within the hour," Zhastra said.

"I'll not leave the Granary."

"You'll do as I say." Zhastra slipped quietly into her daughter's mind, encouraging her family obligations over popular thinking, but there was nothing to manipulate. Emre was strong, as she had been raised to be, but she was also deeply committed to Cance's ideas. She saw Zhastra as a traitor to the Cleave and was ashamed of her raiser's plans.

"Go pack," Zhastra said.

"No."

Zhastra had expected resistance, but Emre was proving a hazard to the rest of the family. She hadn't time to convince her daughter, hadn't the stomach to force or phase her into complying, but when Emre reached for the com, everything changed.

Zhastra pushed Emre into a chair and called to her life mates. They descended on Emre with a gentle fierceness, tying her to the chair with kitchen rags. Before she could cry out more than once, Zhastra gagged her with a strip of towel and slid a binder over her eyes.

"Forgive me, daughter. But they'll see you as innocent because of this." Zhastra kissed Emre on her forehead, nodded to Giana, and then she, her life mates, and three daughters disappeared into the night, keeping far from the pathways.

Chapter Thirty-Three

Duplicity—two; treachery

"Idiot!" Cance cut her twin's bindings and pointed to the pile of clothing by the bedroom door. "Get dressed."

"I can't walks." Brandoff used the wall for support.

"Won't breathes either if you don't finds her," snapped Cance in Autlach as she watched her sibling slip into a set of work leathers too big for her frame. "Let another keeper takes her from us." She kicked a pair of boots toward her twin. "Dosed heavy again, didn't you?"

"I was sleepin' and so was she until that bitch came in." Brandoff dropped to the floor to put the boots on. "You tells someone the code?"

"What a stupid question." Cance opened the door to glance into the hallway.

It was late, and the house was silent save for their voices. Extra guards were posted outside the front and back doors, but Brandoff could slip by them. She'd done so often enough since they'd first met up: keeper and her hunted, wild-woman twin. Everything had fallen into place since their initial encounter. Cance was clan leader, and with the help of Brandoff's blade, had come to the favorable attention of the pedagogues.

Kylis had met with her during her last trip to the Cleave capital, and they'd laughed long about her performance at Chandrey's shunning. Kylis said Cance was going places in the New Cleave, that she knew how to get things done, and had recommended her for a position supervising the six clan cluster the Granary was a part of.

But Chandrey had broken loose and that was solely Brandoff's doing. "What'd that bitch who tooks her looks like again?" Cance hated speaking Aut, but Brandoff didn't understand enough Taelach.

"I fuckin' tolds you." Brandoff pushed her hair behind her ears and peered up at Cance. "It was dark."

"Nothing but excuses." Cance produced a bag of orange powder from her tunic. "You'll get five times this amount when you brings her back." She held out the bag. "Alive."

"Yeah. Yeah." Brandoff pulled herself up and scooted along the wall to take the bag. "Gonna kills that bitch though." She scooped two fingerfuls of the powder and held them to her nose as she inhaled, and then swiped her hand on her leathers and leaned against the wall.

Even though Brandoff was bindered, Cance could feel the drug course through her—the rise, the fall, the numbness. Her twin's leg had almost quit hurting.

"What's buzzin'?" Brandoff asked.

"My hand com." Cance reached into her pocket a second time. "Damned late, Raja. This better be good."

"Central Med wants you, Cancelynn."

"Wake me for that, did you?" Cance appreciated her own ease at slipping between the Taelach and Autlach tongues. She motioned for Brandoff to stay quiet.

"Your lights were still on." Raja hesitated. "Central wants to know why Healer Zhastra isn't answering."

"If I'm lucky, the old bitch died in her sleep."

"They're very insistent you check immediately. There's something wrong with the readings coming from an experiment they've stored with her."

"Experiment?"

"That's what they said."

"Go check and com them back."

"They want you to go."

"Damn. Let me put something on."

Truth was, Cance was still dressed, but few knew about Chandrey's disappearance and she wanted it kept that way.

Two search parties from the Granary were out, and Brandoff would make a secretive and highly effective third. Cance's twin had proven an infallible tracker and had no problems chasing down any quarry she named. If Creiloff had been doable, Chandrey shouldn't be any problem for Brandoff, high or not, but she suspected that depended on who had helped Chandrey.

Zhastra wouldn't leave her brood, not for Chandrey or anyone else. She was far too loyal. So who was she with? No one had been reported missing. Who'd dare help a clan leader's thrall run off? It was more than a Sharing offense; it was a death sentence.

Cance pondered the matter while Brandoff slid between the window bars and scurried out of sight. She continued to puzzle over the unanswered questions as two guards and three of her entourage, sleepy and wrinkled, traipsed behind her on the path to the infirmary. By the time they reached Zhastra's door, she was positively obsessed.

Clan leaders didn't knock, but the silence in the household wing made Cance and her group hesitate in the doorway. Finally entering, she found all the rooms empty save for Emre, bound and gagged in a corner of the main room, and she proved no help at all.

Cance slapped the girl a few times to dispel some of her frustration. Zhastra was gone, Emre said. She and her life mates had fled the Granary, but Emre knew nothing about Chandrey.

Annoyed, Cance ordered her freed and threw open the doors to the infirmary in search of the "project" that Central Medical seemed so concerned over.

Two guards slouched at their posts, sleeping hard. Drugged. Cance could tell by looking, but she'd deal with them later. What they'd guarded intrigued her more than doling out punishment. She slid the door open and peered inside just as her com buzzed again. Central Medical had bypassed channels to reach her directly.

"Is the project intact?" The woman, presumably a healer, on the other end of the call sounded anxious.

"What project?" Cance looked around the room at the empty, unmade bed, the stale food, the stagnant water in the mugs, the monitor showing a pair of heartbeats: one slower, one faster.

"Where's Healer Zhastra?"

"Gone."

"Did she take the project?"

"What fucking project?" Cance waved everyone else away and slid the door closed. "Nothing's here."

"She's not there?"

"Didn't I just say that?"

"The project. Is she there?"

"She?" Cance curbed her urge to hurl the com across the room.

"The monitor's on?" asked the healer.

"Yes."

The healer's voice became muffled, and then she returned to the com. "Turn the monitor off and listen carefully."

Cance's mouth curled. "You obviously don't know who I am."

"The next project if you don't shut up," cried the healer through the com. "That project must be located and—"

"Don't threaten me."

"I guarantee your agony." Another voice came through the com—loud, strong, intense and intent. "This is Tavince. You'll find the woman and you'll *personally* deliver her to Central Medical unharmed."

Cance thought a moment. Practitioner Tavince, a ruthless keeper by reputation, a researcher, head of the breeding program and pedagogue, she was a ruling member of the Cleave, a woman who had the power to enforce every word she said.

"Who am I looking for?" Cance replied at last.

"We'll send an image, but the woman's a slattern. No good aside from what she carries."

"And what's that?"

"That's need to know."

"You want her protected or not?"

"You're Granary Clan leader Cancelynn Creiloff, correct?" Tavince mumbled something the com didn't broadcast clearly, and another voice, just as muffled, replied. "The Missionary speaks well of you so I'll grant you the information. The slattern carries a keeper babe."

Cance laughed. "Pregnant? All this for an Aut?"

"Hardly," said Tavince flatly. "Kinship whore. The name's Belsas Exzal."

The smile slipped from Cance's face.

Chapter Thirty-Four

Conceal—hide, cover up

"Now what?" They were only twenty kilometers from the Kinship border, but it might as well have been thousands, Belsas thought.

Before them stood an open field, a freshly mown field so large, Belsas wasn't certain how to proceed. Worse yet, the field was monitored. Their arrival seemed expected and the welcome, she knew, would not be warm. From her hiding place among the heavy, wild grasses, she watched the blockade for a minute, and then pushed back to where Chandrey hunkered, rocking on her heels.

Chandrey had barely spoken the last two days and only eaten a few bites. She scratched her head now and again, but did nothing else unless Belsas told her to.

They were out of food and down to their last two water bottles. Belsas had found some edible roots the day before, but the fibrous tubers had proven far too spicy for anyone with a limited water supply. She had settled for a handful of half-ripe berries, certainly not enough for a woman on the mend. Chandrey had simply watched her eat.

"They're sweeping the area." Belsas pushed Chandrey to a seated position. "We have to turn back." She decided they would follow the wilds which skirted the enormous field, hopefully finding another spot to shelter before the warm temperatures waned and their body heat could be read from a distance.

Belsas paused long enough to press her head to her knees for a moment. She rose, taking Chandrey by the arm. "Come along."

They slipped deeper into the wilds and farther from the Kinship border.

After a while, Belsas hadn't come upon a suitable hiding spot, but she found water, or rather, a mud hole, which she dragged them through until she and Chandrey were both covered. Broken grasses sufficed for cover after that. They spent a very cold night holding themselves small and still as searchlights moved in every direction around them.

Chandrey panicked when the lights came uncomfortably close, and she sat upright, scattering their cover. Belsas pulled her back, grabbed one of Zhastra's mixtures from her pack, and forced it down Chandrey's throat. The mix proved strong enough to render Chandrey unconscious within seconds.

Belsas spent the remainder of the night silently apologizing as she held Chandrey close to her beneath their grass blanket.

Bedraggled, scraggly, hungry, exhausted—and those are the good parts, thought Belsas in a quiet moment just before dawn. Chandrey lay against her, reeking from what had been in the mud hole. Hopper wallow. A stinking hopper wallow. She should have known. She did know better. Mother above, but they stank.

Belsas had to laugh despite the awful smell. At least it was a small mistake. At least the worst of the filth would peel off as it dried during the day. At least—

Chandrey stiffened and whimpered. The medication would wear off before long, and she would be awake and asking for more. She always asked for more though it was only with her eyes. Belsas wondered how much she'd been force-fed during her time with the Cleave. She wondered a lot of things, but mostly she wondered about their survival.

Morning brought thunderstorms, but with the storms came a reprieve from their pursuers. Belsas knew she and Chandrey couldn't move well in the weather, either, so they huddled together beneath the grass blanket for much of the day, dozing until late evening when the weather settled to a steady drizzle.

"It's going to do this all night." Belsas wiped grass bits from her clothing. "As long as we stay in the grasses we should be able to move unseen. The rain will mask our heat signature."

Later, she wondered why she'd bothered explaining as they pushed along the inner edge of the wild grass plain. At some point, she would have to find a safe place for them to pass into Kinship lands. At some point, the hiding had to end.

Twenty more paces through the slippery grasses, and she and Chandrey went down, clutching dirt, roots and each other as a pit opened beneath them.

They were some ten meters down in the hole, Belsas surmised when she caught her breath. Impossible to climb out, and a Cleave trap if the blinking lights were any indication. She cursed long and loud while Chandrey lay where she'd fallen, looking up at the night as rain washed her face. When lights appeared a moment later, she scurried to hide behind Belsas.

"I won't leave you." Belsas turned to pull Chandrey closer to her and brought her chin up so their eyes met. "We won't be taken back."

The sky above them blazed from a single, powerful spotlight. A behemoth of a launch blocked out the rain. A transport, not a maneuverable search craft, but the underside markings, barely visible through the glare, were Cleave.

Chandrey buried her face in Belsas's shoulder and wrapped her arms around her waist. She was oddly, necessarily calm, thought Belsas, but her fists were also balled. Resistance. Fear wouldn't help, and Chandrey knew that. They'd fought hard. They'd fought well. They'd fought to find each other. Now they'd fight together.

When Chandrey looked up into the spotlight, Belsas brought her gaze back down. "Don't give them recognition." She pulled her blade and held it ready. "Look at me instead." She waved the blade at the blinding light. "Come and get us!" she called.

"Good grief, Belsas!" a familiar voice called down. "Put away that rusty twig and help Chandrey out of that hole!" A line and harness dropped beside them.

"Zhastra!" Belsas wrapped the harness around Chandrey's waist. Two winch pulls later, she and Chandrey were topside and face-to-face with the former Granary healer.

"The borders aren't within anyone's reach." Zhastra quickly examined them when they climbed on board. "You're both a mess, but intact. We figured we'd better find you before the search resumed."

"We?" Belsas looked past Zhastra to the pilot's seat.

"When I told you Sabra couldn't cook, I meant it. But she was piloting for Aut smugglers long before she came to me." Zhastra nodded to her life mate, and the launch's exterior lights shut off. "We fly dark from here on out," she explained. The interior lights cut out as well.

"Where to?" Belsas felt Chandrey's hand slide into hers, a reassuring touch since they couldn't feel each other through the binders.

"I'm not the only one who doesn't believe in this new Cleave." Zhastra sat on the edge of the seat beside Belsas. "You set off alarms when you fell in. Low-tech, but effective, and the Resistance thinks they're necessary with everything that's happened."

"What happened?" Belsas dreaded hearing about whatever had finally prompted the gentle Zhastra into action.

Zhastra gave her a funny look. "I guess you wouldn't know, would you? The Kinship is no more."

Belsas breathed in hard. "What? How? The Cleave?"

"The *New* Cleave," corrected Zhastra. "We'll discuss the unfortunate details when we've safely landed."

Sabra called to Zhastra, who felt her way to the copilot's seat while saying, "There are clean jumpers in the rear bins. Get those ruined clothes into a disposal bag. We'll burn them later." She closed the privacy screen.

Belsas felt her way to the rear of the launch, pulling out the clothing, water bottles and nutrition packs they needed. She returned to her jump seat and handed one of each to Chandrey.

"Eat." Even though it was becoming easier, Belsas hated her keeper role. Still, Chandrey did nothing for herself unless she ordered it. She would ask Zhastra, but doubted a real keeper would see a problem.

"Bel?" Belsas rejoiced to hear her name in Chandrey's whisper. "More water?"

"Get dressed first."

Chandrey nodded, unbuckled her flight strap, and slipped into the jumper, stumbling into Belsas when the launch rocked.

Belsas caught her, mourning the scars she felt when they touched in the dark. "Strap back in." She passed a fresh bottle to Chandrey, and then sat beside her to relish her nutrient pack. She wasn't full by any means, but with food came a new level of fatigue which increased when she slid into clean clothes.

"We're nearing a clan border so prepare to fly low and silent," said Zhastra over the main com. The launch's roar softened beneath them. "One minute until dead time."

Chapter Thirty-Five

Binder—*constrain, control, curb*

The council had been executed one by one, their minds picked for information, their thoughts and bodies ravaged by Sharing until they fell dead. Only Brava had been spared the Sharing portion of the torture. That was Kylis's doing, but her mind had been picked so deeply that she had fallen unconscious, only to wake bindered and bound to a lounger in a seldom used workroom. She'd been stripped of her clothing as well.

They left her there for two days. No food. No water. No way to relieve herself.

When they did return for her, she was escorted back to the Taelach of All's workroom and bound tightly to the lounger.

"How the mighty have fallen." Kylis taunted from behind the worktable. She had shed her Plan robes and dressed for her keeper role. She also wore Brava's military dress jacket. She fingered the epaulets. "Wondering why I haven't killed you yet, aren't you?"

"That'd be too easy." Brava's shoulders ached from the strain.

"True enough," Kylis chided. "We have wonderful plans for all our new holdings. Slatterns will receive their punishment. Keepers will have their pick of new thralls. Daughters will have someone who can teach them the Word as it should be learned." She grinned when Brava scowled. "Aw, not your plans at all, are they, mighty Taelach of All?"

Kylis rose from the table to sit by her head. "Don't worry about that," she said when Brava strained to move away. "I was disgusted by you from the day we met." She patted her heated face. "But try to be more appreciative. I've news about Chandrey."

Brava's eyes widened, but she retained her distance. "Either tell me, or send me back."

"She's not yours anymore." Kylis's smile turned as malevolent as her tone. "She's Cleave property. But you knew that already. I can see it in your face. So how about this—I saw her not two cycles ago. Cance needed help teaching her a lesson."

"No one owns Chandrey."

"She's a beast, your daughter. Wild at heart. Disobedient at every turn. Cance gave up on her for a while, but took her back, spared her from the culling blade to retrain her. And I've helped several times. She was at my feet before the last lesson was half over." Kylis licked her lips. "Very delicious thrall despite your attempts to ugly her head with knowledge. And a real treat after your mind."

"You manipulated my emotions."

"And to think, I brought a souvenir." She held her com to Brava's face as images scrolled across the viewer. Chandrey at Cance's feet, at Kylis's feet. On her back with Kylis's boot to her throat. Chandrey on her knees as Cance—

Brava looked away.

"No." Kylis pushed the recorder into her face. "Take a long, hard look and learn, because this is you from now on. I'm going to train you." She smirked. "In fact, I look forward to it." She pocketed the com and reared back to slap her face.

"You'll be a lousy thrall, one I'd rather beat than fuck. But you see, I really don't care as long as you're miserable every moment of every day." Kylis slapped her again, harder, her nails slicing the bridge of her nose. "You'll be less than a hag when I'm done with you."

"And you're less than one now."

"I'll remember that at your first lesson." Kylis pulled out the com again, moving away from the lounger to record Brava's bondage. "This will be part of my first official message."

Brava tried unsuccessfully to curl to hide her nakedness, but Kylis called in two guards, who pulled her straighter until Kylis finished recording.

"Let her clean up, then take her to my quarters," she commanded.

Brava was granted a quick shower observed by the guards, and then shackled in her former workroom. The space had been transformed in the few days that Kylis had ruled: the worktable and chair of the main room removed to make room for pillows and bedding. A Cleave bedroom. A space for Kylis's more physical "work."

The drapery to the storage space had been tacked back to reveal a second's sleeping space. Brava was left there, chained to a large eye-hook in the floor. She could hobble a few paces when she stood and could reach a blanket if she pulled her chain tight and stretched. Small comfort, but she felt better with her nakedness covered.

This is only a minute portion of what Chandrey has been through, she thought. But the control, the humiliation. Obey or risk a Sharing. How could her daughter not comply? How could she still be emotionally intact? How could she still be Chandrey?

At least she's alive. Brava watched with dread as the outside light began to fade, but her grim thoughts were interrupted when the door to the workroom slid open. The woman who entered—young, beautiful and obviously frightened—sat two mugs at her feet and quickly retreated.

"Sister, please wait." But Brava's words went unheeded, so she turned her attention to the first food she'd had in days: thin soup in one mug and water in the other. Not enough, but something, and she devoured it before the dark encroached any further. She'd need the strength.

Chapter Thirty-Six

Reason—the difference between the Old and New Cleave

When Zhastra told her that the Resistance had just begun, Belsas expected a handful of keepers hunkering in a cave with their life mates, but she couldn't have been more wrong.

The cave was actually a series of caverns formed eons before the Kinship had made Myflar habitable. The caverns sheltered forty or so launches, most heavily armed, and certainly more than a handful of keepers. In fact, there were over a hundred keepers, each with at least two life mates. While these women were certainly not treated as equals, they were obviously aware and taking part in what was happening.

The leader of the life mates, a boisterous woman named Madeleine, came for Chandrey as soon as they landed, but Chandrey resisted leaving Belsas's side.

"Let the keepers talk their business." Madeleine's eyes danced merrily beneath her binder. She was old enough to have lost most of her Autlach accent, but apparently young enough to occasionally test the boundaries of her role.

Chandrey shook her head and gripped Belsas's arm tighter.

"Go with her." Belsas peeled Chandrey loose. "Get some rest."

"Beg pardon," said Madeleine as she took Chandrey's hand. "And you can lecture me later about my mouth if you wish, Adara," she said with a glance at her keeper, a dumpy, glassy-eyed woman who grimaced. "But she needs more than rest if she's been a clan leader's play toy."

After some kind words, coaxing, and a bit more reassurance from Belsas, Chandrey followed Madeleine away from the launch. Sabra followed a moment later, but not before stopping for instructions from Zhastra.

"Good work." Zhastra kissed Sabra tenderly on the cheek. "Once again, you helped the Resistance prevail. Now go help with Chandrey. A familiar face will do her good."

Sabra smiled broadly and turned, hiking up her skirts as she jogged to catch up to Madeleine and her charge.

"You'll make the woman prideful," said Adara.

"You've room to talk." Zhastra didn't sound offended. "Madeleine practically runs this place single-handedly."

"And aren't we all glad she does!" Adara laughed. "Speaking of which, Maddy said she saved you some dinner."

"You more tired or hungry?" Zhastra motioned for Belsas to follow.

"Both." Belsas reveled in the difference in the old-style keepers and those of the New Cleave. Neither was acceptable to her, but at least Zhastra's type was tolerable. Maybe this type of keeper environment would help Chandrey begin to find herself again.

Belsas felt hopeful as she followed Zhastra toward a small side cavern outfitted as a kitchen. Zhastra called for one of the kitchen workers to bring food. Soon, her stomach was silent for the first time in days.

Keeper after keeper stopped by to talk to Zhastra, but they largely ignored Belsas.

"Don't take it too personally," Zhastra explained over their post-meal tea. "They're just not sure how to treat you."

"You mean, am I keeper or thrall?" said Belsas. "Chandrey thinks me her keeper if that means anything."

"For our purposes, it does." Zhastra set down her mug. "I know, I know. You don't subscribe to the thinking. But for now, let them think what they want if it'll help them recognize your potential contribution to the Resistance."

"And what might my 'contribution' be?" Belsas swirled the sweetener in the bottom of her tea. "I'm not one of you."

"But you have access to information we need."

"How so?"

"Chandrey," said Zhastra. "She'll talk to you long before she'll talk to any of us."

"But she knows you."

"And she *loves* you," countered the healer. "I don't stand a chance in her head without you there as well."

"She pushes me out too."

"I can medicate so her protective walls come down, but even that isn't enough without you there to help."

"You want me to help you pick her for information?"

"We need you to help save both the Cleave and the Kinship."

"But what does Chandrey know that would be of help?"

"More than you could possibly imagine." Zhastra stood and motioned Belsas to follow her back to the docking cavern. "Does the name Kylis mean anything to you?"

"She's one of Chandrey's raisers."

"She's Cleave, New Cleave, and the Missionary pedagogue."

"And good at it." Adara joined their conversation. "She in?" She nodded toward Belsas.

"I don't know yet," said Zhastra, but she seemed unconcerned.

"Are you certain you have the correct Kylis?" stammered Belsas. "She's a Mother's Plan member, just like Chandrey's other raiser."

"Kylis worked most of her adulthood under that cover," said Adara. "But with Benjimena Kim for a mentor, she couldn't help but be skilled."

"Wait." Belsas stopped dead in the middle of the cavern. "Benjimena Kim is Cleave? I've worked in her office. She suffers from some dementia, but—"

Adara sped past Belsas to block her path. "Benjimena raised my keeper parent." She tapped the blade at her waist. "No one speaks ill of my lineage."

Zhastra placed her hand over Adara's weapon hand. "Lightly, Ada. Benjimena was Old Cleave like the rest of us. Her ashes would light anew if she heard you challenge a truth speaker." She stepped back when Adara dropped her hand. "Benjimena was ill for a very long time. Her passing was a Mother's mercy."

"Benjimena passed?" said Belsas, feeling avenged by her betrayer's death. "Then who's Taelach of All?"

"No one." Zhastra turned them back toward their target, a grotto on the far side of the docking cavern. "Brava Deb was serving as interim when Kylis took power."

"Brava? Oh, dearest Mother." Belsas stopped again. "Is she still alive?"

"Kylis has seen to it," said Zhastra. She stepped past her to knock on the steel plate blocking the grotto opening. It slid open with a grinding noise, revealing a space crowded with computer equipment and keepers. Low-tech tactical maps papered the walls.

Zhastra entered, but Adara blocked Belsas's path again. "This is my domain." She glared at her. "Respect that, Outsider." She allowed Belsas just enough space to pass.

They regrouped at a small table in the corner. Zhastra let Belsas view Kylis's first official message, a gruesome display of New Cleave vengeance and lessons.

"This won't make Kinship sisters comply." Belsas pushed away from the table com. "They'll fight even harder."

"Kylis doesn't care about compliance." Zhastra turned off the screen. "Total, unquestioned obedience is the New Cleave's only goal." She looked at Adara, who sat on the far side of the table with her arms crossed over her chest, and said to her, "For the Mother's sake, she's keeper. Chandrey is hers."

"She's Kinship." Adara looked as if she'd tasted something bitter. "She'll be a hindrance."

"We've no issue with the Kinship, intact or not," said Zhastra. "And Belsas is pilot qualified."

"For what?" Adara's expression mollified ever so slightly. "Personal overland?"

"Transports up to ten passengers," said Belsas, "and small gunships."

"Weapons?" Adara moved a few seats closer.

"Bow, sidearm, blaster and small ship's armament." Belsas had indeed qualified with all those weapons early in her officer training.

Adara looked hard at her. "So you're what, a third officer?"

"First officer." Belsas enjoyed disproving Adara's presumptions. "Over ten passes of service."

"I didn't lie to you," Zhastra said to Adara while patting Belsas's shoulder. "You wanted another pilot. I got you one."

"I still need at least three more," said Adara. "Four if you want Sabra back."

"For now, Sabra serves best under your tutelage." Zhastra got on her feet. "Belsas can see you in the morning. Right now, we all need rest."

"Some of us have watch tonight," mumbled Adara, but she looked directly at Belsas. "Come back here right after breakfast, and I'll brief you."

Belsas nodded in the curt, keeper fashion. "I'll be here."

"Zhastra." Adara nodded similarly and picked up a tool bag.

"Let's see what corner Madeleine has found for you," said Zhastra to Belsas.

She led the way back across the docking cavern and down another tunnel to a third cavern with a lower ceiling than the others. Canvas tents hung from the ceiling, creating a maze of small compartments.

"You can take your binder off in here." Zhastra pushed hers back on her head. "Now if we can find Madeleine—"

"Right here," Madeleine replied from just beyond their sight. "Be there in a moment."

By the time Belsas had loosened her binder and wiped her eyes, Adara's perpetually merry mate had appeared with a bedroll she held out to her.

"Mitsu's with Chandrey right now," Madeleine told Zhastra.

"So you found a space for them?" The healer stifled a yawn.

"Made a space, Keeper Zhastra." Madeleine motioned for them to follow her. "There's barely room to stand, but enough for a platform."

"They'll need wash water and fresh clothing," said Zhastra.

"Chandrey's already cleaned up and the water's been freshened." Madeleine glanced over her shoulder at Belsas. "I took the liberty of evening up Chandrey's hair after I oiled it. I hope you don't mind."

"Thank—" Belsas stopped when Zhastra wagged a finger behind her back. Keepers didn't thank their life mates, she had said. They praised them, but never thanked them. "Well done, Madeleine."

"And there's more oil by the basin." Somewhere in the midst of the canvas maze, Madeleine pulled back a curtain and stepped aside until Zhastra and Belsas passed through.

Mitsu sat on the floor beside the sleep platform where Chandrey lay awake.

"Come along," said Zhastra, taking Mitsu's hand. "My brood is three curtains down on the right. My marker's on the flap," she told Belsas. "I'll come find you sometime tomorrow to discuss our upcoming work." With that, she and Mitsu left, but Madeleine lingered.

"This space isn't ever truly quiet." A baby began to cry somewhere in the maze, proving her point. "Adara said I should stay to assist if you wanted." Madeleine pulled shears from one of her apron's deep pockets. "Chandrey should do it, but—"

Belsas looked again at Chandrey, her body curled in position, her blank expression. "She can't care for herself at present, so yes, you can assist."

When Madeleine left with the wash basin, Belsas, keeper quaffed, deloused, clean and freshly dressed, flipped out her bedroll and settled beside Chandrey, who was still awake.

"Sleep." Belsas told her simply.

She turned off the light sitting by her side of the platform. Various rustles, murmurs and night sounds combined with the collective mental presence, and under normal circumstances, would have kept Belsas awake, but that night she slipped into a restless, odd, dreamless sleep, waking when Chandrey shivered against her.

"You cold?" Belsas pulled Chandrey into her bedroll and spread Chandrey's blankets on top. "There you go."

"It's not the temperature," Zhastra said, parting the curtain. She held a lantern and a binder in one hand, a mug of orange mix in the other. "Her mind is so restless, it's disturbing others—even you. Sit her up."

But Chandrey sat up on her own when she saw the mug in Zhastra's hand, taking and downing the contents in an eager gulp.

"That was simple enough." Zhastra's mouth drew tight with concern. "How many of my mix packs did you use on her?"

"Most of them, unfortunately." Belsas traded Zhastra the mug for the binder and lay back down as Chandrey rolled to lay against her, mumbling an objection when Belsas slid the binder over her head, but she didn't resist. "She's out."

"Who knows how many times Cance dosed her so she'd obey?" Zhastra's tired frown deepened. "Tomorrow, you two will move to the medical grotto. I've a small room shielded like this cavern."

"We going to begin gleaning her already?"

"Not until this addiction is addressed." Zhastra left, but her mind remained a moment more. *Addiction is a difficult word to process.* Her phase was deeply fatigued. *But this isn't the first case I've handled.*

Did I cause it? Belsas wondered how much more complicated things could get.

I treated her. Cance forced her, you saved her the only way you could, but her own need to dull the agony made her an addict.

There's more to it. Belsas yawned despite herself. *When I took her from Cance, she wasn't alone.*

But you said Cance wasn't there.

She wasn't. Belsas shared her memory with Zhastra.

Sharing. No wonder she hurts so. Zhastra pushed a heavy phase at Belsas. *Sleep. Easing her addiction is going to be the hardest thing you've ever done.*

Chapter Thirty-Seven

Inhere—to dwell or exist regardless

The beautiful young woman was named Rachel. She was sixteen, Kinship born, and Kylis's youngest thrall, Brava learned. Rachel had been seized during one of the Cleave border raids and spared only because of her beauty and naïve mind. That mind wasn't naïve anymore, she thought. Kylis made certain of that most every night, sometimes calling three or four of her thralls to her bed at a time.

While Brava thankfully never had to participate, she heard and shared the second's space with them, though the thralls never spoke to her. Kylis promised violent retribution if they did, and surely meant every word.

Brava was fed once a day, led to the facilities twice a day if someone remembered, and allowed to bathe once or twice a seven-day, but other than that she was nonexistent unless Kylis was in the mood. The torture was agonizing, but at least her words received replies.

Kylis wouldn't kill her, not as long as the remainder of the Kinship still fought, so she took her pain as a sign of hope and savored every word aimed at her, no matter how ugly. Someone saw her, which meant she still existed.

Late one morning, when the thralls had left the second's space, Kylis came to see her: to talk, she said.

"Your nose is crooked." Kylis smirked at her handiwork. "Set it yourself?"

"You know I did." Brava was certain her eyes were black too.

"Who gave you the bandages?" Kylis pointed at the strips of fabric wrapping Brava's right forearm.

"It's bedding."

"Resourceful. But I expected nothing less." Kylis left the room, returning a moment later with a chair, which she straddled. "Chandrey's been taken." She waited for a reaction, which Brava didn't give. "Extremists stole her from Cance's bed."

Brava only briefly glanced up. "May the Mother show her mercy."

"You know what they'll do to her because she's Cance's?" Kylis flexed her hands on the chair's back.

"Sympathize?"

"They'll torture her." Kylis cracked her knuckles.

"So nothing will change."

Kylis raised a brow. "They'll Share her."

"And Cance hasn't?" Brava ignored how Kylis drummed her fingers.

"They'll negotiate with her very life."

"And you haven't with mine?" Brava avoided Kylis's boot toe.

Kylis kicked out again, this time catching Brava's shin. "And to think I came here to discuss my concern over your daughter's plight."

"You came to hang the information over me." Brava glared at her.

"You're the only one who dares a look at me in that manner." Kylis sounded almost amused. "I may be able to rescue her, but I'll need your help."

Brava said nothing.

"Of course, I don't expect you to do it for free. I wouldn't."

"I'm not you."

"How stoic." Kylis rose from her chair to stand over Brava. "Okay, she wasn't taken. She somehow escaped. Now she's lost in the Cleave Wilds, and there's a runaway cull on the loose who'll make ribbons of her if we don't find her quickly." She stooped to touch Brava's face. "You don't want her to die alone at the end of a slow blade, do you?"

"A cull got away with a blade?" Brava jerked away. "And you call your people loyal."

"Nevertheless," Kylis grabbed Brava's chin, making her face her, "you tell me what she knows about the Wilds, what survival training she's had. That'll tell us where to find her. In return, I'll grant you more status. You can have your own space, clothes, time in the daylight, three meals, a private bath." Kylis searched her expression. "I know how you miss the daylight."

"I'll not betray my daughter."

"What do you want? Someone pretty? I can make it so." Kylis stroked Brava's hair with one hand while the other held her firm. "I know how long it's been. Who do you want? Rachel? I've seen how you look at her."

"You see pity for the girl." Brava jerked back with all her might, breaking Kylis's hold.

"Please. You lust like everyone else." Kylis squatted before Brava. "You want her? Someone else? Who? Name her. Name two. You can have them at your leisure in your private quarters. Just tell me what training Chandrey's had." Kylis grabbed the base of Brava's chain and rattled it. "I'll reward you beautifully."

"My reward will be your death." Brava pulled the chain with her legs, ripping it from Kylis's hands.

"Fool." Kylis grabbed the chain again, dragging Brava over to her. "I offer you fantasy, escape, pleasure." She caressed the inside of her leg.

"You offer me the same lies, false hopes and temporary numbness you always have." Brava swung her legs, catching Kylis across the face with the chain. "You could care less about any wild woman threat. You know Chandrey was taught the same survival traditions as every sister." She swung with her legs again, smacking Kylis a second time and knocking her against the chair. "Chandrey's eluding you because she's got help, and you want to know who!"

Kylis rolled out of Brava's reach, but it took a moment before she could stand. "If you think this'll make me mad enough to kill you, you're wrong." She touched the laceration on her forehead. "But I did underestimate you. Lesson learned."

With that, Kylis stumbled from the second's space, only to return an hour or so later, properly bandaged, and accompanied by three guards.

"Take her back to her original cell," Kylis told them. "No food. No water. No anything! That clear?"

"Yes, Pedagogue Kylis."

Brava was returned to the forgotten workroom which had since been stripped its furnishings. There she was left short chained, barely able to sit or stand.

"Is stoicism still working for you? Is it keeping you warm and fed?" Kylis said when she came to see her the next afternoon. "You thirsty?" She opened a bottle of water, took a swig, and then poured out all but the last swallow at Brava's feet. "Oops. Oh, well, here's your ration for today." She capped the bottle and tossed it to her.

Brava caught the bottle in her fingertips.

"I'll be back tomorrow, if I remember," Kylis said, walking away.

Brava didn't call after Kylis. She wouldn't beg. Besides, she was too busy silently cheering her daughter to pay much attention to her own plight.

Chandrey was not only alive, she was finally free!

Chapter Thirty-Eight

Lost—adrift, wandering without; a thrall without her keeper

Freedom, decided Belsas, was a relative term. Chandrey was free from Cance, but caught in the hard grip of withdrawal.

Belsas wouldn't leave her side, but at times she gagged on the stench of sweat and vomit trapped in the critical care room. While Chandrey was bindered, her suffering was overtly clear. When she was awake, she writhed in Belsas's arms. When she slept, she dripped sweat and thrashed free of her blankets.

Zhastra said it was all part of the process, and forced vile-smelling herbal mixtures down Chandrey's throat every few hours until she finally slept soundly, pressed against Belsas.

"The worst is over." Zhastra moved aside as Chloe and another woman cleaned the room. "They'll bathe her, and Chloe will sit with her until you return."

"I'll stay," Belsas said.

"You've ignored your own needs for three days," said Zhastra. "There's a basin and clean coveralls in your cubicle. After that, see Madeleine for some food, then Adara needs to brief you."

The healer left no room for argument, so Belsas nodded and climbed from the tangled sleeping platform. "How long will the briefing take?" She looked down at Chandrey.

"Not long. I told Adara you need rest." Zhastra patted her back. "She'll be okay."

"I'm coming back here."

"Of course. Chandrey will sleep for a day or so, and no doubt you should too." Zhastra turned Belsas toward the doorway. "Go."

Belsas obeyed reluctantly, cleaning up, eating and reviewing her position on the flight schedule with Adara before returning to Chandrey's side. She slept heavily and woke sometime the next afternoon when Chandrey stirred against her shoulder.

"Hi," she said.

"Bel?" Chandrey looked confused. "Where are we?"

"Somewhere safe."

"Oh." Chandrey closed her eyes a moment more. "Where's Wreed?"

"We broke up a while back."

"I must have forgotten." Chandrey nuzzled into Belsas's tunic. "But I'm glad you're here now. I've been sick." Her voice was muffled. "That's why we're here, isn't it? That's why I can't remember things?"

"Yes, you're having problems, but you're safe." Belsas rolled so she faced Chandrey.

"My head."

"No doubt." Belsas wrapped an arm around Chandrey, drawing her up for a long awaited kiss, but when Chandrey moved, she groaned and buried her face again.

"Want me to rub your temples?" Belsas asked.

"I don't think it'll help." Chandrey rolled on her back and looked around. "How long have we been here?"

"In this room? Three, maybe four days." Belsas pushed the hair from Chandrey's face. "Maybe a back rub would help."

"No. I think it might be hunger." Chandrey sat up and moved to the edge of the platform. "My head *really* hurts."

"Zhastra said it would." Belsas moved to sit beside her.

"Zhastra?" Chandrey peered at Belsas through her fingers. "Who is she again?"

"Your healer," she said.

"Most everything's a blank."

"Let me fill you in a bit." Belsas explained the difference between the New Cleave and the Old Cleave Resistance, that they'd fled the New Cleave, but she stopped short of telling her about the Kinship and Brava.

"So Cance owned me and you took me from her." Chandrey rubbed her wrists. "Then are we oathed?"

"For New Cleave's purposes, yes." When Belsas took her hands, Chandrey pulled away. "But no one owns you."

"I'm not certain whether that's true or not at this point." Chandrey moaned and clutched her head. "Why can't I remember?"

"Don't push yourself. Zhastra said your memory will come back slowly."

"Not certain I want it to." Chandrey clutched her head harder. "Is Healer Zhastra around? Maybe she can give me something for this headache."

"I can show Belsas how to phase-ease your pain," Zhastra said from where she stood in the open doorway. "But your system also needs copious amounts of water. Part of that headache is dehydration."

Chandrey looked up. "Are you Healer Zhastra?"

Zhastra started, and then motioned Belsas to move so she could sit beside Chandrey. "Don't you remember me?" She glanced at Belsas. "But she remembers you?"

"Seems so," Belsas replied.

"Interesting." Zhastra pushed back her binder.

"Can I have something for my head?" Chandrey tried to jerk away when Zhastra pulled her head up for examination.

"Be still." When Zhastra raised her brows, Chandrey whimpered and drew back, retreating until she pressed against the rock wall behind the platform.

"Why are you so frightened?" Belsas came to the bedside. "Zhastra's never hurt you."

"It was my expression." Zhastra moved back to the doorway. "I'm certain it meant something totally different to her once. I'll keep my distance," she said softly, "but we'll need to begin phase-gleaning as soon as possible."

"I don't want anyone in my head!" Chandrey wailed from her corner. "I just need something for the pain."

"I'll get her something." Zhastra returned a few seconds later with a half-filled mug. "Small sips, but drink often."

Chandrey took the mug without looking up and hesitated. "Water?"

"You're dehydrated. Drink." Zhastra returned to the doorway. "I've sent Chloe for some food."

"Why can't you just give me something?"

"There's nothing I can offer besides a phase." Zhastra sighed. "I can show Belsas how to or she can simply try, but you have to let someone in if you want any real relief."

"No." Chandrey shoved the mug at Belsas and put her head between her knees. "If you aren't going to do anything, then leave me alone."

"Now, be reasonable," began Belsas, but Zhastra shook her head. "You have duty in an hour. You best get ready."

"But doesn't she—"

"You do your job. I'll do mine." Zhastra waited until Belsas slid on her binder, and followed her out the door. "You won't be respected or trusted if you ignore duty for any more of your life mate's needs. Leave her in my hands and do what's expected of you."

While this troubled Belsas, she knew it was necessary. "Let me tell her I'll be back."

"I'll tell her." Zhastra blocked the doorway. "Go to work."

Belsas flew two security sweeps before picking up a keeper and her family joining the Resistance. At the end of her shift, she unloaded her breathing cargo, prepped her launch for the next pilot, and grabbed a meal mug and water bottle on her way to Chandrey's side. She stopped when she saw that a guard stood outside the door.

"She wouldn't be there if it wasn't necessary." Belsas turned to see Zhastra approaching. "Cance and her helper have positively poisoned her mind." She placed her hand over the door latch. "But we must begin gleaning her."

Belsas knocked Zhastra's hand aside and opened the door.

Giana sat on a pillow by the platform's head, darning footlings in the low light. Chandrey lay on her back with a fluids IV line trailing from her arm. A second line ran from underneath the blanket to a nutrition flask, which had been hung from the ceiling on a protruding hook. A catheter bag hung from the end of the bed.

"Is this necessary?" Belsas took Giana's place.

After a few words and a hug from her keeper, Zhastra's eldest life mate departed.

"I'm strengthening her before we begin."

"She sleeping?"

"Phased. And no, not willingly, but we've no time."

"What's changed?"

"Cance has been named Missionary pedagogue."

"I thought that was Kylis's title."

"Kylis has been named Missionary pedagogue of New Lands. She appointed Cance as her replacement inside Cleave lands."

"From granary manager to pedagogue in less than a pass." Belsas's stomach had turned too much for her to do more than sip from her mug. "So Kylis is in charge of the Kinship, and Cance is in charge of Cleave education."

"Cance has pooled all her new resources into finding the Resistance." Zhastra motioned for Belsas to remove her binder. "And she's spread your image everywhere. You've been labeled a thrall thief."

"Might as well be a murderer." Belsas set the mug aside in favor of her water.

"You're that too." Zhastra sat on the edge of the platform and slipped off her boots. "Cance claims you killed one of her life mates."

Belsas gagged mid-swallow. "I did what?"

"One of her lesser life mates did die the day you freed Chandrey," said Zhastra. "But everyone here knows it was at Cance's hand, not yours." She slid Chandrey over so she could lie down next to her. "I need you on her other side."

"This frightens me." Belsas shed her boots and moved into position on Chandrey's other side.

"It should." Zhastra gently rolled Chandrey until she faced Belsas. "Do what I say, exactly how I say to do it, and without hesitation. This is Chandrey's mind. She can move much more quickly than we can."

"Are you saying she'll try to run?"

"In a sense. She's smart but wounded, and wounded animals run to save themselves." Zhastra looked over Chandrey's shoulder at Belsas. "She'll hide memories she doesn't want to share or address, and those are the ones we need most. Now meditate to calm your jitters."

Belsas closed her eyes and focused on her favorite calming phrase, repeating it until she felt a small nudge. Zhastra had entered her mind.

Don't stop. Zhastra's energy spread through Belsas, and then part of that energy peeled away, taking some of her with it. *Draw her to you.*

Belsas wrapped her arms around Chandrey and pulled her close, but there was suddenly too much going on for her meditation to continue. Images flashed. Sounds cut in and out. Faces came and went.

There was darkness, and then sudden blinding light, then darkness again. The noise was deafening. Zhastra had pulled her inside Chandrey, deep inside Chandrey's mind, to her darkest memories, to her raw, agonized, emotional core.

Chapter Thirty-Nine

Pedagogue—instructor, dogmatist, zealot

Apogee, Cance thought as she stared at the security feed image, looked more like a training base than a bustling capital city. The streets were bare except in the morning hours when the market and stores opened long enough for residents to fill their pantries. Keepers tended that duty and all others which required going outside.

Thralls were not to be seen. For them, going outside was now a Sharing offense. No laundry hung on the lines. Flower boxes had become weedy. The Aut studs were conspicuously absent as well, locked deep in Central Medical with the breeders.

Only the capitol building itself seemed alive. Heavily armed keeper guards circled the building in quick kick-step. Armed launches flew overhead every few minutes. Long-range blaster nests sat atop portable guard towers set every twenty meters. The capital and its center had become a fortress which protected the pedagogues, including her.

Even so, a certain someone had managed to slip in and out undetected, and now lay asleep in a dark corner of Cance's new home, waiting for her return.

Noise from the hallway roused her from her thoughts, and she looked up. *About time.*

Tavince and Jandis entered the meeting room in typical flamboyant pedagogue fashion. They were followed by a trio of keeper attendants specifically assigned to cater to their every need. If they wanted thralls, they had them, as many as they wanted, no matter their keeper.

A pedagogue herself, Cance took advantage of this perk between most every meeting, as did Tavince, but Jandis preferred to spend the time in meditation and prayer.

She scoffed at the aging Harbinger behind her back, but Jandis was a Cleave icon.

"The Missionary should listen to the Harbinger," Tavince reminded her over a mug of liquor during an early afternoon recess. "Or at least make it appear so." She smiled lewdly. "It keeps the remaining elders loyal."

"What good are they?" Cance poured herself another mug. She and Tavince were alone, no attendants or thralls to fulfill their needs. Tavince had insisted on it.

Tavince flipped a speck of dust from the cuff of her fine tunic. She reminded Cance of a much deadlier version of Creiloff. "The elders sacrifice their daughters and granddaughters to defend our ways."

"True enough." Cance leaned back in her seat and began to clean beneath her nails with her boot knife. "You don't like me, do you, Practitioner?"

"Hmph." Tavince flounced her tunic bottom. "Why would I? You're Kinship born, young, inexperienced—"

"But nevertheless, here I am." Cance grinned brashly. "And there's not a damned thing you can do about it." She twirled her blade, and then cleaned under the nails of her other hand. "Besides, Kylis wouldn't have appointed me if I were unable to succeed in the position."

"I never questioned your competency, Cancelynn. I only stated that I didn't like you personally." Tavince's slim upper lip began to curl. "Or your personal habits. The undersides of fingernails are ripe with bacteria. Cleaning them with your personal blade is disgusting." She looked down at her own finely manicured surgeon's hands, her tone smug, her expression demure when she looked up. "No wonder your thralls contract so many infections."

"Fuck you." Cance twirled her blade in Tavince's face.

"With those filthy hands? Certainly not." Tavince tapped her fingers on the arm of her chair. "So tell me, Cancelynn, what do you plan to do with this new power of yours?"

"Serve the Cleave's goals, of course." Cance failed to impress Tavince and she knew it.

Tavince raised both brows at her. "Save the rote for the Harbinger."

"I'm not a thrall you can tame with a look." Cance rose from her seat.

"And I'm not one bit intimidated by your blade tricks or childish displays of temper." Tavince placed her elbows on the table, folded her hands, and rested her chin on them so that she leaned toward Cance. "If we are to be of service to each other, I should know your real plans."

Cance smiled, but proceeded with caution. "Okay, then. I believe the Kinship should be our first step."

"Most certainly," said Tavince. "Kylis will agree."

"And the Harbinger?"

"Ask Jandis yourself at our next meeting." Tavince sat back and waved Cance away. "This conversation is no longer productive. Leave me." She commed her residence, ordering one of her favorite thralls to be washed and readied.

Cance left, puzzled by the finely boned healer. Tavince was a small woman, often shorter than her thralls, but she commanded those around her by reputation alone. She had once doubted the validity of that reputation, but now she believed every word. The Practitioner was cold and clinical, even about sex. She admired her.

Later that same day, all four pedagogues met: the Missionary, Practitioner and Mother's Harbinger in the safety of their Cleave stronghold, and Kylis, the Missionary of New Lands, from her workroom in the former Kinship governmental facilities on Saria III.

After the usual formal greetings and a few moments of informal chat, Cance asked Jandis her views on Autlach domination.

The Harbinger's response was a lengthy rant concerning "those damnable Auts." The only worthy Autlachs carried half of the genetics needed to produce a Taelach. The rest were a waste of resources. The same went for most of the former Kinship. Their spiritual paths were so far removed from the truth that they couldn't even see the Mother, much less know Her law. They had to be lessoned for this indiscretion. They had to be taught. They would pay.

"And they are," said Kylis through the com. "We're in agreement, Jandis."

"Most certainly," added Tavince.

Cance nodded toward the Harbinger.

Jandis acknowledged the gesture and raised the footrest of her oversized cathedra chair. With her shaved head, she was easily the senior pedagogue. Kylis had said that Jandis was past the age of leathers and gathering thralls, well into the age of rigid thinking and rote responses. Cance just thought her old.

"The Missionary must inform us of her lesson plans for the Resistance," Jandis said.

"She has to find them first," said Kylis with a laugh. "It's her initial test of power."

"One I've already conquered," Cance replied.

"You've found their caverns?" Tavince looked doubtful. "You found what the best Cleave scouts couldn't?"

"You doubt me?" said Cance. "I've also found Tavince's pet project."

"How?" Tavince's doubt spread to her pinched mouth.

"I have my sources." Cance briefly thought of Brandoff, sleeping off her latest dose in the crawl space above her master suite.

"Very well," said Jandis. "Then tell us your plan."

"A face-to-face lesson." Cance squared her shoulders.

"Excellent." The Harbinger clasped her knotted hands together. "Kill every thrall. Lesson the keepers, and then Share them until there's nothing left."

"Except for my project," cautioned Tavince. "She must be returned alive."

"No fucking way." Cance sat tall. Her seat had been Kylis's, but would be hers until her custom carved cathedra was completed. "She murdered one of my thralls and stole another."

Kylis's laugh rang through the com. "Having problems with your pets?"

"No more than you." Cance turned to glare. "How's Brava?"

Kylis wagged her finger. "Watch your mouth, Missionary."

"Or what?"

"Enough," said Jandis in a weary tone. "Cancelynn, the Practitioner's project must be handled properly. When does she drop?"

"She's due in three cycles." Tavince sat with her hands primly in her lap.

"Then Missionary Cancelynn shall deliver the project to you unharmed, and you shall return the emptied slattern to her afterward." Jandis glanced to the heavens. "The Mother's law states a thief shall receive her lesson at the hands of the offended. Lesson her well, Cancelynn."

"But if the project is successful, I will need to study her in some detail," began Tavince, but Jandis held up her hand.

"If the project succeeds, the slattern returns to Cancelynn. If the babe has already been born, the slattern receives her punishment. Pick another test subject. You've the entire Kinship to choose from." Jandis looked at Kylis. "And you, Missionary of New Lands, need to explain to us why Brava Deb was not executed with the rest of the Kinship High Council."

"Tavince has her toys, I have mine," said Kylis. "She's good propaganda."

"Her every breath inspires the remaining Kinship fighters." Jandis sank back in her chair. "Execute her and be done with it."

"Absolutely not. She's far too much fun."

Jandis frowned. "You've made your point. I've made mine. Do what you wish, Kylis, just keep her from public view."

"Let them wonder if Brava Deb still breathes," said Tavince. "If this discussion has closed, I've other business."

"Very well." Jandis pulled her lap robe higher and shifted in her seat. "Proceed at your leisure."

Tavince stood and strode to a place where she could see the other pedagogues equally. "We need to address the potential problem of the Training Grounds."

Cance perked up when she heard a familiar topic. "What about them?"

"The infiltration has proved unsuccessful."

"I heard," said Jandis. "They're loyal for slatterns. Missionary Kylis, what can you tell us?"

"I've cut off their supply lines and main power sources." Kylis placed a map on the viewer. "As you can see, Saria IV's weather has been quite problematic."

Cance shook her head. "It won't bother them. The Training Ground's staff is used to it, and most of the base pilots, even the cadets, know how to fly through the storms."

"They can't fly what they can't power," said Kylis. "And starvation will soon set in."

"They've enough stores in those hiding caves to stay alive for several moon cycles and an entire fleet hidden in a deep cavern." Cance used her interface to place a half dozen markers in the canyons surrounding the Training Grounds. "I don't remember them all, but the fleet is housed here."

"Their starvation will prove a most interesting experiment," said Tavince. "I insist on having recorders there when you finally infiltrate."

"Consider it done." Kylis recorded the information with her interface. "It'll take time, but I'll lesson every slattern on that base."

"Excellent," said Jandis. "Any other concerns, Practitioner?"

"A request." Tavince moved to stand directly before Cance. "Healer Zhastra is responsible for my project's escape. I want her thralls Shared in front of her as part of her lesson."

"I'll tend to it personally," said Cance.

"One last piece of business." Jandis scrubbed her eyes with the backs of her leathery hands. "Missionary Cancelynn, since this is your first large lessoning, you must record the entire event for our later critique."

"I want to see Zhastra's face," said Tavince.

"Will be my pleasure." Cance stroked the arms of her seat. "It'll be my supreme pleasure."

Chapter Forty

Paragon—the patient keeper of a troublesome thrall

Chandrey had been made dead by Cance, and then was revived by Zhastra, Madeleine told Belsas in a candid moment, but rage had come with that revival.

Zhastra said it must have derived from Cance and Brandoff being twins, from their dual negative affect on Chandrey's mind, but whatever the cause, Chandrey frightened the other thralls. She growled at them, glared fiercely at them, talked to no one other than Belsas and Zhastra, and bared her teeth at everyone else. The thralls were so afraid of her, their keepers insisted she be supervised or placed in a locking binder at all times.

There was little else Belsas could do but keep Chandrey close. When she did pre- and postflight checks, Chandrey stood on the sidelines. When she bathed and changed, Chandrey was there. They even continued to share the same sleeping space, but Chandrey slept in the corner. Belsas would never have touched her and said as much, but Chandrey still refused, taking two pillows and a blanket every night.

Flight time was the only reprieve Belsas received. Chandrey spent those hours with Zhastra, either beside the healer or locked inside the critical care room.

Belsas loathed the very idea of locking her up, but Zhastra said the only alternative was shackling her. She'd explained and apologized profusely to Chandrey, and never confined her a moment more than absolutely necessary, but each episode left Chandrey angrier than the last.

"You made me serve you." Chandrey told her late one evening after they'd returned to their small sleeping space.

"I didn't have a choice." Belsas sat on the edge of the sleeping platform to pull off her boots, but first she rubbed her skin where her binder had made pressure marks. Bad enough she had to wear it in flight, but she had to wear it most everywhere else as well. Everyone had callouses. "It's what's expected."

"You're acting like the rest of them." Chandrey's voice began to rise and her eyes narrowed, projecting her anger.

"Keep it down," said Belsas. "Only Zhastra and Adara know I'm not keeper. What else was I supposed to do?" She was tired of the argument, the same they had every evening.

"I'll stay quiet for my own sake, not yours." Chandrey sat on the other side of the platform to pull off her hide slippers. "Do you have to be so brusque?"

"You want me to show appreciation like they do?" Belsas slipped her leggings over the top of her boots and took them off as one, leaving them at the ready. "Good girl, Chandrey. Is that what you want?"

"Don't patronize me." Chandrey slid out of her skirt, revealing her under leggings. They clung to her just so, and Belsas forced herself to look away.

"I—" She cleared her throat. "I'm doing the best I can."

"So am I." Chandrey plucked her pillows and blanket from the bed.

"It's damp tonight." Belsas climbed onto her side of the platform. "You know you're welcome up here."

Chandrey answered by flipping one of the pillows into the corner and sitting on it.

"Very well." Belsas laid back and pulled her blanket to her chin. "But the offer stands if you get cold." She lowered the bedside lantern.

If Chandrey knew, really knew, what she thought about her... Belsas sighed and placed her arm over her eyes. As long as they were among the Cleave, be it Old or New, Chandrey wouldn't see anything but bondage, wouldn't feel anything but trapped.

* * *

The next evening, a star-filled sky dominated Belsas's view. It was early in her second security sweep, but so far, the evening had proved uneventful. She was attentive to the sensors, but she also let her mind wander.

She and Chandrey had been with the Old Cleave a hundred days. Zhastra had recently called her a "natural keeper." The healer had even encouraged her to make two recently widowed life mates her own, but Belsas had refused.

"That would push Chandrey over the edge," she'd told Zhastra.

The healer agreed. "They're intelligent, well-trained women. I was just worried about their plight and your personal needs," Zhastra had said, adding that she also understood Belsas's dilemma. "Remember, a keeper's status is measured by counting her life mates. Some are beginning to question your abilities."

"They know Chandrey," said Belsas. "Would they want more to handle than that?"

"Most would have either hagged or culled her." Zhastra held up her hand. "I'm not saying either is right. I'm only saying—"

"I need to keep up appearances."

"Well, your patience does set well with the other keepers. They're calling you a paragon."

"Me?"

Now recalling her incredulous response, Belsas laughed at the humorous memory, but her laughter faded when her launch's proximity alarm suddenly sounded.

The shipboard computer chirped in her earpiece. "Approaching craft. Ten thousand meters north and closing."

When Belsas brought a visual onto her viewer, the alarm sounded again.

"Approaching craft. Twelve thousand meters northeast and closing."

"Damn." Belsas scanned the other crafts' signatures. New Cleave. Small launches. And their heading was very direct—straight at her. She double-checked that her com was set to the Resistance's channels. "Requesting assistance."

"Acknowledged," Adara replied. "Status?"

Belsas held her breath as another launch appeared on the viewer. "Two enemy. Transmitting their heading now."

"Already found them." Adara cursed under her breath. "Hold on. They're drones. No pilots or crew." The com went silent for a few seconds. "What armaments you picking up?"

"Normal guns. Double pulse lasers." Belsas relaxed her grip on the flight stick and looked at her viewer again. The crafts' pulse lasers were front mounted, the guns topside, but what was the dark blip in the middle of each launch? "You see what I see?"

"They're bombing drones." Adara cursed a little louder. "You're armed for the job. Take them out."

Belsas had practiced this type of maneuver during training, but she'd never actually fired from a launch. Sure, she'd blown up lots of things in simulation, but this was—

"Take them down, Keeper Belsas."

"Got it." Belsas opened her targeting computer. She had weapons enough, but she had to get closer. "They're shielded."

"Then you'll practically have to be on top of them."

"Acknowledged." Belsas flipped up her target viewer and threw her launch into a steep climb. She'd drop in from above and fire all her pulse beams simultaneously, clipping both launches' flight stabilizers.

"I don't have a good visual on you," said Adara. "But it looks like you're going in steep."

Belsas said a prayer, dropped the launch down on top of the drones, and fired.

"They're going down. I'm banking out." She shoved the flight stick forward and right, and then up, bringing her out of blast range. What a blast it was, she thought. The explosion threw debris across her launch and rolled it twice before she regained control.

"Easy there." Adara appeared on the viewer. "You still in one piece?"

Belsas waited for her stomach to catch up before she replied. "Believe so."

"There's minor damage to your front thrusters. Fly her back carefully."

"Acknowledged."

Belsas returned to base, receiving roaring applause when she stepped off the launch.

"The Mother had your back that time." Adara patted her shoulder. "But that wasn't half bad for your first major maneuvers outside the simulator."

"That obvious, huh?" Belsas grinned weakly.

"You gave your launch a rookie dirt bath." Adara handed her a bucket and a rag. "Clean her up." She turned away, revealing a line of keepers behind her, each toting a bucket and rags. "And don't ever mud up my fleet like that again, Keeper Belsas."

"Yes, Keeper Adara."

Belsas went to work, laughing and joking with the other keepers as they hosed and rinsed the filthy launch, and then rinsed the muddy water down the grates to the recycling tanks. She hadn't felt so accepted in a very long time. It was nice to be among equals, nice to be—

She saw Chandrey standing on the sidelines.

"Zhastra said I should come congratulate you." Chandrey said when Belsas approached. "But then I saw you with the others and—" Her expression turned sullen.

"I made a rookie mistake," began Belsas. "They were helping me clean the launch."

"You're glad to be among them." Chandrey looked betrayed, even behind her binder. "They treat you like an equal. You're one of them." It wasn't a question.

Belsas was keenly aware that the others were watching. "This isn't the time, Chandresslandra. Return to Zhastra."

"You're one of them," Chandrey repeated louder than before, shoving two fingers into Belsas's chest.

Belsas caught her wrist. "Don't do this."

Chandrey wrenched away from her. "You promised you'd take me home, that you'd never be like them. And now you've become one of *them*!"

"Chandresslandra." Belsas caught her again, this time by the waist. "Your behavior is deplorable. Go to our cubicle and wait."

"Let go!" Chandrey twisted in her arms.

Even as Belsas's heart broke, she knew they had to keep up appearances. She had to lesson Chandrey then and there, an idea which made her very soul ache.

"Chandresslandra Belsas's!" Belsas spun Chandrey around to grab her face, her expression hard, her eyes imploring. "Be silent!"

"Damn you!"

When the others began to mumble, Belsas raised a hand, and then dropped it, instead grabbing Chandrey loosely by the hair and turning her toward the living cavern. "Let's go."

"You need help?" asked one of the keepers watching.

"I'll do it." Zhastra entered the far side of the flight cavern.

"Keep your filthy hands off me!" Chandrey spat at Zhastra.

Belsas was forced to tighten her hold on Chandrey's hair.

Zhastra moved quickly, crossing the launch cavern to grab Chandrey by the arm. "You want assistance, Keeper Belsas?"

"Absolutely." Belsas released her hold as Zhastra pulled Chandrey's arms behind her back. Chandrey writhed for a moment and became oddly still against the healer's body.

"Much better. You need some re-teaching, my dear." Zhastra released her hold and passed the passive Chandrey back to Belsas. "Shall we?" She nodded toward the medical grotto.

"You going to Share her?" asked one of the keepers in a concerned voice. "Cause I don't believe it'll help."

"Definitely not," said another. "What're you going to do with her, Zhastra?"

"Lesson her," said Zhastra over her shoulder. "But know Keeper Belsas doesn't believe in Sharing any more than I do." She slowed to look back. "Remember this one spent time as a pedagogue's plaything." She helped Belsas half-carry Chandrey to the critical care grotto where they dropped her onto the bed.

"Thank you." Belsas, near tears, sagged against the wall. "What'd you do out there?"

"Just a pinhead of sedative." Zhastra pulled the pin from Chandrey's wrist. "I cried at my first lesson too. Giana had badmouthed two keepers, so I didn't have a choice."

"You still expect me to lesson her?" Belsas stared. "You can't be serious."

"Others will ask if you did. We must be able to answer honestly."

"But—" Belsas felt horrified, but she knew Zhastra was right. "I can't hurt her."

"No one expects you to." Zhastra touched her arm.

"Then what do I do?"

"Be gentle but firm." Zhastra leaned over the bed to release Chandrey's binder. "Despite her resistance, she knows you mean well." She motioned Belsas to remove her binder. "You're a good woman, Belsas, and you love Chandrey enough to do this for her. Lay beside her."

"I don't know what to do." Tears streamed down Belsas's face. "Help me."

"You don't need my help," said Zhastra, but she held open Chandrey's mind, easing Belsas's entrance. "Just show her how much you love her. Show her it all, what brought you to the Cleave, what you went through to be with her. Show her every detail." Zhastra touched Belsas on the forehead. "She needs the lesson, my friend, and you've yet to grieve."

"Five," whispered Belsas as she closed her eyes. "Five daughters that weren't."

"The Mother has them now, but they were each part of you for a while," said Zhastra.

Belsas began her first and last lesson for Chandrey, one which was as painful as it was healing as it was needed.

Chapter Forty-One

Lesson—moral teaching, truth

The door to the critical care grotto was open when sirens roused Belsas. An attack was probable. Adara would need her in the air, but she abhorred the idea of moving. Chandrey lay against her, head on her shoulder.

"Hi." Chandrey blushed when she caught Belsas looking at her.

"Hi." Belsas nuzzled the top of Chandrey's head, but pulled back when Chandrey stiffened and slid up to look her in the eyes.

Chandrey examined Belsas carefully, deeply, but at a comfortable physical and mental distance. "They need you."

"But I just found you," said Belsas. "*You* need me."

"We both need a lot of things," Chandrey said. No doubt between them now, Belsas thought, but a million questions still lay in their path. "Can we can talk when you get back?"

Belsas closed her eyes, resisting the urge to pull Chandrey fully on top of her to feel her every curve. "I hope so."

"Me too." Chandrey slipped from the bed as the sirens blasted again. "Go on, before Adara comes to drag you away."

"She would." Belsas stretched and stood. Her clothing was rumpled, but she had no time to do anything about it. "You stay safe." She longed to sweep Chandrey into her arms. Maybe in time…

"You too." Chandrey touched her hand before they parted ways,

Belsas toward the flight cavern, Chandrey toward the thralls' gathering spot where Zhastra would direct them.

"That lesson had better have worked." Adara frowned at Belsas when she trotted into the flight cavern.

All the launch pilots were assembled, Belsas noticed, forty-one counting her, and they were focused on the portable viewer in front of them. Numerous blips blinked on the screen, too far away to be an immediate threat, but the sheer number proved foreboding.

"Live pilots and crews on all the ones we can read." Adara flipped to a new screen which showed Myflar's night sky. "The New Cleave has secured fifty percent of Saria III." She flipped to an orbital map of Saria IV. "And the Training Grounds are under siege."

"We're the only Resistance on Myflar," she continued when the murmurs died. "All Autlachs inside Kinship lands have been disposed of, no matter their genetic possibilities."

"What a waste," said someone.

"I'd say," murmured another.

Adara held up her hand. "Resistance aside, all Myflar Taelachs have either been lessoned as slatterns or added to the New Cleave population." She held up her other hand as well, quieting the discord. "We've a daunting task before us, but we have the Mother on our side. We've stayed true to Her word. True to Her law. We're the only real teachers left. Time we lessoned this New Cleave about straying from the path!"

Making the whoops and calls, each pilot, Belsas included, found her launch and prepped for takeoff.

Belsas had been in more than enough fights since coming to the Resistance, but never in an all-out battle. She shook off any doubt and took the pilot's seat. It wasn't the bulky transport she had initially been assigned, so she wasn't accustomed to the little fighting launch's speed. The launch lurched hard during takeoff, and she couldn't help cursing.

"Careful there, rookie," Adara said in her earpiece, no doubt watching her from the viewers in the command cavern. "She's sensitive at the stick."

"Acknowledged." Belsas leveled out and fell behind the lead line of launches.

Most of the other fighting launches were meant for offense, to descend on attackers before they knew what was happening. Next came a wave of armored launches, modified to carry heavy weaponry. Each held four crew members, two pilots and two gunners. Belsas's group came third, a mix of fighting and mid-size armored launches that served to mop up any enemies that slipped through the first two lines.

Tyenach, a keeper around Belsas's age, headed the third line. "No dirt baths this time, Belsas, understand?" Tyenach joked.

Belsas wished she could imitate that confidence. "I hear you."

She double-checked her weapons screen. Pulse beams, side guns, and a handful of concussion grenades which would crash a fighting launch close to the blast. She patted the blaster on her hip and glanced at the plasma bow strapped to her arm. She doubted the combat would become hand-to-hand, but according to Adara, anything was possible.

"Front wave. We have visual." Belsas was unsure of the speaker. "Great Mother! Their fleet spans the horizon!"

"Keep it under control," interrupted Adara. "They may have numbers, but we have the Mother's law." She recited a quick prayer for her fleet. "No more unnecessary chat. Let the lessoning begin."

"Indeed." A foreign voice intruded into the encrypted communication channel.

"Go yellow," said Adara.

All the pilots, including Belsas, switched channels, re-securing their communications.

"Go whatever color you wish, your entire communications network has been breached," said the same invading voice. All Resistance communications ceased.

"Stars!" Belsas flipped her microphone to the side. The first line of the New Cleave fleet was nearly upon them. They'd have to rely on hand signals.

Tyenach flew up on her right, motioning through her launch's side window. She signaled with a thumb up, spread her palm flat, and jerked it up and down. The third line was going to drop into the battle early. Belsas nodded. Tyenach peeled off to inform the rest of her line.

A moment later, Belsas's group rose from the back of the fleet into Myflar's upper atmosphere so their numbers would be skewed by the moon's thick ozone layer. Low-level clouds blocked any visual communications, but when she saw the drop in engine flames that meant the launches were gearing for descent, she did the same, dropping from the clouds just to Tyenach's left.

Tyenach nodded, made a swooping motion, and pointed down.

Belsas repeated the motion and passed the information on to the pilot on her left, where it continued down the line. A few seconds later, Tyenach dropped her launch into a steep dive.

"Here we go." Belsas engaged the New Cleave's fighting launches with the rest of her group—looping and rolling between and around the larger craft in a dangerous game, but they were woefully outnumbered and outgunned. One explosion at a time, their numbers dwindled.

"No, you don't!" Belsas fired her pulse beams at the fighter swooping toward one of the larger Resistance launches. The fighter exploded into a fireball that streaked across the sky until the debris fell from view.

She swept around the largest Resistance launch and dropped under it, lurking in its shadow as she searched for another target. Tyenach's launch blew past her a second later, two New Cleave fighting launches on her tail.

"Two against one, not fair." Belsas turned her flight stick to join the chase, picking off both of Tyenach's pursuers before they could turn back on her. Tyenach followed her back into the Resistance launch's shadow, presumably to catch her breath and wipe her brow.

She and Tyenach took turns dropping into the battle to catch one or two of the enemy by surprise before returning to the large launch's underbelly. They'd taken down a dozen fighting launches and one mid-sized launch between them before one of the New Cleave fighters dropped in from alongside the Resistance launch and opened fire, hitting Tyenach's fuel cells at the right angle to blow the remnants into Belsas, knocking her launch into a steep tumble.

This was no rookie mistake. Belsas pulled up hard, trying to regain control. She managed to slow her descent, but as smoke started to fill the launch, impact became unavoidable. A prayer escaped her lips. She ejected, the explosion blowing off the front of the launch and hurtling her into the air.

Wind rushed past her flight suit. The first parachute deployed, which slowed her fall until it caught on the wing of a passing fighting launch, slinging her some hundred meters into the open gun house perched on top of a New Cleave's low-flying armored transport. She crashed into the top edge of the front shield and flipped over it, landing on top of the single gunner. Excruciating pain swept through her body and something pierced her shoulder from behind, but she still managed to release her parachute and roll over, ready to fight.

The gunner was already dead. A piece of the high-speed shrapnel had pierced the gun house's shield and run through the gunner's chest, pinning her to the chair. Belsas had landed on the protruding piece when she fell on the gunner, and now felt blood running down her back.

She unstrapped the gunner, pushed her out of the gun house, and slid into her chair. She was certain she'd fractured some ribs in the fall, but managed to buckle the straps.

The battle raged around her, but the adrenaline had worn off enough for the pain to bring tears to her eyes. She wondered how many bones she'd broken.

Doesn't matter. You have to do this, she thought.

She turned the chair in line with the gun. The firing controls were simple, not unlike a fighter, but the gun certainly had greater impact. She rotated the turret in search of a target, locked on a New Cleave fighter, and fired. The concussion sent the dead gunner's body rolling and knocked her deep into the gunner's chair. Everything went black.

She didn't know if she'd hit her target, but when she came to, the Resistance was losing the battle. *Again*, she thought and trained the gun on another target.

Nothing happened. She tried to clear the misfire, but when the safety system suddenly powered the gun down, she had no choice except to witness the battle unfold. What would she do when it was over? Surrender? Never. She'd somehow find Chandrey, and they'd make their escape back into the Cleave wild lands.

From her vantage point, Belsas could only watch and grieve. Over half the Resistance launches were destroyed and many others were damaged. But the New Cleave vessels remained in good order, and another wave of their fighting launches had just appeared on the horizon. This was the end, but the Resistance had tried. The Mother couldn't fault them for—

The engine of the transport beneath her revved unexpectedly. The transport began to turn, forcing her to brace and sending painful spasms through her torso. Why were they turning away?

The battle slowed to a crawl. The New Cleave vessels were falling back. What was going on? A moment later, a passing fighting launch answered her question. Its hull bore two symbols: the Kinship and the Training Grounds.

Belsas belted out a Kinship battle cry as another fighting launch passed. The Kinship was still fighting! Then her excitement waned, replaced by fear as the battlefield faded from view.

She was being carried away from the Kinship's success as an accidental prisoner.

Chapter Forty-Two

*Accord—mutual understanding, the Kinship and Old Cleave
laughing over a mug of wine*

Initially, the remaining Resistance keepers worried about losing
their thralls, but that fear soon faded, Adara's concern included.
Chandrey was the only thrall to be allowed on a Kinship launch, and
at Master Lupinski's request, she was quickly transported to the main
Kinship battleship orbiting Myflar.

The Kinship didn't want their thralls, Lupinski assured them.
They had the same goal as the Resistance: smash the New Cleave. But
a Kinship member had a right to return to her home if she so wished.
They'd let everyone know as soon as they found Belsas.

"So one of your pilots saw Belsas strapped in a New Cleave gun
house." Adara was amused by the idea. "That explains why they shot
down one of their own launches. Mother help her. I suppose that's one
way to infiltrate the capital."

"She'll contact us when she's able." Lupinski glanced around the
Resistance's docking cavern, which now held a mixture of Resistance
and Kinship crafts. "This is very well hidden. No wonder they had
trouble finding you."

"Master Lupe?" A woman Adara knew as Quall Dawn crossed the
cavern in quick strides, her life and battle braids bouncing. "We've a
situation."

Adara turned to see Zhastra standing between a Resistance pilot and a Kinship cadet who wore her hair in a long braid which she'd tucked into her flight suit.

The healer faced the Resistance pilot, explaining, "It's cultural. She's as much keeper as you."

"Then why's her hair long?" The Resistance pilot lunged for the Kinship pilot's collar, pulling out her waist-length braid. "See? They sent their thralls!"

The Kinship pilot jerked her braid away and crouched in a fighting posture. "I'll kick your sorry little keeper ass from here to next cycle if you touch me again!"

"Stand down, cadet!" Lupinski inserted herself beside Zhastra. "Kinship pilots, return to your launches and await further instruction."

"Keeper pilots, regroup in the kitchen cavern." Adara stepped up with Quall. "It appears both groups need a lesson," she said to Zhastra.

"A bit of retraining is definitely in order here." Zhastra looked at Lupinski. "Hello again, old friend." She held out her hand.

Lupinski grasped the offered hand just above the wrist to draw Zhastra into a hug. "Zhastra, old girl, how long has it been?" Lupinski patted the healer's back cordially.

"Let's see. I had just taken on Sabra so, what, fifteen passes?"

Adara exchanged confused glances with Quall.

"At least," said Lupinski. "Still a bastion for change, I see."

"Same as you." Zhastra turned to Adara. "Back then, the Kinship and Cleave conferenced at least once a pass. I served as the Cleave healer of record at several."

"And I served like you are now, Quall." Lupinski's smile recounted the depth of their friendship. "So how do we solve this problem?"

"Through understanding," said Zhastra. "Talk to yours, I'll talk to mine, and then we bring them together under a common banner for a lesson."

"Banner?" Quall frowned.

"The one you and Keeper Adara are going to create," said Lupinski. Zhastra nodded.

"These fingers aren't exactly artistic." Adara held up her calloused hands.

"They'll be proficient," said Zhastra. "As will your co-creator's." She smiled gently at Quall. "You haven't much time. I suggest you get to work."

"As should we," said Lupinski. "Introduce me to your family when this is done?"

"Would love to." Lupinski turned toward her own people.

Zhastra did the same.

"It's First Officer Quall?" Adara motioned her Kinship companion to follow.

"Yes, Keeper Adara." Quall was easily twice Adara's size, but she had to jog to keep up with her. "You have a work space for us?"

"That's where we're headed." Adara found herself doing something she never thought she would: welcoming a Kinship officer into her workroom.

* * *

"We're done here." Chandrey stopped Healer Jacksun mid-question. "Where are my quarters?"

"You're frail, Sister Chandresslandra." Jacksun knew she was not much older than her patient. "I'm admitting you to the infirmary for more testing."

Chandrey peered above her head, no doubt trying to figure out her keeper status before she stopped herself. "Am I a prisoner?"

"Why, no, Sister Chandresslandra," said Jacksun.

"Have I been drafted into military service?"

Jacksun was taken aback. "No."

"Then tell me where my quarters are." Chandrey climbed down from the examining lounger and put on her slippers.

"But you should really talk to—" Jacksun began.

Chandrey cut her off. "I'll talk to an emotional healer when I'm ready. Not before. My quarters?"

"I'll call your escort."

When Chandrey left, Jacksun completed her examination notes, and then walked down the corridor to her superior's office. The door was open. Master Healer Fahari waited for her.

"I watched on the viewer." Fahari motioned Jacksun to sit across the worktable from her. "Your thoughts?"

"Sister Chandresslandra is underweight and damned stubborn," said Jacksun. "She wouldn't undress for her exam, refused to take off her binder, and barely let me take her vitals. Aren't thralls supposed to be obedient?"

"Stars, Jack, what you saw wasn't stubbornness. It was suspicion."

"She's suspicious of me?" asked Jacksun in surprise. "Why?"

"She's long learned to be suspicious of everyone." Fahari backed up the exam recording. "Watch." She indicated all the cues Jacksun had missed—Chandrey looking for and finding the viewer camera, her carefully surveying Jacksun for weapons, and lastly, pocketing the decorative blade hanging on Jacksun's workroom wall.

Jacksun rubbed her chin. "But she had a blade. I saw it."

"A child's blade." Fahari zoomed in on Chandrey's belt sheath and zoomed back out so Jacksun could see how deliberately she moved. "The Cleave doesn't allow thralls more."

"Why didn't she just ask for one? Mother knows there are more than enough on this ship."

"That's not the way her world works." Fahari cut off the viewer. "So how do you get your blade back?"

"Well." Jacksun rubbed her chin harder. "I could call security."

"Not advised if you want to gain her trust."

"Then what?" Jacksun looked at her mentor.

Fahari twirled her braids between two fingers. "You're her healer. You tell me." She rose, sliding past Jacksun to reach the door. "I've patients to check. Make certain you let me know what comes of your problem."

Jacksun frowned as she followed Fahari. This was another of her master's puzzles for an apprentice. But as healer of record, it *was* her problem. How was she going to handle it?

* * *

By the time the transport landed, Belsas's teeth chattered from the combination of altitude, nerves and the gun house's cold steel. She'd managed to stay strapped in for the entire flight, but not without significant pain.

When she'd thawed a bit, she turned on her belly and shimmied across the top of the launch, careful to stay in the shadows so she wouldn't be spotted from above. From what little she'd seen during the landing, she knew Apogee's streets were empty, but there was enough air traffic to give the city life.

She adjusted her binder and slid further toward the front of the launch when it began to unload. A hundred or so keepers in full battle gear came out first, followed by four artillery floats and a string of ground cycles with gun mounts. Apparently, the New Cleave had planned on totally overrunning the Resistance. She was thankful for the Kinship's sudden arrival.

When a fighting launch flew overhead, Belsas pressed into a gunwale's shadow until it was safe, and then peered again at what emerged from the transport. More ground cycles, two floats of random gear and ammunition, and then the crew emerged. Two pilots, three gunners, and, to her surprise, a finely dressed keeper of substantial rank.

Belsas couldn't see the keeper's face, but the build, the balled fists, the red and white striped cloak amid the sea of Cleave camouflage said enough. She was looking at a pedagogue, she thought. She was looking at Cance.

Chapter Forty-Three

Attendant—aide, pedagogue punching bag

Cance strode into the meeting chamber where Tavince and Jandis waited, dropped into her cathedra, kicked her boots up on the table, and began to clean under her nails with her blade.

"Someone mind explaining the Kinship fuckup?" she asked.

"The Missionary blames others for her failures." Jandis leaned forward to push Cance's boots off the table. She had tired of the newest pedagogue and seriously doubted her faith.

"And she actually believes she can intimidate us." Tavince lunged out with her mind to knock the blade from Cance's hand. The knife skidded across the table, where Tavince caught the handle between her fingertips. "You disgust me."

She held it out to Jandis, who deposited it in her belt and pulled out another, which she slid over to Cance, saying, "A child's blade for childish behavior."

Cance bashed the dull blade against the edge of the table, breaking it at the hilt, and slid the halves back to Jandis. "A broken blade for a broken-down keeper." She kicked her feet back on the table, pulled a small dagger from her boot sheath, and began to clean under her nails again.

Jandis brushed the pieces onto the floor. Her disdain was difficult to conceal, but why should she? Cance obviously wouldn't return the courtesy. "Censure yourself, Missionary Cancelynn, before I choose to lesson you."

"You lesson me, old woman? I don't think so." Cance blinked hard, sliding down a pair of amber lenses over her eyes. Jandis had heard of the lenses, but never seen them in use. "But you can try whenever you're ready."

"Kimshee lenses," said Jandis. "And you said you'd abandoned your past."

"Only the useless parts, old woman." Cance tossed her blade from hand to hand. "Ready to try me?"

"Your disrespect is infuriating." Tavince's prim demeanor leaked exasperation. "And Kylis scoffed at our reservations about your kimshee past."

"I told you there was nothing you can do about my being here, Practitioner." Cance settled deeper in her cathedra. "I'm here to stay."

"You are proving the most unpredictable peer," said Jandis with the slightest sneer. "'The power wielder must work carefully or risk falling prey to her own confidence.'" She wasn't surprised when Cance failed to react to the verse.

"The wisest of Mother's Words. Very apropos." Tavince shared Jandis's expression. "Don't you agree, Missionary?"

"Whatever." Cance sheathed her boot knife. "So, let me guess what happened today. Kylis didn't get to the fleet cavern in time?"

"Your warning was for naught." Tavince took a sanitized towel from her side of the table and cleaned her hands with extreme care. "The Training Grounds had already escaped onto waiting Kinship warships. Missionary Kylis had no means to stop them."

"She let the entire grounds get away from her?" Cance let out a low whistle. "Now *that* deserves a lesson."

"We've already demonstrated our discontent. The Practitioner has taken two of Kylis's local thralls for her use." Jandis looked directly at Cance. "And your failure today resulted in two of your thralls being moved to my household."

Cance seemed indifferent, but she asked, "Which ones?"

"The youngest, fairest, sweetest minds you owned," said Jandis. "Your taste is excellent."

"They'll go to waste with you."

"I abstain from random thralling because my home brims with the Mother's best." Jandis let her eyes glaze with satisfaction. "They'll be well cared for on every front."

"Spare me." Cance shrugged. "There'll be more." Her lenses, Jandis noticed, remained in place.

"Then we should be more inventive with our next lesson," said Tavince. "Did you, per chance, obtain or manage a glance of my project?"

"Wouldn't you like to know?" Cance laughed, provoking Tavince into launching a lesson phase at her which bounced back painfully. "Now, now, Practitioner. That wasn't nice."

"Next time, use your blade." Jandis twirled Cance's knife between her fingers. She wasn't as quick as she used to be, but her aim was still accurate. Her palm itched for the practice. "Perhaps Tavince should cut out those lenses in your eyes."

"Temper, temper." A smile twitched Cance's mouth. "I never got to land, much less look around." She turned to Tavince. "Kill me, and I won't be able to destroy the Resistance."

"You've already failed at the task." Tavince seethed in her seat. "What makes you believe we will give you another opportunity?"

"I'm not asking for your permission." Cance swung her feet down from the table, adjusted her boot cuffs, and stood.

"Where do you believe you're going?" Jandis wheeled her cathedra so it blocked the doorway. "We are not finished."

Cance blinked hard, flicked out with her mind to move Jandis and her seat from the aisle, and blinked again, resetting her lenses. "Oh, we're finished," she said, turning back as Trisk, her attendant, opened the door. "I relaunch in ten hours with a fleet capable of solving our problem."

"Is that so?" Tavince smoothed her tunic, and then stood. "Then I have an experiment to finish before we depart." She swept by at such speed, Cance stepped back.

"She is not going with me," Cance said, looking at Jandis.

"Yes, she is." Jandis smiled triumphantly. "The Practitioner seeks to personally claim her special project. Furthermore, since an almost limitless supply of slatterns have taken up residence in our lands, she will claim the best for her research, and then show you how to properly lesson the rest." She rolled her cathedra toward the doorway. "I demonstrated for her many times, so she knows and has perfected some highly effective techniques."

"And a few I probably never considered." Cance shared Jandis's smile. "Very well, then." She stepped back further, to allow Jandis passage through the doorway if she chose. "Are you coming along for the fun, Harbinger?"

"Regrettably, no. Someone must remain here." Jandis drew a hard breath and stood, catching her balance with her attendant's help. She leaned heavily on the younger woman's arm. "I've a prayer service to plan and a meeting with Missionary Kylis in a few hours."

She began shuffling down the hall, and stopped to glance over her shoulder. "Your second effort must be successful."

Cance nodded curtly and pushed past her.

"Your second effort *will* be successful," repeated Jandis in a quiet, tired voice meant for her own ears. "You can bask in your triumph until Tavince demonstrates her scalpel skills on you too." She stopped in the hallway to catch her breath until her attendant looked at her inquiringly.

Despite her attendant's phase blind mind, Jandis knew exactly what the woman was thinking. "I may be old, Drew, but I am very capable of killing you in less than a second."

Drew stiffened and looked ahead, unable to reply if she wanted.

Jandis had seen to that early on, leaving her with Tavince for a series of surgeries. Drew's mind had been made phase blind, her voice had been silenced like an unruly thrall's, she'd suffered through a double mastectomy, and her genitals had been partially removed and cauterized so she found no pleasure. She wasn't the keeper she had been, certainly not a thrall, but no hag either.

Drew and the other attendants, as Jandis often told them, were nothing, only useful to a pedagogue. She'd be culled outside this position, so she stayed, caught in the crux of Cleave rules as were the other two attendants, Gale and Trisk.

"Remove my boots." Jandis stretched on her workroom lounger and pointed at the coverlet, which Drew spread over her. "Ready the meeting room for later, and then return to your quarters until I call."

Drew pulled Jandis's hide slippers from her gnarled feet—she hadn't worn boots in nearly three passes—placed them at the end of the lounger, and turned and walked from the room, her face void of any expression.

Jandis watched her go, content that her attendant remained cowed.

* * *

Inside her mind, Drew crafted yet another horrific way for Jandis to die.

She paused outside the conference room, watching Tavince's attendant, Gale, carrying a large hide case down the hallway. Gale was the eldest of the three attendants, a few passes older than her, which she'd learned through the combination sign and lip speaking system that she and the other two had developed.

She, Gale and Trisk had been roommates too, sharing one of the two small apartments appointed for attendants until Tavince had decided Gale would serve better from her home. Gale had never been the same after that. Not that any of them were right anyway, but Gale didn't really try to communicate these days, giving nothing more than a nod or a shake of her head to indicate understanding. Now Gale walked by without acknowledging Drew's presence.

Drew knew what was in the case, and that might have been why Gale hadn't looked at her. The hide carryall contained Tavince's medical instruments, many of which the Practitioner had invented to use when she lessoned slatterns. She wondered how many of those had been tested on Gale.

Drew tidied the conference room, set the wall com for reaching Pedagogue Kylis, and gladly retreated to her apartment.

Trisk had been assigned to the other apartment, but hadn't had time to move in. Cance kept her busy. Cance, Drew was certain, would be another Tavince as soon as she learned to use the Practitioner's "tools."

She felt a peculiar sense of relief. The Harbinger used her mind and blade—the latter and the back of her hand being the only means by which she could discipline Drew. Jandis had only used the blade twice in five passes to deliver a deep scratch up her arm for hesitating and a gash on her leg for not returning soon enough from an errand.

Gale had sewn up the cut on her leg, but the wound still scarred badly, and her leg ached whenever the weather changed.

Quiet moments were the only upside of serving Jandis. The Harbinger needed her afternoon nap. Drew generally used the time to meditate or read from one of the ten or so texts the Cleave actually allowed. But not today.

Drew layered on both her cloaks and moving swiftly and lightly, exited the pedagogues' inner sanctum of the capital building. She was one of the few women permitted freedom of movement in Apogee and no one dared block her path. She was a pedagogue's attendant. No one got in the way of a pedagogue's business.

Drew smiled. It would take convincing for her target to trust her, so she'd written a message and tucked it into her cloak as she turned to the launch docks. The message read:

I'm First Kimshee Drew Lupinski. My raiser said you might need some help. Follow me, and I'll get you to safety.

Chapter Forty-Four

Silent—voiceless, tacit; quality of a good thrall

Belsas watched as Drew reheated a bowl of steamed dark grains and beans. Drew had dressed her shoulder wound, wrapped her ribs, and cleaned her assorted cuts and scrapes. Every movement hurt, but she knew she'd be okay.

Drew spooned the hearty mix into a mug, poured tea into two more, and then looked at Belsas, moving her hand to her mouth in an eating motion.

"I'm more thirsty than—" Belsas began.

Drew slapped her hand over Belsas's mouth and shook her head.

A voice will draw them, she scribbled on the pad of paper on the table and pointed again at the food.

Belsas nodded and dove into her meal, finishing the simple vegetarian meal and two mugs of tea. Drew watched with amusement, sipping her tea. When she finished, Drew motioned to the bowl.

Belsas shook her head.

In the cooler if you want. Drew moved about the apartment, hanging both cloaks and tucking away all signs of foreign presence until Belsas stopped her.

Lupinski? she wrote on the pad.

My raiser.

Aren't you Cleave Born? wrote Belsas.

Technically. Drew held up the paper before she continued writing. *My keeper parent crossed our launch into Kinship territory. We were captured. My keeper parent died later.*

The Kinship? Belsas dreaded the response.

Drew shook her head. *Her own hand. She left me.* She paused. *I was alone until Lupinski took me in. Good woman. Taught me a lot. I'm Kinship loyal. No worries there.*

How'd you get here?

Volunteered. Prisoner exchange. Drew rolled her eyes. *Once Cleave, always Cleave.*

Logical, thought Belsas, since the Resistance hadn't existed then.

Been waiting ever since. Drew's expression briefly darkened.

As attendant? ventured Belsas, knowing what the role entailed.

Drew looked through her, leaving a great deal unsaid, Belsas was sure. *Thought my efforts were wasted.*

No, Sister Drew. Belsas touched her briefly on the shoulder. *Your plans?*

Drew patted the hand and moved to the other side of the table, where she and Belsas passed the paper pad back and forth until the pen ran dry.

Jandis called.

Sleep, wrote Drew, snatching the paper back to add, Y*ou snore?*

Belsas looked at the corner where the bedroll lay. *You mind?*

Closet, scribbled Drew after she shook the pen. *Stay hid.*

She pulled a tiny blue flask from her pocket, opened two water bottles fresh from the cooler, and carefully dribbled in a clear liquid Belsas couldn't identify. Drew nodded when she saw her watching, set the flask in the drain, and turned on the water.

To Belsas's wonderment, the flask dissolved. Drew left with the bottles, dimming the lights so she had to feel her way to the small closet. She felt around for the linens, pulled them down, and created a nest where she soon slept hard.

*   *   *

The Cleave fleet literally dropped on top of the Resistance during their second attack, leaving them no time to muster defenses, blocking the docking cavern entrance with a literal wall of fighting launches.

What Cance and Tavince found when they landed proved disappointing. The cavern was almost bare. In fact, all that remained were three Resistance launches and one Resistance transport. Eight

Resistance pilots, bindered and bound at the wrists, stood beside their crafts, guarded by a handful of Kinship troopers. Two Kinship Officers—despicable slatterns, thought Tavince—stood to the side with an obvious Resistance leader and Healer Zhastra shackled and sitting on the ground before them.

"I sense no others," said Tavince, taking a quick count of the Resistance members present. "Where's the pregnant slattern?"

"No Auts here," said the tall, fat Kinship Officer in a near perfect Cleave accent. "The Resistance has fallen to us."

"To a band of renegade students and their teachers?" Tavince cursed her body armor, and then pulled a glove to snap her fingers, setting loose a dozen New Cleave soldiers who searched the caverns within moments.

Gale stood behind her, silent, emotionless, holding the oversized carryall.

"All clear, Practitioner," said the lead soldier when she returned. "Lots of remnants, but no thralls or keepers beyond what you see."

"Search again." Tavince crossed the cavern in wide strides to face her opposition. Gale trailed behind her. "Where are your thralls?" She smacked one of the hard-edged gloves across Zhastra's face. "'Where'd you hide them?"

"Ask the Kinship." Zhastra licked blood from her lips. "They took them."

"What an interesting turn of events." Tavince tossed her gloves to Gale and called Cance away from the pilots. She'd been overseeing their searches and balked leaving the task.

"Lessons later, Missionary," said Tavince, tapping her foot impatiently.

"Let me guess, your project isn't here." Cance flicked her striped cloak behind her, catching her attendant with the tip. Trisk stepped to one side, but did nothing else. "Any trace of my stolen thrall?"

"Negative," said Tavince. "But one of these may know where she went."

"I sent all the thralls to our orbiting ship," said the older Kinship Officer.

"And who are you?" asked Tavince.

"First Officer Lupinski. You want them back, you'll give us back the Kinship capital."

"Demands from a dead woman?" began Cance, but Tavince interrupted her.

"What a lovely Kinship accent." She grasped Lupinski by the

collar, pulling her close. "Hello, darling. Shall we play?" The taller Lupinski wrenched away, but Tavince pulled her in again, reaching behind with her other hand to undo the other woman's binder.

"They're locked and coded," said Cance when Tavince cursed and pushed Lupinski away.

"And no one here knows the sequence," said Lupinski, gathering herself from the floor.

"Resourceful slatterns, just like Jandis said." Cance crossed her arms and looked at Tavince. "But I expected nothing less. Belsas fled like the coward she is and took Chandrey with her. I'll catch up with those two later."

"Bind them and take them to the inner caverns until we're ready." Tavince placed heavy emphasis on her last word. "Set up in the infirmary," she said to Gale. "Come, Missionary Cancelynn. Let's retire until preparations are complete. Your attendant can serve us both in the interim."

She turned back to their transport, followed by Cance, with Trisk in their wake.

* * *

"Line them up." The closest guard waved her blaster. The Resistance/Kinship prisoners were marched to the living cavern where they were individually shackled at the wrists and ankles and left one to a cubicle.

"I've been told to tell you to think about your slattern ways," said one of the guards as she eased Zhastra onto a sleeping platform. "Do whatever the pedagogues want, healer. You know what they're capable of." She gagged Zhastra with a piece of bed linen and stood in the doorway, thoughtful until a terse com call from a superior drew her away.

She sounds doubtful, thought Zhastra, trying to find a comfortable position. Mother pray that wasn't too late for any of them. Mother pray it wasn't too late for them all.

* * *

Healer Jacksun adjusted the decorative blade so it hung evenly on the wall.

She hadn't asked for it, but Chandrey had returned the blade the day after Jacksun gave her a well-honed, military issue blade.

"Take it to the scribe terminal and make it your own," Jacksun had said, waiting for the thanks which didn't come. Why should Chandrey thank her? It showed submissiveness.

Chandrey spent hours at the terminal, flipping through the imagery and symbols to find the right combination, the precise representation of herself. She had arrived at Jacksun's workroom door the next day, the new blade in her waist sheath, a printed image of her choices folded in her hand, and the stolen decorative blade tucked into her belt.

"This is who I am." Chandrey tossed the paper onto the worktable, hung the decorative blade on the wall while Jacksun examined her choices, and left without further comment.

"Wait," Jacksun had called, but her gaze was drawn back to the paper.

She thought about the imagery now. A Kinship symbol, the twisting, thorny vines of loss, accompanied by a first name, and a gap where the surname should be.

Chandrey had no affiliations aside from the Kinship. No raisers' names, no life mate's mark—a heart-wrenching combination which defined her emotional state. No faith, no Mother's crest. Lost. Alone against the world.

Jacksun scanned the image into Chandrey's file and tucked the paper into her worktable drawer, thinking about what she could do to help her perplexing patient.

Chapter Forty-Five

Torture—*to afflict, to torment, to teach*

The Old Cleave pilots should have been easy to make talk, easier to lesson, but their binders…Tavince scowled at the woman on the examining lounger. She knew nothing of this technology beyond the fact that it complicated her "teaching." She could inflict physical pain, as much agony as she wished, but she needed to access her subject's mind to make her newest pain tolerance experiment viable.

Tavince screamed for Gale, sending her off to find the highest ranked tech she could.

"What do you know about this thing?" Tavince asked Cance while pulling on her fine hide working gloves.

"Nothing useful." Cance turned the prisoner's head back and forth. "New tech. Double, no, triple coded." She looked at her. "It's armed."

"I want it removed correctly, so we wait on that issue." Tavince smacked her test subject squarely across the mouth. "Tell us your name."

"Mother have mercy on you, Practitioner," slurred the pilot, her eyes closing.

Cance grabbed the lower part of the pilot's face, squeezing until her mouth opened. "Her tongue's orange."

"Zhastra and her fucking potions." Tavince pushed up the woman's sleeve. "It won't spare her." She took a glass syringe with a delicate crystal needle from the selection spread on a nearby table, emptied part of the contents into the pilot's arm, and stood back, feeling victorious. "Wait for it. Three, two—"

The pilot writhed in her restraints, her scream echoing through the caverns as a burnt smell began to rise.

"Yes, let the others know what awaits them." Tavince opened the front of the woman's flight suit to stroke her abdomen.

Her excitement must have intrigued Cance, who asked, "What'd you do?"

Tavince took a small step back, but didn't drop her hand. "Acid injection."

She focused on her subject, unfastening the pilot's flight suit to expose her entire torso. "Skin liquefying, searing your muscles. I know it burns, my pet. But I had undo your numbness. What good is all this if you can't feel?" She slid her hands over the woman's body, soaking in her agony. "That's it."

The pilot shook beneath her touch, eyes wide, breath rapid.

"And she wakes for us, Missionary," Tavince said. "Are you ready for a demonstration?"

"The recorder?"

"Yes, Jandis will want to evaluate your skills." Tavince motioned to Trisk, who stood beside the tripod. Cance's attendant activated the recorder, and then left the immediate area, retreating to a remote corner out of direct view.

"Let's get started." Cance moved to the opposite side of the lounger to look into their keeper prisoner's face. "What's your name for the record?"

"Name?" said Tavince. "Her name is Slattern. All their names are Slattern." The prisoner's cries had reduced to whimpers. "Isn't that right, Slattern Number One?"

The pilot closed her eyes beneath the binder and said nothing. The injection site had been eaten away, burning her to the bone.

"Denial. How predictable." Tavince smirked down at their prisoner. "Tell the Missionary your new name, and I'll grant you some anesthetic for that ghastly pit in your arm."

She stroked the skin between the pilot's breasts. "Come now, my sweet. It's a simple task." She slid her gloved hand up to the shoulder and down her victim's arm to the burn, which she squeezed. "Do it!"

The pilot gasped, but remained otherwise silent.

"Slut," mumbled Tavince in frustration. She slammed the pilot's arm against the lounger until a sticky film of tissue and bone shards smeared the fabric.

The pilot wailed something unintelligible and shook harder.

Cance leaned in. "That's your flight stick arm too. What a shame. What will you do now…er, what was your name again?"

"Say it." Tavince dropped the pilot's arm and took the syringe a second time, holding it so it could be seen. "The next one goes in your face."

Cance leaned in closer, breathing on the pilot's ear. "That'll blind you. Pair that with your bad arm, and you'll never fly again."

"Jezmon. My name's Jezmon." The pilot whispered. "Mother forgive me for complying."

"Incorrect." Tavince pressed the needle against the pilot's temple. "Last chance, my dear. And your name is…"

"Slattern Number One!" The pilot let out low, guttural sobs which didn't stop when Tavince stepped back. "Oh, please, I beg you!"

"And that, Missionary Cancelynn, is how we make a keeper cry." Tavince placed the syringe back on the table.

The pilot breathed a little easier, but hot tears of disgrace continued to pool inside her binder.

"Don't cry, Slattern Number One. It's far too early for that." Cance leaned even closer, grinding herself against the woman's good arm. "Next time, you'll be in my hands. Save something for then."

Tavince called for guards to return the pilot to the holding area.

"Playtime's over," said Cance, closing the front of the pilot's flight suit. "First lesson complete." She released the prisoner's shackles from the table and jerked her upright.

Tavince quickly wrapped the oozing burn, but didn't splint the break. "Take her," she said to the guards when they arrived.

Two guards half pulled, half carried the pilot away while a third waited for instructions "Who's next?" she asked obediently, eying the medical instruments.

"They're cheeking med packs." Tavince pulled off her gloves. "Make certain they swallow them or spit them out." When the guard lumbered off, she threw the gloves on top of the lounger and turned to Cance. "I've a well-aged crystal waiting for us."

"Excellent." Cance reached for the recorder, "Session one end."

Chapter Forty-Six

Substitute—replace, displace; how keepers mourn their thralls

Drew was disappointed by Jandis's lackluster death.

The Harbinger had verbally assaulted her for being slow to an-swer her call, and then taken a bottle of water and downed it in three swallows as usual after her nap. Her medications, given to her by Ta-vince, dried her mouth.

"Another," Jandis had demanded.

Drew was happy to comply, watching as Jandis's head began to nod.

"I'm more tired than usual." Jandis lay back on her lounger, mo-tioning for Drew to pull up the blanket over her legs. "Push back my meeting with Kylis another two hours. Use whatever excuse works," she said, stopping mid sentence to yawn. "Wake me in time," she mumbled. "You're dismissed."

Drew went to the door and turned back, observing how Jandis's breathing slowed to a stop. Too gentle a death, unworthy any of the pedagogues, she thought. She frowned. Now came the difficult part.

She removed Jandis's clothing one piece at a time, from over tunic to leggings, which she folded neatly and stowed in a bag she often carried for Jandis. She removed Jandis's jewelry—rings, bracelets and necklaces—all bearing the Harbinger's emblem. She tucked Jandis's slippers into the top of the carry bag and set it aside.

Lastly, with considerable nausea, Drew used Jandis's knife to re-move her left index finger and left eye, which were needed to access the computer. She slipped the finger and eyeball into separate bags and placed them in her pocket for later use.

Why'd you have to be so fat? Drew wrapped Jandis in the lounger's coverlet and the lap blanket, rolled her with the gentlest thump onto the floor, and dragged her into the closet where the prayer robes were stored, stowing the body behind them. That would take care of things for a day or two, until the stink set in. She tucked a second blanket against the bottom of the door, hoping to stall that issue a day or so longer.

Drew closed the door and flopped onto the lounger, taking in its comfort while she caught her breath. She still needed to move the meeting with Kylis as far back as possible and notify Jandis's house-hold that she'd be staying in her office overnight, a common happen-ing.

Mustering her strength, she stood, swept up the carry bag, and went to the conference room, where she sent the messages.

Belsas was still sleeping when she returned to the apartment. She wanted to let her sleep longer, but couldn't give her more than a cou-ple of hours. They hadn't much time to prepare.

When the time arrived, she tapped Belsas with her toe, startling her awake.

"What—" Belsas covered her mouth before Drew could. She grinned meekly, took her assisting hand, and stood. Belsas moved slowly, she observed, but bore her pain without complaint.

Drew motioned to her and moved to the apartment's small table, where she had set out two mugs of warmed beans and grain and two mugs of tea. Belsas hovered over the latter.

I killed her. Drew wrote on a new pad of paper. While Belsas read, she reached into the carry bag, placing Jandis's clothing between them. *You'll replace her.*

Belsas nearly choked on her tea. *Me?* she wrote, *Why not you?*

Muted. Drew touched her throat.

What does she do?

Senior pedagogue. Drew paused to let Belsas read. *Moved meeting til tomorrow so we've all night.* She passed the pen to Belsas.

I can't do this. Belsas put down the pen, scrubbed her eyes with her palms, and picked up the pen again. *They'll notice.*

Not when I'm done. Drew moved her desk com to the table and went to the closet, pulling out a large, dusty hide bag. She loaded a file into the com, started it playing, and then pulled a razor and scissors from the bag. She moved behind Belsas and pushed her head down just before scribbling on the pad, *Jandis wasn't fully bald.*

Belsas listened to the com, a description of the Harbinger's role in her own words, until Drew held the paper in front of her face.

I'll ready things. You eat. Jandis ate lots.

Can't fatten overnight. Belsas ran her hands over her head and shivered.

Try. Keep watching. Going to the conference room. Be back soon.

Belsas was mimicking Jandis's hand motions when Drew returned. She held out the clothing and Belsas slipped them on.

Big, she mouthed.

Drew held up a finger and went to the closet, returning a few minutes later with the pillows Belsas had slept on. She shoved one down the front of Belsas's leggings, pulled her tunic down over it, and stood back, amused by her handiwork.

Belsas frowned at her. Drew bent over, making the small hissing, gasping sounds that were the only way she could laugh. Belsas began to laugh too, covering her mouth to muffle the sound.

She looked pained, Drew thought, but she still paraded around the apartment, acting the part of a jolly, fat woman until she held up her hand in a stopping gesture.

Belsas waddled over, clearly trying to stay serious while Drew stuffed a smaller pillow into the back of her leggings. She jerked on Belsas's tunic, pulling it above her head so she could stuff two neck rolls across Belsas's shoulders and down her upper arms to mimic Jandis's form.

Belsas apparently found it even more difficult to move. She sat back down, her padding finding the seat before her body, startling her.

Drew smirked and went to the closet again, coming back this time with a small box. She pulled the other dining chair in front of Belsas, her amusement fading.

No binder, she wrote, and reached into the box, producing a pair of lenses the shade of Jandis's eyes. *I've never done this on someone else,* she wrote before she lunged, stabbing a small syringe into Belsas's forearm. Belsas gasped, but Drew clasped a hand over her mouth before she could do anything more.

Sorry, she mouthed as Belsas lost consciousness.

Reaching for the lenses, she went to work.

A few moments later, Belsas woke. Drew had moved her to the floor and now stood over her, watching and waiting. She held up a paper for Belsas to read. *Lenses.*

Belsas blinked rapidly, her eyes watering, but she seemed to see well enough to knock Drew away. *You could have warned me*, she mouthed.

Drew shook her head, reaching to the table to grab the paper. *It wouldn't have helped.*

Belsas snatched the paper and pen from her. *I've worn lenses before*, she scrawled.

Drew gave her a hard look. *Training?* she wrote. *I didn't have anesthetic and couldn't take the risk. The pain will fade.*

Still. Belsas sniffled. *No more surprises.*

I'll try. Drew helped the heavily padded Belsas up from the floor and back into her chair. She went to the closet again, returning with another small box.

Belsas looked warily at the box, and then at Drew, who opened it. Prosthetics this time—cheek pieces to create Jandis's jowls and a forehead piece to replicate her lines and creases.

When the prosthetics were added, Drew could tell that Belsas felt heavy all over. She moved slowly and breathing took an effort, but she did look like Jandis.

Belsas paid close attention when Drew taught her Jandis's walk. Shuffle with the right foot, drag the left. The Harbinger was a woman in constant pain, but her voice was strong, raspier than Belsas's, who touched her throat and made a soft inquiring noise.

Too many piltas, Drew wrote. *Three throat infections last pass. She sounded odd for over a cycle. No one will think much until Tavince returns.*

Then?

Drew made a slicing motion across her throat and sat in her seat to look at Belsas, not entirely pleased with her creation. *Practice*, she wrote on the paper.

For the rest of the night, Drew tutored Belsas in Jandis's mannerisms. She was a difficult teacher to satisfy, one who didn't think twice about cuffing her student to remind her how to sit or move. She wasn't cruel, but Belsas had to be perfect and couldn't give anyone reason to doubt. Their lives depended on it.

Shortly before dawn, she nodded at Belsas.

"Who're you to tell me anything?" Belsas's voice had actually become gravelly from mimicking Jandis. She glared at Drew and reached out, giving her a soft thump on the lip.

Drew grabbed Belsas's wrist with one hand as she grabbed the paper with the other. *Never hesitate.* She shoved Belsas's hand away.

Belsas reacted as Jandis, raising a hand to smack Drew hard on the face.

Better, mouthed Drew.

She worried her jaw, and then smiled and motioned Belsas to the door, where she blocked it for a final moment. She leaned forward, placing her forehead against Belsas's to show her trust, and looked down, demonstrating her subjugation to the Harbinger.

The transformation was complete. Belsas Exzal was no more. Jandis Gladomain, the Mother's Harbinger and religious icon for the Cleave, was ready for the day.

Chapter Forty-Seven

Blockade—impediment, hindrance; a pedagogue nuisance

Most of the Old Cleave prisoners spent time at Tavince's hands.

They'd stayed strong and conscious throughout, frustrating Tavince until she literally ripped the binders from two of them, causing their instant deaths when the broken binders sent lethal electrical charges through their brains.

"An impasse," said Tavince when she and Cance discussed the matter. "My current method gave us some information, but not enough. No mentally Sharing them. No tapping their minds." She flexed her left hand and examined the fingers. "I've been too gentle."

"Jandis called you an expert," Cance snarled around her mug. "Time we tried my way."

"Ah, but I haven't shown you enough for you to strike out entirely on your own." Tavince lounged back in her chair. She'd redressed after her last victim, and cursed Gale for not having a protective frock at the ready when things became messy. She snapped her fingers. Gale rushed to her side. "Have Keeper Adara washed and readied for a demonstration."

Gale's breath caught in her throat.

Tavince laughed. "Yes, dearie. You're familiar with peeling, aren't you?"

Gale nodded fearfully.

"Only took one lesson, didn't it?"

Gale nodded again and gulped.

Tavince smirked and reach a finger toward Gale, who closed her eyes, but didn't flinch, pleasing her. "Good girl. Remember to assemble the other slatterns so they can watch and learn."

Needing no further reminder, Gale moved quickly away from the lounge area she'd assembled for the pedagogues inside the main Resistance cavern.

"She's better trained than Trisk was," said Cance, watching Tavince's attendant scurry.

"Was?" Tavince looked up. "Where is your problematic attendant?"

"Occupied," said Cance, seemingly bored by the conversation. "Or broken. One or the other."

"Is she in need of need my skills?" Tavince flexed her hands.

"Maybe." Cance shrugged. "Or I might need another attendant."

"So you did break her," said Tavince with exasperation. "Good attendants take six surgeries to prepare, then passes to train. Jandis will requisition you another, but she'll want a full disclosure on what became of Trisk."

"When I know, I'll tell you both."

"You lost her?" Tavince was puzzled.

"I know exactly where she is," said Cance mid-yawn. "I just haven't checked to see how broken she is."

"Interesting." Tavince rose, turning to the transport launch. "I suggest you don something warm and waterproof," she said over her shoulder. "Blood won't be the only liquid flowing today."

Cance smirked and rubbed her hands together.

* * *

"Prep the next one." Tavince placed her blade onto the table and motioned to the guards, who unchained Adara and returned her to the rest of the prisoners.

Adara shivered when she was placed on the cold floor.

Zhastra scooted close, aware the infirmary cavern was cooler than usual, but Adara turned away and whispered, "Save yourself."

Zhastra held back, but what could she have done anyway? She looked at Adara's wounds. Tavince had started on Adara's back, working slowly and methodically with a thin filleting blade. She'd peeled each section of skin with precision, and then laid it back where it had been, one long strip at a time.

Adara hadn't cried out until Tavince reached her spine, and then she'd groaned, the sound rising as her skin peeled away from her backbone. Tavince had cut that strip off completely and flung it across the cavern where it clung to the wall—a fleshy streamer above the heads of the other prisoners. That act had proved so satisfying that Tavince had sighed and stepped back from the table, clearly deep in afterglow.

The exposed dermis tissue wasn't at risk for infection, not yet, Zhastra thought. Tavince was a surgeon. Adara her patient. Her experiment. Her toy. Tavince didn't play with dirty toys. That's why she wanted them each washed beforehand with sterile alcohol. That's why she'd given Adara a clotting agent before the torture began.

"Stand, Slattern Six," Tavince ordered.

Adara slowly stood, obeyed Tavince's gesture, and turned with her back on display.

"That'll leave a ghastly scar unless we keep it clean. You want to keep it clean, don't you, Slattern Six?" Tavince grabbed a shock stick from a guard and touched Adara behind the knee. "Answer me, Slattern Six, or you'll be back on my table."

"I will anyway," mumbled Adara when she climbed to her feet again. "Scars are stories where I come from."

"Hmph." Tavince tossed the shock stick back to the guard and called to Gale, who scurried forward, trailing a hose behind her. "Rinse Slattern Six."

Gale stared at her, dumbfounded.

"Do it."

Gale pointed to the specifications written on the hose.

"High pressure," whispered Zhastra to the others. "For cleaning floors."

"You defying me?" Tavince looked hopeful, but Gale shook her head vehemently and twisted the end of the hose, shooting a concentrated water jet which she aimed at Adara. Tears streamed down both their faces, but neither said a word, even as the loosened skin on Adara's back slipped to the floor, exposing raw muscle as the jet enlarged the wound.

Tavince called a halt after a few minutes, leaving Gale to her guilt and Adara to her pain. At last, Tavince allowed Zhastra to help, tossing bandages to her.

"You know a wound like this shouldn't be bandaged," said Zhastra.

"Competency check. Stitches then?" Tavince asked.

"Air and time," said Zhastra, more to Adara than their captor.

"You still have some oomph in you yet, Zhastra—oh, it's Slattern Three now, isn't it?"

Zhastra curled her lip and glared. "For now."

"Good girl, Slattern Three." Tavince patted Zhastra's head and whirled around.

"Ever cleaned a fish? Peeling is almost identical," she told Cance as a Kinship pilot was secured, stripped and washed by two guards who touched her delicately, almost apologetically. Tavince smiled when the pilot shivered from the alcohol's cooling effect. "What's your name?"

"Slattern Eight." The pilot focused over the edge of the examining lounger at Tavince's feet. "Though what's a label forced upon you?"

"A philosopher on my table," said Tavince, setting aside her blade to step closer to the examining lounger. "Keep talking, darling." She ran her gloved hand down the pilot's back, pinching up bits of flesh as she moved.

"You can't force out what's not there. None of us know the binder codes."

"Codes? We're far past codes, dearie." Tavince kneaded the pilot's back, pinching harder with each motion. "We're on to obedience."

Tavince tightened the pilot's binds until she couldn't move, and pulled her instrument table closer. She climbed onto the lounger, straddling the pilot's back. "Poor dear. Look at those freckles. Been in the sun? You know how bad that is for us."

Cance scanned the other prisoners, who'd turned their heads in collective resistance, but Zhastra watched out of the corner of her eye.

"I've seen enough of your technique. Now let me show you how I do things." Cance grabbed Adara's chains, forcing her to stand. Adara stumbled behind Cance, following her toward the critical care room at the rear of the infirmary.

"Take a recorder," called Tavince, bouncing on the pilot when she jerked upright. "The Harbinger will want to see your first solo work."

"Fuck Jandis." Cance shoved Adara into the infirmary's critical care room, closed the door, and turned back to Tavince. "Fillet away, Practitioner. My work will be done in moments."

"Stowing that slattern helps, how?" Tavince returned to her work, injecting clotting agent into the pilot. "Shall we play?" She chose a scalpel, scratching the tip down the pilot's spine.

"You might as well be alone with her for all the others are paying attention," said Cance.

Thumps sounded from the critical care room. Thumps, and then cries, Adara pounding on the door. Cance chuckled. Zhastra listened, as focused on what happened as the other prisoners, and aware the other prisoners were listening too.

Thud. Bump. A voice. Shouting. Then silence within the room.

"Done." Cance sauntered to the door and opened it, stepping aside as Adara fell to the floor at her feet. "Go back to your friends, Slattern Six."

"Yes, Pedagogue Cancelynn." Adara crawled over, collapsing next to Zhastra.

"Bandages and stitching now, Slattern Three?" asked Tavince, throwing the items to Zhastra. "What do you have in there, Cancelynn?"

Tavince sounded curious. She climbed down from the pilot's back, set her tools aside, and came to stand behind Cance, who'd shut the door. "Is that where Trisk disappeared to?"

"Could be."

Now they had their captives attention—and their fear, Zhastra thought.

"Only a beast could do what's been done to Slattern Six so quickly," Tavince said.

Cance slapped at Tavince's hand and pushed her away from the door. "It'll ravage anything I send in there alone. Trisk, slatterns, even you."

"Then tell it to stand down so I can inspect it," said Tavince. "I must be able to report any variances from our expected outcomes."

"You could care less what Jandis wants. You want to know what's getting in the way of your experiment." Cance grasped the door handle. "Very well. We'll go in together." She ordered one guard to the door, the others to oversee their captives, and then she and Tavince disappeared into the critical care room.

"What's in there?" Zhastra whispered to Adara while she stitched a gash in her forehead.

"A whirlwind," said Adara. "Came at me so fast, I couldn't defend myself."

Adara was covered with deep scratches, the least of her injuries. The other prisoners gathered around her, moving carefully so their shackles didn't rattle too loudly.

Zhastra thought the caution unnecessary. The guards' attention was fixed on the closed door. They stood together, discussing the "beast" the Missionary had brought into Cleave lands. Only the door guard and Gale stood alone.

Gale's eyes darted from one group of prisoners to the other.

A single flashing light caught Zhastra's attention. A warning light, she realized, followed in short order by a siren, and then a computerized voice.

"Warning! Multiple targets approaching at high throttle."

The guards started in unison and turned back to their charges, ushering them into their cubicles, including Zhastra, who had just finished stitching a laceration in Adara's forehead.

The guards are confused, thought Zhastra as she sat in her cubicle. *They're so afraid of making a mistake that they'll wait for the pedagogues to tell them what to do.*

She toyed with her shackles. Cance and Tavince were overconfident. With any luck, that overconfidence would be the New Cleave's downfall.

* * *

Gale stayed in place, intent on the door. It remained closed. The guard, the only guard who mattered, still presided. Clearly, the pedagogues hadn't heard the siren or the announcement.

Gale stepped toward the door. Tavince would want to know. She'd punish her for not informing her immediately. Tavince might even peel her for delaying. She glanced about the infirmary cavern, but didn't move, torn between duty and—

"The examining lounger should be the right height to jam the door." The door guard slung her blaster across her back, trotted to the lounger, and motioned to Gale. "We're all tired of the torture. You want to be rid of the real beasts or not?"

Gale smiled for the first time in passes.

Chapter Forty-Eight

Zealot—radical, obsessor; a pedagogue at a prayer meeting

Kylis's meeting with Jandis had been brief and odd. The old Harbinger was sick again and looked like she had lost weight.

She pondered how much time Jandis had left and, more importantly, who would replace her. Tavince had recently brought the subject up, but she hadn't thought much about it then or since. Instead, her mind remained centered on her lowest thrall.

Brava hung limp in her restraints, barely lifting her head when Kylis walked into the room for one of their routine encounters. When the mood struck, she would set a water bottle just within Brava's strained reach. She would stand and watch, amused by the contortions Brava managed for her daily drink. But Brava didn't move much anymore, and she had grown bored.

"I know you're thirsty." Kylis nudged the bottle a little closer.

"No." Brava's voice cracked.

"Now we're committing suicide?" Kylis tore open the bottle and grabbed Brava's face, forcing open her mouth to pour the contents down her throat.

What Brava couldn't choke down, she spit into Kylis's face.

"And that won't work either." Kylis mopped her face with her sleeve. "Spit, vomit, piss or bleed on me. I don't care. I won't let you die by anything but my hand."

She left, returning later that day with a healer she knew Brava recognized, and two guards who dragged a lounger behind them.

"Hydrate her," ordered Kylis. "Nourish her by choice or by force, and treat whatever wounds she has."

She walked away, returning the next day to a better looking, but still unresponsive Brava, who had been returned to her shackles.

"Unappreciative," began Kylis, but was interrupted by a noise. She turned to listen, noticing Brava cocking an ear toward the sound as well. Sirens.

"A test," she said.

"A test?" Brava looked up through her hair. "You keep thinking that." She began to laugh, first in low chuckles, but the sound rose, almost as loud as the sirens. "Go tend your test, Pedagogue Kylis. I'll just wait here until the test is over."

"Fool," said Kylis. She left Brava to her laughter, dropping the water bottle at her feet.

She plucked a sentry from the first group who passed her in the hallway. "Explain."

"The entire Kinship fleet is closing in!" The sentry stiffened and ducked her head when she saw who held her arm. "Missionary of New Lands, let me escort you back to your office."

"I can find my own way." Kylis shoved the sentry aside and walked quickly to her workroom, where her com buzzed across the table. To her chagrin, Jandis waited on the screen, looking just as ill as before.

"Stand down, Missionary," Jandis said. "The time for fighting is over."

"You've gone soft in the head, Jandis. Your brain's a vine plum gone to rot!" Kylis transferred the call to her wall viewer and waved her arm at the screen. "Think of the daughters we're saving from slatternhood. Think of the prayers you'll be leading to the new masses. Think—"

"Enough," said Jandis gruffly. "Do as they say, or you'll be the next pedagogue executed."

"Who?" Kylis dropped her arm, but not her irate tone.

"Practitioner Tavince."

"Wasn't Cancelynn with her?" With two pedagogues dead, her power was almost endless, and would be as soon as Jandis was out of the way. A single leader, that's what the Cleave needed. No opinions, only the Mother's law, the law of one, she thought.

"Captured, as was her twin."

"Twin!" Kylis sat forward in her chair. "Impossible."

"The wild woman escapee from the Granary," said Jandis, her

voice cracking. Sweat trickled down her face. "Surrender to the Kinship fleet, Missionary. We cannot minister if we're dead."

"And we can't teach if we're subservient." Kylis ran her tongue over her chipped tooth, the very tooth she'd broken on her first border raid so many passes ago, as she thought. Jandis wore no earpiece, and the only other presence she could see was Drew, who stood silently behind her master. "Where has your determination flown off to?" she asked. "You too sick to see the path clearly anymore?"

"My body's ill, not my mind." Jandis shifted, seeming uncomfortable in her seat. "Our genocide was never part of the Mother's plan, Missionary, and the Kinship is prepared to do just that if we do not comply."

Kylis looked briefly away as the sound of weapons fire rose from outside. "You may have surrendered Myflar, but the Kinship capital is mine. My soldiers are true believers."

"Then you've sealed the fate of everyone there," said Jandis.

The screen went blank. Kylis sniffed and turned back to her worktable, where she commed her security chief.

"We're under attack," said the security chief without proper protocol. "We're outnumbered and have been called to surrender."

"Surrender nothing!" Kylis activated her worktable viewer, moving the settings to a satellite view, but the hookup wasn't there. In fact, no satellite hookups were available. "Get me a visual."

The security chief appeared on the com. "Visuals have been disabled outside the building." Her voice was flat, and she kept touching her earpiece.

"You've folded to them," said Kylis as she pulled a pair of matching bows from the worktable and began lashing one on. "Coward."

"They've offered those who surrender Kinship status and clemency for our families if we stand down," said the chief. "They'll let us keep our Myflar homes." Her flat tone had turned to resolve. "It's over, Missionary. The Harbinger says we're to give up our arms."

"Hardly," said Kylis. She flicked off the com. Her own troops were turning. And then she knew, she knew what she must do.

"'When ten thousand split a million ways and the world hangs over the rift, one shall shed her disguise—a Keeper strong of heart, strong of faith, a child of the Mother shall rise to unite them.'"

She recited the words a second time, feeling them slip from her mouth and into her heart as she lashed a second bow to her other arm. The Mother's love rose up in her until she was certain she glowed with her Creator's approval.

She ran out of the room, dodging frantic soldiers running in twos and threes down the hallways until she reached Brava's holding room.

"Come on." She released Brava's shackles from the wall, catching her before she slid to the floor. "Get up."

Brava stumbled along behind her, too weak to do more.

A small group of New Cleave soldiers met her in the hall. "We're your servants," said one of them, bowing her head. "Guide us, pedagogue. Show us the light."

"Only one shall rise." The soldiers fell to a swiping blaze from Kylis's left arm bow.

She pulled Brava over the bodies and continued down the hall, down flights of emergency stairs to the building's lowest level which housed a set of escape launches that few knew about. She had specially equipped one early in her reign over the Kinship. She thrust Brava through the doorway of the launch and into a seat.

"Where?" whispered Brava.

Kylis slapped her across the ear. "Not unless you're spoken to."

Brava stayed still while Kylis shackled her to the seat.

Kylis prepared for takeoff, opening the concealed launch bay doors, skimming the interface board with preflight instructions, and slipping on her headset. The launch roared in reply and the landing locks hissed.

"One shall rise—a Keeper strong of heart, strong of faith," she said.

"That's not the right wording," Brava said before she was smashed back into her seat by the launch's sudden takeoff.

Kylis navigated with skill, evading blaster and launch fire, speeding faster than their pursuers, obtaining a pace the launch's G-force balancer couldn't compensate.

Brava blacked out from the stress.

Kylis smiled when the launch broke orbit.

"Cleave launch," issued from the com.

She'd been expecting the Kinship to block her path. No glory was easy.

"Prepare to surrender."

Kylis reached over to shake Brava. "Put on a headset."

Groggily, Brava reached for the set hanging by her head.

"Identify yourself to the slatterns," Kylis ordered.

"They'll shoot you down regardless." Brava withstood a second blow to her ear.

"Did I ask?" She opened the connection on Brava's headset.

Brava glared sideways at Kylis and adjusted her headset. "Kinship forces, this is Brava Deb." Her voice was foreign, shaky, sounding old.

"Registered, Grandmaster Brava. It is good to hear your voice," began someone, but Kylis interceded, smacking Brava's arm again and again to deliver correction.

"Kinship slatterns, this is Pedagogue Kylis, Missionary of New Lands. Slattern Brava is obviously confused as to her status." She gave Brava a final smack. "The Kinship will surrender or face the Mother's judgment."

"Cleave launch, this is Protocol Master Lupinski. Grandmaster Brava, you okay?"

"Holding on," said Brava. Kylis's slapping hand twitched. "Kylis has—"

Kylis lost her patience. "The Kinship hangs over the rift." She rose tall from her seat, proud, untouchable, basking in the glow of righteousness. "Bow to the Mother's Word, Kinship, or know the full extent of Her wrath." She flipped open the armament panel.

"Cleave launch, you are ordered to disarm," came the rote message of a weapon's officer.

"'Ten thousand must splinter a million ways.'" Kylis smiled at Brava, who struggled with a fervor she thought she'd lost. "A child of the Mother, her keeper daughter, shall rise to unite them." She began entering in the launch code for her special cargo.

"Cleave launch, stand down or we will disable you!"

"I am shielded by my Mother's love!" Kylis fired her first missile, striking the Kinship vessel's port side.

"You're insane!" Brava flailed in her chair, and then grew silent and wide-eyed, mouthing a prayer as a Kinship missile bore down on their launch. "Dearest Mother!"

"I'll unite them all!" cried Kylis.

* * *

Brava felt the missile graze the back of the launch, damaging fuel cells, shorting the control panels, and sending the launch into a slow roll which put it within reach of the battleship's debris net. While the roll stopped inside the net, the launch filled with smoke.

Brava couldn't see Kylis, but she could hear her reciting the Mother's Word and singing praises. She also heard the click of Kylis's harness, and her coughing, first at ear level, then floor level, and finally at the back of the launch where the distinct clank of the weapon's bay access door sliding open came to her.

"Kinship battleship Tempest, Kylis is preparing to manually launch missiles," Brava said into the headset, wondering why she felt so calm.

"Do you have visual?" the weapon's officer asked.

"Negative, but I can hear."

"So can we," said Lupinski over the headset.

"I'm shackled in. You'll have to shoot us down to stop her," said Brava.

"We're reviewing the options," said the weapon's officer, but Lupinski cut in.

"Brava? Your daughter's here."

Brava heard the weapon's officer com click out. "My Chandrey girl's there?" she asked. "Can she talk?"

"They just brought her on deck. I'll go offline now," said Lupinski. "Take care, Brava."

"You too, Lupe."

Seconds later, another com clicked on. "Gahrah?" said a familiar voice.

"Chandrey girl!" Brava coughed as smoke caught in her throat. The emergency air tanks were in the back of the launch, far out of reach. "There's so much I want to—" She coughed again.

"Gahrah, I'm so sorry for the trouble I caused—"

"No, daughter, it's me who's sorry. I drove you away. If I had just listened to my heart." Brava wheezed, and then grew quiet, sensing the bump of the debris net's release.

"What was that?" asked Chandrey through the com.

Brava heard Lupinski in the background, explaining, comforting.

"No!" Chandrey cried. "Gahrah, no!"

"This is the only way, Chandrey girl," said Brava softly. "Kylis will blow you, the Kinship fleet, Javicks and half of Saria III away. It has to be done."

In the back of the launch, Kylis's singing had become obscured, no doubt because of an air mask. She seemed oblivious to the happenings behind her. The launch would soon be spinning again, Brava thought, tumbling, and then—

"Promise me something, Chandrey girl."

"Anything, Gahrah, anything." Chandrey sounded stronger now, as accepting as one could be in the circumstance. "Tell me."

"Be true to your heart no matter what others say. Okay?" Brava felt lightheaded.

"I'll try but—"

"Put Lupe on with us for a minute, will you?"

A second later, the com clicked. "I'm here, Brava."

"Take care of my Chandrey girl, Lupe. I know she's grown but—"

"She's still your daughter, I get it."

Brava coughed hard. "I love you, Chandresslandra Brava. Keep that promise you just made." She tasted more than smoke. "Get her out of there, Lupe. Don't let her hear."

"No, Gahrah!"

Both the other coms clicked off, but a few seconds later, Lupinski's cut back in. "She didn't go willingly. Strong girl. A fighter, just like her gahrah."

"Thank you. You're in charge until elections." Talking was difficult.

"I—"

"No time to argue."

"Yes." Now Lupinski grew silent, unsure.

"Was that recorded?"

"You know me."

"Protocol to the end. Thanks, Lupe. I think I'm ready now."

Against the haze both inside and out, Brava clicked off her com and leaned forward, resting her forehead on the launch's front window. Saria III, with its yellow-green landforms and blue splashes of water, was quite lovely, reminding her of a painter's messy palette, of the delightful, sweeping strokes of a child's—of Chandrey's toddler paintings.

Brava smiled against the window. One day, Chandrey girl, we'll meet again. I'll be the one sitting near the hem of the Mother's skirts holding her arms out to welcome you home.

* * *

Healer Jacksun went looking for her patient as soon as the Tempest leveled out from the Taelach of All's sacrifice. When she didn't find Chandrey in her quarters or at the ship's shrine, she began to worry, but that worry, she soon realized, was misspent. A few hallways down, she found Chandrey sitting at the scribe terminal, adding to her personal blade.

"Can I see?" she asked.

Chandrey nodded and pulled the blade from the cutter. The thorns of loss and the Kinship symbol were still there, but two new symbols filled the formerly blank space on the handle. "It's who I am," she said softly, placing the blade back under the cutter to add details.

"It certainly is," replied Jacksun.

She left Chandrey to her work, knowing for the first time that her patient, the intended of Belsas Exzal, was truly going to be fine after all.

Chapter Forty-Nine

Renunciation—renounce, abandon; a new beginning

"Cancelynn Denise Creiloff, stand for your sentencing."

Chandrey could barely contain her emotions when Protocol Grandmaster Lupinski, pro-tem Taelach of All, called Cance to stand. It wasn't that she doubted Cance's guilt. She knew Cance's crimes as if they were her own.

In darker moments, she still actually felt as though Cance's heinous acts were indeed her fault. If she had been a better life mate, a better lover, a better listener…

Belsas said it was Cance's fading influence speaking. Her counselor said much the same. Perhaps they were correct in their assertions, but they also said she'd eventually be able to fully purge the sense of guilt and shame.

Chandrey sometimes disagreed. She had been the favored thrall of Missionary Pedagogue Cancelynn Creiloff, her servant, her property under Cleave law, and property made no decisions.

"Stand, Cancelynn Creiloff," repeated Lupinski.

Chandrey knew as well as everyone else present that Cance would never stand before a court she didn't recognize.

"Do you have any last words before your sentencing?" Lupinski looked at Cance. After a slight shake of her head, she nodded at the guards flanking her.

Two troopers, statuesque in their black military dress, immediately descended on Cance, dragging her to her feet. Cance scowled and spat at the guards, but said nothing. She looked abnormally pale in her dark green, loose-fitting incarceration tunic, but her expression spoke of her ailments and anger far deeper than the sweat which ran around the amber binder keeping her mind phase from others.

"Say something to this piss-poor excuse for a judicial system? Never." Cance pursed her lips to spit, ostentatiously careful to aim just short of Lupinski's feet. "Come here, Chandrey Cances. My thrall will stand behind me."

A murmur rose from the small gallery of spectators who had been allowed to view the judicial sands.

"Chandresslandra Cances, answer me now." Cance's voice rose above the background noise. "You're here somewhere. Show yourself before I lose patience."

"This is the last time," said Belsas softly to Chandrey. "No one can doubt you after this."

"I know," Chandrey replied.

"I feel you, Chandrey. Where're you hiding?" Cance asked.

"Enough." Lupinski raised her hand for silence, a sign that everyone but Cance obeyed.

"I want my fucking thrall. Here. Now!" Cance demanded.

Chandrey sat in the back of the gallery next to Belsas, outside the light of the judicial fire.

Belsas had won the election and would soon be Taelach of All. As Jandis, she had convinced most of the New Cleave to put down their arms, saving thousands of lives, and the new Kinship council had called on her to run for the position of Taelach of All after the story of her survival and heroism surfaced. Belsas had been reluctant at first, but the call to duty had been too great. She had entered the election unopposed.

Chandrey knew that was why they sat at the back of the gallery. Belsas was too close to the Cleave's insurrection to be considered impartial, but she and Lupinski had debated the punishment of the almost thousand defiant New Cleave prisoners for days on end. Their punishment, she'd learned, would be in two parts, the first of which had been the neck branding of every Cleave keeper member who hadn't surrendered.

"Chandresslandra Cances is present." Lupinski knew where she and Belsas sat, but looked the other way.

How Chandrey longed to run, run hard, long, and tearfully from this moment! But she realized she had to sever the last tie. The gallery and Belsas might understand, but the Kinship judicial system and her own conscience wouldn't allow it.

When Belsas touched her arm, Chandrey nodded and rose, slowly crossing the sands in silent strides. She had studied Lupinski's questions for her and rehearsed the answers too many times to count, but to say them, to utter the actual words prompted her to shudder. Cance still owned a part of her psyche. She knew Cance wasn't above using that power even now.

"Chandresslandra Cances is entering the circle," cried the bailiff.

Another murmur rose from the gallery. Chandrey briefly thought them dismayed by her presence, but soon realized the spectators were giving her words of encouragement. They bared their teeth at Cance, and then turned softened eyes on her.

She took heart in their kindness, straightened the brown, calf-length skirt covering her still frail frame, and reached up to adjust her headscarf, drawing her hand back when she remembered she no longer wore the Cleave dictated covering.

Old habits died hard. The Cleave and their laws were no more, but her left wrist, in a sling after surgery to remove scar tissue, bore evidence enough of her suffering during Cance's reign. She also hadn't been able to shed the habit of wearing skirts, but the ones she wore were lighter, wrapped ones similar to Plan robes, and she felt comfortable.

Once on the sands, Chandrey hesitated, unsure whether her place was beside Cance or behind her. The bailiff gently steered her to stand directly before Cance, face-to-face.

"Chandresslandra Cances," began Lupinski, stepping beside them. "Your life mate—"

"The word is keeper," corrected Cance. "As in I *keep her* from the roving eyes of others."

Lupinski ignored the words. Chandrey cringed, her arm throbbing with every syllable Cance uttered.

"Chandresslandra Cances, this judicial circle has found Cancelynn Denise Creiloff guilty of murder, moral crimes against the Autlach and treason against the Silver Kinship," said Lupinski. "Do you understand the ramifications of this decision?"

"I do." Despite her brave efforts, Chandrey's voice shook.

"Do you understand that you must make a choice?"

"Yes."

"Would you please share your understanding?"

"I must..." Chandrey faltered when Cance cleared her throat. "I...I must do one of two things. I must either renounce all ties to my life mate..."

"Keeper, Chandresslandra," interjected Cance. "You know my place in my household."

Lupinski glared. "No Cleave speak will be tolerated on my sands, Cancelynn Creiloff."

"Fuck you," said Cance, but she remained otherwise quiet while Chandrey tried to regain her composure.

"When you are ready, Chandresslandra," said Lupinski with another hard look at Cance.

"I renounce Cance or s-s-share in her punishment," Chandrey said. "I understand."

"Very well," said Lupinski. "Do you also understand that you will not know this judicial circle's decision concerning your—" She paused. Chandrey thought both keeper and life mate must have been too hard for Lupinski to say. "—concerning Cancelynn Creiloff's punishment until after you have made your choice known?"

"I do." Tears welled in Chandrey's eyes, but she was determined to let none fall.

"Then we shall proceed." Lupinski looked at the gallery. "Be it known and recorded that on this day Chandresslandra Cances, of her own free will, made the decision she is about to speak."

All eyes focused on Chandrey. She gulped back her urge to sob, squinting so the tears couldn't escape.

"Speak your decision, Chandresslandra Cances, and may the Mother guide your decision."

"I..." Chandrey's breath caught in her throat. "I..."

"Say it." Cance crooned. "You know we're inseparable."

The gallery grew restless. Several called for Cance to be silenced, but Chandrey knew Cance had the right to speak. Belsas had tried to delay this phase of the proceedings, but the leading sisters of the Kinship wanted swift justice for the New Cleave atrocities. Belsas couldn't protect her any longer.

"Come to me, Chandrey," continued Cance in her most entrancing, sultry voice. "My love, my only, where I end, you begin. You can't deny what the Mother brought together."

"I..." Chandrey swayed. She regained her balance and looked at Lupinski, searching for encouragement, but she found none. Lupinski couldn't help.

"Speak your choice, Chandresslandra," Lupinski said in a gentle voice that few outside the immediate circle could hear. "The time has come." She caught Chandrey by the arm when she swayed.

Cance lunged forward until her shackles strained. "Get away from my thrall, you fucking Kinship puppet. She's mine, my property."

Property. The word lanced through Chandrey's heart and head simultaneously. She was many things, but the term property, even when applied to her in Cance's most delicious voice, was infuriating. She felt her expression darken.

Lupinski stepped away.

"Property?" Chandrey asked in a mumble. "Property." She repeated the word until it became a scream that rose from her gut, venting feelings that she'd long suppressed.

"Property!" She stared into Cance's eyes. "Clothing is property. A launch is property. Sisters are not. I am *not* property!"

She flung herself at Cance, raising her right hand to strike her former keeper across the face. "I am a sister, a sister in the Kinship!" She grasped Cance's throat. "You don't own me!"

Cance didn't try to deflect the attack. Lupinski motioned for the guards to wait.

"See?" croaked Cance. "See, Chandresslandra? We're alike after all. We both hate enough to kill."

Chandrey's grip went slack. She stumbled back into the guards. "No."

Cance smoothed her tunic. "You can hate as much as I do."

"No."

"Come to me, Chandrey Cances. It's you and me. Fuck the rest."

Chandrey peered at Cance, seeking some semblance of the woman she had fallen in love with. If there were any signs, she couldn't see them. They had become lost in a drug-addicted shadow, possessed by a hatred so sinister and bitter that it had spilled onto everything around it.

Chandrey cleared her eyes with the corner of her sleeve and turned to Lupinski. "I've made my decision."

"Then face your life mate and speak your choice."

The sands fell silent except for Cance, who chuckled.

"Why not say it in my arms, Precious?" Cance extended her arms. "Then we'll seal things with a kiss they'll talk about generations after we're gone."

"No."

"I said come here," repeated Cance in a strained tone, but Chandrey kept from her reach.

"I renounce you, Cancelynn Denise Creiloff. My oath to you is no more."

"Bitch!" Cance pulled against her restraints. "After all I've done for you!"

"Our ties are dissolved," Chandrey continued over the tirade. "I feel nothing for you."

"You don't believe in the Renunciation. You promised you would never leave me. You said you believed the oath was for life! You're eternally misery bound. You hear me? *Misery bound!*" Cance howled.

"I still believe," said Chandrey with a resolve that surprised her. "But you broke our mate bond more times than I can count. The other women. The lies. The beatings. Rape. Then you gave...you gave me to your twin! Your promises in front of the Mother were meaningless. I've merely made your action-based renunciation of me public and binding."

"Damn you!" Cance pulled so hard against her restraints, the pins holding her chains to the ground rattled. "You'll pay dearly for this, bitch woman, I promise you that!"

"I've already paid a hundred times." Chandrey turned her back on Cance. "My name is Chandresslandra Brava, and I am Belsas Exzal's intended," she told everyone present. "Chandresslandra Cances is no more."

When the cheers died down, Lupinski said, "So it is recorded." She touched Chandrey's shoulder as she escorted her off the judicial sands.

"Belsas's intended?" Sheer rage distorted Cance's face. "Where the fuck are you, Belsas? Show yourself, you thrall-stealing slut!"

Lupinski motioned for the bailiff to see Chandrey safely through the gallery, and then returned to the center of the sands and Cance. "Cancelynn Denise Creiloff, this judicial circle has found you guilty of heinous crimes against both the Autlach and the Kinship—"

"You're fucking my thrall, Belsas!" bellowed Cance above Lupinski's pronouncement. "You're doing it again!"

Chandrey spun around, but the bailiff took her stiffly by the arm. "Sharp words from a hollow soul, Sister Chandrey. Don't let them cut you."

Chandrey glanced over her shoulder at Lupinski, but duty had cleared the Protocol Grandmaster's features of any emotion as she continued speaking to Cance.

"Your punishment has been placed in my hands," Lupinski said, "and after much deliberation, I have made my decision."

"We all know you're going to execute me so Belsas can have my thrall!"

"I hereby sentence you to lifetime servitude in the Trimar prison colony."

"Belsas, you—" Cance fell silent when the witnesses in the gallery gasped.

"Even justice can find a place in its heart for mercy." Lupinski gathered a handful of sand and let it sift through her fingers, signifying her final decision. "Your sentence cannot be commuted in any way. You will serve until your death."

"She asked you to spare me!" The smirk returned to Cance's face. "She still loves me!"

Chandrey searched for Belsas in the gallery. Her intended's expression was stolid, but behind her eyes flashed something special. Renewal? Happiness?

Whatever Belsas meant with the look, it faded as quickly as it came, but still left Chandrey warmed as Lupinski began to speak again.

"The inmate's launch leaves immediately."

"You still love me, Chandrey!" Cance fought the guards as they undid her shackles from the floor. "You need me!"

"Gag her," said Lupinski. "Her voice pollutes these sands."

"You can't silence the truth!" Cance kicked out in an attempt to knock the gag from the guard's hands. "Chandrey loves me!"

Chandrey could stand no more. She ran from the sands, all the way to her small apartment where she fell into an oversized chair, drew her knees to her chest, and hugged them with her right arm.

Try as she might, she couldn't cry. She couldn't be sad. She couldn't be angry. Everything within her was numb. She had no direction, no purpose. At least with Cance and the Cleave, she had known her place in the world, lowly though it was.

She was fully wrapped in self pity when a scroll on the small worktable caught her eye. Knowing it hadn't been there when she'd left earlier, she slowly uncurled and reached out to grasp the scroll so it slipped tube-like over her fingers. It smelled of old scrolls and hides—Belsas's unique physical and mental marker.

Belsas had rubbed the original symbols from the hide and replaced them with her own, carefully written in her best hand.

Mourn your losses, express your sorrow and pain, but do not let them eclipse your spirit, because your spirit remembers what you've forgotten. Let it remind you and help you renew your faith in the Mother. Listen to Her song. Let Her remind you who you truly are and then remember this—I remember you before and know you now—and I love both unconditionally, no matter what may come. Belsas

Chandrey glanced up to see Belsas standing in the doorway joining their apartments.

"I mean every word," Belsas said.

"I know." When Belsas approached, Chandrey stood and let herself be drawn close. She felt safe and restful in Belsas's arms, but more than anything, she felt like herself. Her mind was totally her own and her body—

"Gahrah told me to always be true to my heart," she said.

"Wise Words." Belsas touched her nose to Chandrey's ear. "And what is your heart telling you right now?"

Chandrey's skin prickled. Suddenly, she knew what came next. It was as natural as breathing and where she should have been all along. "It thinks my blade's scribing will be incorrect by tomorrow. Yours too."

"Well, I guess we could take them to a terminal." Belsas nuzzled into her skin, breathing deep, slow, and silently asking.

"I suppose." Chandrey closed her eyes as Belsas touched her waist. So gentle. So kind. Perfectly right. "But shouldn't they be incorrect first?"

"Yes, there is that." Belsas's other hand slid into her unencumbered one. "But there's no pressure. My election shouldn't make you feel you have to. If you want to enjoy being single a while longer…"

"Every choice I make is my own." Chandrey looked directly into Belsas's eyes, bright and soulful, understanding everything, judging nothing. "And I'm making one right now."

"And that is?" Belsas peered back at her, amused and clearly allured.

"You," said Chandrey, squeezing Belsas's hand. "I make no promises, but I offer everything I can."

"That's all I ever wished for, and all I'll ever need," said Belsas, sharing their first kiss.

The first of a thousand that night, Chandrey thought.

Afterward

"How was your walk?" Belsas asked when Chandrey and Mitsu entered through the open doors off Zhastra's patio.

The aging healer's Vartoch home was much the same as her Cleave residence, Chandrey thought—half home, half clinic, but a special building stood in the corner of the property: a school and dormitory. Three dozen former thralls resided in the dormitory, and three Kinship teachers saw to their education, which would result in their full Kinship membership. Chandrey taught seminars at the school every chance she could, but Belsas's official duties kept her from teaching anywhere full time.

Wreed had taught there for four passes, but had moved to a new position after she'd oathed to Quall Dawn, whom she'd met through Belsas.

Zhastra and her family were Kinship members too, but atypical ones. Old Cleave ideas still existed in the Vartoch sister community they called home, but Cleave traditions were merging with Kinship progress. Zhastra's life mates were discovering interests outside the home, especially the younger ones. While Chloe favored the reasoning of mathematics, Tamberly excelled at drawing and painting, and Mitsu, encouraged by Zhastra, had chosen a healer's path.

Everyone had come into her own, save Emre, Chandrey thought. Since she had still been underage when the New Cleave surrendered, she hadn't been held accountable, but she'd been lost ever since she returned to the family, and left home the moment she came of age.

Emre still struggled with her place inside the Kinship and drifted from job to job, and relationship to relationship. Zhastra worried for her, but there wasn't much she could do since Emre refused her help.

"Mit showed me the medicinal beds she's working. I swear she knows every plant by name the moment it breaks ground. We'd have stayed out longer, but it got too dark." Chandrey dropped into the chair beside Belsas.

"My Mit's quite the herbalist." Zhastra patted the seat beside her, encouraging Mitsu to sit with her.

The group had gathered in the main room of the home. Zhastra's fifth child, Listra, the only one born outside the Cleave, sat at the healer's feet, happily rolling a toy launch into block towers that Belsas built her.

"She likes you, Bel." Mitsu rolled the launch back to the girl, who made rumbling and whooshing sounds mimicking takeoff.

"Listra's a good kid," said Belsas. She built another pair of towers and glanced up when she realized Chandrey and the others were looking at her.

"You'll make a good parent." Zhastra drew her daughter into her lap to whisper in her ear. The little girl giggled, waved at Belsas, and buried her face in Zhastra's shoulder. "She's done a lot to heal this house since Giana…"

"Since she died in her sleep," continued Mitsu when Zhastra couldn't. "Mother's mercy it was peaceful."

"Giana would have adored her," said Chandrey, patting the child on the back.

Listra grinned at her and slipped from Zhastra's embrace to Mitsu's, where she snuggled in the crook of her arm.

"Someone's tired," said Mitsu. She rose, cradling the toddler. "Back soon."

Zhastra touched Mitsu's arm as she passed, and then turned to Belsas. "There'll never be a perfect time, you know."

"I know." Belsas glanced at the trooper guards standing outside the patio door. "But I don't want my daughter to become a spectacle because of my position. I want her to have a normal life."

"What's normal anyway?" asked Zhastra, motioning to the interior of her home. "Look at this family. We're overflowing, yet there's always room for one more." She looked at Chandrey, who nodded. "A regional midwife commed me a couple of hours ago."

"Mitsu told me during our walk," said Chandrey, reading Belsas's confusion. "I think it's our time."

"Now? Tonight?" Belsas appeared stunned.

Belsas had almost given up on the idea, Chandrey knew. She had also been initially reluctant. She had too much work to do on herself, she'd said again and again, and Belsas had so many responsibilities. Someday, she'd promised, but nine passes had come and gone since then.

"Are—what—you're serious?" Belsas stammered.

Chandrey took Belsas's hands in hers. "It's time, Bel. I'm ready. We're ready." She felt so assured, so confident.

Belsas picked up on her excitement. "Is our daughter here?" Where is she?" She looked toward the doorway. "Can I see her?"

"Not yet. The birth family is from a rural community two hours away by aerolaunch," explained Zhastra. "I doubt we'd have heard of her if any other midwife had been in attendance." Zhastra held up her hand when Chandrey expressed concern, echoed by Belsas. "She's healthy, but the midwife insists on secrecy."

"The family is ashamed," said Chandrey in sorrow. "How sad."

"But far too typical." Zhastra looked beyond them to the troopers just outside the door. "The Aut locals list their Taelach births as stillborn to keep them hidden."

"Why didn't the local kimshee catch the pregnancy?" asked Belsas.

"There isn't one." Zhastra shrugged. "Too scattered an Aut population. But the midwife has contacted me several times. That's something."

"That means she cares," said Chandrey.

"No, it means the family paid the midwife to keep quiet," Belsas countered.

"But they care enough to see their child safe," said Chandrey.

"It behooves them to do so. They'll lose most everything if word gets out." Zhastra turned her gaze back to them. "Listra's birth family couldn't afford to pay, so I paid for them. The midwife's costly but trustworthy."

"How long before a kimshee arrives to retrieve the baby?" asked Belsas.

Chandrey shook her head. "We're going."

"I know how you feel about kimshees, love," began Belsas, silencing again when Chandrey frowned. After a moment, she went on, "But the Auts here aren't as open-minded as we're accustomed. I want you and the baby safe. I could call Drew if you want. You like her."

"I've already talked to our detail commander. She assured me that it's safe, and she's set it all up." Chandrey stood, urging Belsas to join her. "We're already scheduled to stay here another five days, so why not use the time getting to know our daughter?"

"Outside the public eye," said Belsas. She turned to Zhastra, whose grin said more than any words. "You're all in on it, aren't you?"

"Of course," said Mitsu from the doorway to the inner house. She held out their cloaks. "We've been waiting for this day. Everyone else is in the storeroom, digging out Listra's old things for you to use until you get your own."

"It's a conspiracy." Belsas laughed as she flipped her cloak over her shoulders. "But what a way to celebrate our ninth anniversary!"

"None better," said Zhastra, ushering Chandrey and Belsas toward the door. "Go now. Your detail knows where to land. The midwife's daughter will meet you and guide you in."

"Thank you." Chandrey hugged Mitsu and Zhastra.

"Thank the Mother," said Zhastra, and she grabbed Belsas by the cloak tie, pulling her into the hug as well. "Fly dark and silent, my sisters. Your daughter is waiting."

"We'll be back before morning," assured Belsas.

With Belsas at her side, Chandrey turned toward the doorway. "Gahrah would have liked to have been here." She looked up with teary eyes. "She'd be so happy."

"She's been watching over us for nine passes." Belsas took Chandrey's arm. They walked toward the launch. Belsas continued, "And she's been watching over our daughter too, keeping her safe until we were ready."

"Are we really ready for this?" Chandrey asked, climbing into the aerolaunch and securing her harness. "Is she the one?"

"Absolutely," Belsas answered, doing the same. "You ready to be a mother?"

"I am. You ready, Gahrah?"

Belsas smiled and clasped Chandrey's hand. "That's what you called Brava."

"And that's what our daughter will call you."

Chandrey looked out the launch window, knowing that Brava walked alongside the Mother, telling her how thankful she was to see her daughter finally claim a daughter of her own.

Bella Books, Inc.

Women. Books. Even Better Together.

P.O. Box 10543
Tallahassee, FL 32302

Phone: 800-729-4992
www.bellabook.com